THE
MAGNIFICENT
ESME WELLS

A NOVEL

ADRIENNE SHARP

HARPER

NEW YORK · LONDON · TORONTO · SYDNEY

HARPER

FIRST HARPER PAPERBACKS EDITION PUBLISHED 2019.

Designed by Bonni Leon-Berman

Library of Congress Cataloging-in-Publication Data has been applied for.

ISBN 978-0-06-268480-6 (pbk.)

19 20 21 22 23 LSC 10 9 8 7 6 5 4 3 2

Praise for
The Magnificent Esme Wells

"Sharp's novel, like Jennifer Egan's *Manhattan Beach*, is propulsive and profound." —*Booklist* (starred review)

"This lovely novel, alternately dark and funny, is a powerful examination of both the nature of love and the will to survive."
—Ayelet Waldman, author of *Love and Treasure*

"Brilliant Esme carries the day in this lush saga of the new American West as she struggles from girl to showgirl to headliner, and the two cities she knows—Los Angeles and Las Vegas— grow up around her. Adrienne Sharp has given us a protagonist to hope for and a powerful new version of the American dream." —Ron Carlson

"In *The Magnificent Esme Wells*, Adrienne Sharp brilliantly recreates the tawdry magic of twin dream machines, studio-era Hollywood and early Las Vegas, in this tale of a boom-and-bust childhood of the scrappy, precocious Esme Wells, her go-for-broke parents, and the toll these dreams took on their dreamers."
—Janet Fitch, *New York Times* bestselling
author of *White Oleander*

"Consider it your good luck to join Esme Wells as she comes of age with the glamour, gangsters, and big dreams of Hollywood and Las Vegas of the thirties and fourties. Like its narrator, this novel is magnificent."
—Ann Hood, author of *The Book That Matters Most*
and *The Knitting Circle*

"Amidst the glittering allure of 1940s and 1950s Hollywood and Las Vegas, young Esme Wells tends to her petty-crook dad and wannabe-star mom, turning showgirl—and moll—alongside a star-studded cast including Bugsy Siegel, Virginia Hill, and Jimmy Durante. Violent and voluptuous; heartbreaking and profound, *The Magnificent Esme Wells* is about the losses we endure—and the love we keep betting on, despite the odds. Truly, a showstopper."

—Caroline Leavitt, *New York Times* bestselling author of *Pictures of You* and *Cruel Beautiful World*

"Adrienne Sharp sure can write! And her newest novel, *The Magnificent Esme Wells*, does all the best things: it transports, amuses, delights, and evokes heartbreak. What a gem of a book."

—Jennifer Gilmore, *New York Times* bestselling author of *Golden Country* and *The Mothers*

"WWII-era Los Angelas. and postwar Vegas come vibrantly alive in this detailed, noir portrait of a *Paper Moon*-style childhood."

—*People*

"Esme is street-smart and tough but vulnerable. . . . A memorable character in an unforgettable era."

—Louisa Ermelino, *Publishers Weekly*

"This glittering noirish tragedy, with its lushly imagined period landscape and subtle feminist trajectory, is both fun to read and sad to think about." —*Kirkus Reviews* (starred review)

"Esme's dramatic and irresistible story sparkles with psychological nuance, sumptuous detail, and vivid historical perceptions as Sharp tracks the high wattage success and violence of tough Jews building movie and casino empires while Hitler bloodied Europe. With real-life figures, mushroom clouds rising from desert test sites, and arresting insights into the power and vulnerability of a daring woman performer, Sharp's novel, like Jennifer Egan's *Manhattan Beach*, is propulsive and profound."

—Donna Seaman, *Booklist* (starred review)

THE MAGNIFICENT ESME WELLS

ALSO BY ADRIENNE SHARP

The True Memoirs of Little K

The Sleeping Beauty

White Swan, Black Swan

For my mother, truly magnificent

THE MAGNIFICENT ESME WELLS

LAS VEGAS
1945

1

MY FATHER AND I first drove out to Vegas with Benny Siegel in late summer, 1945, all three of us covered with fine brown sand by the time we got there. We shook it from our clothes and our hair and swept it from the seats, the floor, even the dashboard of Mr. Siegel's little red coupe convertible. And when we were done sweeping, Mr. Siegel offered me his hand with his manicured nails to help me out of the cramped little backseat where no one but a child could possibly fit, his face jubilant and eager, as if he were about to show us some great prize. I jumped from the car, all excited, only to gaze with my father and Benny at the blank acres that held the ruins of some old motel where the Flamingo Club and hotel would soon be built.

That was the prize. The unformed future.

The landscape was otherwise empty, except for the carcass of a prairie dog, a collapsed bundle of dull fur and bones. I looked around for something else to focus on and when I found it, I squinted to see the shapes better—not cacti, but the El Rancho and the Last Frontier, the casinos built before the war, the only things in sight, little specks far down the highway that would eventually be called the Strip.

It took less than thirty minutes for my face to burn a deep red while Mr. Siegel and my father walked the site. I hadn't worn a hat, just one of my mother's big silk scarves. It was seventy degrees back in Los Angeles, but a hundred and five here. I fanned myself futilely with my hands while Mr. Siegel pointed out to my father where the hotel would lie. They were all smiles, the two of them with their movie-star faces, dark hair combed back, dapper in their checked sports jackets. Jackets! Even as a child, I'd noticed that Mr. Siegel liked to surround himself with handsome, well-tailored men, the better to share his vision of a prosperous future. The war was over, he was telling my father, VJ Day an explosion of flags and confetti and bonfires and cars with the letters VJ painted on them cruising and honking their way down the Los Angeles streets, and now, according to Benny, every G.I. and his wife were going to be jumping into those cars looking for fun and adventure. And the town of Las Vegas was going to be that adventure, a glamorous destination.

Really.

Because to me, Las Vegas felt like a punishment. The dusty superheated ground quickly burned through the soles of my espadrilles. How long could they talk and look at nothing? At one point, I tried to get back into the car, but that was worse. In half an hour, it had become a killing box. There was no shade. None. And we hadn't rented a hydrofan air conditioner to hang on the window of the car, either. We'd driven east with the top down.

My father's face turned death-ray red, but still the men walked and talked. I tried to get my father to look my way, but he wouldn't. He only had eyes for Mr. Siegel. Here be the pool—I wish! I'd jump right in it!—the lobby, the restaurant, the casino where my father would soon manage the off-track betting. An upscale gambling palace, a miracle, certainly, for just when my father had come to understand that Los Angeles was never going to make him his fortune, another city appeared in the east, new mirage, all for him.

Mirage was right.

You have to understand that back then, Los Angeles was everything. Vegas, in the early forties, was not much of anything. A small oasis, a railway depot, a little grid of streets by the tracks and then emptiness. Small town. Big desert. Big sky. Grit. Heat. Distant mountains. Stunted brown-needled cacti. Sagebrush. And Block 16, the red-light district that serviced the workers from the dam and the mines, with its gambling and its liquor and its girls, who sat on wooden chairs by the open doorways of their concrete-block shanties, waiting for customers.

But in Ben Siegel's mind, this highway, Highway 91, sprouted one extravagant hotel after another, all of them in possession of casinos and restaurants and pools. And nightclubs, too, apparently, for after a while, Mr. Siegel called to me, waved me over from where I was pouting and flapping my hands at my hot face, saying, "Esme, come here and have a look at where your stage will be."

I guess it was a given even then that, like my mother, I would need a stage. Partly it was because I wore my mother's gorgeous face, which begged to be looked at, though I didn't know that yet. And partly it was because all the way out to Vegas I'd chattered myself silly as a parrot, as my mother would say, about how I was taking tap and ballet lessons at Daddy Mack's studio up on Melrose and how I was going to dance in the Daddy Mack Revue in August, where talent scouts and casting directors and newspaper reporters made up the audience. Every kid in that revue wanted more than anything to be noticed by one of those men, wanted to be picked to be in pictures. As did I, without thought, without question. Because that's what my mother had wanted.

Yes, I'd talked and talked because the drive was so long, and I didn't even think Mr. Siegel had been listening to me. But apparently he had been.

Hence, his grand gesture with his arm to my square of sand. Command performance. My own fault.

I looked at my father, who nodded.

So, inspired, probably, by the western landscape around me, I refashioned my head scarf into a bandanna and took my place to perform a number to "Ragtime Cowboy Joe," which my class was polishing up for the revue. I flapped my elbows and bent my knees like a bow-legged cowboy and crowed,

> *Out in Arizona where the bad men are*
> *And the only friend to guide you is an evening star*
> *The roughest and the toughest man by far*
> *Is Ragtime Cowboy Joe.*

> *He's a high-falutin', rootin', shootin',*
> *Son of a gun from Arizona*
> *Ragtime Cowboy Joe!*

I went through the entire song, complete with do-si-dos and pretend lasso twirls and a lot of clomping around in my imaginary boots, and when I finished, Mr. Siegel frowned.

A western number was not really part of his vision for his new casino, not really the right sort of bait for the type of person Mr. Siegel was hoping to draw here. In his casino, he didn't want the scruffy locals from the Henderson magnesium mines or the workers from Boulder City who had settled in the desert once the dam was completed or the ranch hands who watched after the grazing horses or the airmen the war would leave behind at the old Las Vegas Gunnery School. Las Vegas was then still pretty much enmeshed in its cowboy past—men with sunburns despite their ten-gallon hats, sweaty, unshaven prospectors— and it had not yet met its future filled with new men, like Benny

Siegel, with their wide-lapel silk suits and shiny shoes, men who imagined a whole city with hotels as glamorous as the night-clubs on Sunset Boulevard, which Vegas would eventually drain of talent and audiences, desert hotels that filled its pockets with human desire.

Right from the start, there was to be nothing of the El Rancho, which billed itself as the Queen of the West, or the Last Frontier, which needed no special billing to explain itself, about Benny's Flamingo Club. There were to be no sawdust floors, no slot machines painted to look like cowboys. The showgirls weren't going to dance like Indians or twirl lassoes and they wouldn't wear sombreros or bandanas. As Mr. Siegel imagined it, a stay at the Flamingo would be a glamorous event, like going to Monte Carlo, but even better, Hollywood style, where guests would rub shoulders with Bing Crosby and Jimmy Durante. The staff would wear tuxedos, and the girls would wear feathers, pink high heels, and glass jewels.

And one day all that would come to be, but right now, even before I yodeled out "Ragtime Cowboy Joe!", took my hee-haw bow, and shook my scarf like a pair of reins, I knew I'd made a mistake. I hadn't given my audience what it wanted. It wouldn't be a mistake I'd make often. Mr. Siegel clapped and winked at me with one of those amazing blue eyes, but it was only to be polite, because when he wasn't being a sociopathic killer, he always displayed the exquisite manners he learned from his fancy lady mistress and his Hollywood friends. He was not enthusiastic, and even at age twelve, I could sense that. I hadn't given him what he wanted. But by the time Las Vegas was finished with me, I would be exactly what he and everybody else wanted. Exactly.

2

JUST SO YOU KNOW, my mother was a showgirl, too, though never here in Las Vegas. She started out as a Busby Berkeley girl, one of the first, a gorgeous thing with a headdress four feet tall, ostrich feathers dripping like waterfalls, and satin bows rippling on her elegant shoes as she walked the great soundstages of Warner Brothers and MGM. She was not quite sixteen years old when Buzz came out to Los Angeles, looking to scrounge up some dancing girls for his first Warner Brothers picture, *Gold Diggers of 1933,* which had been a big Ziegfeld hit on Broadway. At her audition, Buzz called her over, measured her leg from knee to ankle, instructed her to twirl, and then hired her on the spot. That's all it took.

For the Shadow Waltz number in *Gold Diggers* she wore a platinum blonde wig, gold metallic shoes, and a two-layered chiffon skirt stretched over a hoop. In the black-and-white photograph I keep of her in my dressing room, she looks like a little doll, her skin manufactured partly of white wax, partly of alabaster. All she had to do in that number was stand with a hundred other girls on a tall staircase that doubled back on itself like a looped ribbon and pretend to play a lit-up violin while the camera sailed by, forty feet in the air. No wonder her audition was so brief.

Shooting from above was Buzz's trademark; he had done a hundred numbers that way back at Warner Brothers, in picture after picture like *Gold Diggers* and *42nd Street* and *Footlight Parade,* his girls rotating like flecks in a kaleidoscope, making geometric patterns of stars or layer cakes or blossoming flowers. That's all they did, but that wasn't all they wanted. When the camera panned his girls' beautiful faces, they smiled, one by one, into the lens, dying to be noticed. My mother was fourth in line, always yearning to be the first. The only. The magnificent. Just like me.

LOS ANGELES
1939

3

I THINK *BABES IN Arms* was the last picture my mother worked on at MGM, but by the time it was released in October 1939, my father and I couldn't bring ourselves to see it. And even though I was on the lot with her almost every day, I never saw any of the great pictures made at MGM that year, like *The Wizard of Oz* or *Gone with the Wind*, because my mother wasn't cast in any of those. She worked almost exclusively on MGM's B films, like the Andy Hardys or *Babes*, which was shot that summer on Lot One, Stage Eighteen, while I watched it all, settled behind the grips and the boom and the monstrous camera. I was a small blond child with big blue eyes that didn't miss a trick, my limbs as thin as the No. 2 school pencils I never got to use. I was six that year, and I should have been enrolled in school, of course, but as far as the Los Angeles City School Board knew, I didn't exist. We moved far too much for anyone to keep track of me and this suited my parents and me just fine.

At the end of each shooting day, when we finally emerged from General Wardrobe, we'd join the big crush of women making a mob at the counter to turn back in their costumes beneath the big posted sign:

TAG NUMBER
GIVEN YOU WHEN WARDROBE
ISSUED MUST BE ATTACHED
TO WARDROBE WHEN
RETURNED

and my father would be waiting for us, out by the studio's East Gate, by the tall columns with the words NO PARKING stenciled on each of their bases, leaning against the car he'd parked there anyway, when had a rule ever caged him in? our big new green 1939 Cadillac 61 with white-walled tires and a silver grille pushing out in front like the prow of a ship. My father's face was always lit up, agreeable, cut in two with a big smile. Trouble almost never showed itself there. He had dark hair that he wore slicked straight back and he wore his hat tipped back, too, exposing his friendly handsome face, as if he knew it was his best asset.

Yes, my father looked like a movie star, even though he scorned them, thought all actors were puppets and that the movie moguls Louis B. Mayer, Jack Warner, Harry Cohn, Carl Laemmle, and Jesse Lasky were just Jewish peddlers from the old country, like my grandfather, who had dropped their rags, fur pieces, and scrap metal so they could traffic in people, pull their strings, pay their actors by the week at one rate and loan them out to each other's studios at ten times that amount and put the profit in their own pockets. Don't be a puppet, he always told me. Be the one pulling the strings.

That's what he did. Or, anyway, that's what he thought he was doing.

One July day, the day our fortunes turned us east toward the Vegas desert, though we didn't know this yet, I climbed into the front seat of the Cadillac, as usual, and my mother followed, as usual, pushing open the sliding front windscreen so we could inhale the late afternoon air coming in off the ocean, damp and salty, so thick you could almost grab hold of it, the kind of cloudy air that had drenched our cottage every evening when we had lived, briefly, in Redondo Beach so my father could take the water taxis out to the offshore gambling boats. When my father took his seat, my mother laid her head back and stretched one arm behind me so that it touched my father's shoulder. I could see the lipstick mark of her red kiss on my father's jaw, a kiss she must have just given him. Her summer dress was made of a light calico print, the fabric fluttering in a breeze that seemed manufactured just for her by one of the big soundstage fans.

She wore her hair that summer in marcelled waves that rippled like black sand, using a rhinestone barrette to pin those waves back, a bob favored by the twenties flappers, yet a bit old-fashioned for 1939. My mother often said if she'd only been born just a decade earlier, she knew she would have been a great silent film star. A Louise Brooks. A Joan Crawford. A Gloria Swanson. And so, the hair. What else? The black pinpoints of her pupils were surrounded by the discs of two brilliantly blue irises, a blue you could almost see even in the black-and-white films of the thirties. A cerulean blue. I have her color eyes, though I'm blond, my light hair courtesy of my Austrian grandfather, but I have my mother's eyes. And as my father tells me, her face.

What else do I remember? The way my mother walked, which was a cross between a glide and a sashay. And her perfume, Tabu, which came in a small cello-shaped glass bottle, let me conjure it for you, the scent amber and oriental and sultry, and which permeated her clothes like a fuzzy cloud of cloves and oranges. It was a drugstore perfume, but it didn't smell that way on her. Far from it. Nothing about her was ordinary to me.

"Scenic way home?" my father asked and my mother said, "Of course," which meant we were going to drive up into the hills to park and look down at the beads of light that made up the night-time cityscape before heading back down into it, to the Holly-wood flats, to home. We liked to do that. Or maybe I should say, they liked to do that. So I fit myself under my father's free arm, while my mother lit her cigarette and turned her head from me to exhale into the balmy air.

4

AHEAD AND ABOVE US rose the enormous Hollywoodland sign, the letters as tall as five men. Years ago, in 1923, the sign had been lit up with thousands of lightbulbs to advertise a new housing development, its five hundred acres pocked with copies of French chateaus, English Tudors, Spanish haciendas, Italian villas. But now the lights on the Hollywoodland sign were gone and the *H* had fallen down so the word didn't make any sense. And the neighborhood wasn't new anymore. It was all filled up with movie people from the twenties, now retired. Bela Lugosi. Erté. Cedric Gibbons. So, of course, this was the perfect neighborhood for my mother, the perfect encapsulation of her perfect era.

It was still just light enough for my father to send our Cadillac along the steep and narrow roads that threaded the neighborhood's canyons and its cypress, pine, and magnolia trees. Gradually the gasoline and exhaust smells of the cars and buses receded, overlaid by the scents of honeysuckle and wisteria and jasmine and lemon flowers, the air flecked with oleander and jacaranda, the whole city saturated with its trademark scent until we inhaled nothing but its perfume, heard nothing but birds and little animals scurrying all around us through the shrubbery. I thought I saw not only squirrels, but cottontails, raccoons, and what looked like a small red fox dart under some brush, probably to his little home, where he had an armchair and a tea kettle.

And as we drove, my father told my mother what she wanted to hear. "This is where we're going to live one day, baby." And, I suppose, that was the purpose of these visits up to the hills, so my parents could remind themselves this was where they were headed, this was where they belonged. Every place we'd lived in since my grandfather's death two years ago—and we'd lived in a lot of places—was just temporary. Our real house, our dream house, was ahead of us, in the big wide future. Those dreamers called dibs on every house we passed that evening, singing out, "This one. No, that one," each new house appealing to them more than the last. And when they couldn't decide at all, laughing, they turned to me and had me pick.

That night I pointed to the biggest, gaudiest house in all of Hollywoodland, up high on Durand Drive, a three-story castle with a watchtower owned by the gangster Bugsy Siegel, who once ran a speakeasy there. Who knew then we'd ever meet him, let alone that my father would work for him?

My father took hold of my hand with the pointing finger and said, "Castillo del Lago, why not?"

Yes, why not? Why couldn't we live in the biggest, gaudiest confection teetering atop the highest hill?

After all, as we all knew, any minute now my mother was going to have the screen test that would make her a star and my father was going to make a fortune at the track and become a member of the Turf Club at Hollywood Park, where he'd rub elbows with Mr. Louis B. Mayer himself, and we three would move up here to a manor house we would call Wells' Loft for my mother or maybe the Silver Lair for my father. Or Esme's Burrow for me.

My mother hugged me, and my father called me Miss Gold Digger of 1939, but I knew I hadn't displeased him. Far from it. I used to love to listen while my parents talked like that, back and forth, their dreams great puffs of smoke that made a lullaby for me. Soon, soon, soon.

5

AT THE TOP OF Mulholland Drive, my father pulled over onto an outlook to park and the three of us looked down at the city below, the many blinking lights of downtown, the three busiest streets of Western, Vine, and La Brea spread in a wide, ever expanding triangle before us. Looking west there were fewer lights until finally it was just a swath of darkness pushing its inky way to the ocean.

When my parents got out of the car to sit on its hood and share a cigarette and look out over the city lights before them, I swiveled around in my seat to look back at the remaining tall white letters of the Hollywoodland sign fast fading in the twilight. A young actress had jumped off the now fallen *H* to her death the year before I was born.

That had been one of my mother's bedtime stories, however oddly inappropriate for me, and embedded in this particular story was the uneasy conflation of my birth and the lady's death, my arrival and her flight.

Did my mother think my arrival meant she too had to say goodbye? Goodbye, goodbye, to Western, La Brea, and Vine? Yes. She was only sixteen when she had me, my father eighteen. I imagined the actress, Peg Entwistle, who looked, in my imagination then, distressingly similar to my mother, though she was blond and my mother brunette, perched on the *H*, her dress flapping in the wind, as she called out to the world that if she couldn't be a star she would rather be a ghost, a beautiful ghost.

My mother had once told me dead people liked to haunt the places where they died, that she'd seen my grandfather's ghost sitting in the dining room at our old house reading his newspapers the night after his funeral, and that people had seen Entwistle haunting this hill, a sad-looking blonde in old-fashioned clothes who gave off the pungent scent of her favorite gardenia perfume. That, and the scent of regret. Or maybe it was rage. Maybe it was her ghost that pulled down the letter *H* of the Hollywood that betrayed her. Maybe tonight would be the night her ghost climbed down the big hill and across Mulholland Drive to our car, her face white and her hands outstretched to strangle anyone whose face loomed larger than hers once did on the screen.

From the foot of the sign where she had fallen, you could see the big reservoir created by the Hollywood Dam. So the water up here wasn't really a lake, it was a reservoir, but it was called Lake Hollywood, anyway. After all, this was Los Angeles, land of pretend, where houses were castles and peddlers were moguls and reservoirs were lakes. So fine. It was a lake. Make it a lake. Maybe Entwistle had been jumping for that, for a dark, watery oblivion.

I turned back and pulled the car blanket over my body, ready to make myself fully invisible should her anguished ghost float by. Meanwhile, I found the sight of my parents through the windscreen reassuring, the two of them sitting side by side on the hood, my father's arm about my mother's shoulders, keeping her there and nowhere else, their bodies silhouetted against the yellow city lights that winked before them and the white stars that had begun to offer their light from above.

While I watched, my father opened up his free arm in a sweeping gesture, as if to offer all of that light, both heaven and manmade, to my mother. Because those were the terms of their marriage from the start, his promise to provide her the big life she craved. As long as they were both engaged in the pursuit of that goal, all was fine. When I knocked on the windscreen to get their attention, to be part of that embrace, they turned, laughing, and knocked back, and my mother pressed her lips to the glass in a kiss. When she sat up, I could see the perfect red imprint of her lips left behind just for me.

The color? St. Petersburgundy.

6

BY THE TIME WE had finished gazing at the city from our perch on Mulholland Drive and headed down to the Hollywood Flats, to Orange Street, as the fruit trees grew everywhere on our block, the susurrus of the car's motor and my parents' voices had acted on me like a great sleeping draught, my head rocking in my mother's lap. But I roused quickly enough when the car stopped too abruptly and my mother let out an odd cry. My father pulled the brake.

I sat up and peeked over the dashboard. On the front lawn before our flat-roofed duplex, No. 23, stood our furniture as if arranged for a nighttime garage sale—our sofa and tables, our chairs with clothing on hangers hooked to the backs of them, large mounds of towels and linen, stacks of pots and dishes. And set out as if the lawn were a green carpet and the square of lawn a bedroom were my parents' bed and all the pieces of the curvilinear Art Moderne champagne-colored bedroom suite my mother had been so proud of that she had invited in the next-door neighbors whose names she didn't even know to see it the day it was delivered. Now they could see it all just by looking out their windows.

I sat up straighter, looking from my father, who, I could tell from years of carefully reading his face, was not entirely surprised by this course of events, to my mother, for whom all this represented an odd, jumbled, and surprising dreamscape. She shut the windscreen against all that lay before us as if the action might erase the entirety of it. Which, of course, it did not.

She sat silently holding her cigarette for three seconds, five seconds, ten seconds before flicking it out the window and turning on my father, flailing her little fists at him over me, pummeling him, crying, "Ike, what did you do? What did you do?"

I shrank down in the seat between them while he, cigarette between his teeth, held up his own hands to ward off her assault, the slap, slap of flesh meeting flesh continuing on above me. This had to somehow be his fault.

And, of course, as it turned out, it was. As usual.

My father's life at that time revolved around the great magic triumvirate of the Santa Anita, Del Mar, and Hollywood Park racetracks. Every morning when the horses were running, he made the circuit at MGM, taking bets from the bit actors and the barbers and the electricians and the kitchen help on the lot, and he put the money in his own pocket. If a horse won, he paid on the bet. If the horses lost, as they almost always did, my father kept the money, saying, Why should the track get the dough? The track was like a bank and banks go broke. Safer this way for everybody. Except when the long shots came in and my father had to scramble to pay. But he always paid. Always. People trusted Ike.

So what had my father done? It was more what he had not done. He had not paid the rent, had not paid the rent for the past three months, had been planning to pay it all to the landlord tonight after his big win at the track. But in, as he explained, a minor hiccup, he had lost the money he'd collected this morning at the MGM barber shop, at the Mill Buildings, at the kitchen door of the Commissary, when Starlight had come in at 4 to 1 in the fifth at Hollywood Park. And the sixth hadn't gone much better. Or the seventh. In fact, he hadn't done well in any of the races. The horses had come in. And he'd had to pay on those bets. What else could he do? He had to pay the win. From the rent money.

"So what?" my father said. "A temporary setback."

To which my mother replied, "It always is."

She was screaming now, saying she wished they'd never sold her daddy's house. If they hadn't they could be there right now. Inside. In bed. At some point during my mother's speech, I began to wish my father hadn't parked right in front of our house. Not that the neighbors hadn't heard this or something like it plenty of times before.

But my father, who usually tried to mollify my mother as quickly as possible, wasn't backing down tonight, was getting out of the car and coming around to her side to pull her out, too, one of her hands grasping blindly for me as if a fistful of my dress could hold her tight. Like a traitor, I shied away from her, and then she was out of the car where my father could shout right into her hysterical rant that there was gold floating in the dust around the great ring of racetracks and there wasn't anything else here for him in this goddamn parched place. All those big boys—Zanuck, Warner, and Cohn—wouldn't be at the track so much if it weren't a place to make money. Even Louis B. Mayer played the ponies. Played the ponies, hell, he owned twenty-five of them! He spent so much time at Santa Anita his staff at MGM nicknamed his box there Stage 14. So my father was going to make his losses back and then some. Like he always did.

My second wish of the night was that my father hadn't pulled my mother from the car to deliver this speech because now she was trying to squirm away from him, an elbow at his chest, and who knew what she would do if she got loose. I peered at her in the semi-darkness. Her face looked nothing like a doll's anymore, long streaks of wet unmasking her sallow skin beneath the golden powder and her eyes blinking out of a blurred black mask while my father reasoned with her, his voice a comet at the end of its course, all sparks and emptiness. She wasn't having any of it.

"Where's all my daddy's money?" she demanded. "All that money. Where is it?"

Without looking away from her, my father waved his arm vaguely at our furniture, our clothing, even the Cadillac with me in it. "It's all here, baby. Every penny of it."

"It can't all be here," my mother said. She put one hand on her hip and jutted that hip out aggressively at him.

"Gone," my father said.

"But there was so much of it," she said. There was some bewilderment in her voice now, maybe some protest, but more than anything, resignation. "What did you do with it?"

Well. We'd moved a lot. Bought a lot.

He took her hand in his. "Dina, baby, it doesn't matter. Change is blowing down the boulevard. Can't you feel it?" And he gestured, a big sweeping gesture that took in the hills, with the Hollywoodland sign glowing white, minus its *H*, even beyond the hills, as if change were a tumbleweed come all the way here from the desert where we'd end up. "Baby, can you feel it?"

Well, I guess she couldn't because she wrenched her hand from his and pushed herself away from him. My father and I watched her take a few unsteady sashaying steps in those high heels of hers, her cotton dress as damp and weepy as she was. She moved over the grass toward the ragged aisles of our furniture where she paused, as if freshly startled, and then marched onward into the mess of it, running her palm along the tabletops as she passed them, a customer considering a purchase, picking up a glass or utensil to study as if it were some curiosity whose use she could not fathom, patting at her black hair while looking into the big framed mirror. Vanity even in extremis. After one fight, my mother had taken scissors to her own wedding portrait—a portrait they'd sat for at some department store following their elopement—cutting my father's face right out of the paper, leaving a hole below his hat and beneath that hole, my father's suited body. But her own beautiful face remained there by him, intact, of course.

My father, who seemed relieved that the worst was over, leaned against the car to light and smoke a Chesterfield. I watched him watch her the whole time and then he finished his cigarette, ground it out on the street curb, and sighed. "Stay here," he said to me. As if I had any intention of getting out of the car.

I watched him walk to where she now stood, slowly emptying my bed of the pots and pans the frustrated landlord had piled in there, helter-skelter, eager to scrape his rental clean of troublesome us. Without looking back at my father, she put up a hand to keep him away. And when the bed was cleared of its tower of kitchenware, she smoothed my bedspread, printed with its pumpkin carriages, glass slippers, and helpful mice wielding scissors and thread. My mouth opened. Making my bed was not something she did very much. Not when it was in the house.

I couldn't hear what my father said to her then, but I could hear her tell him in a too-loud voice, "This neighborhood is full of thieves."

This neighborhood hadn't been our neighborhood for very long. We used to live in a big house in Boyle Heights with my grandfather until my grandfather died two years ago and my mother had to be committed to Camarillo State Mental Hospital. After the funeral, my mother had stayed up all night talking and talking and talking, and then all of a sudden like a chattering doll run out of news, she lay there stupidly mute on the living-room sofa, unable to get up. One morning when I woke, my mother wasn't there, no goodbye, no goodbye kiss, her dresser drawers emptied. My father told me she was taking a rest for a few weeks in Camarillo, at a special hospital. A doll hospital, where the chattering part, its springs and pulleys, would be fixed so it would run neither too fast nor too slow. She was gone for a month, and the whole time she was gone, I slept with one of her chiffon nightgowns as if it were her shadow I had been charged to keep.

When she recovered, we sold my grandfather's house and blew out of there in his 1936 black Plymouth, throwing my mother's inheritance out the car window, one hundred-dollar bill at a time, two bills, three bills, there was plenty more where that came from, of that my parents were sure. We had lived first in a big Spanish-style house in Echo Park, where my father had taken me on boat rides around a lake from the center of which erupted a fountain, the circumference of the lake sprouting date palms with their thick middles and hairy fronds. After that, we had lived, for a few months, in the aforementioned Redondo Beach, at the end of a long railway line, in a shotgun clapboard shack, perpetually damp, and then we had moved again to a wooden bungalow in the hills and after that to this one-story duplex apartment on Orange Street in the flats of Hollywood, where the yard was overgrown with jasmine and sticker bushes and at the back the wood fence sagged inward like an embrace.

And this was where we had last lived.

Used to live.

It didn't occur to me then that our change of housing reflected the slow decline in our fortunes. I see that now, of course. But back then I thought we'd moved to the flats for good luck, because this was where the early Hollywood studios had once cranked out the silent pictures, the kind of pictures my mother loved. Our move there was in tribute, I thought. Homage.

I saw the curtains move in the front window of the duplex next to ours. I held my breath, not only because we were being watched, but because I wasn't quite sure what my mother might do or say next. Not long ago my father had read me a story from the *Daily News* about a woman who had run naked and screaming along Hollywood Boulevard, the police chasing after her for two blocks waving their hands. He had laughed, but I had not. I could far too easily picture my mother running the white-hot pavement in her bare feet, her bare body luminescent and all too fluid in that steaming urban light.

On my one visit to see her in Camarillo she had whispered to me that the night before she had flown over the unit wall to the main building, the one with the bell tower, and sailed around its courtyard fountain to a big wooden door with iron mountings. Locked, but opened by a wish. Down the embossed floor of the hallway, tiles underfoot made for a saint, through the next door, and up the tightly winding stairway that looped back and forth on itself like a troubled mind and led, eventually, to the freedom of the bell tower, which soared three stories high, the tallest perch on the grounds, save the tops of the eucalyptus and palm trees. The tower archway opened to the black air, the ledge just deep enough for a woman's feet. And there she stood, the hem of her gown flapping, the gown threatening to divide itself altogether from her body, a plastic leash with her name on it wrapped around one wrist. I was four, and I wasn't entirely certain what she told me hadn't actually happened. Was it summer? Winter? Autumn? Flower petals? Red leaves? Snowflakes? Drizzle? Different. Different every time I imagined it.

Was my father watching her also, wary even as he pretended disaffection? Did he worry as I did that she might climb up onto the roof of our house and raise her arms to the moon, pull herself onto it, and walk its surface? And if that happened, how did he plan to retrieve her? As he had retrieved her from Camarillo, slowly drawing her down from that bell tower, away from the great black lip of the Camarillo mission bell, the clapper invisible within the dark mouth itself, a secret, my father pulling my mother down from the sky just as she rose to meet it, her gown a pale bone sail puffed full of air? Once I had been in the Sisters Orphan Home, I came to better understand my mother and the lure of a bell tower, from which it seemed possible to launch an escape from everything intolerable. And after she came back to us, I was careful to watch her, to know where she was, to anticipate what she might do next, so I might catch her before she fell or flew away.

To my great relief, she did not take the opportunity this evening to strip off her dress and run up Orange Street to Hollywood Boulevard or to fly up into the hills to perch on the O or the L or any other letter of the Hollywoodland sign still standing. She simply wandered over to her own gold-spun bed, where she lay down, as if the bed were somehow still stationed in the privacy of her own bedroom, the fact that she left her shoes on her only concession to our peculiar circumstances. I listened to her cry. It was dark but there was a streetlight. So she could be heard and seen. My father began to pace a circle around all that had once been inside our half of the duplex and now was not, and then he stood on the sidewalk by the car, looking up and down the street as if some answer to all this might yet come rolling his way. The night air was purple with jacaranda.

Quietly, I got out of the Cadillac.

I'm not even sure my father felt me, a ghost poking its hands into his pockets to see if he'd gathered any betting tickets from the floor at Hollywood Park. He had. And that was a sure sign that things hadn't gone well at the track today. As if I needed another one.

It didn't look good for a bookie to be scouring the concrete floor for trash. That was usually my job. And as a little girl, I was an expert stooper, slipping easily between the men to dive for tickets, the breeze I made in passing sometimes shaking winning tickets from their careless hands. Those tossed tickets weren't always losers, you understand. The men down on the concourse have been drinking all day, they can't see straight to read their tickets, and they let them drop, running off to lay down the next bet. And they dropped more than their tickets. They dropped everything—bottle caps, stubby pencils, handkerchiefs, wads of spittle, shoelaces, bottles, string, coins. At the track with my father, I'd once found a wallet, which he'd stuffed furtively in his coat pocket with a wink. From him, I'd learned to be stealthy.

I walked over the grass and sat down at our kitchen table with the wad of tickets and my father's notebook, the pages full of the names of horses I couldn't quite read: Chance Taken, Up in Arms, Nobody's Fool, Westward Ho.

That was what my father had done years before, gone westward ho, seduced by the picture postcards that showed Los Angeles as a fragrant green land of palm trees and orange trees, lemons and oleander, postcards printed with green hills and orange groves, even the paper of those cards were made of smelling sweet. When he had gotten off the train in 1930 at the old River Station, he had looked up at the hot blue sky with the big yellow sun in it and in that moment Baltimore and all its memories burned away to soot and that was why he had so few left to offer me. I can't even tell you his mother's name.

I might not be able to read yet exactly, but I already knew my numbers. Methodically, I began to sort the tickets into piles. Race 1. Race 2. Race 3. When I'd gotten everything sorted, I planned to check the tickets against the information in my father's notebook. My father was scrupulous about scribbling down the outcome of each race. His notebook held his little history of the track. Usually there were no winning tickets to be found from the first race or so, but as the afternoon wore on and the men grew drunker, they read their tickets with less and less care, and not often, but sometimes, I found a winner. When that happened, my father would bow and kiss my hand, "Thank you very much, Little Miss," and we'd take the ticket to the betting window and the track paid on it. No scruples darkened our glee. I knew how to please him.

A siren sounded somewhere north of us, heading toward Gower Street, toward Paramount, not in our direction. The paper tickets stuck to my sweating fingers as I sorted, squinting to see the numbers in the almost dark. I felt as if I were in a horse race myself, a race against what might come next. My mother wasn't going to lie there crying on that bed forever. So I sorted the gritty slips with some urgency, while my father sat on the edge of the big bed and spoke to my mother in a low, forceful voice. I concentrated hard not to hear them. Eventually, they were quiet and I supposed the quiet meant my mother had acquiesced to something, probably that she would not insist that we all sleep in our beds out here on the lawn of No. 23 Orange Street, Hollywood, California.

Having placated her, my father came to sit beside me, dropping heavily into the other metal chair, and flipped open his notebook. He understood what I was doing. The tall buildings of nearby Hollywood Boulevard, its street signs and light poles and billboards watched us work. Cross-eyed from looking sideways into the notebook, I found one slip I thought looked good, a possible gem. My father studied it, scanned the notebook, shook my hand, and winked. It was good. It was a gem. I said a quick small prayer to the Gods of the Horses, and then I scampered over to the bed where my mother lay, and I wagged the ticket in the dark air above her.

She stared up vacantly at me, Who are you?, and then coughed, a drowned person coming to. I tucked the ticket behind my ear like an ornamental flower and wagged my finger at her, strutting and clucking as I'd seen Judy Garland do earlier today. I'd memorized all her routines, and not only from today's shoot. Already at six, I was a quick study. And, as well, I'd discovered the pleasures of performing for an audience, which offered both escape from—and aggrandizement of—the self. I used my Judy Garland voice to make my mother laugh as I sang,

He's sweet just like chocolate candy
Or like the honey from a bee
Oh, I'm just wild about Harry
And he's just wild about me!

And behind me, my father, who had calculated the win, sang out, "That's seven dollars fifty," victory!, more than enough money for tonight's hotel room, and my mother smiled at me, her tears dried, and held out her arms. "Well, aren't you my lucky little pony. Comeer."

7

BUT BECAUSE SEVEN DOLLARS fifty only went so far, the next morning my father had to perform his own favorite lounge act, the hocking of my mother's engagement ring, something he had found himself having to do a few times since we sold my grandfather's house, and it was never performed without drama. My mother lay in our bed at the Hollyhock Motel, weeping, as he tried to unscrew the diamond ring from her finger, swearing he would soon enough retrieve it, no harm done, and not only that, he would buy her a much bigger ring altogether once we were in the money again. And we would be in the money again, goddammit. And then, with one swift movement, he had sheared the ring from her finger with a cry of triumph, disinterested in my mother's corresponding cry of pain and insult, holding the ring up to the light as if to take its measure, as if he hadn't seen it every single day for seven years since the day he first put it on her finger.

It was not, of course, the first time he'd wronged her. His initial act of perfidy had been to take her to bed the very day he met her in 1932. She had been only sixteen, a teenager walking down Melrose Avenue in her tap shoes, having just finished her own dance class at Daddy Mack's when my father first beheld her. And she, him. Within the hour she had downed two Tom Collinses at a nearby bar, and by the end of that afternoon, her tap shoes lay, satin bows undone, on the floor by the bed in the rooming house where my father, two years in the city, practically a native, was staying, though not, as it turned out, for very long. After that, my mother was bound to him for life, already pregnant with me while she was filming *Gold Diggers*. And here it was, 1939, and she was still bound to him, bound to him and all his troubles.

"So, here's what we're going to do," my father said to me, after he had the ring in hand and we'd hopped into our Cadillac, leaving my mother behind lying in the sagging motel bed with her fistful of tissues and the few valuables she had managed to scoop up before we had left Orange Street behind us last night. "We're going to find ourselves a nice little pawnshop and we're going to get ourselves a nice bit of cash and then we're going to the races on this fine Saturday afternoon, where all we need is one big win and we're back in business and we'll head back for the furniture."

I said nothing, dubious.

"Look, little girl. Don't give me that long face. When you step out into the world, you've got to step out with a smile on."

I refused to look at the world or at him. I thought he should be made to suffer, even though I usually found my father's insouciance one of his most appealing characteristics. But my pout didn't interest him at all. Nor, to be honest, did our furniture. If it weren't for my mother, I knew he'd leave it all behind without another thought, happy to start over, starting over being his specialty.

My father drove west on Hollywood Boulevard. In our Cadillac we passed the big movie palaces, once arcade storefronts with penny machines showing one-minute silent shorts, now the El Capitan, Grauman's Chinese, and the Egyptian, the neon lettering on their marquees a faded red and pink and green in the morning light. And when the mechanical arm on the corner traffic signal swung down the STOP placard and up the GO, my father turned the car south down Fairfax Avenue.

We passed Gilmore Field stadium, where the Hollywood All Stars played ball, their motto "The Hollywood Stars owned by the real Hollywood stars," because their paychecks were cut by movie stars like Gene Autry and the stands packed with movie stars from MGM and Warners. And then there was the plat of oil fields, Gilmore Fields, once a dairy farm, but there were no cows grazing there anymore, no, only pumps and derricks that winched up the money that seemed to be sprouting everywhere in Los Angeles, out of oil fields, out of the new San Pedro Harbor, out of newspapers and movie studios, out of racing tracks and gambling houses, out of the acres of land not only here on the west side of the city but in the Valley farmland above and in the South Bay down below, once Spanish ranchos, money ready to be plucked from the earth by the clever and the game.

Almost all of my father's fantasies revolved around the idea of being clever and game, like the big boys of Los Angeles, the big, important Jews who were making money not only by making movies, but also by snapping up land, snapping up all the old ranchos that had once belonged to the Picos and Dominguezes and the Figueroas, after they themselves had stolen it out from under the poor Gabrielino Indians, who didn't even wear clothes, for Christ's sake, my father said, just walked around naked, the women in deerskin skirts, weaving baskets at the Missions that enslaved them. And that was only eighty years ago!

Yes, the big boys had been busy, and not with the primitive pueblos and missions and ranchos that had preoccupied the Spaniards, but with setting up hospitals and racetracks and country clubs and housing developments and law firms—everything the old school Dohenys and Chandlers and Huntingtons had, the newly fancy Jews had for themselves now, too. The movie moguls weren't admitted to the Dohenys' country club, so they built their own. Hillcrest. They weren't welcome at the Santa Anita racetrack, so they built their own. Hollywood Park. They needed a hospital? Cedars of Lebanon. Jews weren't stuck in the ghetto anymore. They owned this city, or part of it, Los Angeles, population 1,504,277 and still growing, still under construction. And as my father said, Goddammit if there still wasn't more gold to be mined here by men like him. It was his time, his time to be a big boy!

We passed the brand-new May Company department store with its great gold cylinder rising up the center of the building's five floors like a tall stack of coins to which my father always nodded and said, "Ka-ching, ka-ching," elbowing me, which he did today and at which I refused to smile, and behind the enormous department store rose the stench of the Hancock Park Fossil Pits as if no one cared about the mix of commerce, tar, and bones.

"All righty," my father said when we had traveled so far south that we reached Century Boulevard. We cruised past the double-headed streetlamps and the telephone poles and the date palms, past the Cut Rate Drugs and the Inglewood Laundry, and up to the Utility Auto Park that charged a quarter an hour to park. My father pulled in there, telling the man, "We won't be an hour," giving him a quarter anyway, along with his best smile. "Put me over by the exit where I won't bother anyone and keep that quarter for yourself." At this the man smiled, too, and showed a silver tooth in front.

I followed my father off the lot and down the street. "You see how crowded it is here?" my father said. "No place to park. The cars are head to toe at every curb." And it was true. "A man could make a fortune here with a couple of lots." He tapped his hat. "Something to remember. Always keep lots of ideas up there," and he tapped his head again. It was so like my father to be hatching a new scheme right in the middle of a crisis brought about by one of his other schemes.

My father found a shop he liked the look of just around the corner from Inglewood Boulevard and not too far from the race-track. The painted red word PAWNSHOP was stenciled above the storefront window and beneath that word, two more, CASH LOANS. Clearly, that's what we were after. Cash. We stood outside the window for a minute, looking through the glass. Above us on a high shelf, a long row of guitars stood propped up and ready to play, black polished guitars in which you could see the buildings opposite reflected and warm yellow ones with the wood softly waxed that reflected nothing. Beneath the guitars hung a row of trumpets, and beneath that, on a shelf, lay the humble xylophone and some maracas. The shop looked like a music store. When I said this, my father told me, "Easy things to pawn. Not something you absolutely need." Unless you were a musician, of course.

The instruments were what I was staring at, but my father's attention was drawn by other things, other things people obviously didn't absolutely need, like watches and rings. Rows of rings were set out in velvet cases, a dozen long rows of diamond and gold rings, and nestled in the middle of them, jewelry boxes opened like clamshells to show off watches, mostly thick men's watches, but I could see the slender gold bands of ladies' watches, too. But mostly there were rings, diamond rings, like my mother's. "Each one offered up with a tear," my father said to me. But my father wasn't crying.

Inside, we found even more guitars, these guitars still in their open cases as if somebody had loved them very much. They lay like ladies on velvet. Anything on or in velvet accrues the qualities of it—and stimulates the desire to touch. Velvet. Fur. Feathers. Sequins. The tools of my trade, now. That and flesh. There were also bicycles and luggage and clothing, and in every glass case there was more jewelry, as if people had stripped themselves bit by bit of everything they owned, their playthings, their carryalls, their clothing, and then finally, as they were dropping into the grave, their crosses and wedding bands and watches and pearls. I wondered how long it would be before the rest of our possessions ended up at this pawnshop, or some other one like it. At the counter, my father, who had entered the room with a smile, drew with some ceremony my mother's ring from the pocket of his shirt and proffered it to the pawnshop owner. No handsome velvet clamshell for us.

I turned away from my father's genial face and from the pawn-shop man who was holding the ring up to the light to assess its value, the light that made its way in from the street to shine on my mother's diamond and to alight on her tear, which glistened on the stone's icy surface. When the man pulled out a jeweler's loupe to better inspect both the gem and my mother's despair at losing it, I turned away and walked the length of the counter to the back shelf, my head low, where I discovered all the toys—the trains and cars, the puzzles and puppets, the dolls and dollhouses, the toy guns and the many, many bicycles, and I wondered if children had been pried tearfully from these toys or if these were the toys they had simply outgrown and discarded. Which of my toys might soon wend their way here? For all I knew, some of them were here already.

It seemed with each of our moves, something of ours was lost, or so I had thought. But maybe, just maybe, my missing toys were not lost, but pawned, brought here surreptitiously by my father whenever he needed a few extra dollars. Perhaps this pawnshop had not been selected at random, my father making a big pretense of musing his way along these streets near the track, but through long practice. I know now my father is capable of anything, almost.

So I decided then that I would look for my toys, though I wasn't exactly sure what I would do if I found them. Force my father to buy them back for me? But because the toys were much less well organized than the jewelry—puzzles and cars all mixed up with alarm clocks and radios—my attention strayed. I was an avid ra-dio listener and the dozens of squat radios, all shapes and sizes, distracted me. The most miraculous of the radios was a radio painted to look like a portable American flag, with a blue body and red-and-white stripes and a red-and-white numbered dial and a blue handle on top you used to carry it. I had never seen any-thing so fabulous.

I reached for it, thinking to turn it on, when the pawnshop man called out to me, "That there's a Patriot Radio," and to my father, "New. This year." And when my father didn't say anything and only tipped his head, the man turned back to the ring. "I can give you fifty dollars for it."

In our state, a fortune.

"How about sixty?" my father said. "It's worth sixty." He should know.

The man shook his head.

My father grinned. "All right, fifty it is. And," he said grandly, "we'll take the radio."

Clearly a bribe, but I couldn't refuse it, as my father very well knew. I had proven myself bribable on many occasions. As had my mother. I hate to say it, but my father was irresistible. So even though I knew I should have resisted him, should have made him drive back to the Hollyhock Motel and hand every cent of that money over to my mother, instead, I carried my Patriot radio to the car, dancing a bit, I regret to say, and I allowed my father to take me, my radio, and the money my mother's ring brought him straight over to Hollywood Park, which was, I also regret to say, like a second home to me.

8

AND IT WAS A sunny day, I remember, the sky a perfect California blue, a brilliant Technicolor blue, as if the ocean had been sucked from its bed in the west and inverted over us. You could smell the ocean all the way east to Inglewood when the wind blew right, the air flowing over four miles of farm fields and arriving still salty and wet and full of adventure past the ticket turnstiles, over the paddock, through the great building, and onto the track and the infield, a green mound of grass and a manmade pond. The flamingos with their pink backs and stick legs picked their way through this prison habitat, visited by gulls or pelicans who wandered in from the coast on the breeze. Over a thousand horses were housed here, and when the wind blew the other way, you could smell that, too.

When my father was winning, riding a good streak, every one of his picks coming in big, he would stroll the track, and with each step he took at the turnstile, the paddock, the Study Hall, the grandstand, men called out to him, "How you doing, Ike," came up to shake his hand, asked him who he liked in the fourth or the fifth or the sixth. But when he wasn't winning, he hunkered down in the back corner of the Study Hall on the bottom level, the concourse, like a delinquent student serving detention. He smoked his cigarettes at his table overflowing with racing sheets, made desperate notes with his worn-down stub of a pencil in his lucky red notebook, always the same kind, which was always fat with money in the morning and by the end of a bad day, thin with nothing but its own lined leaves of paper.

On those days, the bad luck days, he wouldn't leave his table, and he'd send me around to bring him his lunch, and when we went crawling home to my grandfather's house, we knew my grandfather would be there waiting, would look at us sternly as we pulled up the drive behind his big black Plymouth, shaking out the cuffs of his crisply ironed pants and fingering his wide checkered tie, his eyes an icy blue and his narrow mouth pulled over his teeth in the grimace of displeasure.

"So," he would say to my father, "Seabiscuit lose again?"

To which my father would invariably reply, "Rome wasn't built in a day," and saunter on past to the garage.

"This isn't Rome!" my grandfather would call after him in his heavy Austrian accent, but my father was gone.

By the seventh race that fine Saturday afternoon, the day almost over, my father was hiding in the Study Hall and sending me out for our late lunch.

So I knew things weren't going well in Rome.

When I ran past the big Negro shoeshine man, he called out to me, "Comeer, Miss Movie Star," wanting me to come visit with him, which I sometimes did, sitting high up in the big chair until a real customer came by, listening to the big man's jokes while he pretended to polish my shoes.

But not today.

I just held up the dollar bill my father had entrusted me with. And the man nodded and said, "Go get yourself your dogs, little girl." Everybody knew what my father and I ate for our lunch, every day, winter and summer. At the time, I didn't find anything strange about this, or about the fact that I spent my days at the track with my father or on the studio lot with my mother. And because I was small for my age, luckily for my parents, it was rare for me to be questioned by some adult about why I wasn't in school. Especially at the track, where everybody was playing hooky from something. But if I happened to be asked, my father had coached me to say I was home sick. And to cough.

I headed to the concession stands far below the elegant clatter of the Turf Club, which was where my father believed he really belonged, with its statues of jockeys and its paintings of horses, where Robert Taylor, Barbara Stanwyck, Clark Gable, and Bing Crosby sat and where we had never been, to the counter that sold the Lunch of Champions. Irma, an older lady with a hairnet, stood there all afternoon with her gleaming forceps, pulling hot dogs from the big steaming vat, shaking the water from them, and sticking them into long warm buns. Above her the sign laid out your choices:

HOT DOGS 10 CENTS.
RELISH
MUSTARD
TOMATO
LETTUCE
ONIONS
CHILI

We always made the same choice.

Before I even reached the counter, Irma had our four dogs ready in their fluted white paper trays, and she shoved the mustard container toward me. "Here you go, honey. How's your dad doing today?"

I looked over through the big windows of the Study Hall and then back to Irma. "Good," I said, even though he was not.

But I would never tell Irma that. I would never tell anybody that. My mother had impressed upon me that we never discussed family matters with others. Besides, it was bad luck to say you were having bad luck. I smiled at Irma. She kissed the air. Sometimes Irma called me around the counter so she could comb my hair, using the tail of the comb to unravel what she called my rat's nest of dense snarls. I can only imagine what compelled her ministrations, what I must have looked like, hair unbrushed, shirt on backwards, my neck strung with a hundred necklaces in imitation of my mother, a silk flower pinned to my wild coiffure. No one at home ever questioned or edited my sartorial selections. Sometimes Irma even washed my face with a soapy dish towel.

"All right," my father said, when I finally arrived with the hot dogs. He slapped his hands down on the table, setting his pile of cigarette ash shaking in its cheap tin tray. He wasn't much interested in his lunch; mine was gone in seconds. I was never exactly sure when I would eat again. "Baby doll, it's Number Four across the board. Win, place, or show. Thundermaker." And with that my father gave me his famous grin, and then we stood in line together to bet, my father pulling that big juicy wad of pawnshop money from his checkered shirt pocket and handing it over to Carl, his lucky clerk, at the window, ready to make that wad of money even juicier.

And Carl, black shoe-polish hair and a toothpick in his mouth he didn't bother to remove, said, "Got a sure thing, huh, Ike? Whaddiya know?"

But my father only smiled and winked and said, "Put it all on Number Four in the seventh."

To which Carl responded, "Magic Ike! Thundermaker going off at two to one in the seventh," and printed out the ticket, handing it over to my father with a flourish. "Strike it rich, buddy," he said, and my father kissed the ticket, putting on a big show, making Carl and everybody else in line laugh and wish us good luck.

I was nervous.

My father didn't usually go in for single bets, didn't like what they called bridge-jumper shots, putting all his money on one horse. If you put enough down, doubling it could mean a fortune.

But if the horse didn't run well, a man lost everything and ran himself to the nearest bridge to jump off.

I tugged unhappily at my father's hand, but he didn't want to look at my pinched face. He'd had enough of that.

My mother had worried all night about our furniture sitting out on Orange Street, picked over by our neighbors, who, transmogrified into hook-beaked vultures, she was sure, were busy pulling at the threads of our clothes and picking at the stuffing of our mattresses before flying off with my grandmother's silver forks and knives, the one part of my mother's inheritance we had managed to hang on to. Until now. My father had had to promise her over and over again that it would all still be there, every twig of it, we would retrieve it all tonight, and we would not have to sleep in that hotel room again. And it was up to him to make it so. So tugging worriedly at his hand made me querulous. Worry was a cloud and my father liked a clear, sunny day. And a smile. A Shirley Temple. Worry was a jinx, as was a frown.

So he ignored my fear, handed me the ticket, and winked. Cahoots, even though I didn't want to be in cahoots. "Hold on to it, baby girl, and wish for what you want." I knew what he was wishing for. Rent money. I knew what my mother was wishing for—the return of her ring. And maybe a new car, a Cadillac just for her. She liked to say, "Cream for me, please. I want a cream-colored ride." What did I want? I wasn't even sure. Maybe to be returned to my grandfather's house of two years ago before my grandfather became a ghost at his own dining room table.

My father folded my fingers around the paper stub and said, "Let's watch this one from the rails."

So I followed him past the concession stands, past my big Negro shoeshine man, who gave us a salute, through the crowd of scruffy men to the fence right by the track, beyond the wooden grandstand into the big open space to the left, to the apron, where rows of wooden benches made up the cheapest seats, closest to the track and the fence around the track, so really they were the best seats, but the poorest people sat in them. Or stood by them. Or milled around close to the fence where they shouted into the wind whipped up by the horses as they ran past the men toward the finish line.

The pavement beneath our feet roiled with paper cups, wrappers, and racing guides, and mixed in with that were betting tickets, just like the one I held in my hand, those losing tickets thrown down and blown in all directions, little white waves making an ocean all their own. We worked our way now toward the fence, weaving through the legs of the men, their faces above me nothing but black shadows made by their hats. They stank when they lifted their arms to push back their hats or rub their chins, laughing, strolling, still hopeful because it was never over until the last race was over. And even then, there was always the next day.

"Well, would you look at that," my father said, nudging me and then pointing behind me at a man who was sitting bare-headed in the first row of the grandstand, the long shadow of the Turf Club just starting its journey over the boxes but not yet reaching that row, which was still glowing with light, light the small man with the barrel chest and the broken nose seemed to have gathered up all for himself, along with the attention of the people around him, their faces turned or tipped toward him as if involuntarily, tulips to the sun. "You know who that is? It's Mickey Cohen," and he winked at me. "I heard Chicago sent him back here to be the muscle for Bugsy Siegel."

Mickey Cohen. My father had told me stories about how Cohen had run craps games and numbers in Boyle Heights during Prohibition while his mother served brew out the back door of her pharmacy, and how he later boxed as The Jew Boy so everybody would know Jews could be tough, tough as nails, how he ran stickups with a Tommy gun in New York, Cleveland, and Chicago for Al Capone's brother—Al Capone's brother! So I knew who Bugsy Siegel and Mickey Cohen were long before we met them, men who made their own way, like my father, Jews who stood up for themselves, refused to be peddlers, pushed back against the world that wanted to hold them down. Boyle Heights was full of those types of men. Maxie, Izzie, and Joey Shaman. Hooky Rothman. Champ Segal, Curly Robinson. My grandfather hadn't approved of any of them, all of those hoods hanging out at Louie Schwartzman's bar on Brooklyn Avenue, making money from running numbers and prostitution now that Prohibition was over and drugstores were drugstores again and Mickey Cohen's mother was scooping ice cream in hers instead of pouring drinks.

All Prohibition ever did, according to my grandfather, was make bootleggers the richest criminals in America. Stupidest legislation ever enacted. Put money and guns in their pockets, and now J. Edgar Hoover's got to run around after them all with a dog-catcher's net. Well, where was J. Edgar with his dog-catcher's net now? In Washington, D.C., while Mickey Cohen was here, glad-handing his way along the rows of the Hollywood Park grandstand, taking his sweet gangster time! And why should he rush? No one was going to trifle with him. He probably had a gun in his pocket. A gun in every pocket. And two big boxer's fists. And a wallet full of money. A gold pinkie ring. He was always a bit rough looking, unlike Benny Siegel, working his charm at the front of the house.

I had actually seen Mickey Cohen once before that day at the track, though I didn't tell my father this. I'd been standing with my grandfather on the synagogue steps when a short man with a thick chest and thick arms and a broken nose that made him look like one of the bad guys in a detective comic came strolling down

Breed Street from Brooklyn Avenue. The man wore a black hat with a big brim and a light-colored suit with padded shoulders, but he didn't look comfortable in his suit, or at the shul, either, where he had arrived, apparently, to escort his aged mother home. "Who's that?" I asked my grandfather, pointing to the man. My grandfather said, shortly, "Nobody. A bum," and he turned and gave me a sharp tug to make me look away. But I couldn't look away, and the man winked and smiled at me, and I couldn't help but smile back. What was it with me and these men? And my grandfather called out to me again, and Mickey Cohen saw my grandfather's disapproving face, and he put a finger up to his forehead in a salute, Boo to you, sucker.

But it wasn't my grandfather who was the sucker, of course.

The uniformed bugler abruptly let out a string of notes that could be heard all over the track. Post time. The horses were led from the paddock down through the concrete tunnel and from there out onto the course. That day each horse looked as beautiful to me as the next, the horses, who, despite their baths and their rubdowns with liniments, gave off beneath those scents a nervous, animal smell. The horses were all much taller than I, with big rump muscles and long backs and snooty heads, and then those long delicate, knee-knobby legs with the splayed hooves, ankles wrapped to keep them from snapping as the horses ran forty miles an hour around the track.

The announcer spoke. "The horses are entering the gates. The horses are entering the gates. Post time one minute." The men around us surged toward the fence, and we moved with them. No more of the man with a white handkerchief and a white chalk-mark starting line. Just this year Hollywood Park had started using an electronic gate, and the instant the last dancing horse was locked into his pen, a bell rang. The gates swung open and the pack of horses broke away almost immediately, surging forward into the straightaway, the shape of the pack gradually thinning into a line, as some horses moved toward the front and others fell behind them, for now. Rabbits and turtles.

The crowd of men around the fence began to yell, calling out the names of the horses they'd bet on, screaming, "C'mon, daddy. C'mon, daddy," pleading with their horse to blow around the track, last chance to go home with money in their pockets, but it was more than that, too, it was the sound of the horses and their beauty and their speed, the comically accelerated voice of the announcer who called the races, the names of the horses spilling rapidly from his lips. You never knew which horse from behind might come up the outside or from the inside to overtake the big horse who started strong. Or when the strong might fail. Last week, in the stable after a race, one of the horses had had a heart attack and died, collapsed on the concrete floor covered with hay, its big eye staring up at his appalled trainer. And he'd just come in at 5 to 1.

The horses were headed around the curve now, their long mouths dripping with lather, the sound of their hooves on the turf beating inside me like a second heart. Like a number of hearts. I put both hands on the fence rail. And just then, as if I'd made it happen, one of the horses stumbled and sent its jockey catapulting from its back like an acrobat shot from a circus cannon, his horse running on for a while without him, out of habit, reins flapping, chasing the pack as it rounded the first turn. And then, a little bewildered without the whip or the spurs or the voice of the man who had guided him, the horse slowed and trotted awkwardly off into the grass. I backed up a bit. At this distance, you couldn't quite see its number, or any numbers, the horses blurred, the numbers at yards and yards away indistinct. The jockey was on his feet and men were running onto the field after the rogue horse, grabbing at the reins while the horse held up one foot. Something was wrong with it. I couldn't watch the race anymore, only that horse and the white ambulance that religiously followed the horses around the track now pulling up next to it.

All around me, men were shouting and roaring because the other horses were still running, still in the game, and they made the final turn and were coming fast toward the finish line, and our horse, the black horse, Thundermaker, Number 4, was first and my father's voice was cracking. He was winning, he was winning, a winner, Magic Ike!, and from my vantage point down below him looking up, his face seemed feverish and crazed, skin reddened, mouth open in a scream. But by the next curve, his voice had faded, and I looked back to the race to see that Thundermaker, too, was fading, suddenly dropping back, losing the lead. I started whispering his name. To no avail. He was second place now, then third, the jockey not even whipping him, not even leaning forward anymore to whisper in his ear, Please, and then, finally, the horse was lost in the pack of turtles at the back. My father had by this time stopped shouting, by this time having figured it out. Another horse, White Soda, had come from the outside and won. Up in the grandstand, Mickey Cohen was shaking hands all around and having his back slapped, and I saw my father looking at Mickey Cohen, too, and then down at the racing sheet. "White Soda. Twenty-eight to one," my father said. "That's got to be a fix."

What wasn't a fix in the world of bettors and gamblers?

I watched my father purse his lips and look speculatively up at the grandstand where Cohen stood winner. I knew what my father was thinking, that he'd lost because Mickey Cohen just happened to stop by Hollywood Park that day and open up his fat wallet to Thundermaker's jockey. To all the jockeys. Tip sheets and racing papers and calculations in the red notebook were really a waste of time, the pathetic fiddlings of a man on the outside and being on the outside was like being a horse on the outside rail. It was just too hard to win from there, the distance around the track so much longer.

Meanwhile, the ambulance team was erecting a white folding screen around the injured horse so the public wouldn't have to see the horse that was no longer a horse as it had been just seconds before but was now just a body without a soul, a carcass to be dragged away by a tractor. My father was watching this, too, shutting his useless notebook, the full magnitude of his losses bearing down on him like, well, like White Soda to the finish, and he said to me, ruefully, "When they're done there, they might as well come over here and shoot me, too."

Las Vegas
1946

9

WE WERE AT THE cusp of a big change out here in the desert, with ground being broken for a whole highway of new hotels. The Flamingo was the first of them, but we wouldn't be alone for long. My father and I had the only two finished hotel rooms in the main building, the one original building and the first one built, and when Mr. Siegel was here, he stayed there, too, on the top floor, in a private suite with steel-enforced walls and a bulletproof office, a suite with its own elevator and secret exit, the existence of which I never even questioned, other than to think he should have worried more about the front way in because the suite door hadn't yet been installed: Benny kept changing his mind about the height of the ceiling. He didn't know anything about construction. He just had visions of how he wanted it all to look. Expensive. Modern. Hollywood.

First, Benny had wanted one building. Then, we were going to have three. Then one, again, a horseshoe design that melded all three pieces together in a way that reminded me of Hollywood Park. And as Mr. Siegel wasn't there all the time, it was my father's job to watch over things in his absence, to consult with the builder, Mr. Webb, about the incessant changes, to keep track of the January plans, the February plans, the March plans, scrolls of blueprints laid out in the hotel lobby that served for now as the construction office. I still couldn't really read, my peripatetic life in and out of schools had left me almost illiterate, but I was always good with numbers, and so I studied the plans and the accounts, all of which were laid out there for anyone to see, which is how I knew Benny was paying out more than he was taking in.

Copper piping, copper wire, concrete, wood, steel, fixtures, everything he needed for his hotel was at premium postwar prices, and he needed more loans, more money, from the Teamsters, from Mr. Lansky and Mr. Costello and Mr. Luciano and Mr. Fischetti and Mr. Trafficante, from friends, from Beverly Hills businessmen, really from everybody he knew, but still we were way behind schedule, the construction money seeming to vaporize as soon as it arrived. Materials came by day and were unloaded from the trucks. Yet, at night, I saw my father open the gates, supervise that same material as it was loaded back onto new trucks, which drove it all away. In the morning, those trucks returned with the same goods, but Ben said they were new and then asked Mr. Lansky for more money. The syndicate liked clever men, but the problem was that clever men were clever enough to look out for themselves first, always. And if they were too clever, the syndicate lost patience, and that was the end of them.

Benny came by every week or so that summer, and I always looked forward to seeing his black roadster, waxed and polished like the dark side of the moon beneath its layer of Vegas grit, pull up by the front entrance. I always hoped he would come alone. He never brought his wife out here, but he sometimes brought his daughters or his girlfriend, Virginia Hill. Virginia was just over thirty then, which seemed to me at the time to be quite an advanced age. And also, it seemed to me, she was not exactly pretty, with her wide, block-like face and her painted-on eyebrows. She was a hooker, my father told me, making the kind of face my grandfather made when discussing something he found distasteful, got her start in 1933, the year I was born, at the Chicago World's Fair, and had been passed from gangster to gangster ever since, Jewish and Italian alike. But Ben, who liked hookers, and who liked her long legs and her red hair, didn't seem to mind any of that. All summer, every time she came with him to the Flamingo, there would be some kind of blowup, often followed by a trip to the doctor. Some of their scenes resulted in her packing her bags and fleeing to Los Angeles. Other of their scenes resulted in her taking an overdose of sleeping pills, an action she visited often in either fury or frustration or regret, I'm not sure which.

But when Virginia wasn't in that roadster, there was always something in there for me, tucked next to the packages of heroin Benny sometimes brought over the border from Mexico, which he told me was dusting powder and, no, I couldn't have some, the bit of overflow his mules didn't have room for—a long black dress, a pair of shoes with tiny gold bows, a silver compact with an *E* engraved on its lid. Having two teenage daughters, he knew how to buy for one, and even if I couldn't wear these things around the burning hot, gritty acres of the Flamingo, Mr. Siegel assured me I soon would in the glamorous environs of the Flamingo Club, which currently existed only in his imagination.

So that afternoon, I got out of the pool with my towel around me, the pool once an old gravel pit before any motel, even that old crumbling one we'd knocked down, ever stood here, the pool Mr. Siegel had ordered filled just for me. One side of it lay razor-blade straight and the other was all angular sawtooth edges, no dull rectangle for the Flamingo, but something clean, new age, sun-bleached, ringed with date palms and cypress trees and grass struggling to grow. I ran eagerly toward the lobby in the blinding heat. The desert sun had turned my hair so blond it was almost white and the sun had darkened my skin so much I looked, my father joked, like a blond Negro or a photographic negative. He told me if I got any darker, he'd have to drop me off in West Las Vegas, on the other side of the highway overpass we called the Cement Curtain, which separated us from the Negro part of town.

A chilling joke, though he didn't know it. Just a half block from my school—I'd spent a few spring months at the Fifth Street school, where the Negro, white, and Indian kids, the natives of old Vegas, fought constantly, and where I hardly learned anything at all—a Negro man had leaned out of his car and asked me to show him my pussy. On the playground, a Negro boy had asked me to suck his balls, two for a quarter. I knew I wouldn't last long on the other side of the Cement Curtain. But I didn't say anything about any of this to my father or Benny. I just kept quiet and waited for summer.

My wet footprints dried instantly now on the concrete in the July heat, and I was happy, wondering what Benny might have brought for me this time. I believe I was hoping it would be a tube of lipstick. Pretty in Pink. Before I even got to the glass lobby doors, I could hear him, though I couldn't see him. I could see only my father, the back of him, shirt back wet, big white fedora with the black band that he wore always dusted with sand. He must have just come in from the construction site when he heard Mr. Siegel had arrived. He might be sweaty, but my bathing suit was already dry, my brittle hair stinking of salt and chlorine, the goose bumps on my long skinny legs having long since gone flat from the heat.

Their voices were loud, so I stayed quiet.

"I'll get the cash from Chicago." That was Ben.

I watched my father take off his sunglasses and wipe at them with a handkerchief from his pants pocket. "Ben, you're already almost $500,000 behind. The contractor can't pay his suppliers or his men."

"I'll get the goddamn cash, Ike." Mr. Siegel thumped his fist on the lobby counter and the scrolls of his many blueprints rattled and rolled. Half the problem right there.

My father said, "We have to stop work. We're going to have to let everybody go."

"I'll go to Chicago, I'll go to Phoenix, I'll go to Utah, to the Mormons, those *goyishe* shitheels."

"You're going to need millions to finish this. You can't get that much money that fast."

It was odd for me to hear my father being practical, the voice of reason.

Mr. Siegel just shook his head. "You let me worry about that. The casino's got to open by the end of the year."

I knew from my father that Benny's investors were restless, harping at him, Just open the joint already, put in the carpet and open, fed up with delay after delay, like the one earlier in the summer, when the federal government had shut down construction for a month over rumors about what had been done to poor Billy Wilkerson, once Ben's partner out here, now hiding from Ben in Paris.

"Can't be done, Ben," my father said, stalwart. "Impossible."

By this point I'd edged up enough to the hot glass, careful not to touch it, so I could see them both as if through a lens. Mr. Siegel was pacing the lobby floor, agitated, his face glowing, the anger within like a pure white light that seemed to suffuse his skin. A camera bulb going off inside him. He wasn't used to being told he couldn't get what he wanted. Didn't like it.

"Don't give me all this cocksucking shit, Ike. I'll get you what you need." He pivoted the glare of himself toward my father. And then Benny paused, a man at a tripwire he both set and set off. "Just don't tell me it's impossible. Because nothing in this life is impossible."

And then, while I watched, nose almost to the glass, Ben began beating the counter with his fists, *bam bam bam*, kicking at the glass cabinetry until it cracked like parched earth, pitching one of the heavy freestanding ashtrays into the front door where I stood, and right before my eyes the plate glass sent lightning-bolt zigzags in all directions from the epicenter of impact. I jumped back. All these things and everything else Ben touched and ruined were now things that would need to be replaced and Benny would have to beg for the money to do it on top of all the other money he would have to beg for, which he must have been aware of in some pinpoint of logic in his brain and maybe that logic simply fueled his frustration. Whatever could be lifted, flung, kicked, or beaten, was. It was the first time I had seen one of Benny's uncontrollable rages, though my father had described them. And I saw it all through that broken glass.

There had always been stories about Benny and the havoc he unleashed in Brooklyn and Los Angeles, about men he'd shot in the street, like James Regan or Big Greenie Greenberg, his head resting by a curb, or men he'd thrown from the top of a hotel like Abe Reles, limbs akimbo. And now there were new stories about Mr. Siegel, Las Vegas stories, stories of his pistol-whipping a clerk at the El Rancho who'd referred to the Flamingo as a gyp joint, stories of Ben's threatening to kill the owner and burn the place down. Our nearest neighbor. As Ben's face flicked from its lightbulb-white incandescence to a meaty, bloody red, my father began edging away, backing toward the doors. Because the next thing Ben was going to strike was my father. By this time in my life with my parents, I had seen a lot, of course, but I had never before seen my father physically assaulted. Ben advanced and advanced and then put his fist to my father's face and sent my father smashing with some finality into the already cracked glass door.

And then it was over. I didn't even have time to cry out. My father made no move to strike back. He made no move at all.

Breathing hard, Mr. Siegel smoothed his shirtfront, smoothed his hair, reassembled, with visible difficulty, the features of his face into what he believed to be a version of normality, of reasonability, of accommodation. It seemed only then that Ben as I knew him was returned to himself, the rage retracted and capped. It was only then that he focused again on my father and whatever expression his face held. Shock? Fury? Fear? Resignation? I couldn't tell you. I couldn't see.

"Give the men a week's break, Ike," Ben said. "I'll have the money then."

My father's back was pressed against the glass front door like a fly to a spiderweb, and by now I was crouched down small as a stink bug behind him. I'm sure at this moment my father quite seriously considered driving away from here, returning us both to Los Angeles, leaving behind the pilings, the wire, the sheet metal, the concrete blocks, letting it all disintegrate in the heat the way the original hotel on these thirty-three acres had disintegrated, crumbling, tiny and abandoned, a neglected home for lizards and insects and a magnet for tumbleweed. Hidden behind the figure of my father, I tightened my towel around my shoulders, though I was not cold. Far from it.

My father, dismissed, moved to open the door inward, and I was suddenly exposed, bare-footed, straggly-haired, hunched like a beggar child, hotel towel twisted around my torso. And my face was exposed, too, revealing my terror, a tiny fraction of, an echo of, a child-sized version of my father's.

My father looked down at me, horrified, one side of his face already swelling. Ben's smile at suddenly seeing me, a genuine smile, slid into an O of regret as he realized by my face and posture just how long I had been there, just exactly what I had seen.

My father took a step toward me. "Esme—" he began.

I turned and ran from him, a flesh-colored rabbit from the

brush, towel flying off my shoulders and blowing white and plush into his face for all I knew, and I didn't stop, even though my father had by now come out the lobby door to call after me, shouting my name over and over, "Esme. Esme. Esme. Come back!"

When I reached the pool, my unconscious destination, I leapt in, dove for the bottom, and stayed down there, arms around my knees, feet on the concrete, rocking the ball of myself back and forth and squinting up at the surface, hiding in plain sight and holding my breath and eventually my father's distorted face appeared over the water's edge. He was waiting for me. He knew I couldn't stay down here forever. And, eventually, of course, I had to surface, though I wouldn't look at him when I did. Instead, I pressed my face to one of the pool lights, treading water and staring into the domed glass that concealed the big lightbulb behind it.

Above me, my father spoke.

"Esme, it doesn't matter. We're here for the big prize, baby girl, and nothing else matters. We're just going to keep our eyes on the prize."

So.

So, while we might have been blindsided that day at Hollywood Park, my father and I couldn't say we didn't know what we were getting ourselves into here in Vegas. We had plenty of warning.

10

BENNY DID MANAGE AS instructed by Meyer Lansky to open for business in 1946, the day after Christmas, even if everything wasn't exactly finished and even if it was practically the last day of the year.

Unfortunately, it was raining that night. The days right after Christmas are always empty days in Vegas—even now, everybody comes in for New Year's—but it was emptier still in the casino that first night as we waited for everyone, anyone, to arrive, the cigarette girls and coat-check girls and all those young, handsome Greek men Mr. Siegel had imported from Havana as his croupiers standing aimlessly by their tables, his men in the counting room with nothing to count, the sun gone, the early evening sky slate-gray with low storm clouds we could see through the windows traveling fast across the flat valley from the hills, heading for us, ready to punish our impudence for even thinking the world would come crawling to us way out here. And at first I thought, Good. Serves Ben right.

The airplanes Ben had leased back in Los Angeles to transport his most important Hollywood guests had been grounded because of the weather, and the movie stars who did come arrived in somewhat less glamorous conveyances, their own dirt-covered cars. Despite the bad weather, a few of Ben's Hollywood friends made it here. And Benny, grateful, stood by the door with Virginia on his arm to greet every arrival. It was a little discomfiting for me to see Virginia wore an evening dress not entirely unlike one of the black dresses Ben had given me. He himself wore swallowtails, white ones, the two of them straight up dandies from nowhere. Which I guess I could say about everyone I know, including me.

I walked the casino floor that night as an underage cigarette girl, wearing too much lipstick, too much eyeliner, legs skinny as an actual flamingo's, those legs finished off with a pair of red high-heeled shoes just a bit too big for me. I'd begged for the job over my father's objections, and Benny interjected, "She'll just be selling cigarettes, Ike. Let her do it. Opening night. Just this once," still trying to curry favor with me since his argument with my father. The fact that I was underage didn't matter much in Las Vegas, where I'd already seen everything was upside down, everything illegal elsewhere legal here, everything shameful elsewhere perfectly acceptable here. Bribes. Battery. Drugs. Adultery. Divorce. All acceptable here.

Laudable, even.

And tonight the finished Flamingo Club was the most laudable thing of all, Benny Siegel's big, beautiful dream come to life, no part of it more beautiful and dreamy than its casino, the ceiling a green-blue pocked lunar landscape, the columns throughout pasted up with desert flagstone, the bar glowing like a universe of stars with its bottles and mirrors, the seat covers a shocking flamingo pink, the spiral staircase made of marble and polished wood, the wall of windows one big square of the shimmering desert.

Because we were the Flamingo, those pink birds stood on one impossibly thin leg on the serving trays, the napkins, the bottoms of the martini glasses, winking at you when you took your last swallow, though the two real flamingos Mr. Siegel imported as test subjects had died in September, in the desert heat. He'd cried over them, had to cancel his order for a hundred more, which he had imagined roaming the grounds like a flock of exotic indigenous animals but which didn't belong here any more than they belonged in the Hollywood Park infield. But, ultimately, the birds didn't matter. The only thing that mattered was the tables, upholstered in traditional green baize, the thick material embossed with gaming grids, and the slot machines, waist-high, silver, like gasoline pumps filled with coins instead of fuel, every deck of cards marked, every roulette table wired, every pair of dice weighted.

In my short skirt, tray of goods strapped to me like a baby, and, as Mr. Siegel requested of all the girls, wearing red lipstick and red painted nails like my mother's, hair coiffed like a movie star's, I circulated those slots and tables with my cigarettes. I felt delightfully glamorous and adult, listening to Jimmy Durante singing "Inka Dinka Doo" and joking into the microphone in the half-empty nightclub and Xavier Cugat leading his band to a brassy racket as if every seat in there was filled. And in the half-empty casino, I pretended the same, pausing by each guest to ask, "Cigar? Cigarette?"

When I offered a pack of cigarettes to Sonny Tufts, he smiled at me, called me a Little Sweetie, and he was so handsome and so blond, it was hard to believe in a few years he'd be such a lush, drunkenly groping at girls' thighs with his teeth like some shark. Benny's friend George Raft, who played gangsters even as he befriended real ones who then copied his movie mannerisms and his style, so much so that who could tell anymore the original from the copy, bought a pack of Lucky Strikes from me, giving me a wink and a smile, saying, "Little girl, let me see what you have there on that tray," and then stuffing his tip into the waistband of my skirt while I flushed. I was close enough to smell the oily scent of the pomade on his hair.

I'd seen movie actors like these men on the MGM lot, but they had never looked my way before and I had never been quite this close to them before. My proximity made me a little clumsy, made me tremble a bit with the coins and the Luckies. The whole experience was like being on one of my mother's soundstages, but this time as a player, not as child, watching. And this frisson of the movie set was exactly what Ben Siegel was after, of course, hoping it would make gamblers lose their minds and their money with the excitement of it all. It was certainly making me a fool.

Mr. Raft had tipped me with a hundred-dollar bill, a discovery that astonished me after the fact, as I thought it rude to look too closely at the tips as I accepted them, peeking at them only as I walked away. The sight of Benjamin Franklin's doughy green face made me stumble. I was rich! Had been made rich in under two hours! This was the moment I first understood that Vegas might hold some benefits for me personally, not just for Benny or my father. My father always said I had a mind like an abacus, just like my grandfather's. I stood there in the middle of the casino, working my beads, adding things up. Then I looked around the room, suddenly all blue and silver and light and possibility, and Benny, across the room, saw me looking, saw my face, and came over to me to say, "So what do you think, Esme?" knowing of course what I would say and wanting to hear it.

And I had to say, "It's wonderful." And then I couldn't help but wag my big bill at him. "Look at my tip!"

He smiled, all gratified contentment as if we shared in all this together, which in a way we did, and Benny peered at my mouth, knowing it was safe to tease me now, saying, "Is that by any chance Passion in Red?" Which was the lipstick he'd bought me on his last trip out and which I hadn't until now had an occasion to wear. Or hadn't wanted to make him happy by wearing.

I laughed.

He leaned over and impulsively kissed my cheek. "You're a good kid. And I promise you, life is going to be a lot more interesting around here, now."

True.

And then someone from behind me yanked at my hair, jerked my head back. It was like being attacked by a dybbuk, and when

I turned to see who it was, I found Virginia's contorted face two inches from mine, that block jaw of hers wide as a wall, her black painted eyebrows jammed together like an automobile accident. She was already screaming at me, and before I could even make my mouth into an astonished *O*, she reared back and her other hand came forward to scratch my face with her long fingernails, raking me from my eyebrows to my chin, and the pain was so astonishing it made me cry real tears, though the shock left me voiceless, a weeping mute.

Not so Benny. "Virginia," he bellowed, "what the fuck are you doing? This is Ike's girl, Esme."

As if maybe he thought in my adult getup, I was unrecognizable to her.

He grabbed at her arms, but he couldn't get both of them, and one of them still flailed and flapped at me, those painted nails, hard as concrete darts, still scrabbling at my face. I tried to duck, but she reached me anyway. Octopus! Benny grabbed her other arm, finally.

"Sure, save her young face, you gangster," she shouted, kicking at him and spitting at me, and the two of them tussled, evening dress and swallowtails a twisted jerking mess that appalled me, as I backed up, my face stinging and my hair unfurling from its inexpert coiffure, feeling humiliated, as any person publicly spanked would feel. But I also felt something else I couldn't quite identify, maybe some pride that I wasn't such a little baby, anymore, after all, if Virginia could be made jealous enough to hit me. I was still baby enough to cry, though.

Grappling with Virginia, Benny managed to jerk his chin at me, which I understood as instruction to flee, and so I ran for the kitchen, my cigarette tray slapping against me, and made it through the kitchen's swinging doors, where one of the chefs gave me a wet towel. From the round peephole windows, I watched as Benny's men helped pin Virginia's arms and, with Benny following, dragged her up the gorgeous spiral staircase and off to, I assumed, Benny's penthouse suite, which just last night had had a front door installed. Good thing. Because behind that door tonight Virginia would be held prisoner.

But she wasn't there yet, and she kept screaming at Benny and everybody else the whole way up that seemingly endless staircase, "Gangsters, murderers, you're all murderers."

We weren't allowed to say that or anything like it in front of Mr. Siegel.

But there she was, saying it.

"Gangster. Murderer," she yelled one last time into Benny's face before she was made to vanish.

She wasn't wrong, of course, though I didn't know that then. The pit bosses, the counting-room bosses, even half the gamblers here or at the El Rancho or the Last Frontier or the casinos downtown I would come to learn were gangsters or hit men or one-time crooked cops who now dealt openly in vice. You had to pity the poor prospectors and ranchers who still thought of Las Vegas as their town. So when Virginia screamed, she screamed the truth.

The action on the floor stopped for a moment.

And then the few gamblers we had here resumed their play, chips laid down, wheels turned, slot machine arms pulled. They would stay, put up with what they had to, in the name of greed. Just like us. And my father, over by the craps tables, hadn't even seen what had happened to me and could hardly believe it when I told him about it later, showed him my scratch marks, the evidence of another one of Virginia's regular breakdowns in civility, a little more public maybe, this time, with a corresponding breakdown in civility on Ben's part, as well. Virginia's tantrum, a full-blown humiliation for me, was just a kerfuffle for Benny, something that hardly retained his attention. Because the real problem for him tonight was the house losses. He didn't have time to beat up Virginia, as he sometimes did. He had business to attend to. And so he came back down the stairway, and I watched from my kitchen porthole as he resumed his perambulation about the casino floor, glad-handing and back-slapping, joking and smiling, offering up gaming chips, gratis. As if we weren't being taken enough. Too many of the players were winning and the swankily tuxedoed Greek dealers were stealing Benny blind, stuffing their pockets with chips they claimed were tips from the gamblers and cashing in the chips at the cage during their breaks.

So maybe it was lucky for us, after all, that this first night the casino emptied out early. Around midnight, the lights in the casino blinked in the storm and then failed, and when it became clear the lights were not going to come back on no matter how hysterical or how imperious Benny became, our little crowd of celebrities and their fellow gamblers drove off down the highway into the distance toward the kitschy El Rancho, Ben's nemesis!, and the neon cactus of the Last Frontier. Because there weren't any rooms here for anyone to stay in. The hotel itself wasn't finished, just the club and casino.

We really shouldn't have opened tonight at all, but Benny was frantic to show his investors a return on their money, to prove his desert dream could be fruitful.

Well, not so fruitful. Not tonight.

So while my father was calculating the evening's losses and figuring out how to best present that terrible information to Mr. Siegel, I went outside to let the wet night air soothe my sore cheek. I could be scarred for life! My mother had led me to believe that a woman's face was her fortune and mine was now subject to a terrible downgrade. I had been maimed. And even if I wasn't an applicant for one of those coveted slots as a Louis B. Mayer screen goddess, I could already see that even here in Vegas, a woman's face would be her fortune. As was her body. I thought about my tips and tried not to finger my raw skin as I meandered around the front of the building.

The minute the main structure was built, Mr. Siegel had the tall Flamingo sign at the front entrance erected so it rose like a totem pole, one letter on top of the other, and at the apex, the talismanic bird flapped its wings. The words CASINO. LOUNGE. RESTAURANT. CASINO. LOUNGE. RESTAURANT repeated themselves along the very edges of the roof above the cypress trees and scraggly desert plants below, just in case the world wanted to know what this building was doing here, the architecture of clean straight angles, as if we could sweep away our own troubles and the troubles of the past decade with a plumb line and a few boxes. I wished.

I sat down on the ledge of the fountain by the front entrance. The mechanisms were not yet turned on. Earlier this week, I'd discovered that the orange tabby cat roaming the construction site, coming here from God knows where, had given birth to a litter of kittens in the bottom of this very fountain, a concrete nest of safety from prairie dogs and raccoons, and I'd begged and begged Benny to let her stay there with the mewing babies, until finally, with an, "All right, Baby E," he had relented, and Benny's three-story-high water show was an empty well, bubbling jets inert, the only water in it the sharp blips of falling rain. None of this would have mattered, of course, if everything else had gone well this evening, but as it was, the dead fountain was just another notch in the tally of Benny's disappointments. All was quiet down there now with the mama and her baby kittens.

I tipped my face up to the raindrops, let my hair flatten and my makeup run. What did it matter? The night was over.

I missed my mother.

And then I saw Ben standing a short way down the drive,

smoking a cigarette, all alone, too, and looking rather wet and vulnerable. Maybe all his bluster and bullying were out of fearful desire rather than power. In that moment he reminded me of my parents, with all the big beautiful dreams they chased with such fervor gone *psst*, leaving them lost and bewildered. The only thing worse than being scared of Ben was not being scared of him. Our fortunes were tied to his. I wiped my face and watched Benny. The end of his Lucky made one small light in the middle of the wet desert.

11

AFTER THE FLAMINGO LOST $300,000 in its first two weeks, Meyer Lansky forced Ben to close at the end of January, finish construction of the hotel, and retool the casino. And Mr. Lansky sent some of his men from the successful casino at the El Cortez in downtown Vegas—Moe Sedway and Gus Greenbaum—ahead of him to poke through everything before he himself flew out in March to review the account books, to check the cameras in the counting room, to rerig the tables and rewire the slot machines in the casino. Out front there were to be no more thieving Greek dealers. No more tuxedos. This wasn't Paris or Havana. We needed to be friendly looking, not intimidating. The new dealers would wear regular suits, just like the patrons. There would be bingo and giveaways, though just the idea of either one of those made Benny wince. And, further, Lansky also wasn't happy about Ben's recent divorce from his wife, Esta, over his affair with the ridiculous Virginia. So there was nothing at all, really, that Lansky was happy about on this visit.

He and one of his men even made a point to watch the dress rehearsal of our new floor show before we reopened. No detail was too small for his review. So we were all nervous. What would Lansky think of us? I'd been promoted from cigarette girl to dancing girl during the closure. When I'd told my father I wasn't going back to school after Christmas, he hadn't objected. I was fifteen. Neither he nor my mother had finished high school, and the Flamingo was just too exciting.

And, anyway, who needed math and history lessons to be a dancer? Daddy Mack had been my schooling for that, just as he'd schooled my mother, and I'd had more of that schooling for sure than my fellow dancers, a bunch of local girls, pretty, but a little clunky, untrained for the most part, the kind of girls my mother and I would have bent our heads together and laughed at if we'd seen them on set. None of them could dance, not that we had much choreography to perform. A bit of strutting, some waving of feather fans, a kick here and there, some tap. Who couldn't do that? Our little numbers were scheduled between the real acts, a sip of water to cleanse the palate, the announcer introducing us with, "And now, from the Fabulous Flamingo Hotel, here's our lovely line of dancers!" The hotel had even been given a new name for our grand reopening. No longer the Flamingo Club, we were now called the Fabulous Flamingo, as if the adjective could make us so.

I don't think we lovely line of dancers was that important to the overall show, but still I was nervous about making a good impression. We could be dumped just like the Greek dealers—and then what would I do? Sell cigarettes. Check hats. Or be sent back to school to keep me busy. So I was watching closely as Lansky, Benny, and a man I didn't know sat on chairs in the empty night-club, the three of them our only audience, their table the only one with a cloth over it, smoking and tipping their ashes into our flamingo-adorned ashtrays. The three kings.

It was the wrong time of day, of course, to see a floor show. You needed night. The sun was bearing in on us despite the draperies, rendering the room vacant and dead, like any theater during the day. And having the men sitting there at the center front table with a tablecloth laid deferentially just for them made the rehearsal feel like an audition. None of the girls were wearing curlers as they usually did for four o'clock rehearsal. No one was wearing practice clothes. We wore our pink feathered costumes, our rubberized mesh tights pulled up high and rolled at the waist, our red high-heeled shoes. I'd Pan-Caked over the faint scar on my face. And what if the men didn't like what they saw? Would the costumes be taken from us? Would the opening be postponed still further? Did these men have sway over everything, even something that seemed as inconsequential to me as the floor show?

Eventually, I would come to understand that our show, or any show here, had just one purpose, a purpose of paramount importance to Lansky and company, which is why they bothered paying any attention to it or to us whatsoever, and that purpose was to send the exhilarated, titillated, intoxicated audience members out into the casino eager to part with their money. Because the casino was the heart of the heart of Las Vegas, the whole point of the whole city.

The baying patrons, flinging their money down, always amazed me. Didn't they know the house always won and the house would always do whatever was necessary to make that so, even if what was necessary was to shut down an entire hotel?

Benny, sitting there between Lansky and friend, looked chastened, his normally ruddy, enthusiastic face a little empty, a little sandpapered, and he looked small, even though he was actually bigger and taller than Lansky, who lacked Benny's, or for that matter, even my father's, sartorial flair and dash. Mr. Lansky wore a shirt without a tie and a herringbone sports coat, his hair combed straight back. He was not handsome. He was ordinary looking, middle a little thick. He could have been a shopkeeper in Boyle Heights. Or a rabbi. The other man, whose name was Nate Stein, though I didn't know this yet, wore a two-toned golf shirt and slacks. He was tall with a broad back and his hair was a black shock of a pompadour before there even was an Elvis Presley to sport one. Not that this man wanted such style. He just had a lot of thick hair. Lansky might look to me like the rabbi at my grandfather's synagogue, but the way he held himself, the way both those men held themselves, the way they smoked, the way they looked about the club said they were not obedient servants of the Breed Street shul, but men who considered themselves as powerful as the God to whom its worshippers prayed.

My father wore a bouncy enthusiasm, always looking for the next opportunity to grab, sure it was coming around the corner. Lansky and Stein had already grabbed hold of opportunity and had twisted it into something miraculous. They were more powerful, I realized, than Benny Siegel, who held his own with Sedway, Greenbaum, and Rosen, but I hadn't yet met anyone more powerful than Ben. I thought bigger than life meant powerful. But Lansky and this Stein lived smaller, they lived quietly, and there was nothing small or quiet about Ben, and for the first time, I realized that might be a liability. Quiet like my grandfather might be better, power hidden up the sleeve, not sprayed all over everybody in sight. I'd only ever seen grandstanding—in Ben, in Buzz, in my father, even in Louis B. Mayer with his big white semicircular desk up on a pedestal in his blindingly white office.

Under Lansky's disapproving gaze, everything around me seemed wrong. First of all, our costumes looked cheap. In this glare, my short pink dress had a tacky sheen to it and my red shoes were silly and the pink feathers I held ridiculous. I'd had a better costume at last year's Helldorado parade, a bluebird flapping my wings as I flitted about our float's silver pâpier-maché birdcage. I wasn't sure the men would even understand that we were supposed to be flamingos, picking our way across the stage after the Andrews Sisters exited and before the Xavier Cugat band played again. Yes, I was finally going to have a chance to put my expensive Daddy Mack lessons to some use, and I should have been thrilled, but our dour audience snuffed out any excitement. For me, anyway. The other girls, scooped up from dry-goods store counters and restaurant cash registers in a pinch to fill the stage, seemed oblivious to anything but the fun of this. We're flamingos! At the Flamingo! Ha, ha, ha. And suddenly, I knew just exactly how my mother felt in her blackface with that spring boinging on her hat in the "Harry" number from *Babes*. Truly humiliated.

So I watched the Andrews Sisters sing "Near You," watched the way they tapped their way toward the proscenium and back, swinging their arms in unison, doing a few step ball changes, singing their little delightful dated songs, and I thought, This is boring. Even their costumes were boring, their hairstyles dated. Early forties. Wartime entertainment. Patrons could get the Andrews Sisters back in Los Angeles or watch them in the movie houses. And they weren't even that pretty, one of them with a big nose. Any extra on the MGM lot was prettier than the prettiest of the Andrews Sisters. This wasn't what people would drive to postwar Las Vegas to see. The stark desert and the luxury hotels would need more riveting entertainment, more beauty. Not this. And not a handful of chorines like me dressed in short pink dresses and red high heels doing some kicks and tap dancing between the real numbers.

Of course, this was 1947, pre–Las Vegas showgirl, before the Copa girls and the Lido girls, before the Moro-Landis dancers and the Rangerettes, before the sky-high headdresses and the sequins and beads. But I could see it all before it arrived—because I had already seen it in my mother's Busby Berkeley films. That was what Las Vegas needed. Goddesses. Long rows of girls descending staircases, curving staircases like the one my mother stood on playing the violin in *Gold Diggers*, girls flying on trapezes, girls turning on spinning pedestals like the ballerinas in music boxes. I didn't know that girls like that were already performing in Parisian nightclubs or in some of the clubs Meyer Lansky was opening in Havana, girls ornamented in every way with the exception of clothing. But I could sense that what we were doing was not going to fly here for long.

And standing there in my short pink dress and red high heels, I looked to Benny. His face was blank, obedient. Whatever Meyer wanted to see on that stage was what Ben was going to put on that stage, no matter how he felt privately. He would watch the cheerful Andrews Sisters retreads. He would cut the paychecks for the twelve of us girls dancing chastely in pink. If Meyer wanted the clean American West, friendly, welcoming, bring us your money, we would present cheerful Americana as we scooped up the tokens and chips. I wrinkled up my face as I watched those Andrews Sisters dancing and singing.

> There's just one place for me, near you
> It's like heaven to be near you
> Times when we're apart
> I can't face my heart

They swayed their arms as if they had no idea their days were numbered and pretty soon they'd be a nostalgia act. I could feel my lips purse as if I were tasting something sour. This act would not interest Buzz and I had cut my teeth on Buzz, on Hollywood, and on the Sunset Strip. Not on a desert backwater. So over to the side of the floor where we girls were corralled waiting for our turn to flip and flap, I quietly defied Mr. Lansky. To "Apple Blossom Time," I did something else. I stretched, threw my leg up, arched my back. I did a slow swirl that started in a crouch and then spiraled upward and ended with a head circle. I did the mincing steps of the high-heeled strip-tease artist, my arms thrown up to the heavens, hands wagging. By the window drapes where nobody could see me, I had my own private ball. And then, slowly, I became aware someone was watching me.

It wasn't the crestfallen Benny or Lansky, the man who'd deflated him with a long silver pin. It was the man beside Lansky. Nate Stein. He wasn't looking at the Andrews Sisters anymore at all, just at me, only at me, and there was no censure in his face. Quite the opposite. He was smoking and watching. I looked back at him for a moment and once I figured out that what I saw in his face was not disapproval, I continued dancing. I pretended I didn't know he was watching, but I knew that he was, and what I felt was entirely different from what I felt while doing my "Ragtime Cowboy Joe" dance for Ben two years ago. From Ben had seeped a gray disappointment, and what emanated from this man was, I understood, the opposite of that. I felt myself tugging on a long fluid string to make his hands and legs and lips move and if I wanted to, I knew I could pull him toward me, though I was too naïve, of course, to have any idea what to do with him once I'd gotten him there.

When the Andrews Sisters finished their number with,

> Spend the rest of my days
> All those happy, happy days,
> So near you!

I stopped, my back to the club floor, and I listened to the men clap. When I turned my head for a peek, I saw Benny and Lansky were applauding the Andrews Sisters, but not the third man. He was looking right at me, all approbation, and when I inclined my head in a small bow to acknowledge his pleasure in me, he smiled, eyes crinkling, all the former harsh severity in his face banished, and suddenly, I liked him. All the men I knew used on occasion what I thought of as the bad face, the tough, unflinching stare meant to intimidate. The man had been wearing that face not ten minutes ago, but now his bad face was gone and he was looking at me as if he were delighted with me, this little girl he didn't even know. And he was the one who tugged at that string between us, not me, tugged me to him with that smile. And then he leaned over to Benny and said something to him and then Benny looked to me and I knew he had asked Ben who I was. And I saw Benny hesitate just a moment before he brought Nate over to meet me.

Maybe it was because I was wearing this costume. Or maybe it was because I was finally grown up, which I'd been trying to do as fast as I could since we'd arrived in Vegas because there was nothing here for little girls and so many opportunities for young women. I didn't know yet how these men were protective of little girls but preyed upon them when they grew up. But you couldn't stop growing up. The transition from girlhood to womanhood turned on a pivot. One day you were a child and then, all at once, you weren't.

Well, that day was my pivot.

The man had a pinkie ring on his left hand and a cigarette in his right, and he transferred the one to the other as he approached, and that's how I knew he was going to touch me for the first time. I could see better now his Roman nose that counterbalanced all that hair. He was handsome, though not in a pretty-boy way like Benny, who once wanted nothing more than to be a pretty movie star. Still, he looked something like Ben, something like my father, some version of them. Without the intemperate rage. Without the failure. He moved with a tall, silky grace that actually reminded me of my old Hollywood dance teacher, Daddy Mack, who might have been short and fat, but when he moved all that weight on his two short legs, he wore his blubber like a mink coat. And that's how this man moved, as if he were wearing a mink coat.

"E," Benny said to me, not entirely happily. "This is Nate Stein."

Nate offered his hand. I took it. It was large.

"I'm Esme Wells," I told him, giving him my stage name, which was half my name and half my mother's stage name. Nate laughed.

He knew exactly who I was, Esme Silver, fifteen years old, practically unschooled, a nobody, but he understood my affectation, even approved of it. All those men approved of ambition. Of reinvention.

Naturally.

And we stood there, my hand in his while Benny frowned, probably because Nate was married, and not for the first time, not that marriage had ever inhibited Benny himself in any way in his various extramarital adventures, but because I was Benny's Baby E and Nate was staring at me in this certain way and Ben could see what lay ahead, and he didn't like it. He cleared his throat. He would have liked to clear the club, or rather, clear Nate from the club. But in the current pecking order, Ben didn't have the power to do this. So the rest of the girls clumped back to the dressing room, where they would smoke cigarettes and drink Cokes, while I stood here. I can only imagine how I looked to Mr. Stein, a piece of candy in a candy-colored costume, my face orange with Pan-Cake and my lashes an elongated black, my hair long as a child's. I didn't want to let go of Nate's hand and he seemed not to want to let go of mine, either. What was happening was perfectly proper, an introduction, a handshake, but somehow it didn't feel proper at all. And Benny, irritated, looked away.

My costume, though actually quite modest, suddenly seemed to feel riskily low-cut and short, exposing too much of me everywhere from my neck to my flamingo-red high heels. I flushed and Nate smiled at my transparency. Embarrassed as I was by my near nakedness, I nonetheless found myself in the grip of an absurd impulse to undress further, and all the while, Nate Stein smiled at me. He's an old man, I told myself. But the fact that he was older was exactly what I liked about him. He wasn't striving to be something, he was already something. If I'd met him when he was twenty, I wouldn't have liked him, wouldn't have wanted him. But I'd met him now. And I wanted him, whatever that meant. I had a feeling about him, the kind of feeling my father had when he knew his horse was going to come in.

But because I was as yet still underage, and because Nate was a careful man, more like Lansky the accountant than the id-driven Benny—who needn't have worried about me, at least, not yet, and by the time he should have been worried, he was dead—it was therefore too early to know what would become of us.

And so all Nate said to me that day was, "Lovely to meet you, Miss Esme Wells." His voice was a purr, with the slightest tinge of something foreign sounding in it, which turned out to be just his flat Midwestern accent, though I was too ignorant to know it.

He was fifty and I wasn't quite a third of that.

LOS ANGELES
1939

12

THE CLAPTRAP TRUCK MY father had hired after our eviction followed us all the way along Wilshire Boulevard, the words EXPRESS MOVING PHONE BOYLE 366 shamelessly, boldly, painted on its side, the bed of the truck piled high with our furniture, which had somehow, for the most part, as my father had promised, remained intact on the lawn, a few pieces missing, my mother speculating which of our neighbors had snuck out in the night to take what. But nothing had been stolen. Whatever was missing had been quietly pawned by my father, shortly after his crushing loss at the racetrack. So most, if not all, of our belongings were now upended in the back of the moving truck, mattresses naked and pathetic-looking in their striped sheaths, a huge jailhouse embarrassment which my parents ignored, pretending that the truck behind us had nothing to do with them.

I couldn't help but turn around in my seat to look at the sight of the swaying mess, so irresistibly wrong, until my father finally rapped me on the head with his knuckles to make me stop. If we didn't look at it, it wasn't there, though we were lucky it was. And he was especially lucky it was. Yet, despite this great luck, I could tell my mother was miserable. For one, she wasn't speaking to my father. Or two, looking at him. We were heading back to Boyle Heights, our horse tails tucked between our legs, retreating to immigrant East Los Angeles, where the rents were cheapest and the scenery most familiar.

I know my father had once appeared to her as if he knew something about the big world, hair slicked back, cigarette jaunty in one hand, the smart Jew on the make who wasn't selling scrap metal or neckties or painting houses or slicing meat in a delicatessen like every other man she knew in Boyle Heights. He looked like a winning ticket, blown into the city from Baltimore's Pimlico racetrack just for her to pick up. Yet this day I'm sure he seemed not so much of a winning ticket after all, not so much a Magic Ike as an Ordinary Ike. Head down, she looked at the naked fingers of her ring hand and chipped at her nail polish, something she did when she was upset, a habit I learned from her and practiced, though not to such an exaggerated extent. I watched while the red paint was slowly nibbled and nicked away until she had nails the same color as my unvarnished child's nails.

We took the Sixth Street Bridge, our own personal bridge jumper, you could say, except my mother, not my father, was the one I worried might jump from it, though it wasn't a very long fall to the Los Angeles River. The water was so shallow you could wade in it only up to your ankles, the banks sharp and sloped, once made of dirt and laced with negligible vegetation, but now newly paved over with cement. The river was being remade into a concrete channel in an effort to control future floods. I peered down now at the angular, empty cement trough as my father drove over it, and he called out, ill-advisedly, I thought, even as a six-year-old, "Hello again, Jewtown. Where Los Angeles rolls its refuse over the river. We're back!" If he wanted to try to soothe my mother, he was taking the wrong tack.

When you first cross the bridge into Boyle Heights, the streets are full of Mexicans and Japanese and Negroes and Chinese, the city's refuse, as my father had put it, who lived here, labored here, and were buried here in cemeteries as segregated as their neighborhoods had been. It wasn't until you drove along Brooklyn Avenue and past the large Breed Street shul that you might understand why the rest of Los Angeles referred to Boyle Heights as Jewtown. It was there that Hebrew lettering appeared along with the open-air markets, replete with barrels of herring and pickles, over which women in housedresses and bedroom slippers bent to take a sniff. We passed Zellman's Men's Wear with its checkerboard floor and Leaders Barbershop with its two long lines of chairs and mirrors where my grandfather used to get his hair trimmed and Cantor Bros. Delicatessen with Jewish stars all over the plate glass, one of them between the two words STEAKS and CHOPS, as if meat itself could chase a religion.

Past the cleaners, the haberdasheries, the drugstore, past the Hoffmans of Coast to Coast Neckwear Company, the Rosners of Rosner's Bakery, the Kartzes of Kartz Appliances, the Abrahams in their dry-goods store, the Shonholtzes at their jewelry store, the Resnicks in their deli, and past Mr. Rael who stood sentry at the door of his furniture store.

Peddlers all, my father would say. Not big boys. These ordinary Jews were the ones who populated Jewtown, and they were not the moguls or mobsters my father admired, the big boys who had sprung themselves from the pen that held all the other Jews.

But this landscape—I can't say it was terribly familiar to me as I was not quite five when we left it, my world at that age consisting of my grandfather's house and yard and the immediate half block of Winter Street on which it stood—was certainly all too familiar to my mother. It wasn't until much later, until after I had things to be ashamed of myself, that I understood how moving back to her old neighborhood was a torment for her. There everybody knew Sy Wolfkowitz's daughter, Dina, too pretty for her own good with the stars in her eyes, always talking about being a movie star. And Sy's son-in-law, Ike, the bum—what kind of a Jew gambled at the track?

And they pitied me, too, though I didn't know it, the little blond urchin dragged around the city by that pair of schemers. We had sailed out of Boyle Heights on a pile of money, but we hadn't been gone very long, and now here we were, slinking back, as I said, tails between our legs, and it wouldn't be but a minute before the Zellmans and the Resnicks and the Shonholtzes and the Abrahams knew it.

My father, who always tried to tease any situation into its best light, had said Boyle Heights was going to be a great choice for us. Boyle Heights! Home! A place to regroup. But I wasn't sure how much of a choice it actually was. It was either Boyle Heights or a boarding house in Culver City. And as most tenants of boarding houses were bachelors or single women secretaries or actresses biding their time until they made married men of those bachelors, what real choice did we have?

We weren't only going back there for the cheap rent. My father was going to beg for work at my grandfather's old company, Wolfkowitz Painting, the company he had been too fancy to own and too quick to sell—as the neighbors would say, back to paint houses for a company he could have run, Wolfkowitz Painting could have been his! his for the taking!, but he had thought he was too good for all that, thought he would hit it big at the races, and now look at him, paid by the hour, Wolfkowitz paintbrush in his hand. Very, very soon my father would be enduring the humiliation of painter's coveralls and a painter's cap.

There would be a couple of escapes for us. For my mother and me, the movie theater. The National Theater on Brooklyn Avenue would become our haunt that summer, even if it showed only second-run movies, some of which my mother appeared in. The theater marquee was stuck to what looked like a storefront, this

movie house nothing like the ornate theme palaces of Hollywood
Boulevard or South Broadway, but it would do. As we passed the
National that day, my mother read the marquee.

CLOSED TONITE
PROTEST NAZI HORROR
OPEN WEDNESDAY
TOY WIFE

And she turned to my father and raised her eyebrows. What?
My mother never knew anything going on in the larger world.
Multiple countries could have blown themselves up or their pop-
ulations died of famine or revolutionaries assassinated all the
kings and queens of Europe, and she would be none the wiser.
But she could tell you every detail of the lives of the movie stars,
gleaned from lot gossip and the studio-generated stories printed
in *Photoplay* or *Screen Romances*.

As we drove past the dark interior of the Ebony Room, Louie
Schwartzman's place, where men played poker and Louie ran
numbers games, a police cruiser made a U-turn in front of us and
parked by the front door, and a group of kids acting as lookouts
scattered, one of them darting inside. My father raised his eyebrows and looked at me. The numbers games were run out of the
back of the bar, and my father always played the numbers, had
played back in Baltimore, along with the rest of his family, all of
whom loved horses and numbers and cards. I knew that much
about them.

So the Ebony Room would become my father's escape hatch,
within which he would eventually meet Mickey Cohen, who always
stopped by when he came to visit his mother in Boyle Heights.

Then we turned onto Winter Street, just to pass my grandfather's old house—two stories, brick and green clapboard, with

a deep porch, red painted concrete steps, and an overgrowth of big blue hydrangeas. For a minute, in my deluded child's mind, I thought we might pull up there and unpack and resume the lives we had lived there before, minus my grandfather, of course, who had vacated the house and was buried next to my grandmother. My mother had my father stop the car so she could gaze at her old home. So maybe it wasn't my father's inspiration to stop there. Maybe she had asked him to do this.

And what did my mother think she would see through those windows? Perhaps she was hoping to see her parents, the two, like Peg Entwistle, clothed in the attire of another age, inhabiting those rooms. My mother once told me that as a little girl and very sick with the measles, she saw her mother's ghost sitting quietly at the foot of her bed in the dark. Like me, my mother lost her own mother young. Perhaps that story was my inspiration, but for years after her death, I used to see my mother sitting by my bed, her dark hair grown out as long as my own, her lips St. Petersburgundy red as she whispered things to me, things I should think of, sequins, fur, fishnets, feathers. It never surprised me that those were the things she thought to tell me, trivial showgirl things.

Maybe she believed, as I did at age six, that even though we and my grandfather were gone, somehow the interior of the house had remained intact, a stage set waiting for the players' return. This was contrary to all evidence, of course. I had seen my grandfather's old-fashioned furnishings sold by my avaricious parents, but despite that, the house and its props remained in place, intact in my mind. Everything about it looked the same from the outside. The dark green trim, the red paint on the cement steps leading to the porch, the hydrangea bushes paired like sentinels, some of the giant blossoms browning in the fierce early August heat.

My grandfather's hat was surely laid on the dining-room table next to his newspaper, the *Daily Forward*, which my grandfather would take with him to the drugstore to serve as an eye chart while he tried on reading glasses, I, functioning as his assistant, Miss Esme, holding up all the various magnifications for him. This one? No. This one? His paper was always folded into a long lean crisp, the latest reading glasses next to it, magnification 3.5. My grandfather went to his office every morning at seven o'clock except Saturday. Behind the swinging door that divided the dining room from the kitchen stood Gertrude, the Negro maid, the polisher of all this furniture and the secretary to all this routine and clattering dishes.

I used to snoop through my grandfather's study as a little girl, looking in desk drawers at my grandparents' old boat tickets for the SS *Adria*, the two of them sailing to America on October 8, 1889, on the Hamburg America line, marveling at their exotic journey and at the neat rubber-banded stack of bank deposit receipts that showed the money my grandfather deposited week after week into his checking account, the small amounts deposited over and over again with such predictable regularity, not the one big jackpot here and there that fell into my father's hands, but many small purses every Friday, and at rings thick with silver and copper keys, some of the keys so old and so weird-looking and so tarnished that I figured they must be keys for locks long lost or never opened. One of those, I had been sure, must be the lock that held my grandmother's jewelry safe from my parents' hands and on which my parents pounced only after my grandfather's death.

On the day of my grandfather's funeral, I had been left behind with Gertrude, and when my parents came home they couldn't find me for the longest time, my mother weeping and calling my name, thinking she'd lost me, too. But I was there. I had crawled under my grandfather's bed and fallen asleep, both my hands slipped into one of my grandfather's gloves, the soft black leather glove with its soft fur lining. Why did he own these? In the over-heated basin of Los Angeles there could be only a week's worth of wearing such a glove. And I remembered, too, how that night my mother had labored so mightily to persuade me to drink my bedtime glass of warm milk, but as she had served it to me, un-thinkingly, in a glass used for memorial candles, I had refused it, no matter how many times she sang an old Nestle's milk ad from the 1920s to a tune of her own invention.

> *Thanks for your feed of Nestle's milk.*
> *It did me good—my coat's like silk.*
> *And now I'm sound in limb and brain.*
> *I'll never drink skim milk again.*

She twirled around the kitchen, putting on a big show, playing at being a cat, her black hair flying. I refused to drink because drinking that milk was like drinking down Death. Plus, she was acting so strangely. At the end of it, she'd said, "Fine," and drank my milk herself. "Happy?"

No.

There had been something almost hysterical about her that night that had unnerved me even more than the milk served in a glass that had once held a candle for the dead. Her frenetic cat-like movements, her creepy eyes lit as if they were stealing light from the big orange moon resting in the purple horizon to the east. At some point that night, she went quiet, all the chatter chatter chatter of that evening gone still. Soon after, she'd been taken to the hospital and from there to yet another hospital, the one up in Camarillo.

So, whatever it was my mother had hoped to see now through

the windows of her old house, she did not see. Her parents were both dead. All the furniture had been sold. By my parents. And so had the house. By my parents. A new family lived there now, with their own furniture, their own lives. Another child's orange-crate scooter lay on its side on the lawn. And while we paused there, car at the curb, gawking, a woman in a duster came out onto the porch to water her potted plants.

Stupendously, surprisingly, my mother started to cry, which was not at all the response my father had expected from the sweep of his arm, all this is here for your pleasure, peruse your past and be comforted. Now his foot sputtered on the gas pedal. When we moved away from Boyle Heights, my mother's sorrow had seemed not to chase her. Now, we were returning her to it. I stared open-mouthed as my mother's face became marked with black tears, which all the speed in the world could not reverse. The Cadillac, and the truck behind us, turned north.

13

WHILE WINTER STREET MIGHT no longer be our street, Soto Street, a lesser street, was. My father turned up Soto for a few blocks and then waved the truck up the driveway of a small two-story house that didn't look all that much different from our bungalow in Hollywood. Spanish-style. What building in Los Angeles didn't at least make a nod to the Spanish padres? This house had all the tropes. It was stucco. Brown. Green shutters and black ironwork. The paint on the railings was peeling. And in the back, I would discover, a strip of grass with a dead fountain. And beyond it, two streets over, the Sisters Orphan Home, a redbrick Romanesque monument to the Depression, which had parents leaving off their children there, children that they could no longer afford to feed. Visiting hours Sunday.

Our chairs teetered and our dressers rocked as the truck lurched its way along the cracked drive toward the back of the house, two Japanese men jumping out before the truck had even gotten all the way there to start unloading. My mother slid out of the car in her pretty sleeveless dress and stood at the curb, squinting at the building. My father and I remained in the car. He looked over at me and gave me a wink. "Let's give her a minute," he said. I nodded, but I didn't think a minute was going to change anything. He gazed conspicuously down Soto Street.

There was nothing to see. My father was stalling. It wasn't about giving my mother some private time. My father just didn't want to live through the next few minutes. Or the next few weeks. I didn't either. If I'm remembering correctly, he did a crossword puzzle, though where he would have gotten the newspaper and a pencil, I don't know.

When he figured he'd given her enough privacy, he put the paper down, said to me, "Ready?" so I knew I had to get out of the car, too, the little child that would keep my mother from killing him. He got out of the car and walked jauntily toward her. You had to admire his spirit. I followed him. Reluctantly. Scraping the sides of my shoes on the concrete, as if that might retard my progress.

As we approached my mother, she turned away from us and said, "I can't live here."

And to that, my father said only, "Yes, you can," lit another cigarette from a fresh pack of Chesterfields, took out his snappy little lighter and walked off in the direction of the truck, and disappeared from view.

Now it was just us two.

My mother crossed her lithe little arms across her chest. She had her deciding face on, as in deciding how much more resistance to put up, how much more of a fit to throw. I think I tugged at her elbow to make her arms uncross. All I wanted was for her to go quietly inside and start telling the men where to put our furniture. But I knew that she wouldn't. Not right away, anyway. Because the minute my mother went inside this new house, it would mean my father had won, that my mother would have to live here. As long as she stood out here by the car, that future was in doubt.

But what else could we do? Go back to Orange Street or the Hollyhock Motel? No, we could not. Go back in time and return to my grandfather's house? No, we could not. And that was why my father had already gone around to the truck. To settle it. So it was settled. My father left us on the drive because he would otherwise have to deal with my mother with her purse in her hand, snapping it closed with a click of finality, saying, We're going back to that motel until you find us a better place. To which my father would say, You think I can get us a palace with the size of that diamond, and my mother would answer, Are you referring to the diamond you bought me?, a variation of a fight I had heard them have many times before. So why would he come check on us? I wouldn't. My mother could stand out here until nighttime with her arms crossed over her chest, pouting with her red lips and gazing at her unadorned ring finger, stand here until the moon rose and all the stars trembled in the sky, but it was settled. There was no one in heaven or on earth to help her. There was only my father. My grandfather had once been the central pivot on which her life balanced and turned. Now, without him, only my father remained, my father, who had tugged her life out of orbit, and me, a small satellite of no help at all.

In fact, I was a burden.

As we stood there, she and I, the Japanese men began carting my parents' bedroom set up the drive and shoving it piece by piece through the front door. I watched my parents' bed, central to all operations, go by. Even as a child, I could sense their bed was the locus of some powerful joyous force that worked like gravity to hold us all together, and yet, conversely, theirs was also a private society that excluded me. I was both in the club and outside it. But that night at bedtime, my father was also out.

Because when he came upstairs, grimy and exhausted, my mother said, "There's no room for you here. You can fix yourself a place to sleep out in the garage."

My father stared at her for a moment, and I could see the flush rising up my father's face from his neck, as if he had been infused with a vial of red dye plugged directly into his heart.

I understood. My father had to be punished. She could not move into this dump with the money her ring had bought—or so she thought—and let him get off scot-free, let him brush his teeth vigorously before the tin metal mirror in the bathroom, and then pop into the champagne-colored bed with her in the master bedroom, that bedroom small by any measure but dwarfed further by the size of the suite crowded into it. No. She might not be able to refuse to live in this house or to insist that she and I sleep in the Cadillac until my father came up with something better, but she could refuse him entry to her bedroom. He would have new quarters. The garage would be his punishment, the couch we couldn't fit into our living room, his bed. This arrangement was not entirely novel. The last year or so we were living at my grandfather's, when my father's obsessive gambling had so enraged my grandfather that he could no longer stand to have my father anywhere in the house, the garage had become my father's bunkhouse. My mother would have to visit him out there, bring him his dinner plate.

I looked up at my father. What would he do? Usually, he never listened to my mother, ignored three-quarters of the ideas she came up with, but this time, this time, my father picked up a pillow and carted it off.

14

I WATCHED HIM CROSS the backyard, pass the dead fountain, slide open one of the wooden doors of the garage, and disappear inside the rickety stucco box that would now house his exile. A light went on, courtesy of a bare bulb with a long string you yanked. My father was smoking, I could tell, for the fog from his cigarettes rose up and seeped through the crack at the top of the garage doors. The moon also rose, above me, a big white moon like a baby's face in the sky, its light flowing down over my body like spilled milk. I was hungry.

I stood still on that scrap of a lawn and concrete. Two birds skittered around in the leaf-filled fountain, looking for a bath, but there was nothing for them there, no water, just dried detritus. An orange tree stood beside me, and I pulled a piece of its fruit from a branch and peeled it to eat. It was sour. I turned to check on my mother. She was still safely in the house. I could see her though the bedroom window. My father, still smoking.

It was as if each of them had spun a cocoon, leaving me unattended and unencumbered. For all they knew, beyond their strange opaque busywork, I could vanish from this spot, run across the Sixth Street Bridge and swim like a dark mermaid along the shallow river. It looked like a small creek now, a rivulet. But last year, during an early spring storm, that rivulet had become a torrent. Mud and rainwater cascaded down the San Gabriel Mountains, ran north, south, east, and west. The towns of Anaheim and Santa Ana and Agua Mansa in the east were submerged entirely. Valley farmland in the north disappeared. All over Los Angeles, south of downtown and west to the beaches, buildings and bridges collapsed and streets turned to waterways. Boulders taller than stranded cars rolled on the roadways beside them. The fronts of houses were sheared off, the water drowning sleeping animals and people before dragging their bodies away in the current.

My parents that night seemed to be preparing themselves, each in his own way, for futures they dreaded and yet found themselves unwillingly dragged toward, and I couldn't help but wonder what future lay ahead for me. Maybe this was the end of all the magical leisure to which I had become accustomed and which other children were customarily denied, and I would now have to go to school and become an ordinary person.

There was no greater debasement in our family. Neither of my parents ever wanted to be ordinary and it was doubtful, I thought, that they could love me if I were. I was the darling baby doll on the studio lot, the tiny baby stooper at the track, the misshapen dream of two reckless parents. If my parents were now en route to disaster, surely I would follow them there, as well, all the way down to a desk at the local school and a dunce cap, tall and pointy, for my head.

But I needn't have worried. There would be no classroom or dunce cap dangling there yet in my future, though it might have been better for me if there had been.

15

LUCKILY FOR ME, BUZZ never minded my being on his sound-stage, because in the morning, my mother and I drove off to-gether in our Cadillac to MGM, leaving my father to snap on his brand-new painter's coveralls and walk by himself over to the offices of Wolfkowitz Paint Co., which had kept my grandfa-ther's name. Could have been Wolfkowitz & Son Paint Co. But it wasn't. There, unlike the track, I couldn't tag along with him, at least not yet, anyway, not on his first day.

My mother was quiet, wearing lipstick and a lot of bangles that made the only noise inside the car, and she kept her lips pursed as she drove. Her thinking face. I could tell she was plotting. MGM was planning a new Busby Berkeley picture, *Strike Up the Band*, and Buzz would need 115 dancers for the movie's biggest number, "Do the La Conga." Paul Whiteman and his orchestra would be playing at the Riverwood High School dance and a band called Six Hits and a Miss would be singing, and Judy Garland and Mickey Rooney would star in the film because the *Babes* daily rushes were looking so good that Louis B. Mayer laid down a commandment that the two should be featured in another vehi-cle. I figured my mother was probably angling for a real speaking role in *Band*, picturing herself on the soundstage in that yellow bomb of light, face flowering before the big, sun-greedy cameras. For eight years my mother had been, like so many others, the cho-rus girl who hadn't broken from the pack, and with Buzz's rising fortunes, perhaps she was hoping so would rise her own. And for that she needed a screen test.

When we arrived at the studio gate, she turned to look at me, and I expected her to tell me then her secret plan to beg a screen test from Buzz, the two of us in cahoots, but instead she frowned at me and said, "You need a haircut," as if the thought that my hair should be cut had never before occurred to her nor had the fact that she should be the one to do it. She wrinkled her nose at me. "Your hair's as long as a little gypsy's. And it smells." Again, my fault. And, of course, in imitation of her, I wore my own sheath of necklaces and wrist bangles so I probably did look like a little gypsy. And smelled like one. And I had thought I looked like a movie star today. I slunk lower in my seat, ashamed beyond measure, and I couldn't bring myself to wave, as I usually did, to the guard at the gate.

I think the reason Buzz never minded having me around was because he, too, had been a little urchin child who followed his actress mother from theater to theater, from show to show, a baby who slept in a dresser drawer turned bassinet in her dressing room. And so he allowed my presence. In fact, he almost always brought some toy for me to amuse myself with while they worked, as if the show in front of me wasn't amusement enough. I remember miniature garden furniture made of clothespins, a cheap carnival Kewpie doll with a thick swatch of yellow hair, and today on the set he handed me a colorful paper bird with sticks to work the wings. In between takes, I played with it, made it swoop and fly. During takes, I used the sticks to close the bird's wings, stroked it to sleep so it would be quiet, put the bird in my dress pocket. Sometimes I would write Buzz's name as my mother had taught me on a piece of paper and keep it in my pocket, too, as if I could put him there, as well, all those z's a comforting snore.

Is it possible for a little girl to be in love with a grown man? Apparently. This was my specialty.

Today, though, I was the only one in love with him. Buzz's girls, my mother included, were furious with him, fidgeting, exchanging glances. Normally, Buzz dressed them all like queens, but that day they were costumed as fools, outfitted in puffy black Negro wigs, black makeup thick over their faces. Their arms were painted black, too, their legs made dark with black hosiery, their feet identical in black tap shoes with black bows. The only thing white about them was their lips, which were clown white, drawn big, giant-sized. The girls looked nothing like their usual ultra-glamorous selves and they looked none too happy about the difference, either. Today they were shooting the number I'd watched them rehearse earlier this week, "I'm Just Wild about Harry." The girls started complaining about the blackface in the dressing rooms, in the makeup chairs, and continued complaining about it as they walked all the way to the set.

There was always some gimmick with Buzz, though usually it was a pretty one—illuminated violins for the girls to play, ten-foot ribbons to be unscrolled from the floor, enormous feather boas for the girls to wave or cellophane-covered hoops for them to jump through, capes made of linked gold coins that clinked when they shimmied, a row of fifty white pianos with fake keys for the girls to pretend to play. Unfortunately, today the gimmick was humble, humiliating even, as was the choreography. All my mother and the other girls had to do in their spongy wigs and blackface was to stand on the rows of a riser behind the girl actually singing the number and to shake their heads, which had top hats with pom-poms on long wires affixed to them, their every move making those pom-poms quiver. If there was ever a day to make my mother rue her lot, this was that day.

Also, unfortunately, Buzz was in one of his moods. It was hard to tell if he was hung over or if he'd had too much to drink already. Even before noon, it was already the umpteenth time I heard him call, "Cut!" This, of course, was squawked from the heavens, as Buzz made it a habit to ride the boom or climb above the set to see what the camera would shoot, walk the girders seventy, eighty feet in the air, camera finder in hand. I saw the girls start shaking at the sound of his voice and look up to the rafters to spy Zeus with his thunderbolt. Make that Apollo. Apollo with what? If I'd ever gone to school, I might know to tell you.

God, or the closest thing MGM had to Him, Louis B. Mayer, had given Buzz this entire picture to direct, his first, a B picture with some song and dance numbers. So Buzz wanted this picture to go well. Needed it to go well. The old-fashioned musical was dying, the big extravaganzas that Buzz had brought from New York to California eight years ago had just begun to fall out of favor, all that gold he'd spun dwindled to floss, and all Broadway's players had relocated here to Los Angeles, it seemed, holding out their hands to the Hollywood gods, the same palms Florenz Ziegfeld once filled with gold. And Buzz liked it here, they all did, liked this brown fragrant landscape where it was always warm. He wanted to stay.

"Cut!" I could hear Buzz's intake of breath from on high. "Do you have any idea at all what you're supposed to be doing?" He hung his sour face over one of those ten-ton klieg lights, the better to see his unfortunate victim, who happened that day, that moment, to be Judy Garland. Garland's face, uptipped in response, was a blank black slate. A damp slate. I could see the sweat beaded up on her forehead. She'd been working hard, despite the fact that she was exhausted and overbooked by the studio, as my mother had told me. In my child's head, I thought, Leave her alone. But, of course, he didn't.

His next words were, "Just what the hell do you think you've been doing?"

Garland jutted her chin at him. Defiantly. And said, "Exactly what you showed me."

Wrong thing to say.

Everybody stirred. Even my own stomach felt the spoon.

Buzz liked humble quiescence. But perhaps because he was so far away, bird on a wire, Garland figured it was safe to say whatever she damn well pleased. She'd only just finished shooting *The Wizard of Oz*, which hadn't been released yet, so she was still just the bit actress, the nice girl who lived next door to Andy Hardy whom Buzz felt he could push around.

"Well, aren't you a silly little bit*ch*?" Buzz barked, red mouth, red tongue, and even from the distance we could all hear the hiss of that digraph, which was nasty, and patently unfair, because Judy Garland wasn't any of those things—silly, little, or a bitch. But Buzz was too worked up to care about the truth. "You're fucking up my number and you're tiring out my girls. And every time we have to do it over because of you, they have to do it over, too."

I could pick out my mother now, the bold one rolling her eyes, bold because after all, she had been with Buzz from Day One, rolling those eyes at the girl next to her, who shook her head in response, pom-pom gently bouncing.

We all knew what was coming. More invective, more takes.

Buzz didn't like Judy Garland, but Mr. Mayer had forced him to cast her. Because of her rolled shoulders, Buzz called her behind her back, as Louis B. Mayer did, "the little hunchback"— and in addition to her posture, he also took exception to the amphetamines the studio fed her, the pills that kept her upright but couldn't keep her legs from going this way and that. In fact she was so stuffed with pills that she had the hollow look of one of those floating ghost women I saw when my mother was confined at Camarillo.

"All right, let's go again," Buzz said and he whirled his arm like he was turning the key on a mechanical toy. And so they all started it up again, Garland shuffling and shucking front and center, my mother and the rest of them standing on their risers, shifting their weight from one foot to the other, pom-poms boinging on their springs, Buzz yelling at Garland, "Open your eyes. Open your eyes! Wide! Left, left, right, right."

And then just as Garland was singing,

> *I'm just wild about Harry!*
> *And Harry's wild about me!*

she stumbled, left foot caught on the right, and simultaneously, Buzz took a sudden tumble from the catwalk, the two of them finally on the same page in catastrophe, his white body making a swoosh, traveling with ridiculous speed, arms and legs spread-eagled as he dropped from the heights, sleeves and pant legs quivering in the cosmic winds.

At first, I thought there'd been an earthquake, like the one my mother described that had sent Buzz tumbling from the boom six years ago, during the filming of the Shadow Waltz number from *Gold Diggers*. The 6.4 tremor had knocked Buzz from his perch and then knocked out the electricity, plunging the soundstage into the blackest black. He'd called out to his screaming girls—some of whom were standing eighty feet high in the air on that winding staircase of his, clutching their now unillumined violins—telling them to sit down right where they were as carefully as they could. One of the grips felt his way over to the soundstage door, which sounded, sliding open, like a metallic earthquake all its own. My mother described her terror that day so well, I felt I was there. And in fact I was, as my mother was pregnant with me.

But there was no earthquake today. Who knows why Buzz fell this time. Maybe he'd seen that misstep of Garland's and his temper tipped him over. Maybe Apollo didn't like him screaming at one of his disciples and leaned down from Olympus to give Buzz a push with one divine finger. Of course, I'd been half worrying this might happen because he was up there in such a state, and I stood up as he fell and ran toward him, screaming, smelly gypsy hair flying, paper robin falling from my hands, having given the gift of flight to Buzz. Everybody was screaming. Even Garland's jaw opened, the musical notes flying from it turning into frightened birds, melody transmogrified into a squawk.

Buzz didn't fall all the way to the ground, of course, because he had tied himself to a rope thrown over an adjacent girder, and the other end of the rope was held by one of the camera grips on the ground, Big Harry, whose job it was to winch Buzz back up to his beam if he should slip, like a circus worker rescuing an aerialist who'd plunged from the high wire. So for better or worse Buzz didn't fall to his death, as Garland was probably hoping, a little less wild about this particular Harry. But Buzz did look ridiculous, the way a director never wants to look in front of his cast, stalled there midflight in his leather harness, arms outstretched, legs kicking in some useless spasm. Distressed, I waved my hands at him, strung up like a chicken four feet above me.

By now, Garland had shut her mouth and pinched her lips together, looking altogether satisfied. Who could blame her?

And all through the hubbub, Buzz was apologizing, "Gee, I'm sorry, Harry," with a humility I never saw him employ when he spoke to his dancers, who were always bitches or idiots, and Harry was calling out, "Hang on, Buzz. I've got ya."

I stood on tiptoe, then jumped, trying to reach him, as if somehow I could be the one to save him.

"It's okay, Esme," Buzz said to me from where he hung, upside down now, face red, my anxiety turning his fury and embarrassment to solicitude. He reached down to me and clasped the hand I held up. Our fingers touched, and he twirled me, then lifted me a little until my feet were an inch from the floor, made a game of it, until Harry finally unhooked him from the harness and

Buzz was upright again, keeping one hand on my little shoulder while he called Garland out as a sorry—and then with a quick look down at me—witch, responsible for his fall and a lost day of shooting.

It was amazing how quickly he made the transition from abject apologist to imperious dictator once his sneakered feet were back on the ground. And Garland just stood there with her rounded shoulders and her glistening blackboard face and all the other girls, about twenty of them, I guess, stood there just as she did, obsequious. Standing there next to him, his hand on my little shoulder, I felt wickedly complicit, as if he were a ventriloquist and I were his puppet and his words were coming out of me.

Discomfited, I tapped on his arm.

Buzz stopped mid-word to stare down at me, stunned or apoplectic, I couldn't tell. His brows were thick as black bristly caterpillars, his face the face of an advisor to a Roman emperor.

He was looking at me and I had to do something. So I said to him, already regretting it, "You're being mean."

Silence. I looked around. Roman statues, every one. My mother's face: furious horror.

Buzz looked away from me then, looked up at the harness still dangling from the rope and for a moment I thought he might buckle me into it and leave me hanging there all night as punishment. But he didn't. He compressed his lips into a long flat line. Nobody moved. Then he turned to Garland and said, "Sorry, dear," and to the rest, "Let's call it a day, girls," and he strode past my mother toward the big metal door of the soundstage. As he passed her, I heard him say, "Don't ever bring her to the set again," and though my mother opened her mouth to answer, he kept walking.

I'd gone from teacher's pet to pariah in five seconds.

"What's gotten into you, Esme?" she said when she reached

me, the wire with her pom-pom swaying like crazy. I stared at her strange black face, not quite sure all of a sudden that she really was my mother. "He's the director. He's a man. He can do and say whatever he wants."

One of the grips scrambled to open the big soundstage door as soon as it became clear Buzz intended to keep walking, that he'd bust right through the heavy barn door if the men couldn't slide it open in time. But the door slid aside almost quickly enough, Buzz just skimming the side of it, the mechanism clanking crazily as it revealed the sun and sky I'd almost forgotten about and which made a bit of a sham of everything within. Buzz was a silhouette and then nothing.

To my surprise, my mother went steaming after him into the sunlight. To apologize? Surely she wasn't going to ask him about her screen test now, with him in this state, after what I did? But you could never tell with my mother—when she got an idea in her head, it was hard to stop her. Or maybe she was just trying to run away from me. Like everybody else.

Because usually at the end of a shooting day, the girls made a big fuss over me as we walked together to the General Dressing Rooms. I always looked forward to that. They'd call out, "Comeer, Little Movie Star," and to my mother, the girls would say, "Dina, what a cute little sister you have." To which my mother always said, "Don't I?" giving me a hard warning squeeze, even though I knew very well I wasn't to say anything to the contrary. On the set, I was my mother's little sister and my father was her boyfriend, not her husband. I didn't particularly like pretending to be her sister or the feeling I had that my mother wished that were actually the truth, but I liked the attention being there brought me, liked the sweat and perfume, wigs and costumes, the way all those pretty girls petted and kissed at me, saying, "Won't be long before you're one of us, honey."

Clearly, I was getting none of that today. Buzz's girls, like my mother, couldn't be scurrying away from me any faster. And I wasn't going to be getting any of that tomorrow or any other day, now that I'd been banned from the set.

There was only one person who hadn't abandoned me. Miss Garland, who, as she passed me by, leaned over and kissed the top of my head. It was so quick, I wasn't sure if it had happened at all or if I had imagined it, but when she turned her black face back to me and winked at me over her shoulder, I knew it had happened for sure. Yes, she winked at me and then she stepped right on top of the paper robin I'd dropped, smashing it. It lay on its side, now, and the highly polished soundstage floor made it look like two robins, kissing. What did I care about that smashed bird now, now that Buzz hated me? I stepped over it to follow her out.

And there, by the soundstage door, I found my mother talking earnestly to Buzz. Lord, what was she saying?

I tucked myself against the side of the building, but I couldn't hear them, so I watched them, and watching them, I noted how my mother had gotten thinner seemingly overnight, her arms and legs whittled away and her full cheeks gone, as if whatever liquid in them had been sucked out with a straw and the flesh had collapsed against her teeth in despair, as if she and my father had drawn some sustenance from one another I hadn't known about and without it, she had shriveled. Instantly. She looked like one of her silent screen icons, that hollow-cheeked Joan Crawford from *Taxi Dancer*. Crawford looked gorgeous. But my mother didn't. She looked desperate. Desperate for some new kind of sustenance.

No, I couldn't hear what she was saying, but in this silent movie, this pantomime, my mother, my beautiful mother, was begging Buzz for something, this I could tell. And I didn't think she was begging on my behalf, but on her own. I think, too, she had forgotten she was standing there before Buzz in blackface,

with those wire springs on her head like Martian antennae bending this way and that as she entreated him, and when she reached
up her hand to stroke her hair, one of her favorite gestures, her
hand found nothing to stroke at but that fat black woolly wig. If
you were going to beg, you couldn't look ridiculous. You had to
look appealing. Especially because MGM was picky about order-
ing tests. They were expensive, $600 apiece, which I knew my
mother knew.

Still, I crossed my fingers. Maybe Buzz would give her what she
wanted. He had given her a nice close-up last month as she ran
by the camera for the titular "Babes in Arms" song with Douglas
McPhail because Buzz was not only good to his crew, handing
them cards as a shoot wrapped, promising them jobs on his next
film, but also good to his dancers, making sure to give each of
his girls her little moment, They're all so pretty and who doesn't
like to look at a pretty girl? And though my mother was a very
pretty girl, almost all of the close-ups belonged to Garland, of
course, because she was the star, even if those close-ups featured
her capped teeth and the nose the studio was always trying to
reshape by making her insert these rubber discs in her nostrils.

Buzz was looking down his own nose at my mother. Don't beg,
I wanted to tell her. Be the queen.

Now, of course, I better understand her. Some things are
worth begging for. Youth and beauty were what she had to offer,
and though that year she was only twenty-three, she must already
have been counting her approach to thirty and its inherent lim-
itations, the horizon that spelled curtain in show business. Who
wants a thirty-year-old chorine? The aging chorine is a somehow pathetic creature. But the thirty-year-old star? Well, she's in
her prime. Ripe. Lush. Delicious. You have to be center stage by
thirty or you'll never get there. And it didn't look like my father
was going to get her there.

But Buzz was shaking his head, turning away. Was this made easier to do because she was masked, concealed by the blackface, not really quite Dina Wells? Or was it just easy to do because he was Busby Berkeley, imperious for the moment, humbled by time soon enough. In a few years, Judy Garland would be a big star, and he would be a washed-up nobody, and she'd have him kicked off the picture he was directing her in.

When he walked off, I called out to my mother, wanting her, but when she turned to me, I went mute. The way she looked at me. Yet, I ran over to her nonetheless. What else was I going to do? Hide somewhere on the lot? Jump in our Cadillac and drive myself home? When I reached her, my mother made her lips into a flat line. "You and your father," she said, "ruin everything for me."

Oh.

Las Vegas
1947

16

UNLIKE HOLLYWOOD, WHERE THE big stars never spoke to the girls who danced behind them on the soundstages, here in the great democratic desert, the stars paid us notice. The Flamingo headliners—Jack Benny, Sophie Tucker, Tony Martin—knew all of our names and they bought us drinks and they sang Happy Birthday and blew out candles on birthday cakes with us and they let us take our pictures with them and they autographed them *With Love*. We weren't studio chorines, we were Las Vegas showgirls. And as such, we were cherished—both on the stage and in the casino.

Pretty soon the stage managers would start keeping us younger girls corralled in the dressing rooms between shows, while only girls of legal age were allowed to dress up the tables, but in 1947, there were no rules until we made them up and that rule about keeping the younger girls in the back hadn't been made up yet. We were all given free chips to play in the casino and a drink or two to sip—even if I was fifteen and wasn't allowed to actually sip from the glass. This is for show, now, Baby E. We were told to mingle with the regular players and smile at the celebrities, we lovely dancers of the Fabulous Flamingo, serving as living, breathing, smiling, ambulating advertisements for the next show at midnight.

My father didn't like me out on the floor and when he caught me there, he waved me off it, didn't like it even when I sunned myself by the pool, where I played the exhibitionist at Benny's request. Ben had seen me one day, lying out on a towel near our bungalow, and he'd said to my father, "What's this?" and my father had said, "What? The pool's for guests now," and Benny had said, "Shit on that, Ike. With her looks, I want her sunning herself at the fucking pool every day. Go on, Baby E. Go find yourself a chaise." Ben thought I was beautiful, an asset to the hotel. And I was flattered. But soon enough I discovered the casino, where my assets actually made a profit. For me. The players, the men, anyway, usually gave me a chip or two as a tip for helping them win at the tables, and I'd been starting to save my money, my own little weekly stash that often surpassed my paycheck.

Anyway, one night in the early summer of 1947, I was on the floor after the first show, leaning over the craps table, bringing good luck to a customer, one of those greasy-haired cowboys the free buffet had dragged in. My father was busy in the counting room and I was taking advantage of the opportunity while he was otherwise engaged. It must have been around eleven o'clock that I looked up and saw Lansky's men from the El Cortez, little Moe Sedway and big Gus Greenbaum—Greenbaum, always red-faced, always bow-tied, cigar poking out of his box face, and his sidekick, the tiny, hand-wringing Sedway with his bashed-in nose, both of them in suits and ties—striding with uncommon purpose across the casino floor toward the counting room.

All the dealers and croupiers were looking at them as they marched across the carpet, barking left and right as they went, "We're in charge here, now," and I could see the pit bosses exchanging looks with one another. An undertow of shock and surprise tugged at the cards and dice and the casino personnel, but not, apparently, at the oblivious customers, for whom Benny Siegel had built this pleasure palace. But Benny himself wasn't here tonight. He'd had a big fight yesterday with Virginia and chased her home to Los Angeles, his car tailing hers west. I looked again around the casino. Sedway and Greenbaum were now pushing open the counting-room door, and after a minute, I saw my father step out from it, his face streaked with distress. He was scanning the place and I knew he was looking for me.

When my father's eyes found mine, he waved me over, but as it turned out, tonight my father didn't just want me off the floor, he wanted me out of the casino altogether. He wouldn't even give me time to change my clothes or find a tissue, hustling me in my teetering heels and my smearing eyeliner and my orange Pan-Cake right through the Flamingo Club and out into the hot June night, while my cowboy called after me, "Little girl, where you going? Don't take my luck with you!"

Then, with my father urging me, wildly, to hurry, while I asked him, equally wildly, "Why? Where are we going, Dad?" he pushed me down the drive, alternately prodding and dragging me, and he wasn't satisfied until I'd folded myself and my spiky red heels and my costume of pink fluff into our Cadillac parked in the dark side lot.

He jumped in the driver's side and then leaned over the steering wheel, a little breathless, trying in vain to light up a Chesterfield. So what was the point of our big hurry?

"Dad," I said, "I have a second show in an hour."

On the other hand, I might not. We might not be returning to the hotel tonight. Tonight or ever. With my father, I never knew exactly. Every few years, it seemed, we were going somewhere new, where life would be better, bigger, full of riches, Magic Ike!, with me sewn into this costume of feathers and chiffon, the two of us saying goodbye to no one on our way out. If my father ever got his cigarette lit and started the car.

When I couldn't stand watching his stupid, trembling hands any longer, I took the gold lighter from him and helped him spark it. He inhaled deeply, able to hold onto the wheel now, and then exhaled a flat sheet of smoke from between his teeth, cigarette wedged like a flaming toothpick. I put the lighter down on the seat between us and it rolled there like a nugget from some long-ago Nevada mine.

"What's going on, Dad?"

He took the cigarette from his mouth. "Ben was murdered twenty minutes ago. In Beverly Hills. At Virginia's."

And then he started up the car.

17

IT DIDN'T TAKE US long to leave the Strip. In 1947, Highway 91 held only the El Rancho, the Last Frontier, the Flamingo, and the soon to be opened Thunderbird with its three angular supersized tricolored Egyptian phoenixes, red, green, and yellow neon, those hotels looking impressively fulsome alongside the skeletal beginnings of the Sahara, the Sands, and the Desert Inn, the latter of which Nate Stein would come out from the Midwest to run alongside Wilbur Clark and Moe Dalitz, with the flying saucer of its Sky Room going up, up, up. But as big as these hotels were, within a minute or two we were past them and past the little motels that trailed them like crumbs, the Pyramids, the Rummel, the Sage and Sand. We found ourselves soon enough nowhere at all in the flat dark desert, which was bigger still, where the moon hung in the sky like a weight, ballasting the many stars pressing down heavily upon us.

Benny. From white tie and swallowtails to corpse in six months.

I put my palms to my eyes, lids heavy with false eyelashes and now tears. I hated to think that Ben no longer inhabited his beautiful body and that I would never again see him climbing out of his little roadster with a present for me, most recently, last week, a mink coat, my first mink, totally inappropriate for fifteen-year-old me.

Yes, I cried there in the car while my father drove, and this was before I even saw the newspaper photographs of Benny slumped on Virginia's couch, his beautiful eyes turned bloody, his beautiful, rough baby face massacred, his hands soft in his lap. He had died thinking himself one who had well pleased his masters. But obviously he hadn't.

I didn't have to ask who killed him. I already knew someone as important as Ben Siegel wouldn't be killed unless Meyer Lansky had agreed to it. Someone—Greenbaum, Sedway, or Stein—must have been whispering in Lansky's ear. The only reason men were killed in this life was over money.

Or for talking to the government.

But Ben despised the FBI and J. Edgar Hoover, whom he invariably referred to as that cocksucking son of a bitch, even in front of me, that's how bad Hoover was. So Ben would never have spoken to one of Hoover's agents. No. So it had to be about money. Though as it turned out, it was about more than that.

I quietly picked at my nail polish.

Lansky's men were forever in the casino conferring with the pit bosses and the shift managers and the box men and the section supervisors and the hard count supervisors in the counting room, of which my father was one. They, not Ben, kept the real watch over the money at play on the gaming tables, over the reported profits and losses. I'd been wondering just how much credit Benny was getting for this great green landslide of cash he'd promised Lansky was coming since 1945 when we first broke ground, a landslide that had finally manifested itself since our reopening four months ago. If Lansky appreciated Ben for having pulled all this off, if he trusted Ben, then why all the oversight?

The answer. He wasn't appreciated. He wasn't trusted. As this night now made clear.

The car plowed on, and eventually my father turned east toward Lake Mead, though we didn't go nearly that far, just toward the mountains that lay before and around Lake Las Vegas, to the Las Vegas Wash, a marshy waterway. He turned onto a long dirt drive, which spiraled upward partway into those mountains and eventually, a few miles up, he parked on a ridge. From here, we could see the Strip, tiny winking colored lights in the west and the low dark purple of the Wash below, the mountain peaks cutouts against the sky. It was like being a Gabrielino Indian squatting at the top of Mulholland Drive before the city ever took its place at the table. My father liked to look at things from the heights.

He got out of the car. I watched him reach into his suit jacket pocket and take out his pack of Chesterfields, shake and smack it, pull out another cigarette, rummage again for his lighter.

He was already smoking a second cigarette by the time I reached him. It was hot, as hot as the day Ben first brought us out here, a furnace-heated wind flowing by us, god knows what animals flowing by us, too, little animals we couldn't see, maybe couldn't even hear. Raccoons. Bats. Lizards. Prairie dogs. Or worse, bobcats. Rattlesnakes.

My father was still looking out into the warm moonlit dark when I came up behind him and said, "Dad, where are we?"

"Home."

I tugged at his hand. Be serious.

"We're home, Esme. I bought this land for us. Look around. The plan was to build us a house here and surprise you." He dropped his cigarette to the dirt, ground at it with his shoe. "I just wanted you to see it. Because now it's not going to happen."

"Why not?"

"Because Benny's gone, and I was Benny's man."

True. Under Ben's aegis, my father had gone from box man, keeping watch over the craps games, to section supervisor and then to shift manager and just last month, he had been promoted to supervising the hard count in the counting room. Whatever sins of theft Ben had committed, perhaps my father had, too. Not copper wire this time, but paper bills. That must be why we had run from the casino, why we were really here, so close to the Wash that I could hear water, where perhaps my father had a boat waiting, tied to some post and ready for us to set sail in the dark to Lake Mead. After all, everybody knew my father had followed Benny Siegel out to the desert and opened his hands to catch the manna falling from the heavens. But so had a lot of other men. And a lot was forgiven them, a lot overlooked by the thieves they served, because they understood a man needed to make a little on the side. Though there was a line, a limit. And my father wasn't a big boy in Vegas. Not yet, anyway.

"So what are we going to do?" I asked him.

"We're going to go back to Los Angeles. Tonight."

A retreat to Los Angeles wouldn't save us. Benny was just killed there.

My father wasn't thinking. But I was.

Because what could we possibly find if we drove south through the vast Las Vegas valley ringed by mountains and then east through the low desert of Palm Springs, the mountains slowly giving way to flat scrubby acre after acre until we reached, eventually, the Los Angeles basin, with its mountains and hills to the north that ran all the way to the ocean, as did the highway? I remembered the route well enough from the treks my father and I made to and from Las Vegas during the war until we finally settled in Vegas for good. I would fidget, opening and closing the windscreen against air that was first temperate and then freezing and then temperate and then freezing as we went up in altitude and then down.

While my father and I had been steeped in this emerging Las Vegas of the past few years, Los Angeles had been changing, too. A chaos of demolition and construction for a new freeway had destroyed much of Boyle Heights, old houses flattened like the carcasses of movie sets surrounded by broad swaths of recently carved earth and stacks of iron pilings. Housing projects for the poor had been built in the Boyle Flats after the war. The shopkeepers who hadn't yet joined my grandfather in Evergreen

Cemetery—the Kartzes and the Resnicks and the Hoffmans and the Shonholtzes—would have grown older, and their children, my parents' generation, would have moved north to what had once been farmlands and were now suburbs, neat rows of identical homes stretching up Hazeltine Avenue to Magnolia Boulevard, all the old stockyards and furrowed acres and orange groves turned to block after block of happy streets and houses, the subdivisions built on land Mr. Mayer had been prescient enough to buy thirty years ago. So what would we recognize? What would be home?

And if we did go back to Los Angeles (with my mother's mirrored dresser), and if Mickey Cohen wouldn't put my father on his payroll again, he would be back to the tracks, back to his race sheets, back to selling tip sheets at the park gate on Prairie Avenue, stones on a milk crate holding the papers from the wind. IKE'S TIPS. Back to his red notebooks full of calculations, to a cheap hotel room on Inglewood Boulevard, where he would sit on a painted metal lawn chair in the evenings, shooting the breeze with the other aging bachelors who had made their unlucky lives revolve around the horses and who had nothing to look forward to but the excitement of the next day's races, the dream of the win, which would do little more for them than provide one night of good drinking and a few months' more rent.

And I? What would I do there? Go back to the track with him, old enough now to lay bets myself? Beg Buzz for a role in some picture, that is, if Buzz even remembered me, little Esme, Dina's baby sister, if he ever even believed that fib? Ask Mickey Cohen if I could dance at the Clover or Ciro's?

If the thought of such a return exhausted me, it had to also exhaust my father.

No. In Los Angeles, my father wouldn't have these beautiful hotels to work in, the silver slots, the green baize, the waxed, paper woven chips of packed clay and sand, the carpeted rooms, the swimming pools, the great vast space of the valley, this site, the first acres of property he had ever owned. We wouldn't have our free bungalow to live in on the Flamingo grounds or our free meals at the hotel restaurants.

I didn't want to go back. And not only because of all that.

If I had come to love Las Vegas, in part it was because it was not Los Angeles, so much of which was colored for me by my mother and my memories of her. This place, this desert, was raked clean of her. She had never stepped foot here, and so nothing, not a single sight anywhere, not a speck of it, reminded me of her. But I couldn't say this to my father.

I looked around at the mountain ridges above me, the valley and the Wash below. Right now, even late at night, it was so hot you wanted to dig a hole to find earth deep enough and cool enough to offer some relief. But in five months, there would be no place more beautiful. And what was more, this place, these acres, was ours. About what other square foot of ground could we say that?

If my father's sins had been too egregious, he wouldn't be left standing here. And if my father wasn't going to be killed, there was no reason to leave. We should stay, take our chances. My father knew a lot about the Flamingo, had been here since the beginning, and that knowledge had to be worth something to the new bosses. Because there just weren't that many men willing to leave the vice-rich cities of Miami, Chicago, New York, Detroit, and Cleveland to come out to this hellhole of a desert with its couple of gaming tables. Lansky thought Vegas was so hot it was the mythical Hades itself. Mickey Cohen couldn't stand the flying grit pelting his clothing and dirtying his skin. At this point in time, 1947, if you were going to drop everything and head for Nevada, Reno was the place to go, not Las Vegas. Only a very few men thought Vegas was going to be much of anything. Ben was one of them, but Ben wasn't thinking anything anymore.

"Dad," I said finally, "all these hotels are going up. Who are they going to get to work all those casinos? Men like you, men who've been here, who know the business. "

My father shrugged. I couldn't tell if that gesture meant he was agreeing with me or not. He looked off, lit another Chesterfield. Like many men out here, he was a chain-smoker. But he was listening.

So I continued. "If Lansky's men are in Vegas, it's because they know something."

My father laughed, shortly. "They know this town's getting ready to blow the hell up."

I nodded and watched him smoke.

He smiled without looking at me. "Well, maybe I can ride this out a little."

Yes.

"See what's coming."

Yes.

I looked down. I was so much better at this than my mother, with her flailing arms and her shrieking. Ike, what did you do?

I came closer to him and nestled myself under his arm. We were an odd couple, to be sure, a man in an overpriced bespoke suit in imitation of his betters and a skinny blond fifteen-year-old wearing false eyelashes and a feathered dress and red high heels in imitation of hers. But I didn't care if we were odd, I only cared that we were devoted to each other. And that I had won. Because despite what my father said about my having my grandfather's mind, I was more truly the product of my parents, those two schemers.

I waited a little before I spoke again. "So where's the new house going to be?"

That got him going. And while my father pointed here and there and took my hand to help me walk the site and talked to me about what room would have been where, etc., if only we could have stayed and built it. Then, as we continued our tour, his tense changed to where this and that will be when we do build it, shades of Benny Siegel with the Flamingo, Here be this, here be that. And that was all Benny Siegel was now, a shade.

The first time I saw Ben was when my father had gone with Mickey Cohen to the track at Santa Anita to take bets from whatever customers they could lure from the windows with the promise of better odds, and I stood near them, dancing like a little monkey on a leash, attracting the eye which was followed soon enough by a wallet. While we were there, we three grifters, Benny Siegel strolled by us on his way to his box, wearing a shiny blue tie, a button-down shirt, a brushed gray suit, a two-toned handkerchief tucked into the pocket of the jacket, his hair lightly oiled and combed back, his face tanned, his eyes two shining jewels. I'll never forget what he looked like that day. He chatted with Mickey and my father, then bent and kissed my hand with a gallantry that made me feel as if a choir of angels had burst into heavenly song all about me. Benny, those blue eyes of his ashine with self-love and ambition.

After that day, there were rides in his roadster, rides on his shoulders, rides on the ponies he rented for his daughters' birthday parties to which I was invited, a sort of third daughter when his girls were in town for summer vacations. My father always looked down at me, bemused, when I asked him each morning if we were going to see Mr. Siegel that day. Tell me, Dad, tell me! But until we moved to Vegas, I saw a lot more of the squat, broken-nosed Mr. Cohen than the glamorous Mr. Siegel. But much as I loved him, I didn't go to Benny's funeral, and I wasn't the only one to abandon him at the end. Benny's sister, his brother, his wife, and his two real daughters would be the only ones there at

Groman Mortuary in Los Angeles to mourn him. Virginia, that other outlier, was in Europe, overdosing on sleeping pills.

Yes, Benny was dead, but we were still here, alive, walking the earth's crust. I stumbled along in my heels, ruining them from the dirt and the pebbles and the creosote and thinking how the dresser at the Flamingo wasn't going to be happy about my needing another pair when we got back.

18

THOUGH THE DESERT INN was called Wilbur Clark's Desert Inn, Mr. Clark was merely the affable casino-floor gadfly with a percentage. Anybody who knew anything knew that Mr. Clark was the front man for the men who were really in charge, Moe Dalitz and Nate Stein, who had moved here to Vegas a few months ago. That's why I walked over to the Desert Inn just after New Year's in 1950 to audition for Donn Arden. The Desert Inn was set to open in April, with the new Donn Arden Dancers. For the grand opening, the Ray Noble Orchestra would perform along with Edgar Bergen, and Abbott and Costello, and the dancers would open and close the show and have a number in the middle, as well, just for a change of pace from the other acts. Book covers and a bookmark, as Arden said, though I wasn't sure he'd ever actually read a book or personally employed a bookmark. He'd spent his whole life in jazz shoes and nightclubs, his biggest vocabulary words being, "a one and a two, step ball change."

Nate, who'd used Arden to choreograph shows for his nightclubs in Detroit, had tasked him with creating something glittery and slick and big-city to distinguish it from the other shows in Vegas. So Nate had thought we Flamingo girls were parochial, backwater! To be one of those glitzy Donn Arden dancers, with my big, childish handwriting I filled out an application that looked something like this:

Name

Age

Height

Weight

Hair Color

Eye Color

Complexion

Bust Measurement

Waist

Hips

Dress Size

Bathing Suit Size

Hat

Shoe

Present Occupation

Ambition

Why did you apply for this position?

Answer to the last: to try to save my father and myself from further degradation.

If my father and I were going to get anywhere in this town, we needed to get away from the Flamingo. Because as my father predicted, he had been punished for being one of Benny's boys, not important enough to be murdered, just demoted to the credit cage. All the hard count workers at the Flamingo had been fired or shoveled into other jobs, under suspicion by association.

It was hard for me to see my father now in the brass cage, no matter how fancy the design of it, pushing stacks of chips across the counter, where he reminded me of his own favorite betting clerk, Carl, from Hollywood Park, rather than the desperately carefree gamblers Carl served and of which my father had once numbered. My father wore a uniform now, not a suit. He looked like a bellman or a valet, and I worried that's where he would find himself next, pushed out of the casino entirely and onto the front drive, a cap on his head, pushing a luggage cart with one hand and holding out the other for his five-cent tip. And, of course, all this was my fault for encouraging him to stay.

And with my father's downturn in fortune, so went my own. I could see how the children of the casino managers were granted all the privileges—they were the ones dancing on the Helldorado floats, they were the New Year's babies in diapers when the hotels held their big champagne-drenched parties, they were the ones sitting at the tables at the Passover seder that gave the floor show the boot for a night at the Last Frontier, matzo balls replacing the bread rolls. When my father's fortunes were rising, so were mine. But with his demotion and Benny's death, I was only one step from ignominy myself. It was too easy now to get lost in the blur of young women and men filling all the spots in this bigger Vegas, in all the bars and lounges and stages. No one paid me any attention anymore.

So I knew we needed whatever grace and favor I could fashion for us to cancel out our having laid our money down on Ben Siegel.

The stage in the Painted Desert room where the auditions were being held was so small it could fit only twelve girls at one time across the breadth of it, not much different from the Flamingo's tiny nightclub-sized stage. A little disappointing. I'm not sure what I imagined, but there would be no more space to dance here than down the Strip. But any extra feet for a stage took up space for a table. The tables brought in money. We girls cost money. This disadvantage Donn, like Buzz before him, would overcome with tiered sets—not that Buzz ever had a problem with stage size—every one of the MGM soundstages was, measured by any dimension, a massive space.

A row of men in rumpled shirts sat before this stage at a long table that had been carted in from somewhere, clipboards and papers and pens before them as if we girls were a list of sums to be added up, their suit jackets laid over the various and sundry round nightclub tables and chairs behind them. Not one of those men was good-looking, but they didn't let that interfere with their ability to judge the beauty and presentability of us girls. Not at all.

After we handed in our applications, we sat down at the little cocktail tables and waited to be called. I gazed at the blue murals on the walls, vaguely suggestive of the mountains around us, the orange ceiling as hot-colored as a desert sunset, the orange and blue braided drapery dressing the stage. The room felt nice, plush, moneyed without the filigree of ostentation that marked Benny's club. I approved.

Then I studied the other girls, my competition.

Some of them wore leotards and tights and some of them were wearing street clothes, summer shirts and cropped pants. I wanted to stand out, so I wore tights with my very high-heeled dance shoes, a half leotard, and a long-sleeved black turtleneck, my hair in a high ponytail, which was not at all the fashion of 1950, where the tightly rolled hair of the forties had turned to loose bouncing curls to the shoulders. I still wore my hair like a child. Maybe it was not the best thing to be, to be different, here among the ponies and stablemates, the regular girls. You needed to match up, not stand out.

Worse, Donn Arden liked tall, classically trained girls, and I was small. And I was trained by Daddy Mack.

I would have been a better match at the Sands, where the showman Jack Entratter preferred small girls with pretty faces. I was Entratter material. And Jack didn't even care if his girls could dance. So it was a plus if you could. All he wanted was pretty. But I couldn't wait another year or two for the Sands to open.

By then my father would be the size of a midget, sweeping the kitchen floors with an oversized broom. So that's why it had to be the Desert Inn for me, the DI and Nate Stein. Because if anyone in Las Vegas could help my father regain his footing, it was Nate. Already, even in 1950, nothing happened in Vegas without Nate's say-so. I only hoped he remembered me.

So I fudged my height on the Donn Arden application and I wore heels, but I was hard pressed to look five feet six inches.

While group after group of girls were called up to the stage, I looked surreptitiously toward the back of the club, quietly turning my head each time the next group of ten girls climbed up the steps at the sides of the stage. I guess I was hoping Nate might be at the audition. But it was just the men at the table and Arden, who wore a suit jacket, a striped shirt, dance shoes, and a pinkie ring on his right hand that held his cigarette. Finally, my group was called, and even though I was watched every night on the stage at the Flamingo, I felt suddenly self-conscious walking up onto this stage, all those eyes assessing me, assessing all of us, calculating the balance of plusses and minuses. I did the Daddy Mack walk tall and when I found my place in the row of girls, I lifted my chin high.

Arden jumped up onto the stage to demonstrate once again the Arden walk, the way he wanted his showgirls to move across the stage, something he had already demonstrated ten times this afternoon. He had patience, I'll grant him that. "Imagine you're wearing a two-foot-high headdress," he said, and he put his hands behind his back, elbows crooked, and stepped forward first with the ball of his foot and posed there before moving farther. I loved it. Pose, walk. Pose, walk. Just the way Buzz liked his girls to walk across the endless polished soundstage floors. And Arden even looked a little like Buzz, with dark hair and a mountainside nose, but with a more reasonable face, no beetle brows, no snarling, a gentler version of Buzz, or so I thought at the time, before I heard him bark at some poor girl, "Get off my stage, you fat cow." These men.

"Okay, girls," Arden clapped his hands, "let's see what you've got."

He jumped down off the stage and began to count. "One, two, three, go. Step. Pause. Step. Pause."

There was no music. Just the sound of Arden's voice, the rustling of paper from the long table, the soft slide and scrape of our high-heeled dance shoes. Think Buzz, I told myself. Think Dina Wells. This was my screen test, or the equivalent of. Would I capture the interest of this man who held such inordinate power, against which, like all aspirants, I was powerless, with nothing other than the weapons I marshaled of hope and desire. Pitiful weapons, enormous odds. I stepped and paused forward and back. I pivoted. Arden watched us all intently, studied me, I thought, in particular, conferred with the men at the table, turned back to us. "You," and he pointed to a brunette with the neck and legs of a giraffe, "stay. The rest of you, thank you very much."

It's never easy, that rejection. It's so personal. You. Your face, your body, I don't like it. I don't like it at all. Get off my stage. Cow.

But there was a sop. As I descended the steps of the stage to the carpeted floor where the civilians dwelled, Arden said to me, "You're lovely, dear, but I want them very tall."

19

WHEN ARDEN DISMISSED ME that day, I went out into the hotel lobby, prepared to wait for hours, if necessary, until Nate came by, which he did, every day, the manager assured me, at least four times a day, as he went from the restaurant to the kitchen to the grounds to his office at the back of the casino to the telephone where he was paged at least three times while I sat there, "Paging Mr. Nate Stein, paging Nate Stein," to the counting room to his own rooms because all the important men at every hotel had rooms somewhere in the hotel assigned to them alone, where guests were never booked. These men lived where they worked, obsessed with every detail of the hotel plant and with the hotel's place in the larger universe ruled by their god. Mammon.

So I waited. I sat in one of the cushioned armchairs that faced the front desk with its wall of cubbyholes that would in a few months hold mail and keys and messages, my back to the big window and the row of leafy plants, all leaves, no flowers, growing in the long stone planter there, and I held a tissue in my hand, ready to hold that pose for hours if necessary, to cry when it was time. I wasn't my mother's daughter for nothing. I'd learned from her how to ambush a man to get what I wanted. And when, finally, I saw Nate—his glossy black hair shooting up high—stroll by the front desk, I stood. This was suddenly terrifying. I had radically underestimated the amount of daring it took to perform an ambush. It was a swan dive, without the certainty of water below. Suddenly, I was filled with admiration for my mother.

Nate turned his head. And having seen me, too late for me to run now, he squinted—I found out later he needed glasses but was too vain to wear them—and then he came over to where I stood, and as he neared, I saw he was smiling, his face soft. "Is this little Esme Wells crying in my hotel?" he asked, teasing me with the stage name I'd given him three years ago, which he had remembered, as he had remembered me. So this wasn't going to be so hard, after all.

I laughed. I hadn't actually managed yet to make myself cry, my big plan, even as I posed, tissue to my face. I tried to do so now. Cry, I told myself. Cry! But no tears came. I didn't feel distressed. On the contrary, I felt exhilarated. Nate remembered me! But when I finally found the words to tell him I'd just auditioned for Donn Arden and that I hadn't been chosen as one of his dancers, my voice sounded convincingly choked up, even to me, each word a reluctant child I had to poke between the shoulder blades to push out.

Nate smiled again and said, "That must have been a mistake."

I folded up my tissue. No longer needed. The prop itself had done the work. Thank God.

"So tell me, Miss Wells," he said, "why do you want to dance in my hotel? Aren't you happy at the Flamingo?"

I couldn't say what I couldn't put on that application. So instead, I answered Nate with an honesty I hadn't intended: "I'm eighteen now. I'm all grown up."

He turned his head from me so I wouldn't see him laugh, maybe at my youth or at my lack of strategic prevarication. And then he turned back.

"Yes," he said. "So you are."

We stood there in the hotel lobby looking at each other. Once again, he was dressed, this time in a dark suit with a tie, the formal costume of a businessman, an empire builder, and I was in the costume of a plaything. A partially dressed plaything. Each time we met, it seemed, too much of me was revealed, reducing me to a state of indignity that should have given him the upper hand. And yet, it didn't feel that way, exactly. It felt as if I had the upper hand. Though I wasn't exactly sure how that could be. Some instinct had me run my fingers through my long ponytail, pull it across my breasts. My mother's special gesture, the touching of the hair. His lip ticked upwards slightly, tugged by some impulse. He bent his head toward me, pulled it back. I stroked at my ponytail, flipped it behind my shoulders. On a conscious level I did not yet recognize the extraordinary power a woman's beauty lent her, but some part of me somewhere must have. I might be eighteen, but I was a young eighteen, despite everything. Because of Ben, because of my father, men had left me alone. But now Ben was gone, my father demoted, leaving me—well, leaving me easy prey.

The quiet hotel lobby, full of winter sunshine and green plants and the coordinated fabrics of furniture and drapery and carpet, waited with us to see what would happen next. The clock over the front desk *tick-tick-ticked*.

What happened next was that Nate took me by the hand, not the one with the pinkie ring, but the one with the wedding band, and this hand was as large and warm as I remembered it. And when he touched me, I let out an involuntary sigh. Which made him smile again. With this hand, he led me back into the club, interrupting the tail end of the endlessly ongoing audition to bring me to Arden's side.

Arden turned, a little surprised, and mid-word stopped his spiel, the one with the Pose, walk. Pose, walk. It was as if L. B. Mayer had walked onto a set. The girls up on the stage stopped moving when Arden stopped speaking, abandoning their showgirl postures now to stare, unabashedly, at me, this important new girl, new to this hour, new to them, anyway, brought in on Nate's arm. I wasn't even sure if Donn remembered me from my audition an hour earlier. I might be new to him, too. All the men at the long table stood up to shake Nate's hand, but still he held on to me, even as he turned to Donn.

"Donn, I think this girl is exactly what we're looking for."

Arden looked at me. Blinked.

"Of course," Arden said, "I'll make her the lead girl, Mr. Stein."

Ha.

LOS ANGELES
1939

20

MY MOTHER AND I were headed over to the Star Suites, the long white building abutting Washington Boulevard. On the other side of Washington, this building would have been an apartment house. On this side, though, the humble two-story structure was the Star Suites. My mother said to me guilelessly, "Let's just go in for a minute. What do you say?" And without waiting for me to say anything, she entered the vestibule, hushed, to study the directories posted on the wall, black boards with white stick-on letters. You could see who was big by who was given an apartment in this modest building, the directory of the Women's Apartments and Men's Apartments constantly shifting, fashion or death prying names from the signs. Hence, the stick-on letters.

WOMEN'S APTS.

First Floor
A Lana Turner
B Jeanette MacDonald
C
D Norma Shearer

Second Floor
  E Greta Garbo
  F Myrna Loy
  G Louise Rainer
  H Joan Crawford

MEN'S APTS.

First Floor
  A Clark Gable
  B Nelson Eddy
  C William Powell
  D Donald Loomis

Second Floor
  E Robert Montgomery
  F Robert Taylor
  G Spencer Tracy
  H Mickey Rooney

While my mother whispered their names, I studied the letters lined up in each spot. By First Floor, Apartment A, behind the white letters my mother told me spelled out Lana Turner's name, I could see where the letters had once spelled out something else, those letters just black shadows now, the sun having quietly faded the background all around the previous vowels and consonants, leaving just this echo.

"Who used to be there?" I asked, pointing at the ghost letters of Apartment A.

My mother squinted. "Jean Harlow."

Harlow was dead then two years. But there was no such shadow by Apartment C. No white lettering either.

"Who's going there?" I asked, pointing at the blank space.

"I bet it will be Judy Garland," my mother said.

So Judy Garland's name might soon fill the blank space by the words Apartment C. Judy Garland. She'd had a horrible name before she changed it: Frances Gumm. Sounded like something you chewed and spit out, stuck under a table. Judy Garland who might be in C had been just one of the Gumm Sisters in vaudeville, Baby Gumm, and Lana Turner in A had been a regular teenager sipping a Coke at the Top Hat Café. I knew all the stars' stories because my mother had told them to me, made them my bedtime stories when she tucked me in, more to amuse herself, of course, than me. Who, really, was Clark Gable, my mother had said, but a nobody from Ohio who had fixed his teeth and taught himself how to talk in a lower register, with a first wife who was more a mother than a wife, much older than Gable himself, who had come all the way out here just to be an extra in an Erich von Stroheim film. Nobody. An extra.

And then they all had screen tests.

Step One to stardom.

The step my mother had the toe of her shoe on. Or was determined to get her toe on. After that, the pictures made them all into somebodies. Which was what my mother was determined to have happen for her.

That's when I said, "Maybe it will be you, you in Apartment C."

A ploy to get back into her good graces after my debacle with Buzz.

I got what I wanted. She looked down at me and gave me one of her rare smiles, rare for these days, rarer still for it to be aimed at me.

Last year, my mother and I had actually gotten inside the Star Suites, into the dressing room of Clark Gable, once a nobody, Apartment A, on the first floor. Gable had invited everyone on the set that day over to his suite to listen to the World Series on his radio, and my mother had gone over to the Commissary, to the newsstand where my father was taking bets on the game, and fetched me. Gable had been nice to me, calling me "honey" and pouring me a soda, and I understood then I served as my mother's sidekick and bait, the little girl who disarmed the prey I emboldened her to stalk.

So. Why were we here? Who were we stalking? Whose Star Suite were we trying to ambush today?

I didn't have long to wonder.

Robert Taylor's.

Taylor was playing an officer in a new picture the second unit had just started filming and my mother wanted to test for it. In *Waterloo Bridge,* Taylor falls in love with a ballerina named Myra during World War I, the ballerina to be played by Vivien Leigh, whom Mr. Mayer admired so much in the soon to be released *Gone with the Wind.* Myra had a ballerina friend from the dance troupe named Kitty and my mother felt she would be perfect for that role, much better than Virginia Field, whom Louis B. Mayer was planning to cast.

All became clear to me. My mother was in the lobby of the Star Suites to lobby Robert Taylor.

"I just want to ask him a favor."

I frowned but she ignored me.

Robert Taylor's dressing room was on the second floor, Apartment F, but we knew he was there because we could hear him talking on the telephone, the *rap rap rap* of his voice followed by a pause and then *rap rap rap.* How did my mother know she'd find him here right now? Witch! Or maybe she was just a fortune-telling gypsy herself!

We stepped outside a moment to the little landscaped walkway, my mother looking up at Taylor's cranked-open windows, her dress blowing in the wind, garters exposed, head tipped up, plotting. I knew her face. At least it wasn't painted black today. Maybe she'd do better with Taylor than she had with Buzz.

"Okay," she said. "Here's what we're going to do. You're going to go up there and knock on his door and when he answers, you tell him you're looking for Mickey Rooney, that you're filming *Debutante* with him and he asked you to come by and run some of your lines together. I'll be right behind you and when he tells you Rooney isn't here, I'll come up and apologize for you and then I'll take it from there."

The ruse was ridiculous—there was no way Mickey Rooney would want to run lines with a child, even if I were in the picture— but I knew protest was useless. Besides, I owed her. Because I'd ruined her chances with Buzz, I was obligated to help salvage matters.

"Come on," my mother said. "Move." And she opened the door to the vestibule.

I trudged up the stairs, my mother a few steps behind me. At the end of the hall, she hung back and shooed me forward with one hand. I stomped forward and knocked on the door of Apartment F.

"Yes?" said a man's voice and then footsteps over carpet and the door was opened and there was Robert Taylor, The Man with the Perfect Profile, the nickname the press had given him, looking down at me.

The apartment behind him was all wood paneled, with a wooden-shuttered standing screen before plaid curtains making the apartment even darker and quieter. Over the low sofa hung two big framed lithographs of horse heads. One horse head faced the other across their frames as if they were lonely for each other. "Don't tell your father he likes horses," my mother would say, later, "or he'll pester Mr. Taylor for a bet," as if what we'd done today hadn't been pestering.

All of Robert Taylor's ashtrays were filled high with cigarette butts, probably the Luckies he got gratis, my mother said, also later, because he shilled for the company. I had seen the ads, the colored illustration of the movie star's smiling face and the words "Robert Taylor tells how his throat picked Luckies—a light smoke." He was incredibly handsome. A real movie star. Not a B movie star. Not at all a regular person.

He had been talking on the telephone while sitting on the sofa, and to answer the door, he had left the receiver off the hook. "What is it, sweetie?" Robert Taylor said to me with his movie-star mouth.

What did I look like that day? What outfit had I selected for myself, what ornamentation for my hair, what color painted on my bedraggled little nails? About one thing I can be certain: my face was unwashed.

"I'm looking for Mr. Rooney," I answered, immediately forgetting the rest of my mother's script, but it didn't matter because my mother was coming right up behind me, her heels going *click click click*, putting her hands on my shoulders as if to stop me from bothering the great man, as if she hadn't been the one to send me right up to the threshold in the first place.

"So sorry to interrupt you, Mr. Taylor," she said. "Mr. Rooney wanted my little sister to run some lines with him. She's working on the new Andy Hardy picture."

"Is that right?" said Mr. Taylor, looking down at me.

I nodded, immediately feeling the discomfort I always felt when my mother announced to anyone that I was her little sister, the discomfort of guilty collusion made worse now by the banishment of my father and my mother's reversal from mother and wife into the young daughter of Sy Wolfkowitz, time sucked backwards so strangely in its bed that I believed I might actually be my mother's sister, my grandfather's other daughter. I felt something ping painfully in my heart and I tapped my chest to make it stop. I knew this was just acting, not real, a small scene in which I had my own part, as did my mother, and Mr. Taylor.

"I think he's still on set," Mr. Taylor said. "Lot Two."

My mother lifted a hand to fan herself as if she were warm and said, "Whew! We didn't know it was so far from Lot Two. We should have taken the trolley."

I stared up at my mother. We hadn't been anywhere near Lot Two.

But she seemed to know what she was doing, because Mr. Taylor was inviting us in to sit down for a minute and offering my mother a drink, and after a few more quick words into it, hanging up the telephone receiver. He had found something more interesting than his phone conversation. Specifically, Dina Wells.

But I, given the way she had lately been treating my father, found her flirtation with Mr. Taylor objectionable. My father had shaved the ring from her finger, yes, but he had not unmarried her. I began to wish for the hundredth time that I wasn't here. I'd wanted to go with my father today to the house he was painting, but he'd told me I'd only be bored, that sitting there among drop cloths and paint buckets and rollers was nothing like enjoying the amusements of the track. Or maybe there was another reason my father didn't want me there. Perhaps he didn't want me watching him paint walls, bossed around by a Wolfkowitz foreman, to whom he could only say, Yes, sir.

He came home every day in the late afternoon, exhausted, after having risen so early, returning to us with hands shellacked white as if the paint had run down his arms instead of onto the walls, his hair speckled, his elephant-sized coveralls dribbled and daubed, his work shoes myriad colors. He would leave those clothes and shoes by the back door, use the shower in the house as a guest would, and then retreat to the garage out back, taking his dinner plate with him. My mother paid him just that much attention—a dinner plate. His garage light was usually out before my own bedroom lamp. I knew because I spied on him from my bedroom window.

So for all these reasons, I refused to look at my mother now, refused to be a full participant in the caper she had dreamed up today. I'd kept my face turned from her on our long trek across the lot to here. Not that she'd noticed. My mother was transformed by her quaff at the flask of possibility, and she pulled me along, ignoring my complaints.

She sat down on the sofa beneath the horse heads and looked over at the end table, which was piled high with scripts. She smiled and raised a hand for the glass Mr. Taylor offered her, her forearm strung with bracelets that slid and clanked against each other flirtatiously as she did so. Unconsciously, I raised my hand and made my bracelets do so as well.

"Is that the script for *Waterloo Bridge*?" she asked, nodding at the pile. "I just love the writer who did that. I think he's a genius."

I doubted she had any idea who had written that script. I had never heard her mention a writer's name in my life. It was always Lana Turner, Norma Shearer, Myrna Loy, Joan Crawford. And we had never walked by the Writers Building to stare longingly up at its windows, the way we did these Star Suites.

"Really?" Mr. Taylor said, putting one foot up on his little coffee table. He wore cuffed trousers like my father, or as my father did before he started wearing painter's coveralls. "I love Sam Behrman, too. He wrote some great lines for *Queen Christina*."

"He really did," my mother said, taking a sip of her drink, which was not water, but something darker, probably whiskey.

I squinted at her and she saw me looking and waved her hand in my direction to get rid of me, extra baggage now that I had done my job.

"Sweetie, why don't you go downstairs and play on the grass? It'll be just a minute until my head clears and you don't want to be cooped up in here."

No, I didn't. And I didn't want to leave her there, either, but Mr. Taylor said, "I'll look after her, honey. I won't let her faint."

So there was nothing for me to do but leave her to her disloyalty to my father. And Mr. Taylor's to his wife, at that time, Barbara Stanwyck. Maybe she was even the one he had been talking to on the phone! But my mother and Mr. Taylor were smiling at each other, clearly making a party of two, so I went outside and ran down the stairs to the little garden area. The grass was all staked off with wire curlicues or landscaped with flowering plants. The grass was just for looks, like everything else on the lot. There was nowhere to play but the street, so I stood in it, at a loss, looking up and down its length.

And that's how I happened to see Mr. Mayer in his vest and tie and suit and trademark round-eyed spectacles riding the trolley away from Lot Two where *Andy Hardy Meets Debutante*, the picture I was allegedly a part of, was filming today. And where Mickey Rooney was. There, not here. As my mother well knew. Mr. Mayer had probably gone there to take a look at the shoot.

My mother had told me that Mr. Mayer was always inordinately interested in the Andy Hardy serials. If a writer dared create a scene in which Andy played a prank on his parents or refused to eat his supper or mouthed off at his mother, Mr. Mayer would cross those lines out with his Eversharp blue pencil. It was supposed to be small-town Carvel, small-town America. Wise Judge Hardy. Maternal Mother Hardy. Good boy Andy. A place where wives slept side by side with their own husbands, not someone else's. The perfect, peaceful life neither Mr. Mayer nor any of his fellow moguls running two steps in front of a pogrom had ever had. I understood his penchant for comfort and order, which I had little of right now, either, on Soto Street in Boyle Heights.

In fact, if I had courage enough to disobey my mother, I'd leave her and this scrap of lawn behind me in a snap, clamber onto the trolley Mr. Mayer had just exited, and ride the car until it headed around again to that sweet spot on Lot Two. I knew the route. I'd ridden the trolley often enough with my mother. I'd even memorized the sign that hung above the driver:

DO NOT GET ON OR OFF
MOVING TRAIN
USE BUZZER

I'd jump off at Carvel. Population 25,000. The *Debutante* shoot would be taking place right there, right now, on New England Street where Andy Hardy and Betsy Booth and Polly Benedict all lived. Behind the camera, canvas chairs with the actors' and the director's names on them would be scattered about beside wooden towers on wheels with white screens mounted on their tops to bounce the light and two big cameras on a long crane, beneath which two men sat on built-in chairs. A tripod with a long crane and a microphone at the end of it would be operated by another man, and cables would lie everywhere on the ground by a long track made of railroad ties. Judge Hardy and Andy would inevitably talk together earnestly, the judge giving Andy advice, which, of course, Andy would take, before both of them went home to Mrs. Hardy's hot dinner. And then at the end of the day, the cameras and chairs and screens and booms and cables would be packed up, and the houses and stores would be left to themselves. And even though I knew very well that behind the doors to those homes, just like the doors to the stores, lay nothing whatsoever at all—the interiors were all shot on soundstages—I somehow still believed that if I pushed open the door to Andy Hardy's house, I could take up residence there, with that better family, that better mother.

But I did not jump on the trolley. I just stood on the walkway outside the Star Suites, waiting for my own mother.

21

MY MOTHER'S SCREEN TEST was six minutes of black-and-white celluloid, a scene from almost the very end of *Waterloo Bridge*, where Robert Taylor as Colonel Roy Cronin, searching for his beloved, confronts her friend Kitty in the small London apartment the two women share. Myra, his fiancée and ballerina cum prostitute, has gone missing and the officer believes Kitty knows where she is.

Costumed in garb so drab it must have pained her—she was supposed to be poor and struggling, though her coiffure was magnificent as there was a limit to how downtrodden Mr. Mayer's goddesses were allowed to appear—my mother faced Mr. Taylor, who had a pencil-thin moustache spirit-glued to his face and who stood opposite her on a small kitchen set on one of the smaller soundstages on the lot. At first, there was just some posing for the camera, my mother instructed to turn her beautiful face this way and that, and then the two actors ran the scene. Take One. Take Two. Take Three.

MY MOTHER

Roy, can you take it? No matter what you find out about her?

ROBERT TAYLOR

What are you hinting?

When they filmed the scene, I thought my mother's gestures were large and fabulous, and Mr. Taylor's were way too small, as were the tics in his expressions, which I could barely see. He was bland and unreadable—what was the matter with him?—and she was impressively alive and dramatic. That's what I thought until I saw the rough cut later in the edit bay, after the film had been developed and its development fixed by its various chemical baths in MGM's Film Lab Building. That's when I discovered my mother was clearly chewing the scenery and Mr. Taylor was utterly authentic. Where Robert Taylor was smooth and buttery, my mother was over the top, her body stiff, her voice forced and shrill, everything about her expressions stagey and unwatchable. She was overusing her face, as if she were a silent screen star who had to do it all without words. And under the sustained glare of the lens, she didn't look as pretty on the screen as she did in real life or as she did when the camera flicked by her in one of Buzz's dance numbers. In fact, she looked a little like Virginia Hill.

That my mother would not be extraordinary in everything she did was a revelation to me. I always thought that if she just had a chance to showcase her talents, she would be magnificent. And that if someone just took the time to look at her, really look at her, he would be entranced. As the camera would be. But exactly what the camera will love is always a mystery. Some performers who look barely interesting at all become vivid on the screen, but then, inexplicably, other actors find their beautiful faces flatten out like the dullest wallpaper. And, obviously, my mother needed some acting lessons.

Mr. Mayer watched the test in the same projection room where he watched the rushes of Andy Hardy. My mother had often pointed out to me the portico at the top of the columns at the east gate which concealed a bridge from Irving Thalberg's old offices to the projection room, the bridge Thalberg had crossed every evening before he died, to watch all the film shot each day, a pedestrian bridge christened the Bridge of Sighs by the nervous, hand-wringing directors. No hand wringing for my mother. She was sure Louis B. Mayer would settle into his seat with the great California light pouring in and watch her face eight feet high on the screen and fall in love with her and make her a star. Mayer had a great sixth sense at picking actors who could be fashioned into movie stars, a talent he would continue to exercise throughout the forties and early fifties, believing in Ava Gardner and Grace Kelly before anyone else did. This was my mother's time to be believed in, to be picked, and to be fashioned.

So Mr. Mayer, small, rotund, wearing his owl-like glasses, sat in the dark, dwarfed by the lot he'd built with his ambition and determination, ready to be astonished. He loved beauty in part because he found himself so ugly, a hideous caricature of a Jew like the ones scrawled on the pamphlets I'd soon see at the Bund rally. Mayer might be small and ugly—like all those squat, ugly men who sat in judgment of me at my Desert Inn audition—but he reigned like a king. By the end of the next decade, he'd be forced out of the studio he'd built, which would teeter like a B movie monster without him and then fall to the ground in pieces, but right now he could pick up a telephone and reach the President or the Pope. He could speak a few words and my mother would play the lead in one of MGM's next films—or the role of Kitty in *Waterloo Bridge*. But none of that happened. Because Mr. Mayer watched the test and shrugged. Eh.

Robert Taylor later said his role as Colonel Roy Cronin was his all-time favorite role and *Waterloo Bridge* his favorite picture. Of course, he didn't act in this picture with my mother but with Virginia Field, who I have to say was really not that much better in the role of Kitty than Dina Wells would have been.

LAS VEGAS
1950

22

AT FIRST I THOUGHT it might just be my imagination that Nate Stein was making a habit of slipping into the back of the Painted Desert Room at the DI at just the second I came on for the floor show, that it might be his shadow I saw as I led the conga line of girls in our classic Step Pause Step Pause with which we crossed from stage left to stage right, a shade that vanished when I myself vanished into the wings. At least, I thought I was imagining this until the other girls began to rib me about it, laughing, "Who's your daddy, Esme? Have some pity on the poor man. Blow him a kiss."

For, obviously, despite Arden's decision to codify our appearances—twelve of us in the same flat Pan-Cake, same brushstroke of rouge, same double sets of false eyelashes, same blond wigs, strands of pearls from our headdresses swinging over those wigs while the metal apparatus of the headdress anchored great poufs of feathers, thick plumes of feathers rising sky-high, a bevy of identically beautiful girls—Nate managed to locate me, even when I wasn't working the line as Arden's lead girl, even when I stood with my sisters on the risers or the portable stair-cases or swung with them on the ropes and trapezes, all tools Arden employed to maximize the small footprint of our stage, confecting engaging numbers like the ones Buzz had once upon a time designed for my mother and her confederates. It was as if my mother and her fellows had been transplanted to the desert, deposited not onto a soundstage but into a shoebox. Yet, unlike my mother, I was not one of the blurred many, not to Nate.

Yes, he came to look at me, standing at the back of the showroom night after night, the red-lit end of his cigarette the only other evidence of his desire, all height and Roman nose and power. Nate Stein, back of the house, Donn would hiss, Nate's appearance setting off a little racket backstage. But whatever it was Nate wanted from me he wasn't ready yet to take. Because he had a wife, a fourth wife. And a son. And both of them had come to the Desert Inn from Detroit for a visit.

When I'd arrived at the hotel for rehearsal this afternoon, I saw them both for the first time. For far too long I'd lingered at the back of the lobby to peer through the window at the utterly amazing corporeality of them—they did actually exist!—his wife lying on a chaise, his little boy in the shallow end of the figure-eight pool with Nate, Nate throwing his son in the air and catching him, embracing him. The boy, from what I could see, seemed to be enjoying himself somewhat less than his father. The look on his face was one of uncertain terror, either from the fright of the water play or from the bodily intimacy with this strange man, which was what his father had become for him, a stranger, during these months Nate and his wife had been living apart while Nate was launching the DI.

Nate's body unnerved me, too. I had never seen him without his clothes on—without a golf shirt or a tie and a jacket—and he had a thick brown back that spread out like a fan at his shoulders and a big chest and he was not soft, not at all, maybe from all the golf he played. Rising waist-high from the water like that he looked naked. I always thought my father was a prude for not wanting me to amble about the Flamingo poolside in my swimsuit, That's what everyone wears at a pool, Dad, but now I understood. It was just pretense that a bathing outfit wasn't provocative. Today, this whole sunny display of almost-nude men and women, in repose or sliding in and out of the blue water, seemed to me erotic. And even odder to me still was the fact that watching a father playing with his young child could be arousing. I hadn't known that it could be. But it was. I could feel that it was. Everything about the scene was arousing me. It was ridiculous.

I turned from the window and resolved right then and there not to look at Nate or his son or wife again during their entire visit here, no matter how long it stretched, a resolution I kept for about six hours.

Because when I walked through the casino after my second show and into the Sky Room, I found Nate and his wife there sitting at a table together, her short dark hair a mass of curls, her neck wrapped up in three strands of a pearl necklace like nothing I'd ever owned, her elbows on the table as she leaned in, bare shouldered. A big white corsage had been pinned to her dress, an enormous peony Nate must have given her. So he liked brunettes. Like my mother. A minus for me.

The Sky Room, like everything else here at the DI, was another of Nate's inspirations. The lounge lunged upward into the heavens like a boxy glass spaceship, three enormous walls of windows showcasing the desert nightscape. The twinkling lights in the ceiling blended with the starlit world outside, all of it twinkling. And down below us, the pulsating Dancing Waters show by the pool leapt orange and red, rising and falling to organ music we couldn't hear. Nate often came here to sit at a table and look out at that desert in the dim interior light, a Mr. Mayer looking over his backlots, though Nate's acres had yet to be filled with façades of distant, exotic places.

I sat at the bar. I always ate dinner here, late, 2:00 A.M., after my last show, too tired to drag myself home yet to my discouraged father, his fingers stained an insoluble black from the paper money and coins and chips he had handled all night at the Flamingo credit cage. That would have to change, but I didn't yet have the power by which to levitate him from that cashier's stool and draw him through those metal bars. I ordered. I waited. Nate would, on occasion, join me at my barstool, laughing as I devoured my usual steak dinner, the steak big and bloody. Nate would tell me, "Slow down, Esme. No one here is taking your plate away," and then he told the bartender that anything I ate, no matter how much, no matter how many godforsaken ounces of cow I ordered, was on the house, making me laugh, too, but the bartender took him seriously, saying, "Yes, sir, Mr. Stein."

But Nate wasn't coming over to my barstool tonight, and tonight I ate slowly because I was afraid I might choke, my throat closed up with panicked jealousy, talking with the bartender who came to visit me down at my end of the bar between customers, the two of us chatting about who had been promoted, who had gotten fired, who had won big at the tables tonight and whose fault that was. A lot happened in Vegas every single day, up, down, in, out. And because I'd been in Vegas for so long, it seemed I knew almost everyone we talked about, everyone who worked the Strip—the waiters and bartenders and valets, the trumpet players and dancers and comics, everyone from the girls who worked the shops to the celebrity regulars who played the stages, any one of whom would be a more appropriate partner for me than Nate Stein.

And all the while I talked and ate, I refused to allow myself to look in the direction of Nate's table, where he sat. With his wife. In fact, I made a screen of my hair to shutter him from view to ensure this. But I'd gathered more than enough impressions of him and of her just by walking into the Sky Room. I saw that Nate's wife looked more like a woman than a girl, though she couldn't have been much older than thirty. And it wasn't just her age that made her more suitable for Nate's delectation. All this dancing and performing had me looking like something hauled in from a circus. In fact, I'd begun to remind myself of the blond acrobat I'd spied once at the Ringling Bros. and Barnum & Bailey Circus my parents took me to see in Los Angeles in early September 1939.

Around the side of the big-top tent, through rigging I wasn't supposed to peek through but which demarcated the backstage area, I'd watched a most extraordinary man take a long drink of water. He wore a white leotard and tights, his hands powdered by chalk, his hair a platinum color I'd seen only on women, his skin an artificial orange-brown, and though all of this was amazing enough, the most remarkable thing about him was his muscles— the enormous bulk of his thighs and shoulders and upper arms, his giant-sized hands—the parts of his body he hung by and swung by and used to capture the men and women who flew to him midair. He had been lathed and tooled toward this specific purpose and to see him in the wings, just standing there in his canvas shoes not entirely unlike my own ballet slippers, was like watching a gigolo stroll through a toy store.

He turned and looked at me, mid-drink, took in both my gawk and awe, and he smiled, even half shrugged, as if to say he couldn't help it if he were superhuman, so extraordinary as to be practically extraterrestrial. It was with considerable effort that I had forced myself to close my mouth, still looking back even as my mother dragged me toward our destination, the ladies' room, if the portable bathroom at a big top can be called that. And now I looked exactly like a female version of that man, my body shaved to my own particular purposes as a performer, just as waxed and polished and not of this world. I wasn't sure how I would look in pearls and peonies.

Then suddenly and all at once, the gamblers guzzling up liquor in the Sky Room let out a startling cheer. I thought someone had scored at the Lady Luck bar, where every hour a big roulette wheel spun and a stream of silver coins poured from the hands of the nude neon Lady Luck. But when I looked around, I saw the room wasn't cheering at that, but at the sight through the big plate glass Sky Room windows of an atomic bomb going off, one of the nighttime tests of the great nuclear secret.

Most of the tests were run at dawn, but it was the nighttime tests that were the most spectacular, the great red mushroom cloud rising up like hell on a stick at the horizon, like the stem of a champagne glass, globe of the glass inverted, pouring down not champagne, but the hazards of destruction. Because a hundred miles north of the Strip that seemed the center of everything, there was another center of everything, the Nevada test site, complete with its own little suburb not entirely dissimilar to Andy Hardy Town, this one ominously named Survival City, with its own dusty streets and little two-bedroom houses and picket fences and kitchens with counters and tables and refrigerators and mannequins of husbands and wives, Mr. and Mrs. America, and their children, sets of families within homes constructed variously of concrete, aluminum, brick, and wood in order to see which substance could best resist the atomic blast.

The oblivious mannequins were posed to watch television or tucked into beds, blankets pulled up to their chins, though why the scientists bothered with this silliness, I couldn't fathom. Other mannequins were dressed in clothing made variously of cotton or wool or linen or silk and lashed to posts at the edge of the city, their blank faces turned toward ground zero. If their eyes could see, they would have been able to take in as well the forest of trees that had been trucked to the desert and bolted to the sandy floor, so the scientists could study what the bomb would do not only to houses and people and the food tucked in tins and paper packaging inside refrigerators and pantries in the perverse life-size doll houses erected in companion with the real houses only a hundred miles away, but also to foliage. And when the bombs were detonated, as they were, with regularity, the force of them blew the trees around like match sticks, tore the houses apart, tossed the Mr. and Mrs. America dolls into the air, rolled the refrigerators across the sand and dirt, irradiating everything there before the winds carried the radiation here. And then all of this chaos would be set right again, pins in a too-hot bowling alley, making ready for the next blast.

Survival City was a peek into the hopeful post-apocalypse, in which the properly built home, the properly suited man, the properly packaged food would survive into some kind of viable future, if one could stand to live that future and find some kind of merry to make there. And people believed there could be. Children were taught to duck and cover, to pull a blanket or even a newspaper over themselves if the A-bomb hit. Bars up and down the Strip concocted special well drinks and served rounds of them whenever the tests went off at night, lighting up the sky more fearsomely than any neon casino sign possibly could. And so now there was a big rush to order the Sky Room's two-dollar Atomic Cocktail or Mushroom Cloud Martini or Radioactive Rum and Coke in honor of it all, and everybody raised his glass to the amazing sight to the north. Drink and toast.

With all that as distraction, I turned on my bar stool, ostensibly to look for my bartender, not because I wanted the cocktail but because I wanted to do what I knew I shouldn't, what I had commanded myself not to do, what I had restrained myself so far from doing with, I thought, admirable tenacity. And that's when I saw Nate was not looking out the window at the great bomb that had just been detonated but was looking right at me, something he had probably not been restraining himself from doing the whole time I was talking to the young bartender.

Nate looked away, then looked back, lit a cigarette, then looked back, and now that I was pivoted his way, it seemed each time he looked at me a little longer as if he couldn't help it, sucking on his cigarette as if he could suck me in along with the vapor, flicking his eyes over to me so much that eventually his wife noticed, and she turned her head from the window and stared flatly at me, her expression a little weary, a little knowing.

But what was there to know? Truly, there was as yet nothing between me and Nate.

And since we were nothing, a zero hanging between us, why shouldn't he bring his wife here, to the popular Sky Room, even if he knew I ate dinner at this time every single evening?

Maybe this meant that I was nothing to Nate or maybe this meant only that he wanted his wife to enjoy the big wide view of the desert and the novelty of the Dancing Waters down below with the music and the colored lights.

I told myself this, and though I knew almost nothing about men despite all these years in Vegas, I didn't quite believe it.

Nate could have taken her poolside to dance or to the nearby Lady Luck bar or to the casino. He could have ordered room service for them in his suite. But he had brought her here and seated her twenty feet from me.

I saw her reach her hand across the table for Nate to take, which he did, and the ease of their familiarity spoke of their history together. Whatever this visit was to the hotel, it wasn't simply to bring Nate his son for a week or two. She wouldn't have come here if not at Nate's behest, and I understood that whatever the two of them decided tonight would directly affect me. She might move here, take her place as one of the ladies of the Desert Inn, link arms with Wilbur Clark's wife and Moe Dalitz's, plan charity luncheons for the Painted Desert Room, the showroom a debauchery by night but a proper Plain Jane by day. And I would remain the acrobat, backstage at the big top. Or. Perhaps not.

I took a minute to gather myself, determined to walk through the Sky Room without looking down or around, as if I were in costume on the showroom stage, where even when we weren't making our perilous descents on a staircase, we were trained to look past the audience, to avoid direct eye contact, to focus on the EXIT sign glowing red at the back of the club. I sometimes ambulated with a bit of wobble because I always wore stiletto heels offstage, still determined, even when I walked casually among the Arden Amazons, to trick them into thinking I was approximately their size. And as I skirted this table and that in the low lights, heading for the exit, Nate called out my name and waved me over to his table.

"I want you to meet my wife," he said when I arrived, and she held out her hand, her eyes tiny, fierce pinballs in a chute.

Her hand was small and warm, which meant my hand must be cold with discomfort.

"Hello," she said.

And we had nothing else to say.

The two of them looked up at me, her face unhappy and Nate's creased with the smile he always gave to me, couldn't help giving me, the smile I worried spelled paternal pride. Paternal. Maybe. Maybe I just wasn't adept at interpreting a man's face. I knew I wasn't any good at conversation, my silence at this table attested to that, and I wasn't exactly sure why Nate had called me over, but I had the uncomfortable feeling I was just like one of those bombs dropped on a target to demolish it beyond recognition.

Viable future? Not for the two of them.

23

THE NEXT NIGHT NATE was waiting for me when I left my dressing room. He took my hand without a word. I was wearing my eyeliner still, and my lashes, and this lent our suddenly fused hands a certain theatricality. He was not shaking my hand, though my hand was shaking, he was holding it, with no intention of letting go, and I understood from it that his wife and son had been packed up and sent off. Because of me.

We walked together through the showroom and the Lady Luck bar where the staff was clearing and re-laying linens and tableware, across the small casino floor where the dealers and players were closing down the baize-covered gaming tables, along the half-abandoned lobby where the desk staff said, "Good evening, Mr. Stein," as we passed, and I felt as much a spectacle as if we were walking a tightrope at that circus before the peanut-crunching thousands. Everyone who was awake and upright at this hour, and in Las Vegas, that number was not small, stared at us as we walked together, hand in hand, our processional a statement, a confession even.

At the end of it Nate said to me, "Esme, you know I'm much too old for you."

Inside his suite—and all the hotel suites at the DI were called, ridiculously, Hollywood Suites—we were alone together for the very first time, and in that sudden privacy, all previous constriction abruptly fell from us, which made me wonder what might have happened if we had ever been truly alone before this.

We grabbed at each other unselfconsciously. Like a Flamingo tabby cat, I rubbed my face in his neck and he tolerated that briefly before taking my head in his hands to kiss me. His tongue was muscular, thick, and intrusive, the entire sensation new to me, but the shock was quick, and then I found myself clinging to him and sucking at that tongue. He pushed us through the living room and into one of the bedrooms, no words between us. The décor was blandly serene, Western, bright carpet, impersonal, the rooms of anyone, the colors and textures of the hotel lobby repeated here, very few personal items anywhere, a watch, some cufflinks, laid on a mirrored tray on the dresser, no photographs at all, as if he'd stripped himself of all the years and days that led to this one. Whatever else belonged to him must be tucked away in drawers and closets. But just those few items gave me a jolt. I was backstage, behind the scenes of Nate Stein.

This violation of his privacy was almost more shocking to me, even, than his naked body, an exposure that happened quickly by our rushed disrobing, the shedding of his shirt, my dress, my somewhat complicated undergarments. If I were seeing the inside and outside of Nate, then he was seeing the inside and outside of me and what if he saw there was nothing much to me, after all?

He was older, his flesh thicker than mine, solid and aromatic, the hair on his body almost a fur of black and silver, and he paused a moment to say, "Fuck. Wait," as he pulled off his wedding band, let that crack of gold drop to the carpet somewhere, roll away even as he brought me near. He was an adult, with the bulk of an adult, and I was really still a girl, bones and a sliver of inexperienced flesh, no matter how I strutted the stage or how I was costumed, and what did he want with that? But I found the very maturity of him arousing and perhaps he found the very childishness of me equally so. Certainly he enjoyed the blond novelty of me, "blond even here," he said, stroking a finger between my thighs.

And then he said, "Esme."

Intercourse felt like being impaled with a thick object, his phallus both soft and hard at the same time, an invasion that made me recoil even as I welcomed it. Nothing I had ever done or known had prepared me for this, and during the odd warm hurtful chafing of that first time, I discovered what else we shared besides pleasure. A terrible loneliness.

From us seeped such a loneliness that it wet first the sheets and mattress of that fine room and then from there, it dripped into the plush carpet, unstoppable. It ran down the thick walls, saturating the decorative paper that covered them and swelling the drapes to double their size, sorrow filling the room to the brim while we lay, punctured and flapping at the bottom of this strange pool. I found myself crying for my mother, my grandfather, my once buoyant and now tattered father, and Nate cried for someone or something, too, maybe for yet another wife he had once loved, now lost, or for his little son lost to him also in this grievous, unalterable way. Because all the love that Nate would have given to his ex-wife he would now heap upon me, now that he would not be seeing much of her anymore because of me. And whatever love should have belonged to Nate's little boy, whom I'd also displaced, I would take in greedily, too, without ever encouraging him to share it. Or perhaps Nate cried for something I was too young to even fathom. It was a surprise to me both that Nate Stein believed he lacked anything in this life and that the two of us had anything in common at all. When we were done with the raw gutturality and the formless squawking and the ragged weeping, we spoke of none of it.

Nate handed me a cigarette, my first since the one I'd tried long ago at the track, one of my father's Chesterfields that made me cough until I threw up, which Nate lit for me, and the foul-tasting smoke of it in my mouth felt somehow like yet another intrusion I couldn't refuse. His robust hair was flattened with sweat.

"I'm going to take care of you now," Nate said, his largesse born in part of guilt, for loving me though I was too young, for loving my body to excess as he did, for loving too much what we did together with my young body and his older one, which made us not so much father and child but something more slippery and less durable. But, if nothing else, I was used to slippery indefinable untrustworthy older men.

24

THE LONG FRONDS OF Benny Siegel's one hundred date palms rustled above me in the wind when I returned home in the early morning dark.

The grounds beyond the pool stretched to the bungalows. I'd thought running from the valet stand through the overheated casino and across the grass would keep me warm, but it hadn't. I was still cold. And I was alone on the concrete paths around the deserted, chilly pool, paths that led to the suite of bungalows Benny had built for the high rollers he imagined would come and stay here. And they had. But since my father and I had arrived long before any of them and because Benny loved me, he had given us one of the bungalows and no one had thought to take it away. Or perhaps someone had thought about it, but because of me, my father had been left alone. I can guarantee you this—my father had never once worried about this roof over his head, though I did, and he would never have seen himself as overstaying his welcome, he who found every insult and assault a surprise.

I used my key. Quietly. I didn't know what I was going to tell my father.

I was so changed that I thought everything at home would be changed, too. But nothing was. The living room and kitchen were in their usual state of disarray, glasses and dishes left unwashed, racing sheets spread all over the sofa, cigarettes in ashtrays that needed badly to be emptied, left like this until finally even my father was bothered and he called for housekeeping.

We had moved in here only three years ago, among the furniture Benny and Virginia, as the Flamingo's chief decorator, the Queen of All That Was Garish, had chosen for the bungalows.

Blue-and-orange diamond-patterned curtains. A lamp with a brass starburst for a base. A larger starburst hugged the wall, in melodramatic echo, as if that were a good idea. A television set, a big box more wood than screen. A few yards away, because the bungalow was, after all, a bungalow and small, stood a circular blond wood dining table and its four matching chairs, wooden backs curved, orange seat cushions to match the orange sofa. The shabbiness of it all made me pity myself and my father, even though I knew my father never cared about any of this, never cared at all about where he ate or slept.

Not that we ate here much. We always ate at the hotel. We did everything at the hotel, which always felt more like home than this bungalow, even though my father and I had lived here together longer than we had ever lived anywhere else. When the hotel first opened, I'd get a key from the front desk clerk and avail myself of whatever room was empty at that hour of that day, climb into the bed and watch television. And when I got hungry, I'd order room service. Pancakes. Even at night, when forced back into this box of a bungalow as if I were a toy on a retracted spring (with orders to call my father down at the casino if I needed him), I'd sit at the front window as if deprived of a party. I'd look down over the pool to the Flamingo, lit like a three-layer birthday cake all night long, but even candles on the brightest birthday cake are eventually blown out.

At the threshold of my own tiny room, a museum exhibit of my childhood, I paused. Bedspread and pillows white and pink, ruffles, my mother's mirrored dressing table, dolls. I had been young enough at twelve to bring dolls with me to Vegas, baby dolls with painted hair, real golden hair, beribboned hair, bonnets. No books, of course. My Patriot radio, of course. A Slinky. A Coloredo game. Dinky Toys Railroad passengers. Fifty Card Games for Children. Ha. As if I needed that in Vegas.

On the dresser, two photographs. One was of my mother, my age now, dressed to the nines to go out, strapless tulle dress, gloved to the elbow, bracelets at her fabric-covered wrists. The other was of me, taken during those weeks my mother wouldn't get out of bed. My father had driven me to the May Company department store to have my photograph taken for its Beautiful Baby contest. I was six, laden for the occasion with my usual multitude of bangles and necklaces, my mother's black orchid pin jammed into my tangled hair, beneath that, my strained, unhappy face. My father had been absolutely sure, given that I was the most beautiful child in the city, if not the universe, that I would win the contest. Which I did not. Most pathetic child in the city, that contest I might have won.

We'd brought here only our clothes and my toys. When we'd left Los Angeles, my father had put all our furniture in storage. "We're starting over," he said. "And you never know, we may need to leave Vegas in a hurry." Prescient. Remarkable. For once thinking more than two days ahead. "We don't want to have to stop and load a truck on our way out of town."

But when the men my father had hired carried my mother's shiny dressing table up the wooden ramp onto the flatbed truck destined for the Boyle Heights Storage Company on Los Angeles Street, I couldn't bear to see it buried as she had been. So I said, "I want that." And my father looked down at me, saw my face, and said, "Okay," waved his arms at the men to lug the vanity back down the ramp.

Benny had had one of his men bring it out to Vegas for us, and the minute the vanity was shoveled into my room I was sorry I had asked for it. There was no piece of furniture more emblematic of her. My father had been right. We should have left it all behind. All memories behind. But Benny was so pleased with himself for having brought it here for me, I couldn't say anything.

He actually came out to the bungalow to see the vanity for himself, as if it were my mother he was visiting. He had always liked her, wept like a fool at her funeral, feeling at fault. And here the dresser sat to this very day, ridiculously at odds with the blond wood of the rest of the room, the vanity all early-thirties glamour, every inch of its surface mirrored, every inch of it reflecting my own wavery image. Girl. Once a girl.

I wished, suddenly, I could talk to my mother, to ask her if she felt the way I did now after her first time with my father. A little unsteady, a little battered. What next. After those Tom Collinses with my father in his boarding-house bed, my mother's life careened off and dragged her in its wake because that first sodden encounter had engendered me. And she'd had to face her father, too, my grandfather with his ironed newspaper who swept a soft brown brush across his hats to keep them immaculate. An out-of-wedlock pregnancy. Impossible. She'd had to elope. But what if she hadn't gotten pregnant. What would she have done? Continued chasing her bright dreams, I'm sure, unencumbered by me or my father. Well, she continued chasing them, anyway, the two of us slowing her to a crawl.

I turned out the light in my bedroom, and in that moment when the light slapped up against the darkness, I thought I saw something flick past my bedroom window. Maybe. Bird? Bat? Palm frond bowing in the wind?

It was Benny Siegel standing out there, shaking his head at the misadventure that carried me on its palanquin to Nate Stein at the Desert Inn. Baby E. What are you doing?

Why had I conjured him?

Perhaps because of the parade of gifts with which Benny had been slowly grooming me, wooing me, waiting until I'd come of age to take me, which I suddenly understood now. Virginia had understood this, intuitively, then. As had my father, I realized. But

Benny had died and now Nate, a different predator, had taken me instead.

But Benny wasn't really out there. No. It was my father who had switched on the hall light behind me and was now reflected in the window glass before me. He was the one shaking his head.

"Make no mistake about it, Esme," he said. "Nate Stein is a dangerous man."

Who wasn't of our acquaintance?

But I didn't think that at the time. I just thought with some relief, So he's already heard. I won't have to tell him, after all.

25

BY THE NEXT DAY what had happened between me and Nate was known all over the Strip and not long after that, Nate moved me into his suite at the DI.

Within the month, my father had been promoted back to box man at the Flamingo.

And from then on he held his tongue about Nate, cautious, perhaps, about what I might repeat to him. Yes, my father held his tongue, though perhaps it would have been better if he hadn't.

26

I RAPIDLY DISCOVERED THAT it was not going to be all that easy loving Nate. He might tell me in bed, "This is how adults fuck, little girl, what do you think of that?" might take too much pleasure in my emerging sexuality and disinhibition, which he teased from me, bit by bit, until to his delight I became reckless in the bedroom, letting him do whatever he wanted with me, might, some nights, sweating all over me, his flesh dripping onto mine, hair a sopping black thatch, say, "This is killing me, E. I'm fifty fucking years old," taking my hand to brush my palm along the gray hair on his chest and at his groin as evidence, but even while I assured him of my affection, I never myself felt entirely assured of his. The vastness of his life compared to mine intimidated me, though surely my short life rivaled his in terms of tumult, which he slowly shared.

Some nights, he would light up a cigarette and tell me about growing up in Detroit, playing handball with the Negroes on his block or the way the sharp wind off the wintertime Lake Erie cut right through your coat, your scarf, your shirt, poked its tongue straight into your lungs, directly disregarding skin and muscle. Once a gang of Negro boys surrounded him and asked to see his circumcised Jew dick, and Nate dropped the plated casserole a neighbor had made for his poor motherless family and used the pieces of the broken plate as weapons, one chip in each hand as he swiped at his tormentors. Porcelain claws. Detroit in my mind was a black city, with black smoke, black factories, black warehouses, industrial plants, Negroes—while the only two cities I knew were sun-drenched, horizontal sprawls. But in that black city, he'd lost his mother just as I'd lost mine in my sunny one.

He told me only a little about his father, who'd gone to prison briefly for stealing a check right out of an envelope in a neighbor's mailbox in 1910, but how that petty crime and punishment couldn't dampen the man's ridiculous swagger. Nate hadn't seen his father in almost twenty years. He distrusted fathers. Even himself as a father. Another failure. "So there you go, E," wincing, "that's my life. Part of the deal. Still want me?"

Yes.

But there were some things we spoke less about—his ex-wives, any of the three of them, now four of them, in particular the fourth one. I knew only that their divorce was final and that she was keeping their son from him to avenge her displacement by me, making the little boy half an orphan.

I told Nate about the Sisters orphanage where I'd spent a spirit-destroying six months in 1939 until my father rescued me there in the dead of a Los Angeles winter, where trees had no leaves and the sky was gray and the rain made enormous puddles in the streets and driveways which had no drainage because most of the year the city didn't need that kind of engineering, and where, from that landscape, the orphanage rose like a black wretch, and Nate took my hand and looked at me with a mixture of pity and comprehension, as if he'd already lived that story, had already lived all my stories, had lived long enough to live them all three times over, as if he'd like to journey to the past and rescue me himself before my father could, and he asked me then what he was always asking me now, "What can I give you, E? Tell me. Tell me what you want."

At that moment in time, Nate could have given me anything and I wouldn't already have had it. I literally had nothing but my theater case, which held my entire soul and all my ambitions, a few items of clothing, and the sequined costumes Donn Arden outfitted his girls in, which, strictly speaking, were not really ours, but borrowed, assigned to us temporarily, mine twenty-two waist, twenty-six torso, with my name, E. Wells, marked in ink on the inside of the bodice. If I left the show, the costume stayed on its hanger on the dressing-room rack. But I knew better than to ask Nate for anything. What he wanted to give me, he would.

His first gift to me was a necklace with a charm, the letters of my name, ESME, the letters pavéd with diamonds.

"Do you like it?" he asked, uncertainly, as if he'd never given a gift to a woman before.

I did. It glittered and my father, mother, and I had always liked glittery things. ESME. He had claimed my name and given it back to me, as if he somehow now owned my name, owned me. From that moment forward, I never took the necklace off, except to perform.

27

BUT IN THE MORNING, whatever intimacy we'd managed disappeared with the light. He was a fifty-three-year-old man, invincible, in charge of everything, and I was an eighteen-year-old girl in charge of nothing. If I was awake, from the bed I'd watch him as he stood in his underwear in the bathroom, shaving away the black stubble that reappeared on his face every day by late afternoon, manipulating his wild hair with combs, brushes, Brylcreem, dressing for his day of business, calling downstairs to his secretary for the location of his first meeting of the day. My first appointment of the day was to look at him. Or for him.

If I woke late, which was often the case, I'd go find him, wherever he was, though I never knew exactly how he would receive me. But I was used to that. That's how it was with my mother. You would think I'd have more self-respect than to go looking for him like this. But I didn't. I was used to vertiginous insecurity. Sometimes Nate would hold out an arm for me, "Come here, baby," no matter who was there with him or what he was doing, whether he was in his office making phone calls or looking over the books in the all-important counting room, which was always hot and smelly, with tobacco butts and paper money glued to the walls by the humidity, or sitting by the pool grousing with various men about the slow progress of the various hotels under construction on the Strip or meeting with his partners, more suits than mobsters, in his new real-estate development company, men who'd look away indulgently while Nate kissed the forehead of his child lover. But other mornings, he was curt with me, dismissive, flapping a hand in my direction. "Go away, E. Go play by yourself. I'm busy." I was not to be included in his business or his circle of men. I was still Baby E.

And maybe that was for the best, because as my father had said, Nate Stein was a dangerous man.

I saw that for myself one morning. Walking into the lobby on my usual search for Nate, I spied him at the front desk, but before I could even move toward him, a Negro man came striding purposefully through the glass doors and into the DI lobby, heading directly for Nate. So I paused. We never saw Negroes here.

In Las Vegas, 1950, we didn't have Negro waiters or dealers or entertainers in our clubs, unless they were stars like Lena Horne or Pearl Bailey, and even then, there were restrictions. When Lena Horne came to sing at the Flamingo, she refused to stay in the Negro part of town, which didn't even have a sewage system, so Mr. Siegel put her up in one of the hotel cabanas and had the maids burn her sheets each morning. Burn them! Washing wasn't even good enough. The Negroes who placed bets or played the numbers did so on their side of town, the games run and money collected by Negroes specially recruited by Gus or Moe or Nate. There were a lot of men, desperate men, in West Vegas, who took on any kind of scrap the casinos or bookies or loan sharks threw at them.

But we did have Negro boxers at the hotels sometimes as entertainment, dark men pummeling each other in a roped-off square, white referees in place to contain them. And I thought I recognized this man as someone I saw occasionally at the Flamingo, talking to one or another of Greenbaum's or Sedway's men, someone who collected debts for the casinos and boxed for hire.

The man was angry about something, I could read his body well enough even at this distance to see that, and he may have been drunk, too, common enough in Las Vegas where drinking went on any time of day, Bloody Marys and Mimosas giving way to Screwdrivers and hard liquor straight up as the hands of the clock wound onward. He had the arms of a boxer and the legs of a drunk, and he made his way across the lobby toward Nate. What could he be angry about? Had Nate not paid him the percentage due for collecting on a debt or not paid him the money for a private fight or stopped using him as an errand boy or numbers runner?

When the Negro reached Nate's side, I saw how quickly Nate's face changed, darkened. The bad face. Eyebrows together. Mouth down, unsmiling. The man leaned in, aggressively, and said something I couldn't hear and then forcefully drew back his fist. I flinched, but Nate didn't. I wasn't sure what the man said, but I could hear Nate quite well, the steely spike to his voice I'd never heard him use before giving his words force. "If you hit me, nigger, you'd better kill me. Because if you don't, I'll make one phone call and you'll be dead in twenty-four hours."

While I watched, the Negro man turned his head and looked at his fist for a moment as if it were a stranger, how did this get there?, and then he looked back at Nate, who stood there still unflinching. And then the man's body sagged, I could see it, all the fierce energy that had driven him across the lobby floor, the grievance that angered him enough to confront a boss as powerful as Nate, both of those, the energy and the grievance, slid down to his shoes and slithered away from him. And then the man himself turned and bolted, following that snake.

It was only then that Nate saw me, the bad face rearranging itself into an uncertain grin, and it was uncertain because Nate didn't know exactly how much I'd seen of this encounter or exactly what I would do if I had seen too much. And then I saw him apprehend that I had seen it all.

"It's just talk, E," he said.

Was it? Was it just talk when he'd made a call, sending two men to the casino manager at the Last Frontier to tell him to stop calling Jews "kikes" or they'd come back to break his arms and legs and the man understood that was not what they meant, not at all, and the man left Vegas never to return? I'd heard about that.

Nate felt for his cigarettes and lighter, watching me while he did so. Would I, like the Negro, bolt from him?

No. No, I would not.

Because Nate and I might have sex and sorrow in common, but we had something else in common much less lovely.

Ambition.

LOS ANGELES
1939

28

WHEN MR. MAYER DISMISSED my mother's screen test with that "eh," she took to her bed in a numb, mindless fugue, her body simply folded up, squeezed together, like a director's chair collected at the end of a long day's shoot. She slept alone, and too much, day and night. Without my father even asking me to, at my own bedtime, I went to sleep in her bed, to keep a watch on her. If she went to the window to throw herself out into the dark, I would know. But she hardly stirred. From noon to dawn, she remained unmoving.

I began to like it in her room, with her there, quiet and malleable, not the usual scrap of trouble my father followed around with a broom and dustpan. Being around her now was easy. I could open her dresser drawers, put on her necklaces and shoes, wear whatever I wanted of hers. Slowly I moved some of my own clothing into her room, folded the pieces carefully and laid them in her dresser drawers. My own bedroom had never been organized into anything resembling coherence, my dresser and bed at stark angles in the center of the floor, dropped there by the Boyle Moving Co. and never touched again, my toys still in boxes in a ragged cardboard wall to one side, a wall I'd barely disturbed. My room's lack of design seemed to speak to my parents' general disarray and disorientation since our eviction from Orange Street, a disarray and disorientation that seemed even more exaggerated now with my mother's perpetual slumber. We were in a lull, but a lull with a certain tension in it, an ebb before the flow that waxed everywhere.

My mother refused, for the first time in six years, to go to the studio—what's the point?—and hadn't shown up to any re-hearsals for *Strike Up the Band.* She shrugged, ignored me when I stamped my feet. "Go away, Esme," she told me, in a heavy throaty voice which only proved she hadn't even really woken up. I tugged at her arms and wailed at her, but she rolled over in the bed, unimpressed, and showed me her back.

I think my mother felt if her fate was to continue to appear on the screen with hundreds of others into perpetuity, well, she didn't want that kind of perpetuity. No thank you. In fact, my fa-ther and I worried that she might not want any kind of perpetuity at all.

Neither of us wanted to see her returned to Camarillo, the hospital wedged between the blue Santa Monica Mountains and the verdant fields and orchards that made a valley to the Pacific, the ocean you could smell and feel from the grounds but couldn't quite see. We didn't want her returned to the courtyards and the whitewashed walls and the red-tiled roofs, all of it promising a sanctuary it did not deliver. It only promised this, as did the Span-ish missions after which the complex was modeled, with its cha-pels, orchards, farmlands, stables, and laundries, and at which by day the patients labored as the Indians once had for their padres two centuries earlier. All the women hospitalized there had been trouble for someone and needed to be remade, like the baptized Chumash and the Gabrielino, to please their masters.

When my father took me that one time to visit my mother, after which I refused to go, she had grabbed at my hand to tell me about the babies who were waiting for rescue, swaddled and balanced on the open palm leaves that tottered at the pinnacles of those tall thin trees on the grounds. The babies slept at the tops of those trees, she told me, their hands fists, their mouths slack, nestled in the long fringed palm leaves or captured in baskets of orange tree branches, almost invisible behind their waxy green leaves, or rocked by the waving branches of the eucalyptus. Cradles. Not one of them cried. The babies were good. Waiting, waiting to be collected. That's why she needed to climb the bell tower and fly, to reach them.

Her rambling had terrified me, and I wasn't entirely sure what she said wasn't true, as everything about the place, with its locking doors and restrained women and overcrowded dormitories and solitary confinement cells and hydrotherapy rooms with their enormous, terrifying bathtubs, was the inverse of normal. It seemed to me, at age five, that babies might very well be placed in cradles in the treetops, out of reach of their disturbed mothers. It didn't occur to me then to wonder why my mother was worrying about lost babies, and, of course, I didn't understand she was worrying about me.

29

WHEN MY FATHER GOT home from work at six o'clcok, he went directly into the garage, still wearing his splattered painter's coveralls and his splattered painter's cap. I hated to see my father in those coveralls, my father's pant legs, his undershirt, even his painter's hat and his face streaked all over with paint that had dripped sloppily from his brush, as if my father cared so little for what he was doing that he took no caution with the paint at all, could have poured a bucket of it over his head for all it mattered to him. Now that my mother never rose from bed, my father brought supper home for us each night, and I'd run out to the garage to eat with him there because I was hungry, even though I dreaded seeing my father's face. His expression, normally so animated, so taut with hope, seemed like a shriveled balloon.

Sometimes I'd interrupt him secretly studying the racing sheets my mother had forbidden him to study ever again, making important notes in his red notebook, which she had also forbidden him. But those notes in that notebook might get us out of here, I hoped, or at least might get my father out of this space in the garage, where he had repurposed the couch as a bed, a kitchen chair for a nightstand, and a tabletop for a wardrobe, his pants and shirts folded on the surface of it, his shoes lined up below. My father would look up blearily at my entrance and mutely offer me a carton, usually of Chinese food, from a restaurant just west of Jewtown. My father never had a good story anymore for me and my father used to always have a good story. In fact, he had started to look like one of the men I would spot on the street a few years ago, men sitting on their haunches and holding up signs, NEED MONEY FOR FOOD, men to whom my mother would always give a nickel or dime, putting the coins in their hands and saying, "Here you go, baby," to which the men would always say, "God bless." Well, no such charity flowed from my mother now.

And so on those summer evenings without her, after my father and I had eaten, I shuffled our worn deck of cards, expertly, with my two small hands, the shuffle, bridge, fan, cut, and shuffle, just as my father had taught me, and on one of those nights I accidentally discovered the secrets he kept beneath his painter's cap, grand schemes that ran parallel to my mother's delusions.

On that night he was absentminded though I dealt out our hands noisily, slapping the cards down on the little table, trying to get his attention. The ploy didn't work. My father still stood at the garage door window, looking out at the street, cracking his knuckles, distracted. He had exchanged his coveralls for a collared shirt and suit pants. He'd recently started going out in the evenings to Louie Schwartzman's Ebony Room, where he kept company with the Boyle Heights bums my grandfather despised—Big Greenie Greenberg, Izzie and Maxie Shaman, Hooky Rothman, Mickey Cohen—and where he played the numbers since my mother had forbidden him the track and horses. Because my father had to gamble. That was understood. Only the breadth of it could be curtailed.

"Come on, Dad," I called out, finally. "Let's play."

"What are we playing?" He turned from the window.

"Acey-Deucey," I said, naming one of the poker games my father had been teaching me. Follow the Lady. Little Chicago. Acey-Deucey. Texas Hold-Em.

My father came to the table and looked down at his cards. "Five and a Jack," he said. "Not so shabby."

"Seven and ten," I said of my own cards.

"Bet low," my father advised.

But since all the bets were imaginary, written in pencil on a piece of scrap paper, which was one reason why my father found our game so dull, the fact that I was the only other participant being the other, I wrote down a big number. Ten dollars.

My father grinned at the audacity. He found that much engaging. "All right, big shot. Hit me."

I flipped my father a card. Ace. He grimaced theatrically. I dealt my own, a three, but before my father could commiserate with me, somebody in our driveway called out his name. "Ike!" And my father didn't seem surprised to hear his name called.

"Who's that?" I asked. Nobody ever came to our house.

But he got up from the table without answering me.

I got up, too, and followed my father to the garage door window. A man in a white summer suit like my father's stood at the end of the drive, by the curb, where a car sat, also white, a Chevrolet, its motor running. Inside the car was another man, hat low over his forehead.

My father nodded to the first man. The man nodded back, got into the Chevy, and drove away. My father's expression changed, no longer distracted now, but tense.

I tugged at his hand to flush that face away. But it stayed there.

My father said, "I've got an errand to run."

"Can I come?" I asked him.

"No." He turned to the clothesline, strung from the standing floor lamp to a nail in the wall opposite, and took down one of the suit jackets hanging on a scraggly wire hanger. He put on a tie, used a towel to shine his shoes, and then took something that looked like four metal rings welded together from the tool box that apparently now served as his accessories drawer. He slipped it over his fingers, made a fist, then slipped the contraption off and secreted it in his left pocket.

"What's that?" I asked.

"Nothing."

So it was nothing. So interesting that it had to be made into nothing. I knew it! I knew my father was not just a common house painter, had not become something so ordinary. He was simply keeping his fabulous new identity to himself, like his racing sheets. And his red notebook.

"I'll be back in an hour or two," my father said, fumbling for his car keys.

He slid open the garage door. "Go to bed now."

But then he paused. He'd forgotten something.

That's when I called out theatrically, "Good night, so long, see you later," and slipped quietly out the open door. But instead of going into the house, I ran around the side of the garage to the back alley where my father kept our Cadillac, which he'd displaced, car doors unlocked. It took me only a few seconds to crawl onto the floor in the rear and pull down the blanket we used for impromptu picnics, or did, anyway, in better days. I made my skinny self as flat as I could beneath the wool.

A few seconds later, my father slid into the front seat and started the car with a roar he quickly choked back, so I knew he was nervous. My father never started the car like that. He was a column of mysterious figures in his red notebook that I was about to add up. Magic Ike!

30

IT WASN'T LONG BEFORE we were out of Boyle Heights. From under the blanket, I heard the rumble of our tires over the Sixth Street Bridge and then the traffic of Grand, Hope, Flower, Figueroa, all the big north-south downtown avenues, east of the long avenues we used to survey from our perch on Mulholland Drive. Horns. The bump of a pothole. Squeaky brakes. My own breathing. I could smell that my father had lit a Chesterfield. I wondered at what point, if any, my mother would miss me, come out to the garage in her negligee to call me to bed, see us both gone, and telephone over to the Ebony Room, scream at the bartender, "Tell Ike Silver to come home. And to bring his daughter with him." And, haha!, we wouldn't be there. But, more likely, she'd never notice my absence at all.

My father turned the car abruptly south. We drove blocks and blocks, hitting too many traffic lights, my father cursing impatiently under his breath at each one, "God fucking dammit," words he never would have uttered in my presence, of course, but how could he know I was here? Finally, with one quick sharp maneuver, he parked and jumped from the car. I waited, then carefully sat up.

We were on a side street. Ahead of me, on the sidewalk, I could see a small group of men gathering, and my father striding toward them with the gait I recognized as his gait of false confidence, the jaunty one he used when he lost big at the track. What was he up to? I climbed carefully out of the car and stood by it, half-hidden. I watched my father stop in front of number 634, and I slowly approached the address myself, uncertainly, careful to halt a few yards back from it.

Six-three-four looked like a two-story stucco house, nestled between two other innocuous stucco houses, but this one had a sign
mounted over the front doors. Two words I had never seen before.
I wasn't even sure the words were in English. DEUTSCHES HAUS.
The words had been painted in fancy lettering that made them
look like the Hebrew in my grandfather's prayer books. For all I
knew, Deutsches Haus was Hebrew and this house some kind of
modest synagogue. Maybe my father was turning to God for help
to get my mother out of bed.

Tables had been set out on the small porch and on the grass
lawn, and those rickety tables were piled high with paper. More
men in suits and hats or workers' caps were milling around on
the sidewalk or entering the doors. There were women, too, in
dresses and hats. I could see when the doors opened that beyond
the vestibule there was some kind of big hall, so though the building looked like a house, it was not a house. A house wouldn't have
an auditorium filled with chairs ready to put on a show. So my
next guess was that this must be a theater and those papers must
be the programs. Perhaps my father had been secretly studying
acting in order to join my mother at MGM? He was certainly
handsome enough.

But somehow all this didn't seem to add up.

First, I could see my father wasn't in any hurry to go in and
start performing, and performers were usually backstage long before the audience began to arrive. He wasn't moving, standing at
the edge of the sidewalk with the other men. They were talking,
tersely, a tight bunch. Then one of the men lifted his head to
survey the crowd and I could see the visage beneath the brim of
his fedora. Broken nose. Thick jowls. I recognized him at once.
Mickey Cohen. The boxer. The Jew Boy. The man I'd seen at the
shul and at the track.

I ducked behind the thin trunk of an impossibly tall palm

tree waving feebly in the dark sky. It looked like Mr. Cohen was giving my father instructions, my father nodding seriously. I watched Cohen nod to another group of men at the right of the porch and then he turned his gaze to the other side of the house and nodded again. I turned my head to look, too, but I saw nothing, only more men in suits and hats. I looked back to Mickey Cohen, but apparently he had finished taking his measure of the crowd, for he jerked his head in the direction of the doors and the group of men that included my father went inside. I should say they strolled inside. Maybe even swaggered. On tiptoe now, I saw the group split up in the vestibule, some of them walking to the right side of the auditorium, some of them going left.

I knew better than to try to follow them in, though I wanted to. Instead, I edged closer to the crowd by the front porch. The amplified noise from within made itself felt all the way out here, where that electrified hum met the hum of this one, men talking, shifting, the backs of their suits wrinkled, their shoes not nearly as clean as my father's. Even emerging from a garage where his clothes hung on a wire, my father looked good. A wallet lay on the grass—no, a little book. I looked around, then picked it up. On the front page I stared at words I didn't recognize, not unusual for me, but still, the formations looked different:

Amerikadeutscher Volfsbund
Bundesleitung
Ortsgruppe: Los Angeles
Mitgliedskarte Nr.: 18952
Name: Charles J. Young
Wohnort: Alhambra, Cal.
Strasse: 29 North Vega Street
Geb. Am.: 16. May 1887

And beneath all that was a signature, Hermann Schwinn, with a long, elaborately drawn *H* and *S*.

A mystery. A puzzle. A code?

I put the little book in my pocket and stepped quietly around the side of the porch. None of the men or women looked my way. After all, I was a slip of a girl, a pickpocket, an urchin, a sound-stage rat, used to gliding unnoticed around the backlot and the grandstand. As I passed the tables, I swiped some papers off one of them and when I reached the side of the building, I leaned against it for a moment to look at my cache.

The first paper was a black-and-white flyer with a picture of a Jewish star, a hook-nosed man and a pretty lady, a snake wrapping its way around her and through the double *o*'s of the word "Hollywood." I recognized that word from the big sign on Mount Lee. I dropped the flyer to the ground, bitten. Next, a small slip of paper, no, a sticker, black and white, meant for a jacket lapel with a drawing of a hideous furry-legged spider and the head of a man with a grotesque nose, beady eyes, and rubbery lips. The head looked something like Louis B. Mayer or Louis B. Mayer's worst nightmare of himself. Spiders. Snakes. Foreigners.

I let go of the last paper, but once it was at my feet, I couldn't keep from glancing down. The words shrieked red and black, half covering a fat man in a suit and a yarmulke leaning forward to shovel food into his open mouth. Greedy. Wanting everything. What kind of show was this going to be? Whatever this was, it was about to begin.

I made myself walk forward, shuffling along the side of the building, the papers I'd dropped sticking to my mother's sandals, which were already too big for me, but I had been wearing them, as I sometimes did all her clothes, not thinking I'd be leaving the house, that I would possibly find myself anywhere else, especially not here. My hands gripped at the ivy that climbed the building's walls, my feet shifting on the uneven, uncultivated surface beneath me. Obviously, people weren't meant to walk here, even people who weren't wearing shoes too big for them.

I could tell I was getting closer to my goal by the noise reverberating through the stucco. I must be approaching the hall and surely I would find my father in there. He would be angry with me, but he could never stay angry with me for long. Unlike my mother with her weeks-long grudges. He would clear off the chair next to him and put me in it, and then when we drove home together in the dark, my father would explain everything to me. By this time in my internal scenario, I had reached a French door.

I was now looking into the large auditorium I had first glimpsed from the sidewalk. From this vantage point I could see a stage—so there was going to be a show!—which had been festooned with red-and-black colored banners, above which a flag of the United States flew. Against a podium leaned a framed photograph of Adolf Hitler, whom I recognized from the newsreels before the picture shows at the National. A winged beast cast in plaster perched on a platform by the podium, its beak turned, it seemed, right toward me, a swastika gripped in its claws. And that was not all.

In addition to the fearsome display of emblems, twenty men in brown shirts and ties stood on the floor before the stage in military formation, their right arms hanging by their sides, their left arms bent, hands at their belt buckles. Above and behind them stood three more men in brown shirts, each holding a different flag, the flag in the middle America's flag, the other two, ones I didn't recognize. Though I had no way of knowing this then, I had followed my father to a Nazi Bund rally.

There was something terrifying to me about the militaristic décor of the stage, and I frantically scanned the crowded audience for my father. But there were so many men dressed like him, so many hats and suits, he was indistinguishable. The arms of these many men were moving like a wave, they were clapping, the show was about to begin.

And then suddenly a woman was by my side asking if I was lost. She had bent down, her face to mine, to better determine my expression. "Are you here with your daddy, honey?" she asked.

"My father's somewhere," I said.

Thank God for my grandfather's blond hair, my grandfather's blue eyes, my sundress, my mother's espadrille sandals, the cloth peony, also hers, pinned in my hair. The woman took me for a pretty little Aryan girl, separated from my father by the crowd, my father, the Nazi sympathizer, come to the Nazi rally at the Deutsches Haus to shout his Heil Hitlers. For all I knew that was why he was here.

If the woman asked me my father's name, I would simply produce the little identity book I was clutching and tell her my father dropped it. Charles J. Young, my absentminded father. Lost his daughter and his book.

"Well, come sit with me, sweetheart. He'll find you. I'm sure he's looking."

Ha.

And she took me by the hand through the French doors and sat me by her in one of the front rows of the auditorium, gave me a little candy from her purse. It was a clear crystal candy that looked like a big diamond, and I, who never turned down a bite of food, even from a stranger, because who knew when I'd next be offered something to eat, unwrapped the crisp cellophane while she twisted her head to scan the crowd as if she had any idea who my father was or what he looked like. Maybe she was simply looking for a man who looked panicked, which my father, who had no idea I was here, of course, would not likely be. I sucked on my sweet, strangely comforted now that I had a chair and a guardian to protect me, even if she spoke her words with a German accent.

I was always searching for ladies to look after me in those days. And I wasn't surprised at all when she pulled a comb from her purse and attempted to use it on my hair, saying, "You want to look your best for Herr Schwinn." She adjusted my pink peony hair ornament, while I smoothed my dress. I knew I was pretty, but unkempt, the first an asset, the second not as much.

A man in a uniform, a brown jacket with a strap across it and a black armband and a cap on his head as if he were some kind of military officer, approached the podium to the sounds of loud recorded music. He had a thin face, a thin mustache above his thin, pursed lips, and as he approached he was introduced over a loudspeaker. "Our Gau West leader, Herr Hermann Schwinn!" So this was the man I had to look my best for. Also the man who had signed the little book in my pocket.

The auditorium erupted in even greater applause, and it wasn't until the crowd had stopped clapping that I could make out what Herr Schwinn was saying. An announcement. Somebody important was coming to Los Angeles, Duke Carl Eduard of Saxe-Coburg-Gotha, to the picnic grounds of Hindenburg Park in La Crescenta, where there would be a big rally to raise funds for the Fatherland! The audience cheered. Herr Schwinn raised his hands importantly and then lowered them to quiet the crowd. A magician. He took some papers from his pocket. He was giving a speech. So this was not a show, but a lecture. No singers, no dancers, no Robert Taylor or Norma Shearer. My father was here for a lecture? He might as well be painting houses.

It took me a while, but slowly I began to understand what Herr Schwinn was saying. It had something to do with all those pamphlets on the tables. The official was giving a speech about Hollywood. About Jews. And I shrank down in my seat as if I'd been found out. The German woman smiled at me, thinking me a bored, squirming child.

"The Jews own all the newspapers. We know their names. Their names are not a mystery. Annenberg. Newman. Meyer. Stein. And the Jews not only own the newspapers, they also control the radio and the telegraph. We know their names, too. Paley. Sarnoff. Jews! All of them Jews. And the Jews monopolize all the movies and the theaters. Ninety-seven percent ownership! Mayer. Cohn. Lasky. Warner. Laemmle. Loeb. Goldwyn. Jewish producers! Jewish picture directors! Jewish actors! The film industry employs thousands of Jews and absorbs its share—and more—of Jewish refugees. How is a star born? Ask the Hollywood Jew who owns one!" Herr Schwinn paused here, reluctantly, to allow for the applause.

I knew what he said was true, at least about the thousands of Jewish refugees. The offices of the Writers Building and the Music Department were chockablock, my mother had told me, with all the Jews fleeing Hitler's Germany, their serious novels and important play scripts and brilliant sheet music all packed up in a hurry in their suitcases and floated across the Atlantic until they washed up here onto these desks, where the Jews sprang open the suitcase locks and set to work translating their sentences from German to English, and changing our motion pictures from nothing much into a lot of something. From drivel to masterpieces. From silents to talkies, the Jews giving all the actors something interesting to say.

But the first things the Jews created in the new world were new names for themselves. Cover stories. Everybody at the studios, whether they were composers, directors, or writers, got rid of their clunky eastern European names tout de suite. And the actors, especially the actors, changed their names immediately upon arrival at the studios. First thing they did, even before the requisite glamour head shot. Kiesler, Levy, Garfinkle, Hesselberg, Loewenstein. Not anymore. Goldenberg became Lamarr, the rest of them Goddard, Garfield, Douglas, Lorre, and Robinson. Did

Herr Schwinn know this, too? After all, this was Los Angeles, so who knew what was real and what was fake? Even my mother had changed her name, from Dorothy Wolfkowitz to Dina Wells. No one was supposed to know who we really were, what we really were. Because of this, perhaps. Because of Americans like Herr Schwinn.

Herr Schwinn raised his hands and lowered them again. "Hollywood is the modern-day Sodom and Gomorrah, where international Jewry controls vice, dope, gambling. A Jew is not an American. He is not a white man. He is a foreigner! He is a Jew, a peculiar, special creature of his own who stands out and apart. He is a parasite! Christian vigilantes arise! Boycott the movies!"

And at this point he looked right at me and repeated, "Rise up against the parasite," and then he gestured at me, waved me to come forward, to come to him, and the woman next to me said, "Go on, honey, he wants you up there," and she pulled me to my feet, gave my back a little push, and I walked, mesmerized, toward Herr Schwinn, who smiled down at me and motioned to his brownshirts to help me up the stairs to the stage. The brownshirts smiled at me, proudly, affectionately, and lifted me up to Herr Schwinn, who took me protectively in his arms and brought me around the front of his swastika-bedecked podium. "Hollywood is dominated by aliens who wreck bodies and souls in a mad lust for destructive power over Gentiles. This," he said, his hands on my shoulders, "this is who we must protect, this child, our children, our *kleine kinder,* blood ripe for the dark parasite. The Jew is a rat. And we must cleanse this city of him!"

I spotted my father then, just for a second, standing up, looking at me, his mouth open at the sight of Schwinn's *kleine kinder,* but then he was lost to me as the audience stood, too, one hysterical body emitting its applause, the woman who had found me applauding, too, nodding and smiling at me, her little adopted

Aryan, so carried away was she and the rest of them by the words of Herr Schwinn. I wish I could say I wasn't thrilled by the applause, by the standing ovation, by all those adults cheering for me, looking at me, but I was. I was thrilled, supremely thrilled, and I bowed my head modestly even though I didn't feel the least bit modest, even though I was a shameless little fraud. I felt fervently alive. And I understood that this fever was what my mother so doggedly sought, the spark that lit it the blind love offered up by an audience, any audience.

And now having made the acquaintance of that red-hot flicker, I would from that moment on begin to seek it myself. What other explanation could there be for my having ended up on a Las Vegas stage strutting beads, sequins, netting, and feathers? Is there any more obvious a plea, Look at me? It was only years later that I wondered what my father thought when he saw me, implausibly, impossibly, up there on that stage of the Deutsches Haus, wearing my mother's clothing, which had to look ridiculous on me, smiling at the misguided adulation of my audience.

But my reign as perfect Aryan child did not last long. Because even as those hundreds of people stood and screamed for me, I saw a group of men peel themselves from the pack hemmed in by chairs and rush at the stage, fists raised, knuckles gleaming ferociously, metallic and alien, ruining my moment, stealing my moment from me, and one of those men was my father.

But I lost sight of him as quickly as I'd found him again as other men ran in from the back of the hall, where they too had been waiting for Mickey Cohen's signal, and still more entered from the doors at either side of the auditorium, baseball bats and iron pipes in their hands, which they raised as soon as they crossed the threshold and began brandishing over their heads like batons. Or like Nazi thugs.

All these men, who had seemed to me to look no different

at all from the men in the audience, began to swing their bats
and pipes at the brownshirts lined up so impeccably before the
proscenium. Down went the brownshirts like bowling pins. Herr
Schwinn and I were hustled hurriedly off the stage by one of his
flag men, while the other two used their flags to poke and flail
at the backs of the intruders. To no avail. The intruders simply
climbed up onto the stage and whaled away at the brownshirts,
beating at them with their bats and pipes and wrenching their
puny flagpoles from them. One man's teeth flew out of his mouth
before he spun and fell to the stage floor, a spray of blood following his teeth.

It was then my father climbed onto the stage, calling my name,
"Esme! Esme!" brass knuckles on his right hand, right hand red
with blood. He looked panicked—and exhilarated. I called to
him, which was like yelling into a storm. Within the circle of his
men, Herr Schwinn tucked me under his arm. While I watched
from my vantage point, I saw the men kicking and punching Herr
Schwinn's men until their knees bent the wrong way and as they
toppled, they were kicked and rolled off the end of the stage onto
the prone bodies of their brothers. Despite their military attire,
Herr Schwinn's men didn't really seem to know how to fight. My
father, I could see, was not very good at fighting, either, but his
eyes were locked on me now as he pushed, kicked, and shoved his
way across the stage toward me in the stage wing.

Mickey Cohen, the ex-boxer, standing in the center aisle down
in the auditorium, knew exactly how to fight, as did his minions.
Even though Cohen was wearing a suit, it seemed not to con-
strain him in the slightest. His burly arms swung about so quickly
they seemed to send his fists in eight cartoon-blurred directions
at once and wherever his fists went, men fell. He seemed not even
to move: he stood like a boulder, while men crashed against him
and bounced off him into the folding chairs all around, which

collapsed and splintered, the Germanic orderliness of the auditorium set all askew.

My father had told me once that Mickey Cohen had been put in a jail cell with someone who hated Jews; Cohen had beaten him senseless, then sat there calmly reading a newspaper until the guard came by. That guard should see him now. Some of the brownshirts down on the ground by the stage had rallied, scrambled to help each other up, a few of them trying to run up the aisle to the front doors but running into Mickey Cohen instead, as if they were blind or The Jew Boy was invisible, others of them pushing futilely at the men with the bats and bars.

The audience, including my surrogate mother, screaming all this time, now tried to flee along the side aisles in a great stampede after the retreating pack of brownshirts, some bulldozing their way directly through the chairs, devising an impromptu emergency exit route right up through the scattered rows. I saw one man climb onto a chair and begin kicking at everybody who ran by him, and then others began to hoist the wooden chairs up in the air and crack them over the heads of anybody they could reach. A pair of eyeglasses flew my way. A hat. A man's shoe. I heard myself whimper. A man big as a refrigerator crashed through the line of seats right by the stage's proscenium.

And then my father reached me and Schwinn's men flattened and scattered and Schwinn himself cowered, using me as a shield to deflect the mighty blow he anticipated would shortly, very shortly, come his way. But no such blow arrived. My father simply snatched me from Schwinn's grasp, spit, and dragged me like a laundry bag out from the wings and down the short set of stairs at the side of the stage and up the side of the auditorium. While what was left of the audience squalled around us, up on the stage the intruders busied themselves disassembling the rally's various props. The banners were pulled to the floor of the stage, the sculptural swastika knocked flat. Then stomped on. Within ten minutes, the auditorium had emptied of most of the able-bodied and left to it were the plenteous injured and moaning. A siren sounded in the distance, coming down Figueroa. More sirens.

This evening may have destroyed the hall but it would somehow right my father, help him find a place set apart from the peddlers of Boyle Heights he despised, law-abiding men who were content to sell shirts, furs, and scrap metal—or paint houses—patiently waiting while their children went to school and became doctors and lawyers, who then moved up to the new postwar subdivisions in the Valley, the vast new housing tracts from which Jews were not restricted from buying a home, leaving Boyle Heights a ghost town of elderly Jews and my grandfather's Breed Street shul a dilapidated monument to a vanished era. No, his new buddies from Schwartzman's bar—Cohen, Rothman, Shaman, like Lansky, Siegel, and Stein—were not interested in sacrificing themselves for the next generation, not interested in being left behind, not interested in timidity.

Mickey Cohen, business finished in the center aisle, jumped up onto the stage, grabbed the microphone off the podium, and faced what remained of the battered audience, blood all over his face and his suited shirtfront. His amplified voice filled the auditorium: "Anybody who says anything against Jews gets the same treatment. Only next time it will be worse for you bastards. Spread the word."

And then he reached into his bloody suit pocket and held up a pistol, waved it like a flag before discharging it directly into the framed portrait of the Führer, the auditorium filling with the gun's banging retort. Hitler stared out of the picture with a bullet hole in his head.

The police sirens wailed at the front of the building, the red lights of the police cars made a dizzying circuit of the auditorium, and The Jew Boy was calling to his men, "We gotta scram!"

My father and I ducked through a side door, my father in his hurry practically lifting me into the air like a kite, my mother's sandals flying off my feet, as he ran and I flew, a dark cobbled-together mess of sweat and panic, streaking through the alley behind Fifteenth Street toward our Cadillac, dark and still, an island away from the chaos we'd caused.

Our ride home was made in silence. What I had seen was too fantastic to be approached by language. But as we left downtown and drove northeast to Boyle Heights, my father began to laugh, to pound on the steering wheel, to look at me with bemused disbelief, and then he made me solemnly promise I would tell my mother none of what had happened tonight.

And that was the first of my father's many gigs for Mickey Cohen, for which he was always paid handsomely and always in cash. Mickey Cohen carried with him a fat roll of thousands of dollars wherever he went. And this gig led, eventually and inexorably, to others, and finally to our trip out to Las Vegas in Benny Siegel's coupe in 1945, and from there, to our life now, such as it was.

LAS VEGAS
1951

31

I DIDN'T KNOW BACK then at the Deutsches Haus what Herr Schwinn was talking about when he ranted about international Jewry, about vice, money, and motion pictures. But I understood it better in 1951. And I suppose you could say that Estes Kefauver of 1951 was just a new version of, a more respectable incarnation of, Schwinn, circa 1939. Kefauver's rant was the same as Schwinn's—Jews, vice, money, Jews, foreigners, parasites, gangsters—minus mention of the motion pictures.

For months, Nate had been dodging subpoenas to appear before Senator Kefauver's hearings on organized crime conducted in St. Louis, in Kansas City, in Chicago, in Philadelphia, in Cleveland, New Orleans, and Detroit. Nate even dodged Kefauver's big day in Las Vegas itself, but eventually Nate and his lawyer decided that since the Kefauver tour looked as if it would never stop, with further dates in Miami, New York, and Washington, in fifteen cities all across the country, Nate might as well appear in Los Angeles, a place out of sight of Vegas and the uncomfortable local publicity that would accompany such an appearance here. Los Angeles was a reasonable distance away and the hearings there were set on a date that was not in the middle of a brutal summer. And so Wilbur Clark, Moe Dalitz, and some of the other Desert Inn crew, who had also been subpoenaed, drove out with Nate to the coast.

All he'd done, Nate assured me as he was packing, was a little bootlegging back when he lived in Detroit, transporting liquor across Lake Erie with his buddies, the group of them dubbed the Jewish Navy and Lake Erie dubbed the Jewish Lake, and with that bootlegging money he'd bought some nightclubs and a wide array of legitimate businesses of interest to any legitimate businessman. But there was something in his voice, the slightest *ping* of mendacity. A legitimate businessman. I knew this was what he wanted to be, what he would try to impersonate, for the rest of his life. So obviously he thought my brain was as childlike as my face. Which was fine. The less he knew about what went on in there, the better.

Because I knew only some of what Nate and all the men I knew like him had done was legitimate. And everything legitimate had been funded by money that wasn't, money from liquor and gambling. But the former was legal now, the latter legal here. Legitimate businessman. Maybe. Maybe now.

But I said nothing.

And Nate said, "Don't watch me on television, Esme. You don't need to see all this."

But, of course, I did watch him. I ate breakfast in the DI coffee shop (where I knew every hostess, every waitress, every busboy, every cook, just as my father had once known every man and woman who worked Hollywood Park) and I watched every minute of Nate's appearance before the Kefauver committee on organized crime on the coffee shop television. My father even came over to join me, taking advantage of Nate's absence to visit me here at the hotel, the one place on the Strip he avoided in order to avoid the man who had gobbled up his daughter whole. Wolf. Wolf with a cock.

But today Nate was gone from the DI and from the desert at large, and my father was here and we watched together the

televised Senator Estes Kefauver, with his big black spectacles
and his many assistants and his stenographers and his piles of
papers and records and recorded testimonies, holding court at
the Federal Building in downtown L.A., not all that far from
Boyle Heights—or from the Deutsches Haus, for that matter.
Nate told me he'd heard that Kefauver carried with him in addition to all his paperwork, his constant requests for girls. The
minute he arrived in a new city, he'd cry, "Get me a girl," Kefauver as promiscuous as any goon, even as he was sharpening his
pencils to hone in on American crime in all its various permu-
tations. And who was supposed to supply him with that girl but
the very goons Kefauver was in Los Angeles to grill, someone
like, say, a Ben Siegel?

Because Ben had always run brothels in Los Angeles, and, of
course, as my father and I found out later and so disastrously, the
concomitant abortion parlors. Even Mr. Mayer had visited Ben's
whorehouses, and when he did, he had the place emptied of all
other customers so it would be just him and the ladies, flowers
waiting to be picked. Yes, even the lion of Hollywood needed sustenance, the particular sustenance provided by a young, beautiful woman, a sustenance I would come to learn all men needed,
though for different reasons, especially powerful men, who sometimes lost their heads in search of it or searched more safely for
it on the screen. And when we came out to Vegas, Ben brought
the business with him, though I hadn't known it then, install-
ing at the Flamingo cigarette girls or hatcheck girls or cocktail
waitresses or showgirls, girls who, when summoned, disappeared
discreetly down the various unsupervised wings of the hotel. All
this was done quietly, of course, with circumspection, through a
word to the bellhops or the valets or the pit bosses or the bartenders, the quiet aside, "Get me a girl," which was another reason my
father never wanted me out there on the casino floor.

It seemed this morning I knew every man who made an appearance on that coffee shop television, all of them men from Hollywood, many of whom had then gone to Las Vegas, as we had, men who had taught me how to play stud poker ("Make it a shutout, little girl. Don't let 'em score a single point.") or who brought me flowering orchids, the pots wrapped with big cheap bows, or who had me run to the kitchen for another slice of cake when they were having a meeting in the Flamingo's offices or who said, "Baby E, be a good girl and go tell Gus Greenbaum I'm here," men who ran the hotels and the casinos and the counting rooms and the nightclubs I called home. Men whose names I'd been hearing my whole life were being subpoenaed and were sitting at tables before microphones, where they dodged questions or pled the fifth, Frank Costello, Joe Sica, and most familiar of all, Mickey Cohen, who had dressed himself in an elegant bespoke suit—I believe by now he owned his own haberdashery—a suit that camouflaged to some degree his burgeoning weight.

When he had fought as The Jew Boy, he had been small and thin, but now he was middle-aged, thickset, thicker than I remembered, his chin and jowls too ample. What would he think of me, now, also changed, Baby E all grown up, too big to sit on his lap anymore, too big to let win at cards, too big to be presented with a cellophane box he'd hold behind his back, making me jump for it, a box from his very own Michael's Greenhouses, a box I would recognize at once? Within the plump innards of the box would be nestled a big peony wrist corsage, all blowsy pink, my favorite flower and favorite color, as Mickey, of course, knew very well.

"Would you like this, Baby E?" And he would wink at me.

As answer, I would grab at the corsage, "Oh, oh, oh," and slide it immediately on my wrist, Mr. Cohen beaming at my pleasure.

But Mickey wasn't being questioned today about corsages. He

was being questioned about illegal gambling and tax evasion, and when he opened his wallet and showed Kefauver the $287 inside the leather folds, saying this was all the money he had in the world, he was broke, dead broke, and had to borrow from friends, my father pounded the coffee-shop table with his fist until his eggs shook and the silverware clanged, laughing at Mickey's bravado. But when Cohen was eventually indicted and sent to jail, as he would be within a few years, it would be for not paying taxes on that $287 and its remaining unreported brothers. My father finished pounding the table and sipped at his coffee, but had to put his cup down when, a minute later, Mickey told the senator that if he so much as spit on the street, it made the front page, and both the coffee shop and the televised courtroom erupted with laughter.

What was it about the public and about Hollywood that so liked the spectacle of mobsters, applauded their theatricality both in its films and outside them?

The actor George Raft had been close to Benny. Hollywood people were always guests at Ben's parties in Beverly Hills. Benny's membership at the Hillcrest Country Club—a country club!, albeit a country club for Jews—had been sponsored by two Hollywood moguls. Harry Cohn was such good friends with the murderer Johnny Roselli that he never had labor trouble at Columbia. Maybe Hollywood saw itself in these men, brothers who'd taken different paths but came from the same place, outliers hacking out their own routes in the American wilderness, like any pioneer, rough and tumble, furious with the obstacles in their paths, utterly determined and ambitious, making themselves kings of their own empires if they couldn't rule the empires already in place.

By lunchtime, Allen Smiley, in handcuffs, was carted out from prison where he had been rendered unable, unlike Nate, to skirt a subpoena. I knew Allen because he had been Benny Siegel's best friend and the two of them were always together in Los Angeles, where they held court at the Brown Derby restaurant. And when he sat down at the long witness table, my father said, "I never liked Al Smiley," which surprised me because my father had always been so congenial around him and because while my father and Benny discussed business, Mr. Smiley would make a quarter appear and disappear between his fingers for my entertainment.

Mr. Kefauver's assistant, Downey Rice, started the questioning, and he first wanted to know Smiley's exact name, his Russian name, which was not Smiley, but Smihoff, which was established as a Jewish name, the Smihoffs immigrants from Kiev, because the first thing the Kefauver committee always did was establish the ethnicity of the person being questioned, usually Jewish, sometimes Sicilian, less often Irish. Implication: somehow not really American. Mr. Smiley, which was how I still thought of him, did everything he could not to answer any questions, but eventually he agreed that Meyer Lansky and Moe Sedway and Moe Dalitz were associates of his.

Then he was asked about the night Benny died, about a long distance telephone call he had made to Las Vegas before he and Benny left their Santa Monica restaurant and drove to Virginia Hill's house, the house where Benny was killed while Smiley sat beside him on the sofa.

> RICE: Think back to June 20, 1947, when you were at the restaurant and see if you can think of making any telephone calls.
> SMILEY: I'm quite certain I didn't make any telephone calls.
> RICE: There is some indication that there was a telephone call made to Las Vegas just shortly before that. Do you know anything about that?

SMILEY: I am sure I did not make it because if it was a long
distance telephone call I would have more reason to remember it.
RICE: You are certain you made no long distance telephone
calls to Las Vegas that night at all?
SMILEY: I am certain I did not.

After the murder, Smiley testified he immediately gave over
his interests in the Flamingo to Gus Greenbaum, saying he didn't
care anymore about the place, that it could have burned up for
all he cared, and even I, sitting here at my coffee shop table, four
years after the fact, could see that Kefauver was implying that
Allen had traded his shares of the Flamingo and even Benny himself to save his own life, and that perhaps he hadn't even known
for sure until Ben's assassins finished their nine shots and had
vanished down Linden Drive that he himself wouldn't be next
despite the deal that he'd made. And that's when I understood
that after Smiley made his call to Vegas, someone in Vegas had
made another call—who?—and the culmination of all those calls
was that Ben was killed within the hour and that's why my father
didn't like Al Smiley, even if my father hadn't said a word about
him to me since Benny died in 1947.

My father had stopped eating and so had I.

Waitresses were taking orders on their pads, busboys were
clearing tables and ferrying glasses of water and cups of coffee,
guests were eating and leaving, eating and leaving. My father ordered a piece of pie, another coffee. He was wearing a new gold
pinkie ring, clunky enough to be ostentatious and monogrammed
with a fancy S with an arrow etched through it, Ike Silver, cupid?
Ike Silver, archer? or whatever that meant, and one of the nice silk
suits he'd taken to dressing in since his promotion to box man.

By the time my father finished his cherry pie, Nate appeared
at the long wooden table where those compelled to testify were

asked to sit, microphone before him, attorney next to him, Nate's legs crossed comfortably, elegantly, as he reclined in his wooden chair, relaxed and smiling his genial, appealing smile, appearing sanguine, his thick silky black hair slicked straight back and flattened with some kind of industrial-strength shellac. He had removed his signet ring, which he and all the men I knew wore, the better to show the senator and company that he was not like Ben Siegel or Mickey Cohen or Allen Smiley or my father. And though Nate appeared on this small screen, Nate's appearance on any screen at all, where usually stars like Clark Gable or Gary Cooper appeared, seemed to conflate him with those men. This was a performance, and though Nate had watched me perform many times, this was my first time to watch him.

Mr. Kefauver himself led the questioning, which made me understand that Nate was considered a big catch, not a little guppy like Allen Smiley, tossed to the assistant, Mr. Rice. Well, surely I already knew this, but still, it made me nervous enough to put down my fork.

> KEFAUVER: You got your start from rum running, didn't you, back in the old Prohibition days? You got yourself a pretty little nest egg out of rum running, wouldn't you say?
> NATE: *(shades of Mickey Cohen)* Well, Senator, I didn't inherit any money.

Certainly not. Not from that father stealing checks out of mailboxes. My father frowned. If he'd enjoyed Mickey's cheekiness, he wasn't enjoying Nate's.

And then Nate was asked about a dizzying number of clubs I had never heard of, the implication being these were gambling clubs, clubs not only in Detroit, but also in New York and Miami and Kentucky, so many clubs that Nate had run or had a percentage in over the past thirty years, clubs that must have housed secret gambling rooms just as the Bacon Club with its two-way mirrors and men with machine guns and mountains of cash had been hidden inside Mickey Cohen's Clover Club, where my mother ended up dancing in late 1939. And Nate was asked not only about clubs, but about racetracks, horse tracks and dog tracks, and hearing the jumble of names and dates made me realize all over again and with a jolt how much older than I Nate was and how long, how many decades, he had been running what all the men I knew called "joints."

> KEFAUVER: Have you ever been investigated regarding your interests in any of these clubs or illegal casinos in this country over the last thirty years?
> NATE: I don't recall.
> KEFAUVER: You don't recall any investigations in thirty years?
> NATE: No, sir.

And I heard in his voice that *ping*.

There were then questions about the many different kinds of businesses Nate had owned, from which I slowly understood Kefauver believed Nate had funneled all the money garnered from that illegal gambling, hence all the surveillance and auditing and examination, as Kefauver noted, of Nate's tax returns for the past two decades or more.

> KEFAUVER: Do you own or have you ever owned the Mason Brothers Plumbing in Pittsburgh, the Southland Meat Supply in Chicago, the Mills Valley Ironworks in Pennsylvania, the Central Hardware and Maintenance in Michigan, the Kildare Catering Company in Ohio, the Tent Taxi Service in Kentucky, the Prince Paper Supply in Miami?

NATE: No.

KEFAUVER: So you had no investments in any of these enterprises?

NATE: I was an investor, yes, but I did not own them and had no control of their operations.

KEFAUVER: May I remind you that you are under oath.

NATE: I do recall that.

There were questions to Nate about investments in larger enterprises like railroads and oil companies and various banks and realty firms, and I understood that Nate was much, much wealthier than I knew, with businesses all over the country, that his interests stretched far, far beyond the perimeters of Las Vegas Boulevard, the perimeters of which might be the perimeters of my provincial world, but not his. Not at all.

Then Nate was asked about his relationships with Mickey Cohen, Lucky Luciano, Frank Costello, Meyer Lansky, Gus Greenbaum, Moe Sedway, and Tony Cornero, all of whom I knew and I knew Nate knew, even though he said he had never met most of them, *ping ping ping*, and finally Nate was asked to account for how he came into his controlling interest in the Desert Inn.

KEFAUVER: How much money did you put in to start with?

NATE: One hundred thousand dollars.

KEFAUVER: What percentage of the company did you receive for your investment?

NATE: Thirty percent.

KEFAUVER: *(incredulously)* For a hundred-thousand-dollar investment?

NATE: Yes, sir.

KEFAUVER: Do you draw a salary from the Desert Inn?

NATE: I don't as yet, no.

Slowly, patiently, Kefauver determined that not only did Nate draw no salary, he was also paid no dividends. Implication: he profited somehow, illegally, from the gambling revenue. From the skim. Legitimate income, legitimate businessman? Not to Kefauver and his fellows.

My father had put down his fork, too, to better listen. "There's a lot of money flowing into the counting rooms, now, E, a lot of drug money. More than when Benny was alive."

Drugs. A new medium for these old bootleggers and one even more profitable than liquor had ever been. And apparently, over the last eight years, the trafficking had gotten somewhat more sophisticated than Benny's carting those bags of baby powder over the border in his roadster.

My father, pushing his pie plate away, told me how Mr. Lansky had seemingly endless suitcases of drug money coming in via bagmen, bearing the profits from his networks in Mexico and Turkey and Marseilles, profits swept into the credit cages and from there out into the casinos and through the counting rooms, where the managers kept watch over all the bills and coins and where they kept two sets of books, a clean book that tracked dollars coming in and going out—some for the casino, some for the government, those dollars going back out into the world again, clean—and then the other book, the real book, that recorded everything, including the secret dollars going in and out via bagmen to Lansky, to be apportioned to everybody who really mattered to these men all across the country—the routine division of this money performed out of sight in the counting room three times a day at the end of every shift, cameras turned off.

I watched Nate step delicately around all these questions, unruffled, perfectly comfortable, polite, until he was asked about his involvement in the murder of a Detroit city councilman in the early thirties, before I was born, that councilman about to reveal, in Kefauver's words, "some crooked deals" in which Nate was involved, this councilman killed by a man Nate shared the company of just a few hours before the murder, an involvement in which Nate vociferously denied.

And then, finally, Kefauver asked about a club Nate had owned in Detroit. Ten men had robbed the backroom of that club, and all ten men were killed, one by one, over the next year. And Nate said he didn't know anything about that. Sir.

Half a dozen other men were questioned next, refusing to answer questions directly, laughing at their own jokes, declining to acknowledge misdeeds or crimes or to be shamed by these men in suits, the establishment's inquisitors they faced across the table. They would not bow and scrape, these men who had, by hook or by crook, chased a caper, a scheme, an opportunity. I could only imagine my grandfather's face if he had been watching these hearings with us. I wondered what my own looked like. I could see my father's.

When the waitress came by to ask if we wanted more coffee, my father said no, and he asked her to turn off the television set.

I understood now why Nate hadn't wanted me to watch him on television. It wasn't so much that he didn't want me to see who he was as that he didn't want me to see the disdain with which Kefauver and the rest regarded him and his kind, and by extension, my father and me. I might not be fully literate, I might read with the sounding-out stumble of a first-grade child, but I could understand exactly what was happening that day. These men, the Cohens and Smihoffs and Steins, were being hung on a cross-continental clothesline where they flapped and preened and joked and bragged about themselves before this senator and this committee and the press. They were defiant. Unrepentant. Disingenuous. They might be enjoying the big show they were putting on, but I understood the contempt with which the Senator and the larger country saw us Jews—as foreign and venal and corrupt. And these men were.

LOS ANGELES
1939

32

WHEN MY FATHER WENT to work now, that summer of 1939 after the big brawl at the Deutsches Haus, he was all purpose and energy. But stuck home with my bed-besotted mother, I was as aimless and out of sorts as she. I would sit outside on the street curb in the late afternoons, waiting for my father to come home and break this monotony, wearing one of my mother's nightgowns and a thick cuff of her bracelets, too miserable even to play with my limp-haired doll in the summer Los Angeles heat, which was so flat and so merciless it drove even the insects into the ground.

I could clearly see the Hollywoodland sign when I looked northwest to Mount Lee. It had never seemed so far away. The Santa Ana winds blew in from the desert, making the city oven-warm and dry and blinding it with sunshine, igniting fires, making the city a place where nobody was ever sick, where a body just wore out, eventually, from all that heat and light, like a piece of paper. I thought of my parents as pieces of paper, too, flapping in that hot wind. Which way would they blow—would my mother fly back up to the roof, my father be swept into the alley?

So I was there to see my father pull up in our green Cadillac, hat tipped back on his head, attired in one of his crisply pressed new suits, one of a dozen new expensive suits, bought in imitation of Mickey Cohen who was himself assiduously imitating

Ben Siegel's sartorial splendor, knowledge of which Ben was busy acquiring from his paramour of the moment, the fifty-year-old Countess di Frasso, whom he referred to as his "fancy lady." The one who came before his painted lady, Virginia. The two had met at Santa Anita, L.B. Mayer's Stage 14, and whatever Ben had subsequently learned from her about class and style was passed from one mobster to another, all the way down the totem pole, and it had, apparently, made its way now to the very bottom spot occupied by my father, who jumped out of our freshly washed and waxed Cadillac to tell me, "Look what I've got for your mother." With a wink, he pulled a leather box from his jacket pocket and opened it to show me a diamond ring. And it wasn't the one he had pawned last month, either.

I looked up at him.

"It's a bigger one," my father said. "Close your mouth. Mickey Cohen pays a lot better than Sy Wolfkowitz Painting Co."

The diamond was three times the size of the other, four times the size of it, with a circle of diamonds winking all round it, the ring I've inherited and still have and keep locked in the hotel vault, a dozen years later. It dazzled me that day. As I've said, we Silvers like all that glitters. I was dazzled but I was a child, a real Baby E, so it didn't occur to me that my father must be doing more for Cohen than taking bets on the Culver City dog track to have earned that kind of money.

"Just wait till your mother gets a load of this," my father said with one of his great grins, the grin of possibility, as if he could see great good luck stepping her way in her high heels right around the corner.

Little as I was, I knew that with a diamond that size my father just might be able to lure my mother from her bed and back to the land of the living in a way all my foot-stamping and arm-pulling and wailing could not. The diamond was proof his fortunes were rising. One of their fortunes had to be on the rise at all times for their marital machinery to clank onward.

"Go on. Go on in and tell your mother," my father told me. "Tell her I've got something special for her and that we're going out."

I ran into the house, into my mother's hushed bedroom, and told her what my father told me to say. The words were like the incantation of a magi. My mother, attired in one of her ice-green movie-star negligees—even in a slump, she looked camera-ready—rose groggily from the bed and slowly, dreamily, brushed her hair. Come on, I thought, but I didn't say it. Hurry up. It was impressive enough that she'd actually gotten out of bed, as if she'd been waiting for this, for something to get up for. And, luckily, it appeared she remembered how to stand. And walk. And put on lipstick. "Where is he?" she asked me. Finally.

I gestured. Out there.

He was at the open front door, kneeling on one knee on the uneven, cracked concrete porch and holding out the ring in a posture I fully approved of. My mother screamed when she saw that big diamond ring, shoved her finger into it, and held it up to the big flat sun in the flat sky, the better to make it sparkle, and I didn't hear her ask a single question about where it had come from or what he'd done to afford it. Nor was there one word about her old ring. If it had been offered up with a tear in that pawnshop, that tear, her whole torrent of tears, was now forgotten. As was that ring. And this wasn't all my father had brought her. He'd brought her an offer, a nightclub lounge act all her own.

Mickey Cohen and Ben Siegel were in the process of taking over the Clover Club, a nightclub up on what was then the somewhat desolate unincorporated Sunset Strip, which was soon to flower in a way my mother didn't live to see, but my father and I did. To come were Ciro's, the Trocadero, the Mocambo, the Chateau Marmont, Sunset Tower, the Players Club, the Garden of

Allah, Club Gala. La Rue's. At this point, though, there was just the Clover Club.

The Clover was a deliciously beautiful place with red lacquered doors and white tablecloths, with secret panels, one-way mirrors, and a backroom illegal casino called the Bacon Club, where men with machine guns watched over the players and the money. The bacon. This was a club where photographers weren't allowed, where David O. Selznick and Budd Schulberg gambled each night, a club Cohen and Siegel were in the process of wrestling from its owners, whereby Mr. Siegel had charged Mickey with wrecking one by one all of their gambling operations. Just as later Benny would later muscle Billy Wilkerson out of his interests in the Flamingo, so now Benny took over the Clover Club. And my mother got her gig.

As my father said that night, "If you're a live performer, baby, then here's your venue."

And at this, my mother whooped again, her malaise of the last weeks thrown off like a useless plaster cast. By this time my father was swinging my mother around on the front lawn, one of his arms about her waist, her bare feet nowhere near the ground, big setting sun now their enormous backlight, while I jumped around them clapping my hands, the two of them loving each other, and all was once again marvelous.

33

AND WHEN WE WALKED down South Broadway later that night to celebrate, the street made a white circus against the black sky, the stars and the streetlights a million colored filaments, as raucous as the Las Vegas Strip at midnight, which hadn't yet been invented. Broadway was our Strip, trolley cars on the rails running down the center of the avenue, automobiles north and south at either side of the tracks, the sidewalks crowded with men in summer suits and white straw hats with striped bands like my father's, older men in dark fedoras like the ones my grandfather used to wear. Women of all ages wore stockings and heels, their hats big or small, plain or pinned with false flowers, their hair curled and bouncing at their shoulders, but no matter what they did or wore, none of them was as pretty as my mother, who, black hair swinging and long legs flicking prettily, strolled arm in arm with my father.

I trailed behind them, blinking my eyes a bit at my mother's abrupt transformation. And I could see my father looked at her as if he couldn't quite believe it, either. My mother had been a flat sheath of bones and skin and now she was suddenly revivified, full and fleshy. And all this had been done by a ring and a promise. Occasionally she'd turn around to me and wink, wiggle her ring finger. Most attention she'd paid me in weeks.

We ducked beneath the yellow-and-red canvas awnings over the store windows and past the doors of Loew's State Theatre, once a vaudeville theater and now, like all old vaudeville theaters, a motion picture theater, its big green-and-blue sign protruding above us, an oval thrust into the space of the street itself, glowing neon and promising riches of entertainment within from Jack

Benny and Dorothy Lamour in *Man About Town*, and the Tower
Theatre, its architectural ornaments gold gilded, and the letters

T
O
W
E
R

spelled out vertically in sparkling silver script down the tower
itself, and the big clock, blue-faced and encircled with gold at the
tower's apex, telling the time, a magical nine o'clock, not too early
and not too late, and at this time of the summer, just dusk.

We passed Tally's Theatre and the new Orpheum and Grauman's, the Majestic, the Paramount, the Broadway, the Rialto,
each of them showing movies with Norma Shearer and Greta
Garbo and James Stewart and Clark Gable and William Powell,
all the Hollywood gods and goddesses come down from the heavens just for their fans, none of whom had ever paid any attention
to my mother on the lot, but they would take notice of her now as
she performed for them at the Clover, and beyond those theaters
lay the Western Costume Company, which had outfitted all the
actors in all the movies playing in all those theaters, actors and
dancers like my mother. Or like my mother used to be. Because
now she would be something else. A solo act.

And for the poor people who played only their own parts in
their own regular lives, there was the May Company department
store and the Broadway department store to outfit them.

Eh.

Not for us. Not anymore.

Anything my mother wanted that night, my father bought for
her, and any movie poster she wanted to linger to look at, he

allowed her to look at, telling her she had more beauty in her little finger than any of those goddesses put together. And when she studied the jewelry in Sifton's Jewelers and declared that the ring on her finger was more beautiful than any ring in the window, and for sure it was bigger, my father smiled his big smile, and when she turned to me and said, "Isn't your father wonderful?" that, I could tell, made him feel better than any long shot that ever came in at any horse park in California. They both held out their hands to me. Even now, eleven years later, that night is edged with silver glimmer.

Far away, two radio towers gleamed in the distance, two promises, two scaffolds with the big letters spelling out the call numbers of the station,

K
R
K
D

At night it broadcast Aimee Semple McPherson's Angelus Temple services, in which McPherson would sermonize about Jesus and the Devil as twin airplane pilots, one flying up and the other down. Sometimes McPherson would speak in tongues or heal the sick or the crippled, who right then and there threw away their crutches or stood up from their wheelchairs, which was exactly what my mother had done tonight.

McPherson was a one-woman show, with a team of artists, carpenters, and electricians on her payroll who built her a new set for each Sunday's big production number and with an orchestra who played while she preached. My mother must have been musing over this, gazing at those radio call letters, because she said, "That McPherson. She's a regular Louise B. Mayer. Must be

nice to have your own stage and hire your own help and star in
your own show."

My own exact thought, eleven years later.

And my father stopped in his tracks then and said to her, "Who
needs Mayer, Warner, or Cohn, anyway?"

And before you knew it, we were sitting in a coffee shop, talking
about buying our own club, the Wells, once my mother had become a draw, and then renting offices back in the Hollywood flats
near Paramount Studios, where all the old production companies had set up shop in the teens, a row of storefronts like those
on Brooklyn Avenue in Boyle Heights, except instead of selling
neckties and herring, they had sold short films, silent films, even
talkies. And I would be Wells Pictures's child star, better than
any Shirley Temple.

My mother said, "I'll take her over to Daddy Mack's for some
real dance lessons. She's old enough now."

I sat up straight. My mother was trying to make it up to me
because she knew how much I had wanted to be a child extra in
the "La Conga" number from *Strike Up the Band*. Its catchy lyrics
and trill of congas and maracas would have accompanied me as
I shook my way with all the others in a snake pattern around
the high school auditorium, somebody's little sister. But when my
mother had taken to her bed instead of dancing in *Band*, I didn't
get to dance in it, either.

Now, though, times were changing. And I was going to find my
way to the other side of the camera and enjoy an early start in the
business, like Mickey Rooney and Judy Garland had, pushed by
their mothers onto vaudeville stages at the age of three. Yes, now
that would happen for me, new child star at Wells Pictures, as
soon as there was a Wells Pictures, where my father would have
a desk bigger than Louis B. Mayer's white one up on a pedestal.
Maybe it would be gold! No, silver!

Who were those studio moguls anyway, but men like us with nothing in their pockets but rags and scrap metal and an initial investment in a nickelodeon or a vaudeville house. Adolph Zukor was a Hungarian immigrant who sewed piecework, bought an arcade filled with nickelodeon motion picture machines, and ended up founding Paramount Pictures. L.B. came from Russia, dealt in scrap metal, bought a burlesque house he turned into a movie theater, and ended up with MGM. The Polish Goldwyn sold gloves. Everybody started from nowhere in this business and ended up somewhere big. Why not us? It was our turn.

That night it seemed to us that we could do anything, run our own nightclub for my mother to headline, start our own studio and make our own pictures, drag a ladder over to the Tower and climb it to stick the letters of her name up on the marquee. And mine. E S M E.

By the time we headed back to our car, we already had the whole thing figured out. All we needed was some startup money. And some talent. And because we had my mother and because that night my father's back pocket was bulging with money, plenty more where that came from, wherever it came from, we had it all, and anything was possible.

And when my father retrieved our big green Cadillac from the Auto Park, we all piled into the front seat, listening on the car radio to Artie Shaw, King of the Clarinet and his orchestra, playing "If I Had You," direct from the Blue Room at the Hotel Lincoln in New York City.

> I could be a king, uncrowned,
> Humble or poor, rich or renowned,
> There's nothing I couldn't do,
> If I had you.

My parents sang over the clarinet and the rest of the orchestra as we headed back over the Sixth Street Bridge to Boyle Heights, the Los Angeles River a dry dark slither beneath us, and when they finished the song, they kissed, and my father said, "You've got legs and pipes, baby. You've got it all and I'm going to make a fortune on you." And my mother kissed him and then me, too—St. Petersburgundy!—she was that happy.

And that night, my father did not sleep in the garage on the couch but rejoined my mother in their Art Moderne marital bed, from which, despite my mother's earlier kiss to me, I was unceremoniously booted out.

So I had to spy.

I waited a bit before I went and put my eye to their bedroom door keyhole, expecting to see some kind of glittering spectacle, the bedroom strung with chiffon ribbons and hung with garden swings, silver poles wrapped in great big bows of shining satin, the ceiling and floor turned to mirrors, maybe. Perhaps my father would have changed into a black tuxedo and my mother would have donned a sparkling evening gown and some sparkling dancing shoes. Perhaps a crown. I could hear their voices singing, roaring, and I couldn't wait to see them waltzing perfectly in unison to some beautiful and clever lyrics.

I could leave the old days behind
Leave all my pals, I'd never mind
I could start my life all anew
If I had you.

But, of course, once I knelt and put my eye to the door's old-fashioned keyhole, I didn't see anything like that at all.

LAS VEGAS
1951

34

THE EL RANCHO HOTEL, once Benny's nemesis, looked like an old-school Mexican ranchero, and it stuck stubbornly to its Western roots, no matter what the rest of the Strip had made its mind up to do around it. The hotel had a stucco exterior, with a tower that sported a Texas-style windmill and Western fences that bordered its lawns. In the Nugget Nell cocktail lounge, the name a nod to Nevada mining, rough stone walls stared at a giant roulette wheel hanging upside down in the dome of the ceiling. Ha. Behind the dining-room buffet line, a painted mural featured a chuck wagon out on the Western plains and two cowboys on their horses about to dismount for the chuck. Diners sat in wood-and-leather chairs studded with brass nailheads. The Old West, American, Mexican, or some mixed-up version of the two, for sure.

Nate and I were headed for the showroom, for years called the Round-Up Room, all lassoes and cattle, and only recently and reluctantly renamed, incongruously, the Opera House. The place used to look like a barn with wooden rafters and bundled hay, but now all that was gone. The wood-planked ceiling had been painted over and embellished with sparkling stenciled ribbons scrolling and unscrolling. Everywhere, chandeliers hung and gargantuan vases of floral arrangements stood, both accents looking as if they came from some European court five thousand miles away. Court or opera house. A gilded and carved frame divided the proscenium from the body of the stage proper, as if the events performed upstage were living pictures. To the right lay an alcove for the band, the Carlton Hayes Orchestra, the men and their instruments situated next to and beneath a swell of pleated drapes that matched the inner stage curtains. A second set of exterior curtains sparkled.

We'd always regarded the El Rancho as second-rate, an early forties hotel, pre-Flamingo and pre-everything else new on the Strip. The pool was pitched only a few yards from Highway 91 and its four lanes, where cars whizzed by at sixty miles an hour. But despite its humble design, the El Rancho brought in top talent from Los Angeles. Tonight's lineup was advertised by the highway sign,

THE HOTEL EL RANCHO PRESENTS
JOE E. LEWIS AND LILI ST. CYR
DINING AND DANCING

the sign's lit-up arrow rounding those words in a constant lasso sweep of neon white.

Nate might make regular rounds of all the hotel offices and casinos and construction sites on the Strip, but I liked to make the rounds of its showrooms, see what the Fabulous Flamingo Girls, the El Rancho Dice Girls, the Thunderbird Dansations were up to. He'd laugh at me, "What are you looking for, E, a second gig?," like the second gigs picked up by so many of the Vegas musicians, who played a couple of shows at one hotel lounge and then another two at a different hotel and then, too hopped up to go home to bed, hung out until sunrise in the parking lot of Chuck's House of Spirits, right by the Desert Inn. We'd see them there tonight, when we drove home, forty men in black suits, sitting on their car hoods, on the parking lot curbs, on the one inadequate bench in front of the liquor store, instrument cases turned to makeshift footstools.

Nate might laugh at me, but he liked it, my ambition, my competitiveness, and he encouraged it, went with me to the floor shows when he could. We both of us liked to keep an eye on the horses coming up from behind. And having grown up watching, always watching, this surveillance felt only natural to me. Tonight I wanted to look at Lili St. Cyr, who'd abandoned Minsky's Follies in New York and coasted west, headlining at Ciro's, one of Mickey's clubs on Sunset, back in the Los Angeles from which Nate had just returned.

Nate grinned at me now, wolf, wolf with a cock, as the maître d' seated us, best table, center front, and ordered a bottle of champagne. The bottle would be on the house, as I'd begun to notice since the Kefauver hearings so many things were for Nate—meals, tickets, chips, drinks, golf games, hotel rooms, travel. Every time he shook a hand, I wondered what deal lay behind that handshake, where the money came from and to whom it was transferred and how Nate would stuff that money down some gopher hole the government would never be able to find. And every man Nate talked to or laughed with or drank beside, I squinted at, wondering exactly who he was behind his front as real estate developer or construction contractor or entertainment director or hotel treasurer. Everybody here had a front door and a back. Watching Nate at the hearings, I had a good view of his expansive backyard.

But if I'd expected the hearings to change Nate as they had changed me, they had not. He seemed entirely the same, his usual even-tempered, unperturbable, sanguine self. Whatever bravado he'd shown at the hearing or whatever triumph he felt at having exited that hearing untouched, he concealed from me, saying only, "E, it's good to be home. Let's go to bed, goddammit." Whatever he was out there away from Vegas, whatever he was in the past, here and now, he was someone else, the version of himself he had always wanted to be.

At some point during my third glass of champagne—when I was with Nate, I was always served, even though I was underage—Joe E. Lewis, black bow tie, black tux, and boutonniere, finished joking and striding left and right across the proscenium dragging his standing microphone with him. The house lights dimmed, and the Carlton Hayes orchestra began to play first a jazz number, then something brightly sinuous, and the curtains of the small stage parted.

Lili St. Cyr, her name as complete a fabrication as her set and her act.

She breezed onto the stage to the applause of the audience, radiant, all smiles, as if after a terrific evening out, garbed modestly in a long coat, long gloves, and a rhinestone tiara, which signaled she was playing a lady, the status purposeful as it made the fact that we were going to see her naked just that much more titillating. Her face, though, was the face of a guttersnipe, catlike, narrow and forward thrusted, all cheekbones and black eyeliner, bubble of bleached blond hair rolled into a twist.

She spent a third of her fifteen-minute number just strutting her person about the stage set, a bedroom—what else?—with its dressing screen, oversize bed, cushioned chaise, and candelabra, its sconces fitted with several long unlit yellow candles—it was as if all of MGM's overornamented props for Rich Lady's Bedroom had been removed from storage in the Mill Buildings and trucked east here to be arranged on this stage. Eventually, St. Cyr began to disrobe, because disrobing was what we came to see, the raison d'etre of her particular show and of all burlesque, ceremoniously removing her coat, then her long gloves, so that we could see her bare arms, and eventually, after much delay, her long skirt, so that we could see her stockinged legs. Finally approaching the point of it all, but I could tell the audience did not want her to hurry.

Her long peplum sleeveless top remained on, one more nod to delay, until she faced the audience and let out a wiggle that allowed this last piece of outerwear to drop into her hands. A trick. Beneath that blouse, not bare skin, but a full armament of undergarments that Playtexed her from breasts to thigh. The audience laughed. Her corset sported bra cups as pointed as the wax paper cups from an office water cooler dispenser, the bottom of the costume a lacy frill. She smiled at us, You didn't think I would make it too easy for you, did you?

"I hear she makes a hundred thousand dollars a year from this," Nate said into my ear, his breath as vaporous with alcohol as mine must be.

A hundred thousand dollars a year.

I earned fifty dollars a week as a Donn Arden dancer. Twenty-five hundred dollars a year.

St. Cyr showed us her back now, allowing us a glimpse of her half-bare bottom before covering it with the blouse she still held, a tease as she walked the Donn Arden pelvis-swinging walk I knew so well. At her chaise, she sat and proceeded theatrically, languorously, to remove one shoe, one stocking, the other shoe, the other stocking. All this movement was stylized, long slow gestures nothing like the hysterical shedding of costumes that went on backstage at the Painted Desert Room between numbers, our dressers shrieking at us, "Careful. Don't touch the fabric with your hands!" bending for what we dropped as we stretched out our arms to be inserted into the next number's garb.

There was more walking, so much walking, and then St. Cyr

vanished behind her dressing screen, various of her limbs appearing and disappearing as she discarded her corset, a quick glimpse of the side of her nude body in profile, split vertically by the screen, so we saw one leg, half her back, an arm, a shoulder, the side swell of her bosom. She emerged, finally, in a fluffy robe with a fur collar, hair down, was moved to yawn, arms stretched up to the catwalk, and then she slid into her bed with a draped headboard and a tiara all its own. Once under her shining quilt, she tossed her robe to the chaise. Implication: I'm naked under here.

That was it. And that should be enough for you, just knowing this.

I would come to learn all her numbers were the same—the dressing and undressing, sometimes requiring the assistance of a uniformed, homely maid, the props of a chaise, a black telephone with its long black cord, a parrot, a trapeze, a $7,000 bathtub reported to have once belonged to Napoleon's Josephine, or the impersonation of various historical figures such as Salome and Carmen for further variation—but all of them were versions of this, her signature number—A Woman Alone in Her Boudoir.

I wasn't sure exactly what St. Cyr was. Not a showgirl. Or what her act was exactly. Not a striptease. Not really even burlesque, with its usual brief climactic reveal of pasties and breasts. Which St. Cyr had tried, at Minsky's, with much less success.

Whatever this was, it seemed clear to me that it or something like it was tailor-made for our undersized showroom stages here in Las Vegas, our little jewel boxes much better suited to this than to the tight row of overdressed showgirls we currently stuffed there, the feathers of our headdresses bristling against each other as we struggled to smile. Vegas seemed intent on sowing and reaping these wholesome showgirls, those friendly faces, open smiles, as if to say, gambling is just as wholesome! Come out to Vegas!

But what if our new city proved more fertile ground for a little perversity in its showrooms? Vegas, after all, prided itself on being a narrow bit of vice-rich real estate, an island alone unto itself, unrepentant. An extension of the old Block 16. That's really what people drove all the way out to the desert for. The vice. Legalized vice. As Nate had told Kefauver. And unlike other American cities, with a stable population in need of constant variety, Vegas hosted an incessant stream of visitors from all parts of the country, an ever-changing audience. A nightclub in Vegas could host the same show for months on end, even for years, and still fill every seat. And judging from the volume of applause in the El Rancho's Opera House, that audience would lap up the whiskey of a Lili St. Cyr.

Or of me.

After all, why should St. Cyr have license to come here and do on our stages what I could easily do? I was already here. And I was younger than St. Cyr, prettier, blonder, with longer legs and a dancer's training. St. Cyr looked a bit squat, hard-muscled, somewhat overpainted. I didn't yet look as if the years had run their tracks all over my face. *Life* magazine had just featured a headshot of me, sparkled and feathered, on its cover, "Esme Wells: The Prettiest Showgirl in Las Vegas," that banner emblazoning the bottom of the page. No need to explain why I was selected for the honor.

I didn't want to watch someone else be what I wanted to be, as my mother had, mooning over the Old Mill Buildings on Lot One, where MGM had once made its silent films in the twenties and which now stored every kind of knob, lamp, table, or couch you could possibly want for any picture set in any time period, Mexican pueblo, Louis XIV palace, Andy Hardy house. At lunch breaks, when everybody else went to the Commissary to eat, my mother would shake her head at the other girls and say she was going to have a cigarette first, and she would head around the back of the soundstage with me in hand. "I'm not hungry," my mother would say to me, "are you?" And I, who was, said I wasn't, so as not to disappoint her. "Here. Take a little smoke," my mother would say, "take the edge off," and she'd hold out the cigarette for me, and then she'd lean back against the concrete wall of the soundstage to smoke and gaze at the many glass windows of the Mill Buildings.

She would stare at them so long, I would turn to stare, too. What was she seeing? I would lean against the wall beside her, a little dizzy from the nicotine. The structures were so large and so light-filled, she said, that they could make many movies within them at the same time, each one in a different corner. Inside these glass structures, Greta Garbo had filmed *The Temptress* and Joan Crawford *The Taxi Dancer*, and in the scene where Crawford lay on the floor, weight on her elbows, tossing her hair, the light had glowed on her face, made it soft and white as a petal, and my mother said there was nothing more gorgeous than that, was there? And you didn't have to be quiet making those films because no sound would ever be heard. The directors could shout at you even while the cameras were going, which, given Buzz, maybe wouldn't always be such a good thing. She smiled wryly down at me. If only it were 1925, she said, she knew, with her face, she would be a great star. Crawford, like my mother, had begun her career as a dancer. You could start at one place and end up at another. My mother's article of faith. But it wasn't 1925. It was 1939, and that was the bitter difference.

So here was opportunity, ready to be snatched up by the eager and the game, my opportunity, my chance, and I didn't want to miss it, the way my mother had missed hers, lamenting later and forever her bad timing. And, really, how else was a young woman in 1939 Hollywood or 1925 Hollywood or 1951 Las Vegas to make her fortune but from her face and body. Nothing was forever, as I saw from my own reading of those movie magazines my mother had loved, *Photoplay* and *Movie Stars*, which the hotel lobby shops here kept so well stocked. Like those vanished silent screen stars, Mr. Mayer, I read, had recently been tipped from his white throne at MGM and sent packing. Mickey Rooney made his last Andy Hardy picture in 1946 while my father and I were out here at the Flamingo and sent over to Fox and United Artists. Judy Garland had been trucked unceremoniously from the lot—too many pills and suicide attempts.

Object lesson.

This was what would eventually happen to me. I was twenty. In ten years I'd be thirty. Too old to be a showgirl. Then what? Cocktail waitress at the craps tables. And when I got too old for that, eventually, I'd end up working the graveyard shift hustling drinks at the casino slots, one of the worst gigs in town. No one playing slots tipped well, you had to be in the pit, by the craps or roulette tables for the big money. No, you had to be young and attractive and you had to stash away your money against the day you were told to go totter around the slot machines. Or worse, told to put on sensible rubber-soled shoes and go wait tables in the coffee shop.

Why should St. Cyr get to plant herself here in Vegas and rake in all the profits when I knew Nate could somehow make her contract with the El Rancho—or any other hotel here—disappear and make a contract with my name on it appear in its place. I wasn't going to be on Nate Stein's arm forever, if his marital history was any indication, which was exactly why the shade of Benny Siegel had shaken his head at me so sorrowfully. But while I was still gripping his coat sleeve, I could make use of my position.

"Tell me what you want," Nate was always saying to me. "Tell me what I can give you."

Until now, I had nothing to ask for.

So when the curtains closed on St. Cyr, I turned to Nate. Maybe it was the champagne. Maybe it was the memory of my mother's sigh. But I said to him, "I want to do that."

He blinked at me. What?

I wanted that second gig. With any luck, it would soon be my only.

He didn't like it. But Nate nodded. "Okay, E."

Done. Simple as that.

35

MY FATHER AND I drove over to the brand-new Las Vegas Jockey Club racetrack northeast of the Strip on its opening day in early September just to see the clubhouse, the concourse, the grandstand, all of which I thought we had left behind forever when we left our old Hollywood Park racetrack in Inglewood. Just the sight of the new track going up in the distance had made me homesick for the green-and-black tile of our old concourse, the low-fenced paddock with its saturated green grass where the horses were shown off, up close, a few feet from your hand, before they were led down to the track itself, the old-school oil paintings of horses and jockeys, never of bettors or owners, hung everywhere on the concourse walls, the betting windows that received and delivered the money that drove this whole endeavor. The track's buildings here had been painted a dusty pink, in homage to the famous Hipódromo Rosado racetrack in Buenos Aires, minus the ornate flourishes of its Spanish colonial style or the high-flying Argentinian flag. Like everything else built out here in the desert, we wanted it modern, concrete, clean-lined.

It was hot, of course, because it was September in the desert, 97 degrees, the heat made worse by some bottleneck of a snarl at the parking lot gate, which created a backup of cars that stretched from that misbegotten entrance all the way down to the street and beyond. Nothing was moving, and the survival instinct soon had people climbing from their cars to fan themselves with whatever they had at hand— newspapers, hats, I saw one woman flapping a child's diaper—and as the minutes crept by, plenty of those cars turned around and headed home. But it had been a long time since my father and I had gone to the track, and apparently we had both missed it, and so we were determined to wait, getting in and out of our Cadillac, standing beside it and fanning ourselves with paper maps of California and Nevada we unfolded from the glove compartment, and then jumping back into the car any time there was an opportunity to roll forward a few feet. Yes! We were ridiculously grateful for those few feet!

Eventually, people began walking up the drive, having abandoned their cars at the side of the road, a road we could no longer see, but we were too far up the drive to do that and so we were trapped, inching forward, my father cursing the goddamn miserable heat. And it was true—the heat was terrible, no breeze, just that desert sun like a giant atomic ball of fire in the sky, and while I flapped my paper map and climbed in and out of the car, I worried about the horses who had to race in this heat, just as I had worried about the horses at Hollywood Park during the big Los Angeles rain of 1938, when I'd imagined them swimming, panicked, as the water rose, lifting them from their stables, the swell carrying them up to the Turf Club heights where they'd never been. In this heat, though, the horses wouldn't swim, they'd suffocate instead their stables, stroke out before they came anywhere near the finish line.

And some beautiful Thoroughbreds had been trucked out here to the desert from the balmy, oceanfront Del Mar track to run, prizewinners, horses like Lefty James and Blue Reading, and with them came star jockeys like Tony DeSpirito. Old habit. I still followed the races, quietly, easy enough to do out here, with all the sports books. I wondered if my father did, too. We didn't talk together about the horses anymore.

Once we had finally parked, waved in by one of the sweaty, exhausted uniformed attendants who looked as if they'd been beaten up and probably had been, having fielded a multitude of curses thrown at them by the attendees, curses that could batter you as much as a punch, and once we had gone inside to wander the concourse, to inspect the paddock and the track and its green infield, which did not host a flock of Inglewood flamingoes or any birds at all, for that matter, I opened up my purse. But my father told me, "I don't want to bet today, baby girl. Let's just watch the horses run."

My father didn't want to lay a bet? He never passed up a chance to put down a dollar or two or twenty. I stared at him. He took off his fedora and wiped at his face with his white cotton handkerchief, monogrammed *IS*, black thread against the white. His face was lined now, I saw suddenly and too clearly, as he passed the handkerchief across it. Two deep grooves had impressed themselves into his flesh, the grooves running from the sides of his nose to the corners of his mouth, and the flesh around his mouth and jowls had thickened, perhaps in response. And sometime over the past six years, his hairline had gradually receded both left and right so that now only a peninsula of dark hair remained up top. Why hadn't I noticed this before? Because I rarely saw him by daylight? He put his hat on. I looked down at my hands. Okay. So he didn't want to bet. Because today he was not Magic Ike, Lucky Ike. Or maybe it was because if we'd learned anything from our years in Vegas, from all that my father had seen on the casino floors and in their counting rooms, it was that the house always wins and that everything was a fix.

And today at this track, not only was everything a fix, but also everything was a mess—and not just the parking. Even before the first race, the tote board bearing the odds broke down, its glowing white numbers blinking, vanishing, reappearing, flickering, and then gone for good, and the crowd on the concourse let out a collective moan. While my father went off to buy us hot dogs to take down to the grandstand (my old job!), the machines at some of the betting windows went on the fritz, and I watched as all the high rollers in their summer suits scurried to stand in line with the common man at the one-dollar windows, the big daddies with rolls of fifties and hundreds in their fat impatient hands chocka-block by the low rollers with a jumble of coins in theirs.

My father laughed when I reported this to him, back with our tray of dogs, still served in fluted paper, I saw—at least that was the same—and we went all the way down to the first row of the grandstand to sit, careful to stay beneath the shade offered by the enormous concrete overhang. It was like sitting in a hot cement cavern. I could see the open standing room area right by the fence, where, when I was so little and so eager to please, I had stooped for those breeze-driven discarded tickets, my tangled hair flying while I said my little prayer, "Please God of the Horses, please God of the Horses." I hadn't changed much, even if today I wouldn't be stooping. I was still praying for luck of some kind for my father and me.

I looked behind us. The grandstand was only half-filled, if that. Apparently, no one wanted to leave the casinos to waste an afternoon here. Race after race with lulls in between could chew their way through your whole afternoon. You could throw the dice thirty times during the wait between races, another few times during them, which was why Lansky and company had little interest in supporting this track, which had other investors, or in bailing it out when it failed. So there would be little roar of the crowd today, which had beat in my ears as a child in Inglewood.

My father and I bent over our hot dogs in the still heat, waiting for the bugler's trilling call that signaled the starting time of the first race. And we waited for the announcement, "The horses are on the track. The horses are on the track," in from the paddock, led toward the gates, both the Thoroughbreds and their stablemates, the latter to calm the nerves of the former. Which was I of our odd pairing, racehorse or stablemate?

My father ate quickly, hungrily, in a hurry, dropping his fluted papers to the ground as soon as he was done, and then he lit up one of his Chesterfields, adding heat to the heat. He seemed troubled, on edge, even though our outing was supposed to be a lark, a slice of the sweet cake of our past.

He dropped his cigarette butt on the ground, put his heel on it, lit another, and he didn't look at me when he finally spoke. "When we came out here, Esme, it didn't even occur to me to worry about what would become of you, what there was for you here. You were such a little girl."

I widened my eyes at him when he turned his face toward mine.

He was going to lecture me about my burlesque act, again, the act I had already begun rehearsing. He had been unhappy with even the prospect of my act, saying when I first told him about it, "I don't know why you want to do this, baby girl." Baby girl. Exactly what I didn't want to be any longer, with its concomitant powerlessness. I was tired of being Baby E, baby girl, baby doll. He, jostling among all those big boys, should be able to understand that. "Why can't you just go on being a showgirl?" he'd said, which he hadn't been happy about, either, if I remembered correctly, back when I first put on my pink feathered costume at the Flamingo. When I told him, "I'm still a showgirl, I'm just a solo act now," he pulled a face at me. But I knew he'd eventually come around. My act wasn't all that much different from what my mother had confected for the Clover.

But it would take time. Because now what he said was, "Don't do it, Esme. It's not going to turn out like you think."

And from the look on his face, I could tell he didn't think it was going to turn out well, and that what came after this would not be any better than what I was serving up for myself right now. Worse, probably. In his mind, worse definitely. Harold Minsky's bump-and-grind worse.

"I'm going to be a headliner, Dad." Something I'd said, oh, roughly a hundred times to him already.

But he just shook his head at this as if I were a big fool. "Tell me. Have you been happy here in Vegas?"

I shrugged. Unanswerable.

"Because you know what I've been thinking about? I've been thinking this place is a lot like Hollywood. You give the big boys everything you've got, and they make their money off your back or your brains or your looks or your talent and then one day, they're done with you. Boom. You're out. Used up."

He gestured. It seemed to me that he wanted to say something further. But he didn't.

Instead he just stood and stretched, the backs of his trouser legs damp and wrinkled. I looked up at him, at the back of his head, his creased jacket, his hat, the way I had looked up long ago at all those men holding their tickets while they rushed the fence, shouting, "C'mon, daddy, c'mon, daddy," before they threw down those tickets, time up on their thirty minutes of value. Over. Gone.

Too late for us to get back in the gate now.

The bugle sounded.

My father looked down at me. "Let's go stand by the fence, baby girl. Like old times."

And he held out his hand.

We left after two races. The track lost money that day. And the next. And the next. Then it closed for two weeks to fix the erratic tote board and the broken betting machines. It opened again, briefly, in October, then closed. For good, it seemed. The horses had run for thirteen days.

36

NATE STOOD RIGHT BEHIND me, whispering to me in the wings as the club slowly darkened, his voice a sound meant to reassure me, but I couldn't distinguish his words over the buzz in my own ears and the ambient noise out front—the chalky murmur of the patrons, the chime of the silverware, the slow beat of the jazz music because there always had to be music, something singing alongside the eating and the drinking and the unfolding of menus. I could feel Nate's hands at my ribs and my thigh and the crisp cuff of his tuxedo sleeves against my bare arms. My ears and wrists and neck were heavy with glass and paste jewels, I was suffocating, my long hair fashioned into a helmet so stiff with hairspray—because Nate did not want anyone to see my hair—it almost bent my neck with its weight. How had my mother made her transition from the closed soundstage of the studio to the live stage of a Sunset Strip club? From chorine to solo act? I wished I could ask her. I wished I could be a Donn Arden dancer again, one of a dozen girls, having just finished my last show, peeling off my eyelashes and wiping at my Pan-Cake with a cotton ball.

I should have listened to my father.

At dress rehearsal this afternoon, I had needed oxygen. Nate himself had sprung up from his table on the floor to wheel the tank out from the wings, handing me the rubber mask and pulling the elastic bands secure at the back of my head, pushing my coiffure up into a poof, Ah, his face a raisin of concern. "E, you okay?" And at that rehearsal Nate and my band and my dresser had been the only ones there, a tiny attendant audience but one before which I had felt so unbearably naked. And now, tonight, I would be revealing myself before hundreds of eyes. What would happen when I was out there on the small stage that suddenly seemed so vast? I'd probably need two tanks of oxygen. A trucker tank full.

The anticipation of the audience began huffing and pawing at me now through the closed curtains. Interest in my act had drawn a herd of my former colleagues. So the eyes out there weren't entirely anonymous. Or friendly. They belonged to some of my old sisters at the Fabulous Flamingo, to my envious current fellow Arden dancers, to Donn Arden himself, all high forehead and greased hair and pissed-off expression because I'd told him I wanted to choreograph my act myself, why did I need him telling me what to do?, even to some of the celebrity headliners at the various hotels, because Vegas was suddenly exploding now, in the early fifties, with entertainers like Frank Sinatra and Milton Berle and Vic Damone and Red Skelton and Rosemary Clooney and Eddie Fisher all on the Strip all at once, and when they finished their own gigs, they headed out to the other clubs and lounges to see who was doing what at 2:00 A.M. and no one went to bed until the sun had bleached the neon to a pathetic pallor.

The one person who wasn't here tonight, by mutual agreement, was my father.

My cue.

Nate squeezed, then kissed, my gloved hand.

When the curtains opened, and when, as I had to, I left the wings behind, it seemed my spirit left my body, as well. My fear was so acute it was as if some part of me was looking down at myself from the catwalk, where I could see myself moving out into the black-and-white flickering light, could see that white train, that blond head of hair, those arms and legs, that torso and those breasts, which the audience would eventually get to see but not for long, and for Nate, that brevity was important, because my body, like my long blond hair, belonged to him and he wanted to ensure that only he would ever fully see it.

But on this stage my body was not really his anymore nor was it entirely my own—it was a tool, separate from me, an object I manipulated to entertain. The audience was a necessity—I could feel it out there, a large, warm mass—and so was the stage that separated me from it, and both the crowd's size and anonymity and my distance from it offered me a privacy I hadn't felt at my dress rehearsal, privacy and the freedom of display.

For my debut, we decided for reasons of economy to keep the stage almost bare. What we lacked in props, we'd make up for in daring. And, after all, I, not the stage set, was the show. So for me, a soft dark of twinkling lights suggesting a winter evening, early dusk, winking stars, and a man-size fan in the wings blowing my winter wind. As I crossed the stage, my long white satin gown with its chiffon train no longer than the gown's hem lifted behind me as if a child's hands carried it. After my quiet parade through this suggestion of a windy winter landscape, I stepped into the suggestion of an interior, just three hinged flats paned with glass and a single armchair.

Behind the small panes illuminated snowflakes fell, or were made to seem to do so, and the little bulbs above me flickered quietly, starlight now made candlelight, and the music flickered quietly in concert. I slowly unbuttoned my gloves, unhooked my train and laid all three over the back of the chair, and turned to my invisible lover, my partner in all this, who now bid me to undress further for him, this private moment enacted in a public venue. I lowered my head obediently, looking for his direction and approval as I progressed, slowly, shyly, until I stood garbed only in undergarments, the brassiere and corset and garters, massive and impenetrable contraptions of elasticized fabric, and yet, as undergarments and despite the coverage they offered, still agents of the erotic. And I could feel that the audience was as torn as I had been that night at the El Rancho, by the exquisite tension between the degradation of the performer's self-exposure and the power of her absolute command. She could not lose the latter. The audience wanted both on display, simultaneously.

Under these glimmering lights, what Nate and I had once kept private between us, the only sexual experience I had, was about to be as unmistakably revealed as my flesh. Beneath my chiffon train, I freed myself first from one undergarment and then another. The most difficult part of this whole undertaking was to make these maneuvers look graceful—no wonder St. Cyr had used a standing screen for the final part of her act—but I wanted this opaque cloth to suggest my desire for my lover's body against mine. Disrobing this way was difficult to do despite the innovations of my costume designer and the tape that replaced the usual hooks and eyes and snaps. When I stood, finally, in profile, draped only in the soft, translucent material of the train, I offered to my lover and to my audience an obscured view of my naked flesh.

I leaned then against the back of the chair to watch what appeared to be my lover's slow crawl across the floor to me, an inversion of the usual trope of the burlesque artist crawling the stage in garters and heels. Any performing I now did, I did solely with my face, with the expressions I allowed to shade it, the faces I had worn with Nate as he had supervised my sexual initiation, and this, more than my body, was the private core of my most private self and therefore Nate's, and yet I had to draw on it. No one comes to the theater to see a performer restrain herself. I looked at the floor. As my lover reached me, I mimed accepting his lips and hands at my face and torso and then his head between my thighs, remembering the strange wet strength of Nate's tongue bearing down on me for the first time. My head went back. The black-and-yellow lights above me seemed to swell, rhythmic as a heartbeat. What I became on this stage was what I had imagined myself to be when I danced for Nate Stein those three years ago in that empty Flamingo showroom, making my body undulate to those Andrews Sisters dated show tunes, making him want me. Would the audience?

The drums throbbed steadily and my fingers fluttered against the fabric of the chair. The music built in pace and volume. With my upstage hand, the one invisible to my audience, I found the edge of my chiffon fabric and gripped it tightly, at the ready. And then I let this mock cunnilingus go on, searching for the pulse of the audience, for the sounds of them, my band watching me, awaiting my signal. Then, simultaneously, I thrust my hips forward, opened my mouth for the trumpet's libidinous squawk, and tossed the chiffon to the catwalk above me, a triple play that left my body naked for just an instant before the stage went black.

I waited, terrified, in that darkness. A few seconds later, the chiffon garment I'd flung to the skies plummeted back down onto my sweaty, garnished face. I swiped the thing away. I couldn't breathe.

Was I ruined? Had we gone too far?

No.

As Nate had assured me, This is Vegas, darling.

There was no too far to go.

37

AND NATE NEVER LEFT my side when the pounding on my dressing room door began, with every entertainer and VIP wanting to personally congratulate me, a crush, a crowd at the open door, a pack in the narrow backstage hallway. I knew Nate had coaxed and cajoled most of these celebrities to the Desert Inn, as Benny Siegel had once done at the Flamingo, with offers of free rooms and airplane travel and thousands of dollars of free chips because Nate knew a celebrity presence would legitimize my act, burlesque as socially acceptable entertainment, and that presence would legitimize me.

And Nate knew better than anyone my relative lack of sophistication, and in my dressing room he kept an arm around me, a cigarette in that hand, holding out my hand as if I were a mannequin when he saw someone wanted to shake it, speaking for me or prodding a few words from me when he saw that what he said was not enough, did not quite satisfy the well-wisher. I admired, as always, his social ease, his genial smile, his effortless chat, his warm handshake, his nod to me with a gentle incline of the head that signaled I must step into the circle of conversation with whatever vocabulary I could muster. I was somebody, now. The baskets of fruit, the bottles of champagne, the bouquets of flowers and stems wrapped in paper, all spoke to that—or to the fact that Nate was somebody and because I was somebody to him, these courtiers were prepared to flatter him through me.

Whatever the reason, it was after this night that everyone, even Donn Arden, began calling me Miss Wells, treating me with a deference I had never before been shown. Nor had my parents.

My mother watched all this from her photograph tucked into

my dressing-room mirror, eyes hooded beneath her platinum wig, body hidden behind her wide-hooped satin skirt, posed up there in the altitudes on her winding staircase of the Shadow Waltz, and I wasn't sure if she was proud of me or envious. I knew how my father felt. Neither proud nor envious. Distressed.

Pride, envy, distress, no matter. Because right out of the gate, I became one of the Strip's high-grossing acts—there was no one else on the Strip like me, Nate saw to that—and Nate raked in the ancillary income in the drinking, gambling, and prostitution that followed my performance. Get me a girl. It wasn't long before I asked him for a percentage of the showroom tables. And he laughed and gave it to me. Baby E.

38

FOR MY NEXT NUMBER the following year, I stole my material not from St. Cyr—who had, I learned later, stolen hers from an old 1897 burlesque film entitled *After the Ball*—but from the great Buzz Berkeley, who better?, creating for myself a water show somewhat like the one I read in *Photoplay* he was doing at MGM, confecting for Esther Williams the Fountain and Smoke number in *Million Dollar Mermaid*, shot at the Lot One saucer tank, surrounded by scaffolding and wires and stairways so cameramen could be stationed above the water, at the water's edge, at the portholes below the waterline, so every gizmo and gimmick and girl could be filmed—it was all the business he'd done with his dancers on the soundstages and now would do in a pool. So.

My new act would feature not a pool but a giant martini glass, in a nod, after all, to where we were, its rim and slopes devices for my choreographic inventions, as were the olive on a stick and the stick itself, the stick which made a pole for me along and around which I slithered and slid, a phallus I straddled and rode. At the finale, I sank into the glass's stem, bathing beauty at last, my pale hair loosed in defiance and floating upward, my flesh pressed into the tight column of glass, arms raised above me so the audience could fully take its pleasure in me, though I made them wait, because after all, the long joke is the essence of burlesque.

39

I SHOULD ALSO MENTION this.

That night of my debut, Virginia Hill herself made a congratulatory appearance at my dressing room door, along with her escort, the mobster Joe Adonis. She too had just been called in front of the Kefauver committee and had testified there before all witnesses about her skills at fellatio, which had made her so essential to the syndicate men Epstein, Nitti, Accardo, Costello, Siegel, Adonis, and company, in that order, with some overlap, testifying about the capabilities of her lips and tongue and teeth, doing so all while wearing a mink cape and silk gloves. And a hat. None of which could buff away her rough manners in the same way that none of Benny's fancy suits could buff away his. Afterwards, she had slapped a woman reporter and told her she hoped an atom bomb would fall on her. Virginia. Yet another piece of trash flapping on Kefauver's wire.

She stood flapping in my doorway now, and there was something about the way she greeted Nate, the way they looked at one another, the way his hand stayed a second too long on the sleeve of her dress that recalled for me the rumors I'd heard back at the Flamingo, that Nate Stein had had Virginia when she was very young, when she'd made her initial appearance at the World's Fair in 1933, a red-haired, pale-skinned sixteen-year-old girl, wobbling through Chicago in her big sister's heels, trying to act as if she wanted to be passed around from one man to another. Epstein, Nitti, Accardo, Costello, Siegel, Adonis, and Stein? It was possible. And I'd also heard Nate and Lansky didn't like the way Ben treated her. So there was more they didn't like about Ben than just his Swiss bank account. And that June day after Ben battered

Virginia for the last time and then chased her all the way home to Los Angeles, and that day after she called Joe Adonis and flew to Paris to get away from Ben, Al Smiley made his call to Vegas. And someone with a soft spot for little girls like me took that call and made another.

I narrowed my eyes at Nate, and he pivoted to introduce me to Virginia, as if we'd never met before. Did Nate not know how much I saw at the Flamingo, how much I knew about Benny and Virginia?

She didn't remember me, of course, as the little cigarette girl she had scratched all those Decembers ago—a habit of hers, apparently—but I remembered her only too well. She looked as if she had aged fifteen years in the last six. While Mr. Adonis shook my hand, all pinkie rings and cigar, Virginia told me if she had done my act, she'd have gotten down on her knees on that stage and pretended to suck the hell out of a cock. Which she then demonstrated.

Nate's face tightened with offense, his affection for Virginia gone. He now wore almost, but not quite, the bad face.

It was directed at her, not at me, but both it and she served their purpose, which was to remind me exactly who and what I was. I was not and never would be again my child self, Esme Silver. I was some concoction now of the fellater Virginia Hill and the stripper Lili St. Cyr, a stage-show vulgarity in a satin dress and glass jewels, just one step away, okay, maybe two, from a cot on Block 16. Or a hotel room at the World's Fair.

LOS ANGELES
1939

40

MY MOTHER NOW—TO KEEP me out of her hair while she prepared for her debut at the Clover—allowed my father to take me with him on his errands for Mickey Cohen and Benny Siegel, despite their questionable nature. When he made the rounds of MGM or Warners or Columbia, picking up the checks written by the reluctant moguls in order to keep the unions of carpenters or electricians or extras from calling a strike, checks my father delivered to Mr. Siegel, I showed my father the way. I knew the layout of MGM and Warners by heart. Lot One. Lot Two. Lot Three. Etc.

Soon enough, my father found himself promoted from Cohen's errand boy to his bookmaker, because, after all, that was his métier. No longer a bettor, he now took his place at the other side of the window, taking those bets, working out of Cohen's Stratford Coffee Shop downtown or his Le Grand Prix Barber Shop in Hollywood or the La Brea Club on Beverly, with its $20,000 stakes and a crowd of mobsters or later still at his Dincara Stock Farm up in Burbank, a horse farm with a casino in the stable, one block from Warners, where actors still dressed in costume would come to play roulette and blackjack at the end of a long day's shoot. Occasionally, my father worked nights helping out with the craps games Cohen hosted for his friends at the Ambassador

Hotel. Better for my father to take the bets than to make them himself on races fixed by Meyer Lansky at tracks as far south as Agua Caliente in Tijuana and as far north as Santa Anita, which is where I had my memorable first sighting of Benny Siegel.

Eventually, by the end of the summer, my father ended up, more or less permanently, working at Cohen's ratty little Kon-Kre-Kota paint store in the middle of nowhere on Beverly Boulevard, a store with rows of telephones and a walk-up window, where I was treated like a little queen in a hive of hatless men, green chalkboards, and ringing telephones. I'd fool around with all the phones, which were there so bets could be laid, making pretend calls to movie stars. There was also a back window where I could stand and spy on the men who walked up to put a dollar down on the dogs or the ponies or a ball game. I liked the paint store. It reminded me of my grandfather's paint store. Mr. Cohen's office was at the back, where he always managed to find a Three Musketeers bar or a Clark Bar or a pack of Rolo chocolates in his desk and where after proffering one of them up, he'd pat my head and pay me some kind of compliment. "Baby E, you're one cute cookie!" and then run off to wash his hands.

Cohen was always making for the nearest bathroom so he could wash his hands, which he did, religiously, an obsession that started at nineteen when he contracted gonorrhea and continued ever after through the years. As a little girl, I found his whole washing routine hilarious, Mr. Cohen's taking another shower?, Mr. Cohen's in the bathroom again scrubbing his hands?, though now that I'm older, I understand it better. Three times a day he showered and powdered his entire body and put on fresh clothing. On the hour, he soaped up his hands. Almost every other mobster in town would eventually crawl out to Vegas where vice had made itself a comfortable home, but Mickey Cohen would stay in balmy Los Angeles with its clean ocean air and its sanitizing sunshine, and where, ultimately, he'd fill the vacancy left by Bugsy Siegel's death in 1947. Fill it and expand it.

Anyway, the bathroom was where Mickey was standing, hands under a stream of hot water, when Maxie Shaman burst into the Kon-Kre-Kota one afternoon, his big body seeming to break through the doorframe and his anger over who knows what pushing him like a storm past the rows of paint cans and rollers and brushes and dust cloths and the racks of cardboard paint samples, where I stood, picking out the colors for my new bedroom in the Hollywood Hills house my father told me we'd be moving to soon, now that he was making so much more money and we needed to be closer to my mother's club on Sunset. My plan was to paint each wall of my bedroom a different color, so I had all various shades of pink, purple, yellow, and blue in my hands and laid out like playing cards on the counter before me, weighing my serious decision.

And I seemed to be the only one to look up at the entrance of Maxie Shaman, who made directly for Mr. Cohen's back office as if he knew exactly where it was—and in fact he did. His agenda? Fury over Mickey's bodyguard Hooky Rothman, who broke a chair over Maxie's brother's head at the La Brea Club the previous night. For this disrespect, Maxie was going to hold not a chair but a gun to Mr. Cohen's head.

It was the second time in my life I heard a gun go off. The sound was unimpressive, nothing like the impressively loud and crisp *pop pop pop* on my favorite radio show, *Gangbusters,* not even much like the ringing echo and zing of the bullets from the pistol Mr. Cohen used to shoot at Adolf Hitler's portrait in that Deutsches Haus auditorium. But Maxie's emergence from the back office was not unimpressive.

If he had rushed in like nature's whirlwind, he lurched out like a crime against nature, moving quickly at first and then not so quickly, and then the big man fell, gracelessly and all at once, hitting the floor with a thud, his face a few yards from my sandaled feet, and it seemed to me that Shaman looked directly at me before his eyes turned blank, the floridly colored cards in my hands fluttering onto the floor beside him, the blood that still pulsed forcefully through him also pulsing out of him onto the tiled floor, inching toward me and soaking my little cardboard paint samples red. I took a step back. All the while, his eyes looked into my eyes. He said something to me. "Little girl."

I turned slowly to search out my father by the betting window where he stood, frozen, some green bill making a feather in his hand. The men at the telephones had gone suddenly mute. I looked back down at Maxie Shaman. My sandals were wet now with his blood. He wasn't trying to say anything to me anymore. Around me, telephones rang and rang. Why aren't you answering, answering, answering? I looked back at my father. He hadn't moved.

And then Mickey came crashing out of his office, a squat hulk in a suit, and it was he who took my head in his hands and turned my face away, saying, "Don't look. Don't look, Esme."

But in Vegas, there would be no one to turn my head away. Far from it.

LAS VEGAS
1952

41

I KNEW OF TONY Cornero from Los Angeles, from the gambling boats he ran, where my father had played before the city shut them all down—the *Monte Carlo*, the *Rose Isle*, the *Johanna Smith*, the *Rex*. And I knew of him also because he'd tried to set up shop in Mickey Cohen's territory, and Cohen had bombed Cornero's house to discourage him, which it had. So Cornero, like so many other crooked men, had come here to Las Vegas to build himself a casino, which he called first the Starlight and then the Stardust and for which he had borrowed over four million dollars from Nate and still the place wasn't finished and hadn't yet opened. And I remembered, when I walked toward the casino on my usual morning hunt for him, that Nate had told me Tony was coming over today to ask for more money and he wasn't planning to give Tony one more dollar, was going to watch him fail, and then buy the place out from under him as he crumpled, gravity a slingshot, sending him out past his star-dusted galaxy.

The casino doors were closed and locked, I discovered, and I had to knock to be let in. Inside, the casino was deserted, obviously purposely so, except for Nate, who stood at the bar, stone-faced, a bartender behind him, and an impassive-faced croupier at one of the craps tables where a flushed, frantic-looking Tony Cornero was playing solo. All the other croupiers and dealers, even the box men and pit bosses, were absent. Sent away. It was clear to me when I saw Tony and his red face that Nate's unwelcome news had already been delivered and that Cornero was trying to have his vengeance at the craps table. But vengeance was not his. Not yet.

Even at 10:00 A.M., the casino was dimly lit, as if gamblers needed to play in an eternal night because if they knew what time it really was, they would surely gather up their chips and head to bed. The casino wasn't a large one, just five craps tables, three roulette tables, four blackjack tables, and seventy-five slot machines, but it made Nate a fortune every month, raking in $750,000 a week from the first moment the casino opened, unlike the take at the opening of poor Benny's Flamingo Club. Or the poor Las Vegas Jockey Club. So the house was winning and Tony was losing. But something else was going on or Nate wouldn't be here. Or the casino so empty.

"He's down thirty thousand," Nate told me when I reached him at the bar.

"You should stop him," I said. "Send him home."

"Oh, I'm gonna stop him."

So it was going to be a curt morning, a Baby E, go away morning. There were fewer of those now, but they still happened on occasion. Except that Nate didn't wave me away.

Because then Tony—overheated, black hair glistening with hair oil and sweat, dressed in a suit and tie because after all he had come to beg for money, spiffy on arrival, I assumed, but now a disheveled mess, his collar turned up out of his suit jacket, shirt as crinkled as if he had taken it off and folded it a thousand times before donning it again—raised his arm and flicked a finger at the bartender behind me, signaling for another whiskey.

Nate said to the bartender, "I'll make him the drink."

And I thought, That's good. Nate will take it over to Tony, calm him down, put his hat back on his head, and send him home to the Starlight or the Stardust or the Starglow or whatever it was being called this week, let him sleep off his disappointment and his anger in his bed there in his vast unopened hotel of a thousand rooms in which he'd been hoping to book all the low rollers who wanted to stay in Vegas for five dollars a night.

But after Nate had gone behind the bar to pour the drink, he pushed it across the bar to me and said, "E, give him this, and this," and next to the glass he slid the bill. Twenty-five dollars. A bill?

I stared at Nate. No matter how many drinks Tony had ordered, drinks were always on the house for gamblers.

Nate smiled at me. "It'll let him know it's time to go."

"Nate—"

"Go on."

Reluctantly, I took the tumbler with his 7 and 7 and the slip of paper over to the craps table and put the latter under the former, hoping maybe Tony would think it was a cocktail napkin and never even know about Nate's intent to insult him.

But, of course, that didn't happen, though I got away with it at first. Tony snatched up the whiskey, drank it down all at once, glittery-eyed and reckless, set the glass on the wooden ledge of the table by the very few chips he had left, the greater mass of them, a massive mass of them, stacked neatly on the other side of the table under the jurisdiction of the croupier. Tony's face was wet, his eyes a little wild, but he still managed to say to me, gallantly, "Thanks, honey," before he looked down and saw the soggy bill.

And at that, he started to rant, to scream, to pound his fists on the table, shaking the chips, and then he began to lumber, still yelling, pushing past me toward the bar where Nate stood immobile, watching him—Benny would have gone off like a bomb at

Tony's ferocious approach, if it were Mickey, he would have already shot Tony dead, but Nate was always controlled—and halfway across the casino floor, Tony grabbed his chest, screamed, and fell over, hitting the ground with the thump of the dead, which he was, the second man in my life to fall dead at my feet.

At this, Nate said, "Get out of the way, E," and I, who had taken a step toward Tony with some thought of aiding the man, cradling his head or taking his hand or checking his pulse, abruptly stopped walking, and Nate, who had been striding toward Tony to do the same, or so I thought, didn't pause at all, not even for a second, by Tony's crumpled body. Instead, Nate moved swiftly past him to his goal, the glass that remained on the craps table, a glass he whisked up and took back to the bar, where he washed it and dried it and put it back on the shelf with the hundreds of others and where it became an ordinary glass instead of the poisoned chalice I now understood it was.

The chalice he had had me in all my ignorance ferry over to the luckless Tony Cornero, who lay motionless on the plush carpet of Nate's casino.

Because a drink delivered by me merited a "Thanks, honey," but a drink and the tab smacked down on the table by the irritated Nate would have been perceived as insult enough that Tony might have refused the whiskey and the bill and strode from the casino. Only to be faced again some other time. And Nate didn't want to see Tony again, ever. Hence, Nate's, Take this over to him, E.

No, it wasn't the first time a dead man had lain at my feet, but it was the first time my own actions had brought him down.

What if I hadn't happened to walk into the casino just now?

Or.

Worse, what if Nate had been waiting for me to find him wherever he was, as I did every morning at this hour, had planned ahead in bringing whatever nugget of poison he'd added to Tony's whiskey at just the right moment, so I could perform this service.

No.

Surely my appearance was a happy accident. For Nate, not Tony.

I sat down on one of the tall-legged leather chairs by the craps table, at a bit of a distance from the dead Tony, who had in one hand, I could see now, the dice he had been making ready to throw. Nate had the croupier and the bartender, who said nothing and who kept their faces deliberately blank, stand by the casino doors. He made two calls while I sat there studying Tony, his purple mottled face, the scraped worn soles of his shoes making pathetic contrast to his fine suit, his tie a fabric arm begging for alms from the plush carpet, the ducktail of hair at the back of his neck that needed a trim. And I smelled his loosed bowels. I looked up at the bar. Nate had his broad back to me. And though it took many long minutes, he never turned around to face me while he made his calls, one to a Los Angeles mortician and the other to Cornero's physician in Vegas who was Nate's and everybody else's doctor out here. Why not.

When he was finished, he came and stood beside me in his own five-hundred-dollar suit, silk tie swinging giddily, took my hand, and said, "Don't look at him, E. A heart attack is an ugly thing." And there was that *ping* in his voice again, the *ping* I recognized. He jerked his chin at the barman and pantomimed that he should grab a towel and lay it over Tony's head, which the bartender did and which somehow made everything worse, Tony a macabre spaceman in his helmet, with dice. And as the bartender backed away, Nate said, "I'm sorry you had to see this, Esme."

I turned now from Tony's white-sacked head to look at Nate. So. He was going to deny, prevaricate, pretend. With me. I've never had a poker face. It used to infuriate my mother when she was up to one of her capers to see on my face the contrary emotions coursing there—anger, shame, incredulity—emotions I could not seem to bleach away. She'd look right into my face and say, "I didn't do that," when she clearly had. But worse was when she made me an operator in her trickery, as in, "Go tell Mr. Taylor you need to run lines with Mickey Rooney."

In those situations, I became the golem my grandfather had told me about, the monster made out of mud who couldn't speak for itself but could only lurch around. To make it move, you wrote the Hebrew word for truth on its forehead and then you wrote what you wanted it to do on a piece of parchment and put the paper in the monster's mouth and the golem would do what you told it to do. And when you were finished with it, you erased the word and the golem and the parchment turned to dust. And that's how Nate had used me, too. Except that I hadn't turned to dust. And I wasn't sure there was any truth here between us.

Nate let go of my hand.

The doctor Nate had called arrived within a half hour with a death certificate and a medical bag, for form's sake, I suppose, because he never opened it, and he told the security men by now stationed at every door to the casino that there was no need to call the Clark County coroner, Mr. Cornero had clearly suffered a massive heart attack, no need for an autopsy, and the doctor himself then called for an ambulance to take the body for transport. Maybe Tony did have a heart attack. Maybe the bill for the drinks and not that last drink itself was the catalyst for Cornero's plummet to the floor, dead on arrival there. Maybe, as Nate told me after I overheard him threaten that Negro boxer, his threats were just talk. Just theater. For effect. But something had had an effect here.

And once Tony had been lifted from the carpet and laid on a stretcher, Nate followed the body, making, I imagined, a ghoulish processional through the kitchen and from there out the back of the hotel, the industrial, all-business part of the hotel, with its metal roll-up doors where deliveries were made and its blank locked doors where back-of-the-house employees arrived for their shifts and where the counting-room cash made its exit. In that back parking lot by the delivery trucks and the laundry trucks the ambulance waited, motor running, and I'm sure Nate made certain Tony's body was loaded, hurriedly, into the back of this particular delivery truck with its big red cross.

It was only after Nate left the casino, with a terse instruction to the doctor, "Give her something," that the doctor turned his attention to me. Like Tony, I had to be lifted off the casino chair and half-carried, to the bar, though, not to an ambulance, because, like Tony, I seemed to have been robbed of my ability to walk, my legs going this way and that. I was instructed to take some of the tranquilizers in the bottle the doctor pulled from his black bag, a bag that made itself useful in some way, after all.

I sat on my barstool while the doctor opened the vial of Miltowns and broke one of the tablets in half. I swallowed it with some warm water the bartender gave me. Soon, I would be helped to my bed, bottle of Miltowns in my pocket. Yes, Baby E would have to be carried. Behind me, a small crew was wiping and vacuuming away all traces of Tony Cornero, spraying something sweet into the air and onto the carpet fibers. It was almost noon and the casino needed to be reopened, the players and their fresh, green cash admitted. There were two hundred and twenty-nine rooms in the hotel, with men and women in and out of each one, each night, two hundred different people every night, three-hundred and sixty-five days a year, seventy thousand people a year, each one with his own story. Of that number, I wondered how many brought with them shame, guilt, disgrace, humiliation—or acquired these here, as I had.

Tony would be buried in Los Angeles before nightfall.

42

WHEN I WOKE IN the afternoon, upstairs in Nate's Hollywood
Suite, all alone, it was almost four o'clock. The half Miltown I'd
swallowed had turned me into a corpse, though only for six hours,
not for eternity like the unfortunate Cornero. If I'd been given
a whole pill, I'd probably have been out for twelve, which I'm
sure Nate was counting on, busy as he was vacuuming up all
the celestial particles Cornero had left behind. Better for Nate to
have me unconscious for a while, strapped into some metaphoric
Viking rocket, temporarily spinning in some outer orbit where, at
least for now, I could make no trouble. In what heavenly orbit did
Cornero circle?

I still felt too drugged to move, so I simply shut my eyes again.
Goodbye to a sunlight so brilliant it hid the stars and planets
right there in plain sight. This must have been what my mother
had felt like, the version of her that had been unable to get out of
bed our last summer together, and who, when I had tried to talk
to her, simply rolled away from me without opening her pretty
eyes, unable to utter a syllable or to lift a heavy arm even one
inch, no matter how much I pulled at her hand or put my little
mouth to her ear and shrieked for her attention. "Wake up!" Yes,
I understood now what I couldn't possibly have understood then,
that my mother had been swallowing tranquilizers to obliterate
all the days and all the hours within them that now held nothing
she wanted, nothing she'd been wishing for on a star since she
was a child led by her first-grade teacher from one classroom to
another throughout Sheridan Elementary School so that all the
other teachers could admire the extraordinary beauty of Dorothy
Wolfkowitz, certain to grow up to be something out of this world.

And then she'd grown up.

Well, I'd grown up, too, though not in Boyle Heights. I'd gone to the Desert Inn to do it. So I was grown up, now, Vegas-style. And if there was something I wanted to obliterate, well, there was a pill for it.

Maybe Nate didn't think what he asked of me this morning would bother me much, given that I was a burlesque act, a tawdry one, and a half orphan, the daughter of a stooper, a failed one, and a hoofer, a common one.

I opened my eyes.

I wanted to see my father. If my legs now worked.

They did.

I got up and drew the curtains against the massive hotel parking lot and the eighteen-hole golf course beyond it, someone else's wish on a star, one that had actually manifested itself. Slowly, carefully—how had my mother sprung with such alacrity from her bed the day of her inexplicable resurrection?—I navigated the room, my body remembering itself, my limbs remembering their functions.

I washed my face. I dressed.

Before I left, I took my manicure scissors and sat on the end of the bed I'd shared with Nate this past year, where I could almost feel our shades cavorting at my back. This is how adults fuck, little girl, what do you think of that. Here's what I thought. I used the scissors to cut off all my hair, a long painstaking process with such a tiny tool, but I persisted, working the small blades very close to my scalp so the hair fell from me in the longest possible strands, covering the foot of the bed and the carpet at my feet, and when I was finished, I laid the scissors on the bed over the strands of my blond hair for Nate to see. Because eventually, reluctantly, he would have to come back here, and then he'd discover I'd left behind only all that long hair of mine he loved so much, the troublesome remainder of me having vanished.

43

WINTERS ARE COLD IN Las Vegas. Ten thousand years ago, the climate had been more temperate. This desert had been mild and black at night and by day a lush place of green grass and blue lakes, of mammoths and camels and saber-toothed tigers, if you can believe it, and then nature did an about-face and ravaged the valley with heat, and the oven it became burned away all life, leaving behind animal bones and mesquite and creosote, and a disorganized mesh of rivers that didn't know which way to go, and sandstorms, after which shone the endless sun. And it stayed this way, an abandoned wasteland, for centuries, until Rafael Rivera wandered with a scouting party off the Old Spanish trail and stared into the valley at Christmastime 1829 when the weather was cold and the winter grasses were blowing and he named this spot the Meadows—Las Vegas.

Those meadows and marshes were fed by springs so powerful a man could not even dive into them without being repelled immediately to the water's surface. By 1950, Las Vegas had pumped those springs dry.

And now in that spot lay the extraordinary impudence of the Strip.

I stepped out onto it. The Flamingo was a mile away, and it would take me maybe a half an hour to walk there. In my state. In the cold.

I left, hatless—a mistake, given my shorn head that made me doubly vulnerable to the low temperature—wearing fur-lined winter boots and the mink coat Benny had given me, around my neck the diamond ESME pendant big as a doorknob—I was still not that many years from my overadorned childhood self. Or maybe, just in case I froze to death, I wanted the passersby who found me to know I was a person of value to someone, Send this frozen corpse to the Desert Inn, care of Nate Stein, giver of this necklace, even if I didn't feel very much valued by him right now. Quite the opposite.

On this late, late afternoon, the Strip had not quite yet met the dusk that roused the hotel neon. Vegas always looked so stark and plain by day, a little embarrassed to be seen, its neon melted away to tubing and poles, its lightbulbs sheepish glass shells. Despite the raucous neon brawl, it was so easy to feel alone here. Even into early 1953, the Strip was still nothing much but motor courts. All you had to do was turn from the hotels and casinos of the Strip, look over any wall that surrounded any one of the hotel swimming pools, and gaze at the vast empty sand-strewn valley, which we were slowly taking over, bit by bit.

To the north of me lay the El Rancho, the Thunderbird, the Sahara, and the construction sites of the Riviera and the Stardust of contention, on its site the wooden tracks for carts, the cranes and tractors and ladders and wooden planks demarcating the areas left to be finished. And near that site, another, completely empty but for a battered sign that read:

ON THIS SITE WILL BE ERECTED
THE 1000-ROOM EL MOROCCO HOTEL.

Opposite me at the end of the Desert Inn drive stood the Last Frontier, where in 1947 Adolph Schwimmer came from Palestine to say the Irgun needed machine guns and got fifty-eight crates of them from the Vegas big boys, and from Schwimmer's pitch to the Los Angeles big boys, which put Louis B. Mayer and Mickey Cohen in the same banquet room for an evening, millions of dollars. Then Cohen had held a fundraiser of his own for the Irgun in Los Angeles at his Slapsy Maxie's, because once Mickey heard that there were Jews in Palestine fighting for independence, for survival, Jews? Real Jews with guns?, he raised money for them from every mobster and mogul he knew. South of me stood the newly opened Sands, its façade desert-dirt red.

I started walking. Long undeveloped acres of land extended themselves beside the highway. I passed tumbleweed after tumbleweed, each of which always seemed to find some edifice, however small—a post, a wire, a plank, a creosote bush, a cactus—to halt its otherwise endless sojourn. I passed an abandoned boat, its provenance a mystery, broken and cooking in the sun. I passed a For Sale sign:

HOTEL SITE
THREE MILLION DOLLARS
ENQUIRE AT THE EL RANCHO

Sand and grit, cacti and creosote, concrete and lawn chairs, cinder-block motels and blue-painted swimming pools, some of those pools, like the El Rancho's, right by the highway.

Cars whizzed past me, in a hurry to bring their occupants to the casinos, in too much of a hurry to worry about a girl walking by the side of the highway in the winter cold, in too much of a rush to lose money with a gaiety men never normally expressed when losing money, in a rush to the beds, where these men could make love to their wives, or if they desired, to a stranger, in a rush to the bars where they could drink, incessantly and uncensored, to the clubs, where they could feast on flesh and color.

Around the bend in the highway ahead of me rose the construction site of the partially realized Dunes and shortly thereafter the lushly landscaped site of the fully realized Flamingo. But now it seemed the Flamingo was to be reinvented; plans had been drawn up, my father told me, to build an addition, a tower of rooms—in fact all the extant hotels were drawing up plans to abandon their old-style motor courts and embrace new many-storied towers, blocks of guest rooms stacked one on top of the other up to the night sky. Beyond the Flamingo and the Dunes, too far in the distance to see, reared the billboard advertising the Tropicana Hotel soon to come, with its Three Hundred Luxurious Rooms, and its Desert Oasis theme.

And in every one of those hotels Mr. Lansky or his associates Stein, Greenbaum, Dalitz, Rosen, Berman, Adler, Roen—even Mickey Cohen back in Los Angeles—had a percentage. All the big boys. Yes, Nate had a stake in every one of these hotels, every one of them but the Stardust, which now, with Tony's death, would belong to him in some way or another, some front man installed, perhaps, but with the profits flowing to Nate and from him to Meyer Lansky and from Lansky to men like him all across the United States. Nate wanted them all, every hotel, each one a piece of his empire. Without his careful tending and Lansky's, how long would it take for these hotels to be abandoned, to decay, to stand sand-blown and desiccated? What if Nate and the men like him should be swept out of here by God's rake since Kefauver's wasn't up to the task? And what would these carloads of guests do then, when they saw these wrecks, our pyramids, our desert.

What else? Turn around and go home.

44

EVERY AFTERNOON AT THIS time, an hour before his shift, my father took a swim in the Flamingo pool, through the 120-degree summer, even through the winter in the 40-degree cold, the temperature dropping as soon as the sun started to go down. And sure enough, when I arrived at the hotel, I found my father, alone, doing his laps in the otherwise empty pool, his dark body seal-like as he swept up and down its length. He didn't do the crawl, but some stroke of his own invention, an amalgamation of underwater kicks and paddles that occasionally brought him to the surface for air. The stroke of someone who'd never had a swimming lesson in his life. Like me.

I sat myself down on the cold concrete ledge of the pool, took off my shoes, and stuck my bare feet into the water, which felt warmer the longer I sat there until finally the water felt warmer than the air. I let my feet dangle, studying the distortion that made my shins look as if they'd been broken in two. My bunions, massive creations formed by a decade of dancing in high-heeled shoes, looked exaggerated, too, underwater. The bottom of the pool was a deeper blue than its sides. My father swam on through the cold, through the blue. Around us, the metal umbrella stands rattled, the pink plaster flamingos rocked on their metal stakes.

Somewhere on the grounds, the Flamingo cats were yowling through the wind. The small litter of kittens Ben had saved for me those six years ago had, in just this short time, grown into a feral pack of thirty tabbies, the mouse- and rat-killers of the hotel grounds, who, for variety, occasionally lapped milk from the bowls set out by the back door of the hotel kitchen. First family of the Flamingo. No. My father and I were the first family of the

Flamingo, those cats the second. They sounded off close by, a Greek chorus of panic, turmoil, and need.

What could they possibly have to complain about?

Slowly, eventually, my father came to understand that the girl with no hair, wearing a fur coat and sitting awkwardly at the pool's edge, was actually his daughter, and he swam up beside me and hung from his arms at the deep end.

"What's going on, Esme?" Meaning, what have you done to yourself, meaning why have you taken scissors to your hair the way your mother took scissors to my face in that old photograph, meaning are you unraveling just like your mother and where will I put you if you are. There was no Bedlam in Vegas.

Unraveling? Maybe so.

I shrugged.

"When did you do this?" he asked me, gesturing with one wet, dripping hand in the direction of my head.

"An hour ago."

"Don't you have a show tonight?"

"My day off." The casinos and counting rooms, my father's habitats, were never dark, never shuttered for a night, and soon, with the Stardust, they would never be shuttered at all, not even for an hour.

"Well, that's good," my father said. Meaning, you can straighten out this mess with your hair before tomorrow's show, send your dresser scouring the costume shop for a wig. He was looking at me, waiting for some kind of explanation as to why I was here, in a fur coat, feet in water, hairless.

Why was I here?

Because, really, how could my father possibly make right any wrong done by Nate Stein to me or to anyone else. My father could not fix me with the monster-size diamond ring and a stroll along Broadway, tools he had wielded to fix my mother. My father could only do what he had already done, which was to try to avert this disaster before it arrived by telling me that Nate Stein was much too old for me, that he was rapaciously greedy, that this affair could come to no good end. My father had known that I would be hurt by Nate somehow. He just didn't know exactly how. Or when.

I could not bring myself to say anything, so my father made a stab at what had upset me. "You know dirty hands are just part of life out here, Esme. You know that."

I nodded.

"Don't study anything too closely. Just keep looking ahead, straight ahead."

That was what he did, of course, what he had been doing since I was a little girl. Did he ever feel this credo had failed him? He was too smart not to know that it had.

And then he gave me that grin, the magical grin that showed off his small, white, even child's teeth, and with the palm of his hand, he smoothed his own dark hair back, as if to reassure himself that he, at least, still had a head of hair, and he pushed himself away from the concrete rim of the pool, away from me, to continue his laps.

I watched his brown back, black hair move through the water, merman maybe, maybe more like a trapped animal in a small enclosure, forward and back, never out. A trapped animal, perhaps, but even with no way out, my father would never do to me what Nate had done. And though what was good for me over the years might often have played second to what was good for my father, there were still limits to what he would ask of me. I could call Nate "Daddy" from dawn to dusk, but he was not my daddy, and therefore if I could serve one of Nate's needs, no matter the tenor of it, then I was called to serve.

Baby E, take this drink over to Tony.

I'd huddled at the bottom of this pool years ago, hiding from Benny after his blowup with my father. That day my father had peered over the edge of the pool, the distortion of the water making his face loom way too large, trying to explain to me why sometimes a man had to take a hit. Even as a little girl, I knew something was wrong with Benny, something sick in him that his charismatic charm could conceal but not cure. Yet I loved him, with a little girl's perspective I'm sure I would have lost quickly enough as I grew older. Something was wrong with my father, too, and with Mickey Cohen and Moe Sedway and Gus Greenbaum and Tony Cornero, with all the men I knew out here. Including Nate Stein. And maybe it would have been better for me, much better, if I'd stayed at the bottom of this pool in 1946 and never came up.

45

I WAS SITTING OUTSIDE the bungalow, 3:00 A.M., in my mink coat for warmth and with my short hair standing up in tufts, the shorn head of a sorry French aristocrat about to be made sorrier when her tumbrel stopped at the Place de la Révolution. I'd filled a bowl with milk, and I sat with it in a chair by the front door, calling for the cats with the kissing noises and the soft hisses that usually drew them to me. Eventually, two of them came to drink, one cat a rusty-colored orange and the other black-striped, but they wouldn't sidle anywhere close to my outstretched fingers, wouldn't let me handle them. They even stood back from the bowl, as far back as they could manage, heads and necks stretched forward to lap quickly at the white contents, looking at me only briefly before darting away. They didn't know me, and I didn't know them. I'd named the seven kittens of that first Flamingo litter—Winter Paws, Pussy Showgirl, Madame Victoria, and other fancies of a fifteen-year-old mind—but after that, there were too many cats to keep track of and each successive generation of them became more feral and less domesticated than the last, until finally they were wild cats and suspicious of us all. Around me and the empty bowl the date palms shook their fronds.

It was dark, cold.

At this hour, my father was still in the casino, watching over the blackjack tables—Hit me. Seven. Bust. Goddamn. Double down—working his shift. Then, maybe, he'd be home. Sometimes after his shift, he had a quick drink at the Players Club, a shack on a lot by the Desert Inn, the club soon to be demolished, but until then nicknamed the Flamingo Annex because you could find half the Flamingo staff there after hours, whooping it up to Dorita's congas and maracas. Or maybe he would drop a token in some Flamingo slot machine and the bars would line up BAR BAR BAR 7 7 7 and he would play on his win, play on and on with the extra credits and free games the machine offered until he'd lost everything.

It didn't matter. I didn't mind being alone, a rarity in a Las Vegas so crowded with people. I sat here quietly in my painted metal lawn chair, the back of it shaped like a seashell from some very distant ocean body. The cheap windows of the bungalow rattled in their sashes. No clouds. Only stars, the moon. The same miracles I'd taken in as a child in my grandfather's house, continued to take in from every godforsaken place I'd ever lived in Los Angeles. And here.

I was just about to go to bed when I saw Nate walking up the path by the pool, heading my way, sure-footedly, though he had never been here before, had never come to this bungalow. He must have just discovered I was gone, had finished saying goodnight to the bartender and the manager in the Sky Room, had finished his one last tour of the Painted Desert Room to see it was properly cleaned and the kitchen spotless, was done nodding at the front desk with the stiff mail and the metal keys slotted in the cubbyholes, done checking that the lobby ashtrays had been polished, all lint vacuumed from the carpet and chairs, making sure the smudges on the shop windows had been wiped away, the shop doors locked. Nate could never come to bed without one last sweep of the hotel property, to see that the colored Dancing Waters had been shut off, that the dancers by the pool had vanished, the music turned off for the wee hours. Because even Vegas has its wee hours, of sleep, of desperation.

I gathered my fur coat more tightly around me to watch his approach. He couldn't see me, but I could see him. He walked

purposefully, hair a raised spike in the wind. He was wearing his
trench coat, the dark wool one, I saw, when he finally reached me
and then stopped abruptly in front of me to take me in, a little
surprised to find me sitting outside here in the dark, hunched in
a metal chair, instead of, perhaps, tucked into bed with a doll. Or
another Miltown. Without a word, he sat down in the flimsy chair
beside me, his body so big the chair back all but disappeared behind him, as did the seat beneath him.

He put out his hand.

I shied from it.

Nate used the outstretched hand I wouldn't take to touch my
skull, to finger the short hair standing away from my face, his
own face pained.

I edged my chair sideways along the concrete a few inches until
I was out of his reach, and eventually Nate dropped his hand.

"Come back home with me," he said.

I shook my head. "I'm not coming back."

I'd already observed that no woman seemed to stay with these
Vegas big boys for long, for more than a handful of years, that
they all eventually walked away. The wives didn't like what they
could not help but to learn, what they heard, what they saw, even
if all of it lay to the periphery, supposedly out of sight, out of ear-
shot. Benny Siegel's wife stayed behind in New York even after
Benny came out here. Dave Berman's wife left him and Vegas
altogether, so sickened by her husband's life she never recovered,
living as an invalid in one Los Angeles apartment or hospital after
another until she died. Gus Greenbaum's wife hadn't ever come
to Vegas with Gus, remained in Phoenix while he ran the Flamingo and now the Riviera. All these women had done the walk
away. And now so had I. And the men consoled themselves with
second and third wives, and when they walked away, with whores
or with mistresses who had once been whores. Nate had already

been married four times, and I suppose in me he thought he had found that girl of last resort, a girl at the sight of which my grandfather would draw his lips together.

Nate was staring at me in the dark. I thought at first he was bemused by my childish defiance, my skirting of his hand. But he wasn't bemused. I could feel that my lips had assembled themselves into an approximation of my grandfather's when confronted with a contaminant. And while I was certain this wasn't the first time Nate had seen that look directed his way, it was the first time he had seen it from me. And he didn't like it.

He stood up, a giant who forbade the wind to pull at his black coat. "If you're going to leave me, Esme, you might as well leave Vegas, too, you and your father. Because there's not going to be a place left here for either of you."

And he walked back down the path toward the Flamingo, head bent. And when my father got home an hour later he told me, "Esme, I've just been fired."

Los Angeles
1941

46

THE FACT THAT WORKING for Mickey Cohen might be a dangerous venture for him personally was something I don't think had ever occurred to my father before the day Maxie Shaman was murdered, the first of many murders to follow, men dropping dead all around my father through the years, victims of bullets, bombs, icepicks, knives, garrotes. I think my father saw just once an opportunity to escape all he had unthinkingly taken on.

We were climbing the Hollywood Hills one day in December, which we did sometimes together in reminiscence of our old drives through the narrow lanes of Hollywoodland, still dreaming, I suppose, of Castillo del Lago, of Wells' Loft or the Silver Lair, my father marveling even after his dozen years in California at how flowers still blossomed and fruit still grew even in what should have been winter, what was winter everywhere else. And as we climbed the slope of Mount Hollywood, my father pointed out to me the television towers that had recently been installed at the top of it, metal trees at the hill's peak. Some enterprising businessman had bought that property and put in towers and antennae and a pool, from which he was planning to broadcast a show called *Bathing Beauties*, which would feature young women in bathing suits swimming in the water and sunning themselves on chaises, a sort of Esther Williams free-for-all, sans Buzz's choreography. "By the

time you're old enough," my father said, "all the girls will be dancing on television. You won't even need MGM."

And I thought, Forget dancing. I would love to swim in a pool
all day, flowers in my hair, cameras filming me as I flicked my
limbs prettily through blue water and pointed my toes.

So I begged him to hike with me to the top of the hill, so we
could see up close the agent of this great emancipation from the
movie theaters. At this point in time, my father couldn't deny me
anything, we two still shell-shocked survivors on our own without
my mother. And so with the passing of another hour, by which
time I was panting and silently regretting my request, Who cared
about seeing some steel skeletons and an empty concrete bowl?,
we made it to the summit.

The shining silver television towers rose from bases so enor-
mously broad that I never would have guessed from down below
that my father and I could walk beneath them without stooping.
And what looked like narrow strips of metal and spindly pinnacles at a distance were in fact substantial structures designed
to send invisible and inaudible signals through the Los Angeles
skies and down into the television sets that would soon sit in the
living room of every fake thatched-roof bungalow, every fake two-
story Tudor with its black trim, every fake palazzo and *maison* in
the city, and the owners of these homes would watch the tales
spun by these new dreamers of the small screen, even if their
dreams were as thin and unimaginative as the simple broadcast-
ing of young women swimming around in scanty bathing attire.

But before we could even approach the fence around this
property, two men with rifles and Army uniforms appeared at
its perimeter and told us to go away, that the U.S. Army had
commandeered this property. There would be no swimming, no
pretty girls, no bathing beauties today, just men in army green.
We turned and headed back down the hill, my father in a hurry

now, saying, "Something's going on, something's up," brambles, grasses, stickers scratching at my bare legs until we reached a roadway, but it wasn't until we ducked into a diner by the Hollywoodland jitney stop that we found everyone in there huddled around a radio listening to the news: the Japanese had bombed Pearl Harbor.

And when my father had heard enough about the torpedoed battleships, cruisers, destroyers, and aircraft, all the American war machinery laid out in that harbor and picked off piece by piece, he took my hand and soberly led me back to our Cadillac, which he had parked, poorly, on Beachwood Drive. Once we were in the car, though, my father seemed strangely ebullient, slapping his palms on the steering wheel as he struggled to get the car off the gravel shoulder and back onto the road. "There's going to be a war, E! This'll be my way out! I'm going to join the Navy." It was a way out of this life and into another, and furthermore, joining up was noble, even mobster-approved. After Pearl Harbor, a lot of them enlisted. And when my father was discharged, he'd be free. He'd just be taking a different path, a new path, after the war, no offense, big boys.

"And then when the war's over, you and I will settle in the Valley and I'm gonna run my taxicab company!"

The taxi company was an idea my father trotted out periodically, an idea at which my mother had always scoffed. During and after the war, Standard Oil, Firestone, and General Motors used shell companies to buy up all the electric trolley lines, and then it was buses and taxis cruising everywhere, built by GM, fueled by Standard, and rolling around on Firestone tires. And then the airport was built and everybody needed a cab to get there with their suitcases, so actually my father was prescient, as prescient as, if somewhat less powerful than, John D. Rockefeller, Harvey Firestone, and William C. Durant. That afternoon, my father even came up with a name for this incarnation of his cab company—Veterans Taxi—and it would be staffed, he said, solely by vets coming home from the war, so a call to Veterans Taxi would be a patriotic choice!

Actually, it was a great idea.

But my father didn't end up enlisting, the plan foiled before it could even begin to be enacted. My father had been arrested a few times by then, so the Army wouldn't have him, declaring him an undesirable, mentally unfit, 4-F. Not that my father liked the idea of active service. He just liked the idea of being a veteran afterwards, with all the honor and respectability and new opportunities that implied. For the duration of the war, he carried his papers around, proffering them to anyone who asked why he wasn't in uniform. Of course, he could have founded the taxi company even if he weren't a veteran, but Mickey Cohen (also 4-F) was a sure thing and the taxi company an uncertain venture, and therefore, like so many of my father's ideas, this one flitted like a moth about our heads and finding it dim in there, flew off.

LAS VEGAS
1952

47

MY NAME HAD NOT yet been picked off the Desert Inn's marquee, I saw, when I arrived at my dressing room the next afternoon, but surely that was to come, the beak of some vulture, *caw, caw,* pecking away at the letters. Nate's next move. My things still stood on the ledge before my mirror—my portable plug-in coffeepot, my Morphy Richards iron, my tissue box, Aqua Net hairspray, alarm clock—the photographs of my mother were still thumbtacked to the walls, my costumes still hung on the portable metal rack, my tool box–size makeup case still parted to reveal its three levels of red, blue, and black paints. I knew my timely appearance backstage would already have been reported to Nate—or rather that my lack thereof would have been.

I took a deep breath. I was in full makeup for my midnight performance, orange face, false lashes, red lips, hair lacquered. In my hands, the vial of tranquilizers the hotel doctor had given me only yesterday morning. My plan was to take all the pills, just as Virginia Hill had done time and again. Her version of the walk away. Or the drift away. Or maybe it was just her way of trying to transmogrify Ben's anger into compassion, my purpose now, with Nate's. Either way, whatever way, I had to time this correctly. My dresser would soon be walking the hall to this room, to this chair, to me, to sieve me into my costume of velvet and fur. And there had to be pills to pump from my stomach when she arrived and when Nate eventually followed her here, as I knew he would when called. I checked the clock. 10:45 now.

I had to drink two glasses of water to down the twenty-nine and a half Miltowns left in the prescription bottle, and when I finished doing this, almost immediately I had to pee, more from nerves than from the water. Did I have time? I wished I could ask Virginia—or any of the young Hollywood actresses or actors who had swallowed pills or rat poison or alcohol in some paroxysm of lost hope. I knew I didn't want my dresser, the stage manager, or Nate coming in to find me slumped on the toilet in my blue cotton robe, half-undressed, or worse, toppled over on the bathroom floor, sash of my robe loosened, hem hiked in a rumple. Undignified. I had a different tableau in mind. So I scurried to the bathroom with more haste than was necessary and then ran back to my chair, where I unhooked my ESME necklace and laid it across my lap. A private message. Then I let the pill vial roll from my hand and take its theatrical place on the floor beside me. The big bright lights around the mirror made the bottle glow against the dark linoleum. I didn't want Nate to miss seeing it. Because that was the whole point of the exercise: for Nate to see this and let me go.

This had to work, because Nate had shown me unequivocally that without his beneficence, my father and I would find our cupboards bare. Yet if I managed this right, Nate would leave my father alone, perhaps out of guilt even let him back onto the Flamingo grounds, allow him to climb its ladder all the way up to the *F*. And perhaps, also out of guilt, Nate would let me keep my place here on the Painted Desert stage, permit the continuance of those regular deposits into my bank account, like ones my grandfather made weekly into his own, courtesy of Wolfkowitz Painting, these courtesy of my own business. Esme Wells, Orphan Burlesque.

I leaned back in my chair and looked up, ceiling low overhead, the pattern of dark and light against the exposed pipes and tubing both familiar and strange. I was a little nauseated, though whether from all the water or all the pills or my own thoughts, I wasn't sure. I imagined I was already feeling sleepy. Maybe I really was. The green face of my alarm clock on the dressing-table ledge seemed to glow as the red minute hand did its sweep. Once. Twice. Again.

I wondered how Virginia had felt as she waited for the pills to make her insensible, corralled up there in Benny's suite or in her bedroom on Linden Drive or in some hotel room in Europe. She had done this so many times in so many different places. Had she gobbled those pills down in a single minute or had she walked and walked the room until finally she said, "Goddammit, I'm going to kill myself," fumbling through her drawers and suitcase for her own bottle of Miltowns. Or her own bottle of whatever. And then what. Peace or terror? Or perhaps the repetition of this practice had dulled both for her. If I changed my mind, I could put a finger down my throat, turn back the clock. I'd wait fifteen minutes. Then I could do it or not.

But in fifteen minutes I didn't want to put a finger down my throat. Each one of my fingers had become too heavy even to flick, let alone lift to do something prescriptive. I was barely conscious enough to hear my dresser knock and say, "Miss Wells?" whatever time it was she said it. Her subsequent shout was from someplace far away and then a hub of noise crowded at the dressing-room door and fractured as it bore down upon me. When I opened my eyes, it was only because Nate, big face in my face, was using one arm to hoist me up out of my chair, shaking all ninety pounds of incredibly heavy me, while he stretched his other arm toward the rim of light behind him, wagging his fingers and bellowing, "Get the doctor!" Then he brought those fingers toward me and forced them, bulky and bad tasting, down my throat. Which produced nothing from me, my muscles too limp to respond. I was so weighted down by the pills, pills that themselves weighed almost nothing at all, that my body found itself utterly incapable of mustering the simplest involuntary response.

So Nate started walking me about my small dressing room, or rather, his feet were walking left, right, up, back, two steps in each direction before a wall loomed up and he had to turn, and my feet were dragging, my hip on his hip, his arm at my waist, my head hanging, my sash hanging, swinging left, right, left, right, as we passed the couch, the chair, the door, the little tables, the costume rack, Nate folding my arms around him the way I had folded my mother's limp arm around me at the National. And he was saying my name, "Esme, Esme, Esme," over and over and over. Shut up.

When the doctor arrived along with the stage manager who'd escorted him directly, hurriedly, here, dressing-room door opening with a bang, Nate screamed at him, "What took you so long, you goddamn fucking shitheel?" And the manager backed up, terrified, and then disappeared down the backstage hallway as if it were his hide that needed saving, but the beleaguered doctor stood firm, his face flushing, poor man called here at all hours to fix the dread deeds Nate had wrought. The doctor was the same one who had prescribed me the Miltowns, now here to undo their damage.

He waved his fuzzy arm, pointing to the bathroom, and Nate dragged me there, a sack without volition, and propped me up by the edge of the toilet as the doctor directed. The doctor drew a red rubber bag and hose from his black satchel. He threaded the hose into my nostril, an invasion against which I could not protest, not in the slightest, and so I just closed my eyes. I couldn't move even to gag, the big white floor tiles flickering at my feet, and as the doctor pushed that rubber tubing down my throat, Nate shouted, "You're too late, you're too late. Why don't we have a goddamn fucking hospital in this city?"

And the other thing Nate kept saying, over and over, was directed at me. "Come on, Esme, come on, come on." And I couldn't answer him, of course, nor could I silence him. I couldn't even turn my head. I shut my eyes so I wouldn't have to see him. Be quiet. With a syringe, the doctor sent water coursing through the tubing and into my stomach where it sloshed in that vacant tomb and then he worked the pump at the head of the tube. Nothing.

And then I felt a hand on my wrist, nails in my skin. I opened one eye. My mother was standing there with a blackened face. She put her red-lipsticked mouth to my ear. "Wake up."

I could smell her.

She pulled on my arm.

And whatever was left inside me was suddenly heaved up and out and I vomited liquid and powder even as the doctor was still pumping my stomach, and as I splattered his shirtfront, the sink, the floor, everywhere but the toilet, he cried, "Good girl," triumphant and relieved, of course, that once more he had come through for Nate, had not let Nate down.

And Nate sat on the bathroom floor in all that mess and cried.

Afterwards, I lay on the little dressing-room sofa like a deflated plastic doll, a single millimeter thin, while Nate sat on a chair by me, his hand on mine, repeating over and over to the flattened girl I had become, "Why did you do this, E? Don't you know I'll always take care of you?"

Well, yes. I knew that now. Now that I had assured it.

48

BY THE NEXT DAY, word had gone all around the Strip that Baby E had tried to kill herself because Nate Stein was leaving her.

So be it. Better than the truth.

49

WITHIN THE MONTH, MY father had moved us out of the bungalow and off the Flamingo hotel grounds, the first time since
we'd come to Las Vegas that we wouldn't be living in a hotel. He
had bought us a house, price tag $21,950, to keep me away from
the Desert Inn, away from the Strip, and away from Nate and his
influence. Or so he thought. It was hard to get very far away from
Nate. Because, laughably, the house my father bought for us was
in Paradise Palms, one of Nate's recent real estate ventures with
Moe Dalitz and Irwin Molasky, his ingenious new suburban tract
just north of the Strip, right next to what would soon enough be
the Stardust Hotel's golf course. As for my father himself, after
first reinstating him at the Flamingo, Nate then moved him to the
newly opened Riviera, along with Gus Greenbaum and company,
and promoted him to shift supervisor in the counting room. So
after seven years in Vegas, my father was back in the counting
room. Price tag for that trajectory: twenty-nine and a half pills.

When we closed on the house, my father, triumphant, bottle of
champagne wrapped in a white hand towel and tucked between
us, drove me over after his shift to see it. I was no longer working.
I was supposed to be recovering, quietly, out of sight, from my
alleged nervous breakdown, while still on the Desert Inn payroll.
The disabled list. We rode in the new 1953 black Ambassador
Nate had bought for me, which was more than a car, it was half-
car, half-spaceship, like the Viking 7 rocket, the car showy with
its white top, white-walled tires, white details. It was a get-well-
soon present, an act of penitence, an apology, metallic evidence
of Nate's unspoken regret. Tell me I didn't ruin your life. Take
this fun car.

And, of course, I took it.

The streets of Paradise Palms bore the names of the Indian tribes who had once been the sole inhabitants of Paradise Valley before the Spanish arrived here, before we arrived here—the Paiute, the Shoshone—and even the names of some tribes that had never lived here—like the Seneca or the Comanche or the Pawnee. The new neighborhood had baseball diamonds and Little League teams, playgrounds and volleyball courts, Boy Scout troops, an elementary school. The streets and lawns were landscaped with date palms and creosote and Joshua trees, with grass and with gravel. The houses were made of concrete, some façades ornamented with rock, some sporting fences of filigreed cement blocks like a child's tower, and Models 2A, 2B, and 2C featured variously a flat roof or an A-line roof or a double A-line roof, with the option of a garage or a carport. The windows were big and tall, like the windows of the Sky Room, and every house had its own little pool in back, accessed by sliding glass doors. And whichever way we turned, left or right, I could see the site where ground had been broken for Nate's latest project, Sunrise Hospital, for which Las Vegas had me to thank.

Nate's advertising pamphlets for these neighborhoods bore the slogans "Here Is the Better Life" or "A Place in Paradise!" And the houses were filled with band leaders and bookies, musicians and comics and singers and their families seeking just that—families from an upside-down world of some new kind of Americana where the vices of alcohol, gambling, heroin, and girls were now just the workday norm. And many of those big windows, I saw, were lit up even now, at 4:00 A.M. Most of working Las Vegas was up at night and asleep by day after they got the kids off to school.

We drove north on Seneca Drive and turned west on Sombrero, north on Pawnee and then left on Silver Mesa Circle. My father parked in the driveway of one of the houses. A few cars were parked on the street or in driveways. The house was a one-story flat-roofed box, Model 2A, with the carport option and a concrete-block fence running halfway across the front of the modest house to shield it from the view of passersby. This was it, our house, all 1,000 square feet of it, not quite, not anything at all like, the showy mansions we'd once dreamed of owning in Hollywoodland, our Castillo del Lago, or even our Wells' Loft. And it was located not on one of the lush peaks of the Hollywood Hills but on this tiny dry lot in a desert valley 260 miles east. Ah. I know. The Silver Folly.

But all I said was, "Dad, this is great."

My father said, "Come on, E," and jumped from the car, eager, ridiculously eager, to show me the prize he'd procured for us. He put the key in the lock and flung the front door open with a flourish, saying, "After you." I swear, he practically bowed. And after he'd flipped on the lights, with some ceremony he handed me one of the two keys he'd had made.

"Ours," he said. "I paid cash."

Cash?

Inside, the concrete floors were the temperature of ice water and the color of the giant gray moon that hung every night in the east before crossing the sky. Nylon carpets were coming, my father assured me, to be installed soon. He gestured at the big space around us, pointing out all the latest, most modern fixtures, the Tappan oven and fridge, the Whirl-a-way disposal, the Rheemaire's heating and air conditioning, the Kentile vinyl-asbestos tile, the aluminum-framed windows—none of that old-fashioned splintering wood that constantly needed painting—the luminous ceilings, the wood beams that clung to those luminous ceilings.

I wandered the long, flat space, my father hovering close behind me, watching me as I inspected the vacant living and dining rooms, one wall all brick fireplace, the other all glass, which framed the golf course and beyond that the desert valley and mountains. The sliding door opened to a small oval pool, not yet filled. Sliding doors from one of the bedrooms opened to the pool, as well.

"This room can be yours," my father said. "I'll take the smaller one in the back." He waved his arm to the little bedroom down the hall.

Everything we did echoed, every step we took, every word my father spoke.

"So what do you think, baby girl?"

"It's nice." And it was. It wasn't grand, but it was nice.

"We can turn the fire on if you're cold. It's gas."

I shook my head. "I'm not cold."

But he turned it on anyway. I think he wanted to show it off.

Then he went off into the kitchen, made some noise there, and when he reappeared, hatless, coat shed, dropped to the concrete floor or onto one of the fabulous Formica counters, he was ready for fun, the opened bottle of champagne under one arm, two glasses in his hand. To all the fabulousness around us, my father said, "Let's drink! Come on outside, see the pool up close."

He opened the sliding glass door and stepped out first. I watched him pace around the small empty blue-painted cement pit, which I supposed we would soon fill. How? Was there some hose, a spigot? I couldn't tell. I went outside then, too. The pool, one day, filled with water, would reflect that moon and those stars, but for now it stood like an empty gaping ditch, reflecting nothing. Some kind of debris skittered along the concrete bottom, stirred by the wind. Music from the house next door. Or maybe it was music from the Strip, notes also carried by the wind these few blocks. An organ. The Dancing Waters at the Desert Inn. My father circled the pool a few times, one hand in his pants pocket, other hand still holding his champagne glass. While I watched, he toasted the moon, what was up there of it. No. He wasn't toasting the moon, he was toasting my mother who sat up there on the moon's rim, dark hair shining, smiling down at him and at her daughter, more like her than either of them could have known.

He drank his champagne and then my father cleared his throat. He wasn't looking at the moon anymore.

"I want to tell you something, baby girl. I went to the National after the funeral. I sat here, I sat there, I think I put myself down into every godforsaken chair in that godforsaken theater, but I just couldn't quite figure out where you two might have been sitting that day. My plan was to watch *Gold Diggers*, the picture the two of you saw. But I couldn't do it. I had to get up and leave halfway through."

He stood there watching me across our crater of a pool.

"Don't leave me the way your mother did, Esme. Don't leave me half the way through."

And how could I tell him then that swallowing those pills had been a trick, a stunt, a grift, like his pocketing all the money from the bettors at MGM and hoping none of the horses came in at Hollywood Park, their losses his secret win, as my pocketed Miltowns had become mine. But I didn't want my father to think less of me, to know that I could be so calculating, that I could gamble like that with my life. I'd rather have him think of me as an unmoored girl in distress, like my mother. And who knows, maybe I really had thought I deserved to die. So I said nothing.

But he saw something on my face, and he misunderstood that, too.

He put up a hand, ready for an argument I wasn't planning to make.

"I didn't mean to leave you alone afterwards for so long, baby girl," he said. "I just didn't know it would take me that many months to persuade myself to go on."

LOS ANGELES
1939

50

ON THE EVENINGS MY mother wasn't dancing at the Clover, my parents went out, often to Benny Siegel's Holmby Hills home, for which Benny had forsaken his Castillo del Lago and where Benny had gone on a decorating frenzy in imitation of the Countess di Frasso's own mansion. Cary Grant and Clark Gable and Marion Davies and Loretta Young gathered in the evenings to enjoy some mobster company, whatever of that company was presentable enough, and there were some members presentable enough, like Al Smiley or Ike Silver. Mickey Cohen, at that time not yet sufficiently polished up, was invited there as entertainment—to box in a hastily erected exhibition ring—and my parents would gather shoulder to shoulder with movie royalty to applaud the show, after which there was drinking and dancing and gambling. My grandfather the Austrian had left the old country around the same time as Goldwyn, Mayer, Lasky, and Cohn, but it was his daughter who grasped and reached and twisted and connived like the moguls, and now she was partaking of the sweets.

For these occasions and others, my mother had a new dress or costume made for herself every two weeks, all of them tailored especially for her by the woman next door to us on Soto Street, Mrs. T., I never learned her last name, an extraordinarily inventive seamstress from Paramount who created these marvels on the side, fabulous concoctions of feathers, spangles, and satin. The garment bags my mother stored them all in could barely contain them, so stuffed were they with the combustible energy of those fabrics and ornaments. Mrs. T. herself looked like a mouse to me, small, stooped, with hair that was neither brown nor blond, pink-rimmed eyes, their vision assisted by a pair of reading glasses poised halfway between her nostrils and the bridge of her nose. A mouthful of straight pins. Not a movie star. Definitely not a movie star. Yet from this nondescript person erupted a flamboyance worthy of my mother, who for all I knew might have represented Mrs. T.'s secret vision of her secret self in which she was no longer a mouse but a lion.

Standing on the small platform before the triple mirror in the living room cum fitting room of the bungalow next door, my mother modeled Mrs. T.'s confections and ignored the two of us, we small figures in the background of her own reflection, two mice, I a tinier version of Mrs. T. and equally unworthy of attention. Mrs. T. never swallowed a pin, though I waited patiently for this to one day happen. What did happen was that Mrs. T., taking pity on me, made me a skirt and two cuffs of stiff black tulle from the leftover fabric she'd used to make the tail for my mother's peacock costume—I was noticed by someone!—and I wore the stuff always, a constant accessory, as if I, too, were nightclub entertainment and this were the sliver of some larger magnificent me I was yet to become. I was six, but it seemed I'd already heard the call.

And when Mr. Cohen saw the bedraggled black tulle I wore so religiously, he started giving my father weekly wrist corsages to take home to me from his latest business venture, Michael's Greenhouses, the corsages made up sometimes of roses, little miniature baby roses, other times peonies, flowers of every color, red, yellow, once baby blue, sometimes the palest pink to an almost, almost white. I saved the wilted browned corsages in a box in my room as if they were coins in a piggy bank, but unlike pennies, those old corsages infused my room with a reeking flower smell I thought divine.

I longed to grow up and join my parents at Benny Siegel's place, but until then, I would be left behind. So on their evenings out, I lay on my bed, as usual, latest corsages on each wrist, smelling them alternately, listening to Mrs. T. who enjoyed no nightlife whatsoever of her own and who was therefore paid to keep an ear out for me from across the narrow walkway between our two houses: my bedroom window opened onto hers and I could hear her working on her sewing machine, the whirr and the stop of it. I think she took in mending, too. I'd listen to her and gaze at the ridiculous colors of my ceiling and walls that I had selected from the Kon-Kre-Kota and that my father had purchased and, using the skills acquired during his brief stint at my grandfather's company, had rolled up over every surface. It was like sleeping in a circus tent. As a joke, my father would put a hand up to shield his eyes every time he walked into my room. But I loved it. It was a preview, I suppose, of the neon-gilded Las Vegas I would also come to love.

That night, I lay in bed and listened to my pawnshop Patriot radio, waiting for my favorite show, *Gangbusters*, to start. I sniffed both my corsages at once and scratched at my arms, which had lately begun sporting a horribly bumpy red rash, which my father had diagnosed as an allergy from Mickey Cohen's goddamn gardenias and roses, but which would take the nuns at the Sisters Home to diagnose as impetigo from my not having been bathed enough. For weeks to come, my arms would have to be washed twice a day and painted with gentian violet so that I looked like a space alien—as if those weeks to come would not be traumatic enough. For now, I scratched and waited for my program.

Gangbusters always began, as it should, with the sounds of sirens and machine-gun fire and a man's portentous voice. "Calling all police. Calling all G-men. Calling all Americans to war on the underworld!" More sirens. "*Gangbusters*! Brought to you, the men and women of America, by the makers of Sloan's Liniment, with the co-operation of leading law enforcement officials of the United States, *Gangbusters* presents the facts of the relentless war of the police on the underworld." And the program always ended the same way, too, with the announcer booming, "Crime does not pay!"

Though that had not yet been my experience.

I hadn't even gotten very far in the program when my parents pulled their Cadillac around the back of the house. They were home early and they were arguing as they got out of the car, and their voices woke me up or mixed in with the radio I'd left on under the covers, a blur of sounds that were no longer dreamy or smooth. The sewing machine was silent, which meant either my next-door neighbor had already called out across the driveway, "Good night, Esme," and gone to sleep or was quietly listening to my parents alongside me. I sat up in my bed.

My mother was speaking outside, loudly, indiscriminately, of course, in that way she had, her words ricocheting between the garage and the back of the house. I got out of bed and went to the window just as she walked around the car to where my father still sat in the driver's seat, door closed against her in a futile effort at self-protection. She had her shoes in one hand, the spiky heels a black corsage. A dog barked from somewhere down the block. A car drove by, its radio leaving a trail of notes in the Soto Street hemisphere. The moon and the streetlamps faced off in the night sky. Camellias and hibiscus unfurled their blossoms. The Cadillac gave off a mechanical hiss.

"You'll just take a year off," my father was saying from behind the wheel.

"I'll be a year older."

"It's just a year."

"And who's to say what I'll look like when the year's over. Or if I'll ever get the stage back?" my mother said, and she set her shoes down on the hood of the car, as if those shoes were the problem. They faced two different directions, north and south.

My father got out of the car now, the better to reason with her. "If not that stage, another one, all right? The boys are opening clubs all up and down Sunset." And he waved his arm as if Sunset were right up at the end of Soto Street here in Boyle Heights.

That just made her hiss at him, "You want to tuck me away like Ben's wife, Esta."

My mother, tucked away? I wasn't sure that was even possible. My mother once said that if it weren't for me she'd rather just live in a hotel, not be bothered with laundry and pots and pans. Not that she bothered much with them anyway. And I doubted my father wanted her to be a housewife, a Betty Crocker. He took pride in her beauty and her talent, loved to stop by the Clover to see her numbers, though he told me later she wasn't a headliner as I had thought, but just an entr'acte, her dances wedged between a singer and a jazz band.

"Dina, you know that's not true."

And I knew that it wasn't, that my mother was being unreasonable. For a change. Not that this stopped her.

"And who's going to watch the baby?" she said.

"We'll find someone."

"Really? The way we found someone to watch Esme? Because I feel like I've dragged her behind me for a thousand miles. A hundred thousand." My mother's face was stretched tight, the face of someone starving. "I'm not letting you push me into having another child. One's enough!" and she pointed at my bedroom window, which made my father turn to look, and that's when he saw my face framed there, looking out at them.

He put up his hand to my mother, who turned her head. She didn't seem pleased to see me.

"Esme." She waved her pointing hand with the bangled brace-lets. "What are you doing up?"

"Go back to bed, E," my father said, and he took my mother by the arm, picked her shoes up off the car hood with his free hand. When he saw I was still at the window, he jerked his chin at me to make me do what he wanted, and I retreated.

I took my corsages off my wrists and dropped them into the box with the others, fresh little roses crowning a pile of brown-petaled bracelets, which made me think of my father's saying, "Gather ye rosebuds while ye may," each time Michael's Green-houses delivered me another corsage. I looked around. For the first time, I saw how garish the colors were I'd chosen for my walls. I would tell my father tomorrow I wanted to paint them over. White. And I wanted to throw out my flowers. They stank. I wanted to throw out everything. I wanted to run to Union Sta-tion, that station at which my father had long ago arrived, and buy myself a ticket to somewhere else. Maybe Baltimore, where my father had come from and where his family still lived, all the way east, next to that other ocean. But I wasn't sure any of them even knew I existed. And I was in my pajamas. So instead, I crawled under my bed, an action I promptly regretted—under there dust had formed its own layer of crusty earth—but re-fused to reverse.

When my father brought my mother and her bare feet inside, their fight raged on. Even from my impromptu burrow, Esme's Burrow, I heard them through my bedroom wall. I wished my parents were dead so they'd stop talking or better yet, that I were dead so I didn't have to hear them anymore. Better than that, that I had never been born, all the miles my mother had so resentfully dragged me rescinded. And, eventually, somehow, I fell asleep.

But I wouldn't have slept at all if I'd known everything was going to be over so quickly.

51

THE NEXT MORNING WAS Saturday, the day my father always went off to one of Cohen's bookie joints to monitor the racing results and the betting, but my mother was gone, too, I discovered, when I woke, a little dust-covered, and crawled out from under the bed, and that was odd. She always slept in on Saturday mornings. I wandered the house, a little bewildered by the wreck of it, the bottles, the glasses, the cigarettes, as if there had been a big party here, but I knew there hadn't been. It had just been a party of two, a long, drawn-out bedraggled party with two reluctant guests, both of whom were now long gone. So I sat amidst the disarray and waited.

At noon, my mother drove up in the Cadillac, and without emerging, honked, called my name, and told me to get dressed. We were going to the movies. She sat in the car waiting for me, smoking a cigarette, a yellow seated statue in the expansive front seat of our car parked behind the house. I kept checking on her as I dressed and I could see she barely moved, that arm with the cigarette dangling out the driver's window, and I thought, I need to hurry. I'm pretty sure she picked a day at the theater to keep me quiet so she could rest without being bothered by me, and what better way to amuse me than with a newsreel, cartoons, and two movies. Outside it smelled burnt, the sky brown, and on the ridge of one of the hills to the north a wildfire showed itself, a slight orange glimmer. Little bits of soot and ash fell from the sky as I ran to join her in the car.

We could spend all day in the cool of the National Theatre on Brooklyn Avenue, which everybody in Boyle Heights called the Pollyseed House, because its patrons brought sunflower seeds with them to snack on during the shows, even though everybody ate popcorn at the theaters downtown or up in Hollywood. But this was Jewtown. The theater had a storefront marquee crammed in between miscellaneous signage—NEW YORK CAFÉ, MALTED MILK 10 CENTS, BOYLE HEIGHTS CLEANERS, and, simply, TAILOR. Ducking beneath it all and paying your quarter, you could stay there all afternoon in the dark under the big ceiling fans, watching the pictures flick by on the screen, and when we came out, my mother said, the sunlight would have grown thin and a lot less warm, the sky a yellow-brown rather than hot blue because even though it was mid-September, autumn everywhere else in the country, my mother said, this was southern California and September was our hottest month, fire season.

And all around us, of course, sat the neighbors my mother had known since she was a little girl—my mother couldn't walk anywhere without somebody saying hello to her, asking her if she was a big star yet, as if ambition were something to jibe about. At the National, we always sat to the side and toward the back in what we had come to call our seats, I don't know why my father didn't know this, bristling if we found the seats taken by others. But today, no bristling. My mother hurried me as I tried to linger looking at the lobby cards for the soon to be released *Gone with the Wind*, six scenes of Clark Gable in a frock coat and Vivien Leigh in a hooped ball dress and gray-coated Confederate soldiers lying dead on Civil War battlegrounds or in happier days smoking cigars on the porches of old southern plantations, but even so, no one had taken our seats.

She sat down with a sigh and said, "Stop scratching, Esme."

I stopped. It was hard, but I stopped.

The National showed older movies; in fact, that day it was showing *Gold Diggers of Paris*, the picture my mother shot last year with Buzz when he was working at Warner Brothers. In the picture, a man named Maurice comes to New York from France to gather some ballet dancers for a Parisian dance competition, but somehow he ends up not at the ballet company's rehearsal hall but at a nightclub. And because the nightclub is about to go out of business, the wily owners pretend they run a ballet company. On the ship crossing the Atlantic they have to teach all their strutting showgirls how to do ballet, and my mother was one of those showgirls.

The theater grew dark and my mother put her arm around me and squeezed, telling me she loved me, something she didn't say often, and after last night, I wasn't sure I could believe. We settled in for the newsreel, which was always first.

UNIVERSAL NEWSREEL
SPECIAL RELEASE

EUROPE AT WAR!
NAZIS ATTACK POLAND AND
BOMB CITIES IN LIGHTNING
COUP—FRANCE & ENGLAND
PREPARE TO STRIKE

A man's voice intoned urgently, "On September the first 1939 the German army smashed into Poland," and the picture accompanying it featured cartoon drawings of a big boot crushing the grass beneath it. The soundtrack was full of cymbal crashes and ominous music, followed by shots of a rally, an enormous version of what I had seen at the Deutsches Haus, the arena hung with swastikas and an eagle and flags and bunting, with hands shooting into the frame as the crowd saluted. Heil, Hitler. Then a new scene. Rows of men in uniform were marching down a wide dirt boulevard, rows of goose-stepping men, and then in a quick change, a group of planes flying in formation, making three vees, like a flock of birds.

Then it was back to a cityscape. The theater echoed with the sound of air-raid sirens. I shrank down in my seat. Men and women in hats and coats were running to air-raid shelters. Then the camera showed what happened while they were inside. Bombs dropped and the streets and buildings of that city exploded in smoke and flames. Afterwards a woman in a kerchief and cloak, an old country woman, sat on a step with her head in her hand. A baby cried while having its head bandaged. People stood on ladders to pile sandbags up against buildings, even though some of those houses already had holes in what used to be their ceilings and rooms with piles of broken wood in them that once was furniture.

I looked at my mother, but she had closed her eyes. Off duty.

I turned back to the screen as the camera showed bodies of people lined up on a sidewalk right where people had just been walking, the dead people lying there in rows still wearing their pants and dresses, some of them with their shoes blown off, their bodies not even covered by sheets. Water. Boats with cannons. Explosions. Fields. Men on horseback. Horses pulling carts. The men stopped and loaded the cannons right there on the field. Men saying goodbye to their families through a wooden fence. Horses having shoes put on their feet, the hot iron, a puff of smoke. Men piling up bombs, smoothly metallic.

The narrator's voice intoned, "World War II has begun." Someplace else now. Thatched roofs a muddle, holes made by something bigger than bullets in the plaster façade of a building. Women in dark coats and kerchiefs read a Proclamation posted on a wall. My grandfather had told me that in Germany the Jews were no longer allowed to visit parks, cinemas, or restaurants, that Jewish children could not go to school, and that stores and synagogues had been vandalized or burned to the ground. But here, on Breed Street, rose the intact structure of Congregation Talmud Torah, its brown edifice curved at the apex. A big stained-glass window above the double doors bore a Jewish star, and above that, embedded into the brick were the two tablets of the Ten Commandments. There, tanks moved through city streets, shooting, and then those streets turned to flame. The Führer jumped out of a car that had barely stopped moving and above him all along the street the second-story windows projected flags with swastikas. The newsreel drew to its scratchy close.

The theater was silent.

The cartoon started and the screen exploded in color. Inside the purple, green, and yellow target were words.

WARNER BROS PICTURES INC.
PRESENTS
MERRIE MELODIES
A DAY AT THE ZOO

Bugles and xylophone. Two men named Bill, doffing their hats at each other and shaking each other's hands, "Hello, Bill." "Hello, Bill." "Hello, Bill." Monkeys in a cage throwing peanuts to the people outside it, who caught the nuts in their mouths. A man with a face so much like a baboon that the zookeeper put him in the cage and let the baboon itself go free. A bird in a black-and-white-striped prison jumpsuit and matching cap pacing a cell, saying, "I didn't do it, I'm telling you, I didn't do it." Next to him, a pigeon sat on a stool, saying, "He did it. He definitely did it. I saw it with my own eyes." A wolf sniffed at the locked door to a cage where cows stood mooing and camels were smoking Camels. A joke.

It was when the lights went on briefly, gently, at the intermis-

sion between the cartoon and the feature that I saw my mother
had somehow over the last hour become a wax doll, a figure as
beautifully white as she was limp, her head resting against the
seat and turned to one side away from me, so all I could see was
her jaw and her cheek. Although her lap was dry, the hem of her
dress was soaked through with blood, blood that had pooled beneath her and then with nowhere else to go had slowly dripped
over the sides of her chair and found its way to the floor beneath
where it had set some seed shells afloat. They spun, lazily, black
coats among the red liquid. I understood immediately that my
mother was dead, her arms at her sides, her palms turned upward
to the big fans making their slow spin through the thick, hot air.

My father would find out later that she'd gone that morning to
Long Beach, to one of Benny Siegel's many abortion parlors, and
that, even as early as her drive back north to us, she had begun
slowly hemorrhaging, which is, from what I understand, a pain-
less death. You don't even know you are dying. And I believe she
did not. She had made no sound beside me. And so now I made
no sound beside her. Somehow I knew that this was my last time
to be alone with my mother, and I didn't want to be separated
from her. If I cried out, they would take her from me in the en-
suing stir. So I said nothing. I used two hands to turn her head
toward me, her pretty face expressionless as it never was in life,
and when the lights went down again, I curled up next to her and
carefully arranged her right arm over my shoulder.

Up on the big screen *Gold Diggers in Paris* laid open its great
big silly self. I watched my mother on the deck of a fake ocean
liner, the Warner Brothers version of that half ship landlocked
on MGM's Lot Two, saw her strolling behind Rudy Vallee, bundled up in a fur-trimmed coat and a smart fedora and smiling.
I watched her do the Can-Can, wearing a beret and tap shoes,
kicking the sky, and I watched her do the Charleston on the

stage set of a Parisian street, and she appeared again in a Hawaiian number, wearing a patterned bathing suit and lei, with a big flower in her hair, and then she was tap dancing up and down a long, low staircase built to measure in one of Warner Brothers shops and erected in its sky-high soundstage, attired like fifty other girls in a strange long-sleeved black leather top, with a matching black leather bottom and a floor-length swirling black skirt, the girls' movements syncopated with those fifty boys in tails, arms up, arms down, arms up, arms down, Buzz's tap shoe-clicking, rhythmic coordination ending when the girls did a backwards swoon, one after the other, into the arms of the boys, all that youth, all that energy, all that eagerness, all that life. The girls fell back, the boys pushed them up, and I watched my mother dancing with them up there as intently as I knew how, as if I could make what had fallen down spring back up, will my mother's spirit from the celluloid back to her beautiful body. You only lived forever on the screen.

And when the picture was over, the Betty Crockers all around the huddle of me and my mother started to cry and shriek and wave their spoons.

That my mother might not have died if I had said something, anything, to one of them between *A Day at the Zoo* and *Gold Diggers* was a thought that didn't occur to me until years later.

LAS VEGAS
1953

52

ALTHOUGH I AVOIDED THE Strip now, I still kept nightclub hours, to bed at 5:00 A.M., up at 3:00 P.M., which in February was just a couple hours from dusk, when small children, the almost invisible inhabitants of Las Vegas, made their way home from elementary school, tiny chorines with book bags in a sidewalk parade. Their parents and almost every other adult in Paradise Palms worked the Strip and my neighbors kept my time clock. To amuse myself, I'd watch their lit-up windows wax yellow late into the night until suddenly they blinked and went black, snuffed out, just before sunup. Whatever news of the Strip that found its way to me came, though, not from my neighbors, but from my father, who arrived home each night with tatters of gossip stuck to him as if he'd walked through some salacious tickertape parade. That's how I kept up with everything, and that's also how I learned Nate had begun dating Milton Prell's secretary from the newly opened Sahara, news about which my father was clearly happy, though my own response was somewhat muddled, a hash of pain and relief and disbelief, because he had found someone new so quickly and because I wasn't there to see it, and therefore, as I'd learned from my parents, what you didn't see wasn't entirely real.

My father came home almost every day just before dawn, every inch of him and every pore stinking of cigarette smoke, something that had not really registered with me before as it was as much a part of my environs as chips and dice, but now the smell made itself quite distinct here away from the Strip. He would fall onto his bed at the end of the hall into a rumpled, reeking sleep. Occasionally, he didn't come home until late in the day. He, like Nate, was seeing someone new, though he never said so, another someone I would never meet, other than to run into, accidentally, in a casino, as I had met, once or twice, the others. He never brought women home, not to the bungalow, not here to Paradise Palms—at first because I was a young girl and now because he didn't need to. If Vegas had anything, it was a surplus of hotel rooms. Seven years ago, his girlfriends had been young women, but as he had aged, so had they, as if he were dating serial versions of my mother, as if she were growing older alongside us. The women had looked somewhat like her, young, white, dark-haired, and they were, as she had been, either dancers or singers. Then, as my father got older, he seemed to tire of the constant replication of the young Dina Wells, all those reimages of her in some crazy Busby Berkeley reprise, and these later girlfriends looked tough, weather-beaten, soft-jowled, as if worn down by the heat and the smoke and the late hours. And they were waitresses.

Whether my father slept here or elsewhere, he made it a point to spend the late afternoons and evenings with me, the hours we had together before his shift started at 10:00 P.M. I'd sit out on one of our aluminum and plastic-slatted lawn chairs and watch him swim his steady awkward feet-flapping laps and when he was finished, he'd shower and cook us dinner on the rickety three-legged coal grill we had out by the pool. Steaks, usually, often my only meal of the day. I had little appetite. I'd gotten thinner. I'd taken up smoking, which seemed to have supplanted my need for food. I understood now why all the Donn Arden girls had smoked, especially the ones who'd had children and whose bodies had changed and wanted to thicken under that biological imperative, an imperative it seemed only tobacco or diet pills could undercut.

When it got too dark and too cold to sit outside any longer, we went in to watch the new television programs exploding over all the new networks, better programming than the fledgling producers of *Bathing Beauties* could ever have imagined. Girls swimming and lolling about? No. Not at all. We watched *The Adventures of Ozzie and Harriet*, a radio show I'd listened to in the forties, now reformatted. In real life, Ozzie Nelson was a Los Angeles band leader and his wife, Harriet, a blond bombshell of a nightclub act, but on this show, they were homebodies, as the fifties seemed to demand. If the Andy Hardy serials had been television shows, they would have looked like this.

And vaudeville, too, had found its way to the small screen, some Ozzie and Harriet sanctioned version of it. *The Jackie Gleason Show* had Jimmy Dorsey and his Orchestra and the June Taylor Dancers, both sandwiched between comics and singers. Ed Sullivan's *Toast of the Town* had the dancing Toastettes pinched together with singers, comics, puppeteers, and circus acts. Their chorus girls did on television what we girls did here in the desert showrooms, what Hollywood did in its thirties musicals, what girls in the teens and twenties once did in New York's cavernous vaudeville theaters. If the Nelson family could watch this now at home, what new and different thing would Vegas find to fill its seats in all our new hotels?

For the Riviera had opened, the Sands had opened, the Sahara had opened, and the Dunes, the New Frontier, and soon the monstrosity of the Stardust. Every one of these hotels would need a draw—not only headliners from Hollywood and Broadway, but also some new kind of showgirls and novel extravaganzas for their lounges and showrooms. Rumor had it Harold Minsky was negotiating with the Dunes to bring out his Follies, his revue of topless girls, but that Jack Entratter, who liked pretty faces and securely costumed bodies and who was president of Nate's newly built Temple Beth Shalom, was balking. But surely that was one way to differentiate ourselves from the girls on CBS. By our costumes—by what they were or were not.

So somehow I wasn't entirely surprised when Donn Arden knocked on the door one evening after my father had gone off to the Riv. Not entirely surprised to find myself summoned, but surprised by the messenger. Donn Arden? Donn Arden in Paradise Palms? I think I'd only ever seen him in the hotels, in their showrooms or stages or wings or backstage hallways. I didn't even know where Donn lived. For all I knew, he could be my neighbor here on Silver Mesa Circle. He wore a jacket and tie, because, apparently, this was an official visit, his dark rumpled hair oiled almost into submission, and he shifted his choreographer's feet uncomfortably on the concrete slab that served as Model 2A's unceremonious minimalist front porch. He seemed nervous, something I never was anymore, now that I was a Harriet Nelson housedaughter, albeit one who had discovered Miltowns.

"Esme, may I speak with you?"

I let him in and we went to the living room, which held just a single couch and our television set, rabbit ears of its antennae askew, box tuned to one of my programs, blue-and-black television screen flickering almost like neon. Donn seated himself on the sofa, pants hiked up to show his blue socks, but not, thank God, anything further. I sat on the fireplace's low brick hearth, gas fire warming my back. Have I mentioned I was in pajamas? I didn't always dress, left the house only for cigarettes and groceries and doctor appointments. In fact, the past month or so I'd talked to no one but my father or the grocery store salesgirls, so I wasn't entirely sure what would come out of my mouth when the time came to speak.

Arden cleared his throat, little of his usual arrogance in evidence here. So I was right, he was nervous. What he eventually said was not, How are you, Esme, or Nice to see you again, Esme, but, "Mr. Stein would like to know if you're ready to come back to work."

Donn may have blurted this out, but he sounded dubious about the prospect, now that he had seen me. And smelled me. I might have been wearing this particular set of pajamas for a few days.

So Mr. Stein wanted to know if I was ready to come back to work. Apparently, I hadn't been entirely drummed out of Nate's mind by the glamorous clamor of Milton Prell's executive secretary at the typewriter keys. He had read her memo that told him I had become a recluse, a pixie-cut in a nightgown, one who ate smoke instead of food. And so he planned to draw me out, a little desert animal coaxed forward with a berry. Don't you know I'll always take care of you?

"Mr. Stein has taken over part ownership of the Stardust."

Of course he has.

"And the plan is to bring in sixty dancers and singers from the Lido club in Paris for a permanent engagement at the hotel."

For which, apparently, Arden's talents had been commissioned.

Lido de Paris. It sounded continental, by which I meant it sounded racy. Racier than the Ed Sullivan or the Jackie Gleason television shows.

"The show will be called 'C'est Magnifique' and the nudity's going to be classy, European, no bump and grind, just a seamless part of the show. Some girls will be topless, some not, you definitely not."

So some covered wagons, some not, as we girls referred to the bra portions of our costumes. I'd be in a covered wagon. Covered by Nate's orders. As if my bare skin had been the factor that had unhinged me.

"And Mr. Stein would like you to be the headliner."

Ah.

Also Nate's orders.

"It will be a big show, Esme. The Stardust is going to be the biggest hotel on the Strip."

Yes, so I'd heard, with more rooms to fill than any other hotel, two thousand rooms, as the Stardust had been put together somewhat haphazardly, stolen out from under Tony Cornero and then bound with boards and nails to the hotel standing next door to it, the failed Royal Nevada, the two big hotels now conjoined. That's why it was so massive and why every single element of it therefore needed to be larger than life, a display colossal enough to fill up the skies, galaxy-size, to rival the brilliance of the stars.

The hotel already boasted the biggest sign on the Strip, the word STARDUST repeated twice, this STARDUST STARDUST stretching itself across the entire front of the building, which featured a huge pastiche of a mural with every planet and star in the solar system spackled colorfully across endless blue space and crowned by rays of golden light. The buildings were to be named for the planets, the swimming pool christened the Big Dipper. There were to be lounges and restaurants and shops and salons and cafes, and they and every other aspect of the hotel would operate around the clock, always open, unlike any other hotel on the Strip, but like the universe itself, no wee hours for this place.

At the parking lot entrance to what was now the biggest parking lot in Vegas rose yet another sign, the STARDUST this time mounted above the blue globe of the earth itself, with satellites orbiting endlessly about it, the satellites captured by earth's gravity the way we earthlings found ourselves captivated by green tables and one-armed bandits. And within that orbit, black letters across the blue earth would soon advertise the biggest show on the Strip. Because as befitted the largest hotel on the Strip with the most hotel rooms and the largest casino, the king of the Strip hotels, the showroom would need a great big new king-size spectacle.

ESME WELLS
LIDO DE PARIS
C'EST MAGNIFIQUE
ADULTS ONLY

So.

I lit a cigarette and said nothing.

Donn looked at me somewhat apprehensively, more so, I thought, than my silence or my garb could account for. Why could this possibly matter so much to him? Only because it mattered to Nate. And judging by Donn's expression, it mattered to Nate a lot. And if Donn failed here in his entreaty, perhaps he thought Nate would scratch him from all the shows he ran, have Jack Entratter and Harold Minsky take over what were now Donn's stages, Donn's domains. And whom Nate might send out here next to reason with me.

I put my cigarette out on the fireplace brick. "What's my salary?"

He told me. Stardust-size.

Another unexpected gift from Nate, like the Ambassador. Or maybe it wasn't a gift. Maybe it was what I was worth. I was a draw—and Nate liked a draw, because a draw brought money to the casino, whether it be a cheap buffet, a Bingo game, free drinks, or a burlesque act. The Lido would be a new kind of draw, the first French revue in Vegas, soon to be copied, of course, by the other hotels—who would hastily concoct the Nouvelle Eve at the El Rancho, the Folies-Bergère at the Tropicana, the Casino de Paris at the Dunes.

Minsky's Follies with its jiggle and grind would have to wait.

I looked down at my fingers, at the hearth, at the living room stretching out before me to the ends of this big wide earth. What else was I going to do with myself? I wasn't six anymore. Or twelve. Not any longer a soundstage rat, a stooper, a cigarette girl. My mother hadn't lived long enough to lay track any farther than to the nightclub stage. What was out there beyond the footlights? TV, groceries, and boredom.

So I nodded. A small nod.

"Still have your dancing shoes? You didn't throw them out?"

Ah. Arden was joking now, relieved. He could go back to Mr. Stein and say, We got her out of her pajamas. She's coming to the Stardust.

And so Arden designed his new Lido de Paris show with me as its centerpiece. Which was only fair, I supposed, as I had, however unwittingly, helped clear the way for Nate to secure the Stardust for himself.

53

FOR THE STARDUST'S JULY opening, at the giant ribbon-cutting, I joined the Lido's cast of sixty. We appeared in our costumes, top hats and tuxedos for the boys, feathers and sequins for the girls. And right alongside Governor Charles Russell and Senator George Malone and the Hollywood VIPs imported for the occasion—Jack Benny, Milton Berle, Carol Channing, Ethel Merman, Bob Hope, the McGuire Sisters—stood the full panoply of the hotel brass. Hyman Goldbaum, John Factor (né Iakov Faktorowicz), Morris Kleinman, Nate Stein. Look how high the Jewish big boys had climbed. Right up to the stars they'd been dreaming of for five decades, up high enough to see their brothers the moguls, 260 miles away in Hollywood. A hundred newsmen covered every event of the day and every facet of the ten-million-dollar hotel and its million-dollar stage and its million-dollar show.

The Stardust's massive Café Continental stage was larger than a basketball court, with an Esther Williams–like swimming tank for summer shows and a Sonja Henie–like ice skating rink for winter ones. The pipes secreted in the catwalks created rain or snow on demand. The backstage machinery included forty scenery lines, six descending stage units, three hydraulic lifts, sixty fly-loft lines, and a sound control booth that looked like the controls of the Viking rocket itself. The showroom seated seven hundred people and the cavalcade on the stage almost matched that audience in size.

For the summer show, Donn posed girls in sequined G-strings and shimmering headdresses on a score of platforms suspended from the ceiling, platforms that hung low over the showroom tables, but just out of reach. On the stage, girls dove into our aquacade, complete with waterfalls, smoke plumes, swings, waterslides, spar-klers, and our water nymphs, girls who smiled and swam and never resurfaced and who made their exits through special channels at the bottom of the pool. Other girls entered from those ducts to drift a moment, bare-breasted (the Adults Only portion of the show), and then to disappear again into those tunnels. The wings were a mess of mats and sloshed water, stagehands in rubber boots manning the wet mops.

For our finale, two dozen barely clad boys lined the winding staircase that wrapped the pool, a construct not entirely dissimi-lar to the set Buzz designed for his long-ago Shadow Waltz num-ber. And I was suspended above this all on a Lucite trapeze that rose higher and higher, my gold sequined ersatz bathing costume and gold turban glinting as I ascended. My eight water nymphs down below wore pink and ocean-green costumes and turbans of their own, but mine hosted a silver crown, to mark me, I suppose, as their water-logged goddess queen. When I was six feet from the catwalks, I dove into the water, into the center of my back-stroking girls. Thank God for all my swimming at the Flamingo pool, my shenanigans in the martini glass at the Desert Inn. At the close, the entire ensemble waved to the audience. Above us fireworks crackled.

By Christmastime, the aquacade was stored away and the ice rink unveiled. In the icy winter world of Donn Arden's great imagination, I was now drawn on a sleigh pulled out onto the stage by two girls wearing headdresses made to look like reindeer antlers. Crystal earrings dangled like long icicles from my own headdress. No antlers for me. On the back of the sleigh perched my attendant, a footman. At my arrival, the girls in satin skirts and golden sashes paused their skating on the ice pond, girls in headdresses of plumed feathers paused in their labors of pulling at ski poles, girls draped in crystals and long crystal wigs posed

quietly in their white jeweled G-strings and bejeweled bras. Scattered amongst them, other girls with sparkled tights, fur hoods,
fur muffs, and fur skirts stood stationary, bare-breasted in this
pretend winter freeze.

On a raised platform reached by white filigreed stairways a
dozen men snow-dusted white made a row, and across the front
of the stage stood another two rows of men in white swallowtails.
At the finale's climax, I twisted myself into a horizontal spindle to
be thrown from one partner to the next as the men stood in a circle center stage. Eventually the men held me, straight up, above
them. Only God and Arden knew exactly what kind of winter
treat I was supposed to be. A wind-driven snowflake? A splinter
of hail? A flying icicle? It didn't matter, just as long as it all looked
magnificent.

54

BACKSTAGE TONIGHT, AS WE left behind our winter set with its icicle-hung stairways, gazebos, and igloos, the stagehands met us, rolling out a giant, Stardust-size cake on a cart borrowed from the kitchen and covered with a white tablecloth, its naked utility disguised for the occasion. My birthday. I'd told no one, yet the cart with its cake stopped before me. The cake was tall, three layers, like a wedding cake, the top layer thick with pink candles, one for each year and a few extra for good luck and good measure, the little flames almost obscuring what was beneath them, my pink name and the words:

HAPPY BIRTHDAY, ESME!
YOU'RE 21!
FINALLY LEGAL!

Yes, I was twenty-one, now, an age of no small significance in Vegas. The cast was laughing and clapping, even before I held back the icicles of my headdress and bent to blow out the candles, singing "Happy Birthday to You," sixty men and women in shimmering partial costume, another thirty men in tuxedos joining in from the pit with their brass and strings and a drum roll, the conductor, Johnny Augustine, waving his baton to make them play the birthday song for me. Even Donn Arden stepped up from behind a white-painted scenery flat, bearing Nate along with him. So that's who had orchestrated this, Nate of whom I now saw little and spoke to even less.

He came up to me after the cake had been cut and while I was handing out slices of it on little paper plates, some of the girls helping me, our headdresses clinking and clattering as we turned this way and that, and standing there in my jeweled covered wagon and G-string and sparkly fishnet nylon tights, naked before him, or almost, yet again, I offered Nate a slice of cake. It had enough whirls and filigrees to rival my costume. But he shook his head, no thanks, saying only, formally, "Happy birthday, Esme, dear," before turning away, leaving me standing there holding that paper plate, heading off, probably, to prowl the henhouse of the Sahara's secretarial pool.

Since I had reappeared again in all my uncovered flesh this summer, Nate had been cautious with me, keeping his distance. He never brought his new girlfriend to the Stardust, and if our paths crossed, he treated me with a certain gallantry, as if I were his grown-up daughter, which was probably as it should always have been. A formal, "How are you, Esme?" Or "Is Donn treating you well?" A nod. A quick walk away. Perhaps the sight of me reminded him that I was capable of sudden and unpredictable implosions, ones he was capable of triggering. Yet, from afar, he kept a protective eye on me, as did the men he tasked as my bodyguards. One of his men stood at the back of the showroom when I rehearsed, guarded the hallway outside my dressing room when I was made-up and costumed, walked behind me through the Stardust. No one ever approached me, no one ever bothered me. If a man sent flowers to my dressing room, the card was quietly removed. Gifts were returned or thrown out. Visitors were discouraged. It was just like being fifteen again and at the Flamingo, where if any man got too close, the floor manager would escort him away. And so I understood in part why Nate had wanted me back on the Strip, to put me under his purview, to supervise me because he didn't trust my father to do it properly. The price I had to pay for Nate's continued beneficence was loneliness. Fine.

In my dressing room, I didn't see Nate's note for me right away.

Not until I'd put down my paper plate of cake crumbs with its too-sweet inch-thick white icing, not until my dresser had taken away my last costume of the night, such as it was, to be cleaned, not until I was sitting in my old blue robe in front of my big mirror, peeling off my lashes and wiping at my face with wet cotton pads. Propped up on my dressing table, there it was, a plain envelope with the big black scrawl of Nate's handwriting across the front of it, an envelope someone, possibly even Nate himself, had placed here at some point while I was onstage. Or while my cake was being wheeled in from the kitchen. The envelope leaned against the emptied Maxwell House coffee jar where I kept my makeup brushes.

On the front of the envelope he had written only my initial, a giant black "E." Four scratch marks, a single vowel. A birthday card? I tore open the envelope and drew from it a piece of stiff paper, a correspondence card with the words Desert Inn imprinted across the top of it over its Joshua tree logo, and I read what Nate had written below it:

> *Gus Greenbaum's dead.*
> *Where's your daddy?*

Nate should know where my father was, at his shift, at the Riviera. He was there. Surely.

Breathe, I told myself.

My hand was afflicted with a sudden tremor. The caged bulbs that rimmed my mirror seemed to glow too brightly and spew flickering stray black marks, like those at the end of a movie reel. The photograph of my mother in her blond wig seemed to spark beneath its yellowed piece of tape. Outside my dressing-room door roared the usual post-performance pandemonium, the pounding feet, hoots of laughter, screams, the screech of costume racks dragged down the hallway. Someone yelled, "Wasn't that cake good?"

I had to put down the card, push it away from me a little, slide it under my makeup tray of paints and powders, make it disappear, find one of my precious Miltowns, which I now begged off my fellow showgirls and hoarded for just these kinds of occasions, which presented themselves more frequently than I could have imagined, and kept with its sisters inside an empty silver tube of lipstick I'd cleaned out for this purpose.

Never let anybody know what you're thinking, what you're doing.

I stuck my head under the sink faucet to swallow the pill I could no longer find any doctor to prescribe for me, not even the house physician here at the Stardust. Especially not the house physician. Hence my begging and hoarding. "I'm gonna lose my job, Esme," the girls would say, "I'll be fired if Mr. Stein finds out." Everyone knew I was watched and to whom the watchmen made their reports.

Then I slid Nate's note out from under my makeup tray and read it again.

Gus Greenbaum's dead.

Had Gus died here or in Phoenix, at home with his wife? What I knew about Gus, other than the fact that he was now dead, was that he owed money everywhere, to Nate, to Chicago, to Lansky. And on top of that, Gus had been stupid, shoveling even more of their money off the counting-room tables into his own pants pockets, stealing from the very men he already owed. Everyone knew that Gus Greenbaum, stupid on heroin and made stupider by all his gambling and whoring, was unraveling. My father had told me Nate had tried to buy the Riviera out from under him, but Gus had said, "No, no, no, the Riviera's my house," that's how unraveled and how stupid Gus had become. Johnny Rosselli had sat him on a bar stool for hours and begged him to sell to no avail. And so now Gus was gone, knocked off his bar stool, if not by a heart attack or a stroke or liver failure, then by someone like Johnny Rosselli, if not by Rosselli himself. And if so, the only people who would know this right now were the big boys, men like Nate, who knew tonight what everybody else would find out tomorrow morning.

Gus's house? Not anymore.

Nate was scrubbing it down, getting ready to move in.

For it was clear to me now that the Riviera management was being cleaned out. Over the past year, one by one the men from the Flamingo who'd moved over to the Riv alongside my father were being killed. Big Davey Berman had died in the hospital, ostensibly after surgery. Moe Sedway of a heart attack. The entertainment director, that slimy Willie Bioff, had been killed by a car bomb. Now Greenbaum, somewhere, somehow. It seemed everyone associated with the Riv, anyone stirring so much as a pinkie finger in the Riviera skim was vulnerable.

I looked down at the note.

Where's your daddy?

Solicitude?

Warning?

Threat?

As soon as I could stand and shower and dress, I headed with Nate's note out into the casino, which was banging tonight, fools throwing chips as if they really were just circles of sand, chalk, clay, and paper, as if they were not at all the hundreds of dollars dropped onto the table where they would subsequently be swept up by the croupier, all the while the cash that bought them being stacked up in the humid counting room, so wet in there that hundred-dollar bills would stick to the walls and flap in the breeze from the ineffectual fans. It was brilliant, really, the whole idea of chips, the way it was so easy to forget what you'd paid for them. And the slot machines tinged and tinged, though little of consequence was won; but now and then there was the occasional great rustle and clang of a great burst of bells delivering a big win and the promise of more of the same to every hapless player in the room.

The Stardust held inside its bowels over 16,000 carpeted square feet of luck, good and bad. And the bell-ringing, chip-clacking furor, I no longer found exhilarating, not after more than half a decade of listening to it. Tonight all I heard was a tin buzz, partly from panic, partly from the Miltown, which had by now laid out the white carpet of its calming effect. Most of the players here had never even heard of Gus Greenbaum nor would they care if they had about what happened to him, but everyone who worked in Vegas, every dealer, pit boss, and box man, knew who he was, one of Meyer Lansky's men and one of the most experienced casino managers in Vegas. And when they found out he was dead, everyone would want to know what the news meant for them, just as I wanted to know what it meant for my father.

I walked through the drape-lined, carpeted casino, no clocks, no windows, no clue as to the passing time, past every table, past the bar, past the slots, past the little starry Christmas trees propped up everywhere and green-and-silver tinsel hung like boughs and sparkling white reindeer with pink-feathered headdresses turning circles on a music box–like platform past throngs of people, but I couldn't find Nate, so I went up to the pit boss, who knew me, everyone in Vegas knew me, had known me since I was fourteen years old, and who, when I asked, called over to the Riviera's counting room.

He spoke into the phone and then he said to me, "Your father didn't show up for work tonight."

Where's your daddy?

If my father wasn't at the Riviera tonight, there was a reason for it and it wasn't going to be a good one. Had my father, following Gus's example, mopped up too many of those sodden paper bills from the counting-room tables, and if so, how many, and based on that answer, I'd know how long he had to live. Because if my father were already dead, Nate wouldn't be asking me where he was.

At my terrified face, the pit boss pulled a concerned one in concert. "What is it? What's going on?"

I couldn't speak. It was so much like the terrible night at the Flamingo when my father came up to me in the casino to tell me about Benny Siegel's death that for a moment I felt I was fourteen years old again, the world tipping, sickeningly, beneath me.

"E?"

I couldn't answer him.

He took my hand. "Do you need to sit down?"

If only my father hadn't gone to the Riviera with Gus. If only he had stayed back at the Flamingo. My fault. I'd bitten off that promotion for him from Nate, too guilty at the time to refuse me anything.

"Esme? Do you need a drink?"

Because today I was finally old enough to be served one.

I smiled at the pit boss, shook my head again to let him know this was nothing, it didn't matter, I was silly. He smiled back, reassured. I turned away. I had to find my father before anyone else did, but I couldn't run out of here like a crazy person. So I walked through the Stardust casino and out into the December night like a queen, because after all I was a showgirl, a headliner, the pride of Las Vegas.

55

THE STRIP, LIKE THE casino, was decorated a bit sadly for Christmas, layered over in tinsel, tinsel Christmas trees in metal stands lining the curbs, stars and bells and ornaments strung on wire swinging above me in the December wind. Silver tinsel and red bells shook on their wires across Fremont Street, too, over the old Block 16, over the older casinos, over the depot for the San Pedro Las Vegas Salt Lake Railroad that started it all. Was it all so frugal-looking because the decorations had been ordered by Greenbaums and Dalitzes and Lanskys and Sedways and Steins, Jewish men to whom the holiday meant little? Because compared to the jewel-colored lights running up and down each hotel's exterior, the tinsel seemed like a Tiny Tim afterthought. Oh, yeah, it's Christmas, string something up. Or perhaps it was just that there was nothing, no star, no bell, no trim that could possibly compete with the gleaming neon already in place.

If Nate didn't know where my father was that meant he wasn't anywhere here on the Strip. He wouldn't be anywhere he could easily be found, not at the Flamingo, the Riv, the Players Club, the Glitter Gulch. He wasn't likely to be at home, either, so I wasn't surprised to see when I pulled up into the carport that my father's car was gone. I sat in my Ambassador for a minute looking at our front door, at the strand of red-and-green Christmas lights, unlit, sagging across the top of the casing, our little nod to the holiday for the sake of the neighborhood. I was afraid to go any farther, afraid of what I might see inside the house.

Eventually, I made myself get out of my car and unlock the front door. At least it was locked, possibly a good sign. I leaned in. "Dad?"

No answer, though I hadn't expected one.

We had, still, despite living here almost a year, little furniture in the living room—because just as with the bungalow at the Flamingo, we spent so little time at home awake. The television screen was dark. No sound came from it or from anywhere in the house. My father wasn't here. I could sense it. The house was empty. No one mixing drinks in the shiny kitchen. No one swimming laps in the pool, the cheap rubber raft lying on the cement beside it. No one singing in the pink-tiled shower. But every cupboard in the house was open, every drawer emptied, the items in every closet dropped to the floor, as if these were my childhood closets. And when I went down the length of our short hallway and reached my father's bedroom, I found the pull cord in the ceiling of his closet had been yanked and the ladder unfolded to the small crawl space above.

I stood there a minute in the tiny closet, my father's suits around me, redolent with his cologne. Cold dank air shuttled down from the opened hatch. Then I climbed halfway up the ladder and looked, tentatively, across the attic floor. We'd put the boxes of my old toys up here, an immediate bore once we'd hit Vegas. I could see their battered cardboard sides with my name written on them, as if we might somehow one day forget whose property those boxes contained. They lay on their sides now, though, flaps open, my dolls and cards scattered across the splintery plywood subfloor. My mildewed board games, my Coloredo card tricks, my dolls flat on their backs. Had they squawked a protest for me?

The men who came here looking were, I understood, looking for my father's rainy-day stash, his get-out-of-town stash, his leave-the-furniture-behind-in-Vegas and get-going-quick stash, his portable version of Benny's half-million-dollar Zurich bank account, the one Nate Stein had found out about in 1947 when Meyer Lansky sent him to the Flamingo to sniff around the losses, the bank account being Siegel's final nail-in-the-coffin. To take a little from the skim was the norm. To take too much was a death knell. Nate, like Lansky before him, needed this money returned because with its return, the big boys regained what was more important to them than the actual cash—their authority and control—without which every casino in Vegas would be stolen blind. Like the Flamingo had been, opening night. Like the Flamingo had been earlier this year, when two armed men had robbed the counting room, and within a month both men were hunted down and shot dead by Jimmy Fratianno in Hollywood.

My father, nose to the ground, nervous as the racehorses he once bet on, must have picked up the scent, early, somehow, about tonight's slaughter, and had run off to hide. Siegel. Cornero. Bioff. Berman. Greenbaum. Silver. My father clearly thought he could outsmart, out-survive them all. Because my father always believed in near escapes and miraculous transformations and second chances, always had faith that a bet would pay off, a horse would come in, his luck would turn. Magic Ike.

No winning horse this time. This one was going to be shot if I couldn't fix this. Shot if he was lucky. If he wasn't, he would die slowly, painfully, after which his body, or pieces of it, would be ferried out past Paradise Palms to a stretch of the Paradise Valley desert with mesquite scrabbling for life, put into ground just deep enough for a sandy covering.

This one was a bridge-jumper.

I climbed down the closet ladder and sat on the edge of my father's mattress. Forlorn without a headboard, it floated aimlessly in the center of the room as if it didn't matter at all where it was positioned, like that rubber raft lying askew in echo outside by the pool. I could hear the night insects, their chatter spiky and indecipherable, the low groan of the pool pump as caution. Think. Where would my father have stashed the skim. He wouldn't have had time to come by here to get it. By the time he heard about Gus, he would have known men would be watching him, watching the house. My father was too smart. He hadn't swum this long amongst these men without being smart. The pump throbbed. And then it came to me, stupid as my mother.

I went back to the living room, opened the sliding glass door and stepped outside, looked around. Concrete. Everywhere. A concrete-block fence enclosed the entire backyard. No grass. Just concrete. The concrete around the pool itself was all shadow, but the round lights set into the walls of the pool itself—like the camera portholes of Esther Williams's Lot One saucer tank—glowed a gentle sickish yellow. One of them was out. An oddity. My father took care of this pool the way he took care of his Cadillac or my Ambassador, always waxed, always polished. The Silvers had to look sharp.

I knelt down, took off my shoes, and slid down into the pool, the water making quick work of saturating my dress and turning the skirt of it into a weight that held me back. But still I made the long, slow walk against it toward that broken light, my legs pushing forward through the heavy water. The water pushed back at me. But I got there, eventually, to the light. With my fingertips I grasped the aluminum frame around the glass cover and pulled. Stuck tight. I twisted. Pulled again. The frame and the glass bowl within it came suddenly and easily away from the pool wall, along with a tangle of wires all taped up blue and red. One wire was loose. I lowered my body, nose level to the water, until I could put my eye to the interior recess. A dark huddle of clear plastic bags. I reached in a hand and tugged at the first one, cautiously, as if it were a joke somehow and coiled fabric snakes might jump out at me. Nothing jumped out. No electric shock. The bag floated out, gently, the other eight of them following their leader like a school of obedient aquatic students. I peered at their translucent bodies as they floated by me. Each bag held stacks of bills, each stack bound with a paper band stamped "$10,000," each group of stacks wrapped tightly in a plastic sheath of its own inside the outer bag. Which my father must have pumped full of air. Because the bags continued to float.

I'd been in casinos and credit cages and counting rooms, so stacks of hundreds had lost the ability to astonish me, but these stacks, packed here so tidily, did more than astonish me. They terrified me. There was easily a hundred thousand dollars in each bag. Maybe more. This had to be a couple of years' worth of serious skim, from the Flamingo and from the Riv. Or maybe it was all from the Riv, all since my overdose, too much in way too short a time not to be noticed. Maybe my father and Gus Greenbaum had lost their minds in there together, dipping deep, too deeply, into the Riviera's green swift-flowing river of cash, deeper, much deeper, than Lansky and company wrote off as the cost of doing business. Just look at the price Gus Greenbaum had paid for his green hands.

What price would my father pay for his. A similar one, certainly. Because nobody was allowed to steal from Nate Stein's casinos and get away with it. Nobody. Not even Baby E's daddy. House rules.

I looked at the light cover, dangling beneath the water now but kept from hitting bottom by the limits of the wires fastened to it.

What if.

I looked around the pool. Eight lights.

I had to know.

I slugged my way over to the next pool light, yanked on the cover with my glowing hands, looked inside the recess past the wires. Bags.

Of course.

There were bags behind every light in the pool.

It took me only a short while to pry off all the covers, which then hung like tentacled octopi down the pool walls. I stood there a long time in the water, very cold, breathless, my back against the cement wall of the shallow end, watching as the scores of bags bobbed and turned, stupid, oblivious, on the surface of the blue-black water.

56

I ROLLED SLOWLY ACROSS the Desert Inn parking lot at the side of the hotel, sending my Ambassador stuffed with my father's stolen booty past all the white lines marking parking spaces for all the guests the DI hosted and all the guests the DI one day dreamed of hosting, certain the appeal of Las Vegas would only grow greater and greater, stratospheric. And who's to say Nate and the rest of the big boys weren't correct in their assumptions? More guests. More money. Into infinity. When I arrived at the lot's most deserted section, the farthest corner of it, I parked by the low concrete-block wall that separated civilization from the undeveloped valley. From this vantage point, I could see nothing of the Strip. It was still dark, but in another couple of hours it would be dawn, and my father would be exposed, caught, made visible by the rising winter sun. Whatever could be settled needed to be settled tonight. Whatever strings still bound Nate to me needed to be tugged on tonight.

Happy birthday. *Where's your daddy?*

Why had Nate ordered that big cake for me on exactly the evening he was hunting down my father? To distract and disarm me? Because even as he had wished me a happy birthday, even as he bid the candles be lit up on my cake, he knew his note in all its dark unpleasantness was waiting for me in my dressing room, and he knew I wouldn't be happy for long.

My father. To know him, to know the full dimensions of his folly, could not erase my love for him. Nate had once told me my father reminded him of his own, which was not a compliment, each man being a bit of a talker, a flashy dresser, good-looking, full of swagger but not in possession of that many smarts, ultimately small-time. I had protested, but Nate had held up his hand. No arguing. My father was small-time. Always and forever. And the paper doll of my father turned and twisted in my mind's eye, not that his image hadn't already been diminished by our years together in Vegas, by his demotions from floor man to box man to credit cage and then his slow, creepingly slow, rehabilitation back to the counting room, courtesy of me. How much mercy would Nate be likely to grant his father's doppelgänger?

I slipped down in my car seat. I just wanted to be small, invisible, a dot unnoticed at the far end of a large parking lot, but I wasn't, I couldn't be, because as small as I was, I was here. Or maybe it was more my father I wanted to be made invisible, unnoticed. But he couldn't be effaced either. We were both here. He was alive, or so I believed or so I would soon find out.

I stayed in my car, motor on, so I could run the heater against the December cold, the radio playing holiday tunes.

> *Remember Christ our Savior*
> *Was born on Christmas day*
> *To save us all from Satan's power*
> *When we were gone astray*

December. Christmas. Where would my father and I find ourselves in twenty-two days?

The song ended, and shortly thereafter, I saw in my rearview mirror Nate's Cadillac making a dark crawl across the lot toward me, and I panicked, suddenly, wondering if I had done the right thing in calling him. Too late now. But who else could help me untangle the nightmare my father had gotten himself into? No one. Well, maybe it was a good thing my father hadn't been able to get to these plastic bags, maybe I could still fix everything.

Nate pulled up in the parking space beside me as if we needed to be slotted in an orderly fashion here at the end of the world. I almost laughed. But wasn't that exactly what was happening here, the orderly process of exchange and restoration? Nate rolled down his passenger-side window. He was hatless, the wind now blowing through his car and tugging at his dark overcoat and his thatch of wild hair. Dark meadow. He gestured. I didn't move. So he got out of his car and walked around to my window, motioned for me to lower it while he looked first into the backseat, then over me to the passenger side of the front seat, as if he might have missed what he wanted to see at first glance. My father.

Well, I was bringing him my daddy, or the part of my daddy Nate and the big boys wanted. And in exchange, I wanted the part they didn't care about. The actual man.

"E?" He raised his gloved hands in question. Impatiently.

No more birthday wishes. This was business.

I got out then in my heels and my cape coat, my short hair blowing around me, blond gossamer, what was left of my *kleine kinder* hair, now, over the past year, slowly growing in. I walked around to the back of my car. How could it be getting colder as we edged toward sunrise? Maybe it was going to snow. The hem of my cape flew up around me, the petals of a day lily closing up to wilt, wool cloth slapping at my chin, hitting the back of my head. Nate looked at the crazy spectacle of me and smiled. Thank God. For a minute, we stood there looking at each other, wind whipping debris across the lot, across our bodies, twigs, sand, dust, the two of us alone here together. We two had not been alone together for some time. He took a step closer, used two hands to batten down my cape. I could smell the wool fibers of his winter coat, the leather of his gloves, the scent of his skin. He bent his head toward me just a moment, then pulled back. A kiss, rethought?

He released me and stepped back, and I took my keys and

opened the trunk, then the brown leather suitcase, my father's suitcase, into which I had dumped the bags holding the hundreds and hundreds of thousands of dollars, the deep trough of the trunk illuminated by the stars, the moon, the Milky Way, the white bald light of the parking lot lamps.

Nate looked down, unsurprised, at the stacks of cash wrapped in plastic. "Why is it wet?" So, apparently, something about this had the ability to surprise him.

I made a gesture, Who knows?

"Is this all of it?"

"Yes." And then I decided to qualify my answer, just in case. "I think so."

Nate looked up at the black sky. "So where is he?"

"I don't know."

Nate looked down and studied my face as if he could read every calculation that crossed it, and who's to say he couldn't after all his years in the casino pits reading the faces of every gambler and cheat, deciding who got an additional line of credit, a thumbs-up, and who was cut off, a thumbs-down, who got another drink and who was thrown out of the casino on his ear. He read my face and then his own face relaxed.

"You know your father's finished in Vegas."

"I know."

"He has to leave."

I nodded.

"Tonight."

Yes. So the strings that bound us, whatever was left of them, were worth a travel pass. For immediate use.

He sighed. "All right. Well, give me a hand with this."

And so Nate and I ferried the plastic bags from the heavy leather suitcase in my trunk to his trunk, and I noticed not for the first time the flinty gold monogram stamped between the handle and the latches, *IS*—my God, he had taken the trouble to have that done—and I felt as if I were digging down into my father's grave to exhume him, where I would find him somewhat diminished but still alive, possibly furious, but, hopefully, grateful. Thank you, thank you, E.

Because the question now, of course, was had I saved him and his monogrammed valise for a life he could stand to live?

For this life must now be played out in some other city and in some other world, the world of civilians, not the world my father knew, not at all, but the world of humble office workers and shopkeepers, my grandfather's world, the world he and my mother had always thought too dull to ever want to join. My mother had operated in a world of backlots and soundstages, dreams and pretend, and my father's world, the one I had to operate within, the one my father had brought me to, was a world of greed, violence, and death. And so the upshot of all of that was here I stood, Esme Wells, headliner of the Stardust's Lido de Paris C'est Magnifique, in this parking lot, with Nate, mobster king, his car full of money.

Nate shut the trunk of his car, then mine. "Take a ride with me, E."

So we weren't finished here.

I had never felt frightened of Nate before, but neither had my father nor I ever taken anything from him before. Or taken this much. Nate liked to give, liked to offer patronage. He didn't like to find his cupboards forced open.

Nate unlocked the passenger door of his car for me, then got into the driver's seat, leaving that other door open as if there was no question but that I would do what he said. And when had I not?

Where's your daddy?

Which one.

I got into his car.

He turned it around and drove through the parking lot and

around the back of the hotel and from there onto the golf course he had built, black tires crushing the beautiful fairways over which no one but Nate would ever dare to send a car, until we reached the finishing hole on the course, Hole Eighteen, with its long 400-yard green from which we could see the back of the hotel and beyond it, the Strip.

It was a beautiful course, not that any of the big boys could play well enough to even enjoy it.

They hated to lose at anything and they had no patience, no skills. They'd come from the streets, not the country club. They rode slowly around in their carts with their caddies, growing redder and redder-faced with fury at their terrible swings and disobedient balls until somewhere around the tenth hole, they'd erupt, throwing their clubs into the sandpits, across the greens, into the rock-faced artificial waterfalls, up a palm tree, cavemen bellowing and throwing jawbones. Or else they'd break their wood clubs over their knees. And when they played cards with each other, even a genial game of gin rummy, it was worse.

Nate rolled down his window a crack to an instant sliver of ice served us on its icy plate and lit one of his noxious cigars, looking outward beyond the tip of it as if he could see something. The future. Maybe if I squinted I could see it, too, in it my father, running, hunched over, running for his life, like all the little ground animals at the Nevada test site, the field rats and raccoons and snakes, the lizards and ants. Did the first great tremor of the bomb, the sudden bright crack in the dark world, give them warning enough to run, burrow themselves safely away? Or did they melt in an instant, turned to fat and ash. Gone.

"Can you see them?" he asked.

I turned to him, startled, then understood what he was asking me. Before us, in the dark, lay the neighborhood of fancy new homes Nate had constructed right in the center of the golf course, with its perpetually tended grass and its ten thousand imported trees, new homes for the casino managers and hotel management and their families. These golf course homes were almost finished, and all the DI brass were preparing to move out of the hotel rooms and suites they had made their temporary homes and into this new neighborhood that would offer all of them greater respectability, a bit of burnishing. A respectable neighborhood with a capital *R*. Compared to these fancy houses, Paradise Palms was worker-housing.

Nate gestured toward the homes, a half wave.

"You'll be alone, now," Nate said. "So you'll live here with me."

So. If this was the time for all trades and exchanges, it looked like it was also the right time to trade in the executive secretary for the showgirl, to whom he felt better suited, after all, now that I was walking and talking again and was, for all he knew, Miltown free. It would be an easy exchange. I was as vulnerable for a takeover as the Stardust or the Riviera.

So.

Was it possible Nate still loved me, despite everything, despite what he'd done to me, despite the fact that a man like him shouldn't be able to love and that he didn't deserve to be loved in return?

And was it possible that I still loved him, that I could love someone I didn't trust?

It was possible. I'd been doing that my whole life.

Nate was looking at me. What could he read in my face now?

"So, Esme. Tell me. Who have you been with since me?"

No one. But he knew that. Because he made it his business to know everything about me.

"Who have you been with?" I said.

He laughed.

And then the sprinklers went off suddenly around us, set by timers to water the course religiously, day and night, summer, winter, spring, and fall. We were pelted with droplets. I sank down and used my arms to belt my cape more closely around me.

Nate rolled up his window, stubbed his cigar out in the car's ashtray.

"Esme," he said, his voice a purr.

And then he reached for me, pulled me on top of him, and without much preamble, pushed his engorged phallus inside me.

Given the circumstances, of course, I couldn't deny him.

Survival City.

57

WHEN NATE DROVE ME back to my car, somewhat blindly because our moist heat had fogged the cold splattered windows of his Cadillac, his disheveled drive a mirror of our disheveled selves, he said to me as I stepped out into the chill, "Go find your father, Esme."

And it was only then that I understood where my father might have gone.

58

AFTER NATE CAREENED OFF, I had to sit by myself for a moment in my big black Ambassador in the big black parking lot, still flushed but cooling fast, waiting for the vaporous warmth of Nate's body and breath that still clung to me to crystallize here in the freezing air of my car and then drop to the floor of it like a small hailstorm. I had to be free of him to think straight and I couldn't think straight with that wet thicket of him laid all over me, the bodily memory of what we had just so unexpectedly done, the sounds he'd made reverberating still in my ear, Esme, god fucking damn, I've missed you. And I had missed him. Despite my best intentions, if I had any, which I had begun to doubt. Or maybe this wasn't such an unexpected reversal, after all. Why else had he been keeping me under such close watch except to have me returned to him one day, *virgo intacta*, or almost.

Eventually, I was able to start my car and edge it up close to the Desert Inn. I was planning to go directly to the hotel vault. Because even after the move to Paradise Palms, I kept my valuables here, where Nate said they would be safest. I could only hope they would all still be there, that Nate, wolf with a cock, vulture with a beak, hadn't plucked them one by one out of the vault while I wasn't looking, just as my mother feared our neighbors had done when our belongings lay in open display on our lawn, Nate leaving me with nothing, leaving me as he'd found me, a blond child in Benny Siegel's mink. But despite his urgent exhortation, "Go find your father," I couldn't get out of the car just yet. Inside my skirt, my thighs were sticky with Nate's ejaculate, the lining and wool fabric soiled with it. Nate had always been so careful to use a rubber, the rubbers the other girls complained about in the

dressing room—along with their complaints about bladder infec-
tions and the clap—about having used those rubbers and getting
knocked up anyway and now having to find some doctor with a
hanger and a bottle of bleach. But Nate had not wanted to be
careful tonight. And everything Nate did in this life was planned.

I got gingerly out of the car and walked with as much grace as I
could muster to the lobby where I had the desk clerk pass me the
key to my safety deposit box. And I found, when I opened the lid,
every piece of jewelry Nate had ever given me, velvet boxes and
soft leather envelopes of pearls and minerals, as well as the small
red-and-gold leather box with a gold latch that held my mother's
ring, the big diamond with the many other diamonds trying to
crawl all over it, the ring my father had given her with his first big
payday after he started working for Mickey Cohen and the only
thing he himself hadn't pawned during the months right after her
death.

I took a breath. So. I still could help my father. We had pawnshops all over Las Vegas, both on the Strip and downtown on
Fremont Street, and here you could find well-organized stores,
unlike the crowded Inglewood Boulevard pawnshop I visited so
long ago with my father to hock my mother's modest engagement
ring. That place had been filled with household items, radios, musical instruments, toys, but Las Vegas pawnshops were different,
less of that sort of stuff, more of what a gambler had on him at
the moment he needed more cash so he could get back into the
casino.

Here, the locked glass cabinets showcased almost exclusively
jewelry—rings, watches, necklaces, cufflinks, stripped off in the
passion of addiction, in the rush to get back to the tables, the
cards, the dice, the ringing bells, the wheels turning, the glasses
clinking, the roar of the win. And when those gamblers had nothing left but debts they couldn't repay, they were conscripted as

bagmen, smuggling cash in suitcases to cities all over the country, working off their debts at 7.5 percent per trip. If they wouldn't serve and couldn't pay, they were maimed or killed, whether they were big boys or small-time crooks. Or my father. That was the gospel. Debts had to be paid, one way or another. Theft had to be punished.

There was no way I could sell all of my jewelry tonight. No shop had that much cash and I didn't have time to visit them one by one. So I piled everything into my black satin evening purse, a clutch, just about big enough, and decided on one item to rid myself of, my name necklace, the gold chain with the diamond charm that spelled my name, Nate's first gift to me, the one I had stopped wearing after Tony Cornero's death. It was easiest to let go of this first, these diamond-crusted letters. ESME.

And then I left the DI, left the Strip, and drove downtown to Fremont Street, where I pulled over to the curb in front of an all-night pawnshop not far from the Golden Nugget, the big sign, Golden Nugget Gambling Hall, like a bloated sun, red and yellow, and like the pawnshop, perpetually open.

I got out of the Ambassador, carrying my swollen purse close to my chest like a child with a treat she doesn't want anyone else to have, and pressed the pawnshop doorbell to be buzzed inside. I waved through the glass and grating at the tired man with rumpled hair the doorbell had roused. He stood up from behind the counter—was he wearing pajama bottoms?—and he opened his mouth at the sight of me, then came over to the door to open it for me himself.

"Miss Wells!"

The owner called me by name, of course. I'd have to drive to Salt Lake City or Phoenix or Los Angeles if I didn't want to be recognized. But I didn't have time for that.

He looked a little puzzled as to what was I doing here, though he stepped back to let me enter. "How can I help you? Buying or selling?"

"Selling," I told him.

I followed him to the counter, still clutching my purse with both hands. I saw then he had a cot unfolded behind the counter. I'd interrupted his sleep. Well, I supposed if you weren't at the casinos or the showrooms, the Las Vegas night in winter could be very long and very dull. Soporific. I opened my purse. I'd never actually done a transaction like this before, though I'd certainly watched my father do it, again and again, with my mother's engagement ring and sometimes, even, with her wedding band. He had hidden his panic and desperation so well from me that I had never known of it, looking up at him from down below counter level, but now I did, and so I attempted to hide those same emotions from myself and from this man.

I moved to lay my necklace with the ESME charm on the glass. And simultaneously, like a magician, the man slid a square of black velvet beneath the charm before it ever even hit the glass. The minute I saw the diamond ESME lying there on that velvet I thought this was a stupid thing to sell. It had my name on it, and I had an unusual name. Who would want this? Who could give this as a gift to another?

The owner's thoughts seemed to echo my own. "Are you sure you want to sell this, Miss Wells?"

I nodded. I was going to tell him that the diamonds could be pried out, repurposed, and I made ready to persuade him with my own charms that this charm could be refashioned to his benefit, but once I saw his face, I understood he wasn't entertaining any of the thoughts I'd worried about, but a separate set of concerns all his own.

"Mr. Stein won't be upset that you're selling this?" He rubbed a hand through his hair.

Ah. So he was worried about fallout, not about resale. Did the whole world know my business? I straightened up, and stood, as Daddy Mack would say, tall. Very tall. I smiled. "Only if you don't pay me what it's worth."

He gave me a small unhappy smile in return. Because, truly, there was nothing funny about any of this. With this charm, I'd wipe out his bankroll tonight—his bankroll for the week—and I'd endangered him with my plots and plans.

But I'd get a fair price. A better than fair price. The man didn't want Nate sending anyone to his shop to complain. In fact, I doubted he'd even display the charm. He'd probably lock it in his safe, keep it hidden.

Because after all, it was better for both of us if no one knew what I'd done or that he'd had a part in it.

59

THE SUN STILL HADN'T quite come up when I finally sent my car, its tires crackling, on the long twig-littered road, the *krik-krak* making a victory over the sounds of winter insects and the lapping water from the Vegas Wash. If my father wasn't here, then I didn't know where else he could be, and I would just have to wait here for him to find me, as I knew he would. Eventually. For this place was known only to the two of us.

In the six years since that night Ben Siegel was killed and my father brought me up here, my father and I had never spoken of this property to anyone, knowing instinctively somehow that we might one day need a safe house, a place that was wholly ours and wholly our secret, our own Flamingo penthouse emergency back exit. Of course, there was no penthouse here, no anything, as we had never built our house, only dreamed of it, but perhaps it was better this way, because if we had built our Silver Lair, then someone would have known about it and about these acres.

My two headlights flickered weakly up the long drive, up the hill, lost their way for a second or two at the bend, and then pushed onward. If my father were here, he wouldn't be able to see the car or see me behind the wheel. All he would see was a dark shape approaching, two headlights, two white circles of glare, which could belong to any car, any owner.

But when I reached the top of the drive, I was the one who didn't recognize the car there before me, a gold Dodge Dart, parked a few yards up ahead, so I stopped quickly, quietly, engine a purr now, though soon enough I recognized the driver inside the Dart. It was, thank God, my father, revealed in a sudden flash of color when the car door opened and the interior light went on.

There he was, in his long winter coat and his fedora with its green feather, his tan leather gloves, his red plaid muffler, ready for the cold but not much else.

Maybe the Dart was a stolen car, maybe a borrowed one or one hurriedly bought at a used car lot somewhere, but it was a nondescript car, clearly a safe car he'd gotten and had kept hidden in some rented garage, hidden from me, along with everything else. Or maybe he'd traded his Cadillac for it earlier tonight. But at least he'd had the sense to try to make it a little harder to be hunted until I could flush him out of here.

Because that was now my unhappy job.

"Esme?" he called out.

I could hear the wariness in his voice.

"It's me," I called back.

" You alone?"

"I'm alone," I said, and I got out of my car.

He trudged toward me then. He was wearing rubber boots, unhinged metal buckles flapping and chattering. Maybe he knew it was going to snow. It did that sometimes in winter. You could often see snow on the mountains but sometimes snow fell even across the valley. The winter after Benny died, it had snowed and snowed, but our streets and sidewalks and our car roofs and the flat roofs of the few hotels we had then on the Strip had turned only a momentary white before the soft layer of snow disappeared like some desert mirage. I remembered thinking then it was a sign from God of the afterlife: Benny's with me now, little girl.

My father came up close to me and kissed my cheek. "Smart girl. Didn't expect to see you up here until tomorrow."

I studied him in the pale beams cast by my headlights. The big yellow moon was setting low now in the west. I'd left my headlights on so I could see better, but given that moon, I didn't really need any other light. Up close my father looked as he hadn't at a distance—greasy, sweaty, unkempt, not his usual sweet self— and I figured I probably looked the same, having been running around all night, too, in my ridiculous stilettos, in and out of casinos and cars and swimming pools, squatting on top of a man, skittering across the linoleum of a pawnshop. And, suddenly, I understood I was exhausted.

My father stepped back to take my measure. "So," he said, "if you're here, that means you've already heard about Gus."

I nodded.

"Gus was a thief. But every man working Vegas is a thief, of one kind or another."

"Even you."

He shrugged. "The minute you took up with Nate Stein, I started saving for a rainy day. After your pills, I really started shoveling. And now, it's that day. Raining cats and dogs, baby girl." He rapped his gloved fist on the trunk of my car. "I need you to go by the house for me."

"I've already found the money," I said.

"Well." And he looked at me, a little astonished. "I'm giving you an A-plus for today's work. It's in your car?"

"It was." And then I was a little afraid to say this, but I did. "I gave it all to Nate."

My father stared at me, blank as a school blackboard at midnight, and then his shoulders went round under his wool overcoat. Anger and something else, despair? "Now, Esme, that wasn't smart."

"I had to do it, Dad."

He shook his head. "You can't buy your life back from a man like Nate Stein, if that's what you think." He stood there, looking at me, shaking his head, and then, oddly, he grinned. "You're still a child."

He turned from me and walked up toward the summit of the hill, to the site where we had once imagined our house would eventually stand, more Wells' Loft than Silver Lair, perched up high with the birds, a nest from which we could look down on the Gabrielinos, or, from this eastern Nevadan perch, the Paiute, I guess. After a moment I followed him. Through a crack in the mountains, where in the daylight we could see the water, I could now in the dark only smell it, wet and fragrant. My father reached into his pocket and took out a pack of Chesterfields, shook and smacked it, pulled out a cigarette, rummaged for his lighter. He lit the cigarette, took a moment to smoke at it, opened his mouth to expel a mass of blue fumes. Only then, it seemed, could he bear to face me. But I was the one who spoke.

"You have to leave," I told him. "Tonight."

"That's exactly what I was going to say to you." He headed back toward me in his boots, his traveling boots, his overcoat. "But I'm not leaving without you."

"I can't go with you, Dad."

"What are you talking about?" His boot buckles clicked sharply, impatiently.

I shrugged, and when I did that I could smell Nate's Brylcreem on the collar of my cape, in my own hair. God fucking damn, Esme.

And my father guessed then at the real reason, or maybe he figured it all out for certain right that minute.

"Oh, no. You think I'm going to leave you behind here, at the mercy of this place, at the mercy of these men, at the mercy of Nate Stein?"

And I thought, When haven't I been at someone's mercy? I've been at yours most of my life.

"What exactly did you hear about Gus?" he asked.

"Just that he's dead."

"He was ambushed at home. In Phoenix. A few hours ago. In bed, in his pajamas, holding a heating pad, TV on. They almost cut his head clean off. They were probably trying to cut it off, put it in his lap. And nobody knows but you and me and a few of the big boys."

So Gus was right now and would remain until he was discovered by someone this morning—by his wife, perhaps, or by his housekeeper—propped up in his bed with his heating pad and his television on, suffusing the room with the warmth of the living, even as the heating pad warmed Gus's stilled flesh. Heating pad. Pajamas. Bed. Television aglow. All the creature comforts of a man in need of comfort no longer. My father, with his head in his lap. No. My father was still alive, standing here in his overcoat, smoking a Chesterfield. Because of me.

But my father wasn't finished. "They left his wife hogtied, face down on her living-room sofa with her throat slit. She bled to death into a towel. What kind of man does that to a woman? Or sends someone else to do it?"

I imagined myself tied up, my throat slashed while I bled helplessly into a bath towel, not even a hand loose to wag in ineffectual effort to stop my life from dripping from me.

"You remember what happened to Nick Circella's girl, the cocktail waitress?"

Yes. She'd been tied to a chair, beaten and tortured to death with a blackjack and a blowtorch. Someone found out she'd been talking to the FBI.

"It's not safe for you here anymore."

My father's point? Gender was no shield, if that's what I might mistakenly believe, from my association with men like him, from my association, in fact, with him. I think then I began to reek, like him, with panic.

My father shook his finger at me. "And Gus wasn't just killed over the skim, Esme, if that's what you think. He was killed because Nate Stein wants a piece of every goddamn pie in Las Vegas, and that piece of pie, that pie, belonged to Gus. And there's no limit to the mayhem Nate Stein can wreak when he doesn't get what he wants."

Because that was how Nate took care of business. With mayhem. Set in motion by telephone.

My father gave me a crooked smile. "Nate's already got you hogtied, doesn't he, Esme?"

More than my father could imagine.

"I'm not leaving you to him. No matter what. So what do you say we go try to find ourselves a little peace and happiness before it's too late. Even if we have to leave here the same way we arrived, a couple of coins jingling in our pockets."

Jingling. Yes. That reminded me.

"Dad, I have something for you."

I crunched my way back to my car, reached for my heavy black purse in the front seat, and shook the thing in the air above my head so he could see how full it was, how heavy it was, a real treasure sack.

He looked at me, at the gentle clatter. "What's that?"

"I pawned one of my necklaces tonight," I told him, "just enough to get you out of here. The rest is worth at least thirty thousand dollars." I put the purse down on the hood of his car. As if to say, Take it. This is for you.

Not what he'd wanted, not what he'd scraped from the counting room. But it was something. With it, he could reconfigure his scheme, last minute, on the run, seat of his pants. Not ideal. But he was good at this. He'd had lots of practice. He put his hat back on. He studied me, impressed. Impressed that I was like him, the old Ike, unstoppable schemer.

"All right, Esme. All right. You go home and pack. I'm gonna

get going, and I'll wait for you in Los Angeles, at the train station, and we'll head out together. Plan was we were driving out of
here, rich. What you've got isn't a fortune, but it'll do. It'll get us
to Mexico City."

"Mexico City?"

"New plan."

I knew what the new plan was. Same as the old. I'd already
lived it. Horses and cards.

But he surprised me. "Maybe your grandfather was right all
along, Esme. Better a shopkeeper than a big boy."

Okay, so maybe no horses, no cards.

A shop instead. A cash register. Boxes, cans, and bottles on
shelves. Better, maybe. Safer, certainly. But how long before my
father tired of dusting tin cans and putting pesos in the till and
ran off with some of that money to the Hipódromo de las Améri-
cas to put it all down on a quarter horse?

He'd be a shopkeeper for about a Mexican minute.

"We'll build ourselves a house on a hill over Mexico City, baby
girl, on El Dorado Road."

Hollywoodland.

When he put his arms around me he felt huge to me, a giant,
albeit one that stank of anxious sweat. I clung to him, inhaling
the scent of him, the panic, the aftershave, the French cologne,
and the Chesterfields, suddenly overcome because he was alive
and because though I held him now, I wasn't sure when I would
again. But he was impatient with me, with my clinging, and he
pulled back. Or maybe he was simply in a hurry, business to attend to.

"You keep the cash from your necklace," he said. "I'll take
this." He picked up my purse from the hood of the car, gave me
a salute, two fingers to his forehead. "I'll see you soon, baby girl.
Go home. Pack. Los Angeles. Union Station."

The station he'd arrived at twenty years ago, called River Station then.

"I don't know, Daddy," I said.

"Sure you do, baby doll. I'll be waiting."

And then he got into his car and drove down the hill.

60

I WAITED WHILE THE moon dropped slowly behind the mountains to the west and seemingly in counterpoint a pinkish light began to suffuse the sky. I slipped my hand into my coat pocket. Because, of course, I hadn't given my father everything, every single piece of jewelry I owned. My fingers blind in my dark pocket figured out the clasp of the leather box, out from which I brought my mother's ring, which I held up while I examined the enormous diamond surrounded by all the little diamonds, baby spiders crowding around the big mother spider, pregnant in the middle. I turned the stone, the tiny flames imprisoned in its many facets flaring up, pinkish, then vanishing.

If only my mother had had the baby she was carrying in 1939. Then I wouldn't be alone here now. The four of us would still be living in Los Angeles. If only we had stayed in my grandfather's house instead of moving all over town. If only my mother had been a different person, a Betty Crocker. Okay, a glamorous Betty Crocker. If only she had made my father take over my grandfather's painting business and renamed it, made it his own, say, called it Wolfkowitz and Son-in-Law, or, better, the Silver Brush. But my mother wasn't that kind of a person and if she had been, my father wouldn't have fallen in love with her. Still. What if she had been? What if we had moved up to the new tract houses in the Valley alongside all the other young Jews when they crawled out of Boyle Heights after the war, leaving the older generation behind? There, my little brother, thirteen years old by now, would be riding his bicycle along Hazeltine Avenue, my father running his Veterans Taxi, my mother, a Harriet Nelson housewife by day, a club act by night. And I, who knows what I would be, but I wouldn't be this, wouldn't be here. If only we'd done any one of those things, my father and I would never have found ourselves in Vegas. And now running from it. If only. What if. I put the ring back into its box and closed it.

I had been this alone only once before, after my father had dropped me off at the Sisters Orphan Home in September 1939, the day after my mother's funeral. She'd been buried next to her father and mother, in Evergreen Cemetery, in the Boyle Heights she'd wanted so much to escape. With my mother's death, my father had become the chattering doll grief had once made my mother, insane, saying over and over, "They took her from me, took her from me just like she was nothing," incapable of taking care of me, weeping and packing random clothes and toys into a suitcase and dropping me off in the middle of the night at the Seventh Street Sisters Orphan Home in Boyle Heights you could see from our backyard, four stories, with a bell tower at its center just like the one at Camarillo, the orphan home where he would leave me for six long months without a word of explanation. It was one big blow to me following another.

It was all dark that night he dropped me off, and no one was there at the Home. He'd wanted to just leave me off on the step, as if I were a baby in swaddling clothes some wayward Catholic girl might deposit at a convent door, but the night watchman told my father all the construction on Sixth Street had damaged the foundations of the Home and now the children slept at night at St. Vincent's Hospital. So my father carried me back to the car and drove the few blocks to the hospital, so determined was he to rid himself of me that he made the choice a second time over, palming me off on a nun with a wimple big as a serving bowl and just as white who led me down into a makeshift basement dormitory room and past a long row of beds with a coursework of pipes hanging thickly above us from the low ceiling. The children were all sleeping and so she had me step quietly, and she held one finger to her mouth, a signal for me not to speak. Not that I could have. I was too bewildered to have anything to say.

I'm not sure I spoke a word my entire six months there. I found out later my father had left me far behind, had gone back to Baltimore, to the family that must have been missing him, as I was, his old family in the East that didn't know anything about his new family out West. If I had known how far he'd gone from me, I think I would have died. As it was I'd already gone mute with shock.

Because of my impetigo, the nuns had bandaged my arms like a mummy's, and they had shaved off my hair, saying it was too full of bugs and tangles to bother with. I had no idea if my father would ever return for me or if he would recognize me when he did. I certainly looked like no version of myself I had ever seen before. But when he did return for me, suddenly, without warning or fanfare, he recognized me at once. I still remember how he looked walking through the tall doorway, with a jaunty step as if a tall doorway could not dwarf him nor his action of six months ago shame him, taking off his fedora and stooping down to me, hand out, certain that after all this time, I would run to him and grab his hand, which, of course, I did.

After all, you have only one great love.

I couldn't be left behind again. To be without my father was simply unbearable for me. And if I were going with him, as his apprentice escape artist, I might as well go with him now, while I still could, before Nate could tighten the ropes at my neck and wrists and belly any further.

I got into my car, turned it carefully around, and headed back down the hill. He couldn't have been gone more than five minutes, starting his flight across the desert, likely to be singing to his radio, preparing for his next great adventure, once again, the unformed future.

61

MAYBE A HUNDRED YARDS from the bottom of the hill, I saw
my father's Dodge Dart parked at the side of the road, driver's
door wide open, but no driver in sight, motor running, headlights on but boring into nothing now that the sun had just begun to rise. I pulled up behind the Dart and turned off my car.
No one. Nothing. Dirt and brush. I got out and looked around
me. Nothing. No sound. And then I looked back and in the red
gloaming of my taillights, I saw the tire marks of a second car,
not mine, mine being the third, a second car that had veered off
the road onto this shoulder and stopped behind my father's. Had
he thought that car was mine, that I had decided to follow him
right now, this minute, tonight, just as I had? After all, he knew
me as well as I knew him.

The treads were crisp, recent, the wind not having yet had a
chance to blur or efface them.

Wobbling a bit in my high heels, I walked up to the open door
of the Dart and turned off the ignition. The keys had been left
in the car but there was not a single other personal item within
it, not the fedora my father had been wearing, not his plaid muffler, not his leather gloves. I leaned in. And that's when I saw
my purse, fat as a baby, sitting there on the front seat. I pulled
the purse toward me. Still heavy. Still chockfull of rings and
necklaces and bracelets and earrings. It hadn't been overlooked.
Whoever had taken my father had left it there for me to see,
along with the car, whenever I came down the mountain. And
then I saw that my ESME necklace, the one I'd pawned not two
hours ago, had been reclaimed from that pawnshop near the
Golden Nugget and had been strung over the steering wheel,

my name dangling just beneath the horn, the letters pavéd with diamonds. E.S.M.E.

And abruptly, I had to sit down on the ground. Inside my coat, I was all wet.

Ten minutes went by. Fifteen. Nothing. Dark. Quiet. Animals scrambling in the brush. Lizards. Rats. Bats. Raccoons. Ants.

I waited. Come and get me, I thought.

But nobody came. Slowly I understood nobody would.

And while I sat there, dumb as a doll, sprawled in the brambles and grit, my back against my father's open car door, a bomb went off miles northwest of the Strip. Its specter rose into the sky in silent opposition to the sun, which was itself rising up over Lake Las Vegas and the Vegas Wash and sending the shadow thrown by the mountains down over the valley floor. I watched the sun tick instant by instant higher in the sky until the shadows across the valley floor shrank away and the dust created by the great explosion spread far and wide. And the red ball of the explosion shifted in the wind, one red eye above the dusty earth opposite the yellow eye of the sun.

62

AN HOUR WENT BY before I could stand. By then I could just make out the motor courts and the columnar towers of the Strip, the little blue swimming pools, the miniature suburban neighborhoods, everything flat and small in the just-there light.

So it looked as if my father hadn't left this place, after all. Well then, let him stay, let him lie somewhere in this godforsaken valley. I'd never know where. In a thousand years, his bones, bleached and clean, might be found next to those of the mammoths and tigers, that is, if the atomic bombs didn't first incinerate every trace of us.

In the pocket of my coat I felt again for my mother's diamond ring, slid the ring onto my finger. Then I climbed back into my big black Ambassador, headed down to the bottom of the hill, and drove away from all the dirty radiant light.

AUTHOR'S NOTE

Readers familiar with the history of early Las Vegas will note that I have compressed events of the 1950s into the space of a few early years of that decade. As well, much, but not all, of the actions the historical personages take in this novel are based in fact, unless, of course, for reasons of story, I required them to do otherwise.

ACKNOWLEDGMENTS

I'd like to thank my backstage personnel: my extraordinary editor, Sara Nelson, who loved this show from the moment the curtain went up; my agent, the amazing Gail Hochman, who sat through its dress rehearsals; and my husband, Todd, and my children, Madeleine and Aaron, my all-too-fabulous crew.

ABOUT THE AUTHOR

ADRIENNE SHARP is the critically acclaimed author of the story collection *White Swan, Black Swan* and the novels *The Sleeping Beauty* and *The True Memoirs of Little K*, which was translated into six languages. Her short fiction has appeared most recently in the *New England Review* and *Lilith*.